Alison Roberts has been lucky enough to live in the South of France for several years recently, but is now back in her home country of New Zealand. She is also lucky enough to write for the Mills & Boon Medical line. A primary school teacher in a former life, she later became a qualified paramedic. She loves to travel and dance, drink champagne and spend time with her daughter and her friends. Alison Roberts is the author of over 100 books!

Award-winning author **Louisa George** has been an avid reader her whole life. In between chapters she's managed to train as a nurse, marry her doctor hero and have two sons. Now she writes chapters of her own in the medical romance, contemporary romance and women's fiction genres. Louisa's books have variously been nominated for the coveted RITA® Award and the New Zealand Koru Award, and have been translated into twelve languages. She lives in Auckland, New Zealand.

A PARAMEDIC TO CHANGE HER LIFE

ALISON ROBERTS

CORNISH REUNION WITH THE HEART DOCTOR

LOUISA GEORGE

MILLS & BOON

First Published in Great Britain 2022
by Mills & Boon, an imprint of HarperCollins*Publishers* Ltd,
1 London Bridge Street, London, SE1 9GF

www.harpercollins.co.uk

HarperCollins*Publishers*
1st Floor, Watermarque Building,
Ringsend Road, Dublin 4, Ireland

A Paramedic to Change Her Life © 2022 Alison Roberts

Cornish Reunion with the Heart Doctor © 2022 Louisa George

ISBN: 978-0-263-30129-8

06/22

MIX
Paper from
responsible sources
FSC™ C007454

A PARAMEDIC TO CHANGE HER LIFE

ALISON ROBERTS

MILLS & BOON

CHAPTER ONE

THE FIRST CLUE that it might be harder than usual for Dr Joanna Bishop to ignore the significance of this particular day of the year came in the form of the rather startling noise of a nearby car horn.

Not that she had any premonition of the ripple effect the noise might have, of course. All she was thinking about, as she looked through the glass doors of the exterior entrance, was why someone might have parked a car at such an odd angle in the ambulance bay of Dunedin's Princess Margaret Hospital's emergency department and why they were now leaning repeatedly on the horn. Clearly, assistance was needed. Urgently.

Pulling on gloves as she moved swiftly to follow a triage nurse and registrar through the double sets of sliding doors, she could see frantic movement around the car as the driver jumped out and opened a back door. A security guard was opening the other door. By the time Jo reached the car, the male driver was halfway into the back seat on the driver's side. A woman had one leg out of the vehicle on the other side but was clinging to the sides of the passenger seat in front of her. And screaming.

'Oh, my God…the baby's coming… Like, right *now*…'

'She started having contractions all of a sudden.' The

man sounded terrified. 'About twenty minutes ago. I didn't think we were going to make it. I didn't know what to do…'

'You've done exactly the right thing,' Jo told him. She tucked the front locks of her short, dark bob behind her ears, bent down to the woman, who was still lost in her pain, and put one hand on her back to let her know she wasn't alone. She put her other hand on what looked to be a belly in the late stages of pregnancy to feel the iron-hard clench of contracting muscles. They couldn't try moving her from the car just yet but they would need to be ready when the contraction ended because an upward glance revealed clouds that looked threatening enough to be about to resume the heavy rain showers they'd been having on and off all morning. Jo turned to the senior triage nurse beside her but she didn't need to say anything.

'I'll grab a wheelchair,' Hanna said. 'And an obstetrics kit—just in case.'

Jo nodded her approval of Hanna's initiative. She needed to raise her voice to talk to the woman's partner over the sound of the loud groaning. 'How often are the contractions happening?'

'I dunno. Every couple of minutes?' The man wriggled further onto the back seat and sounded as if he was on the verge of tears now. 'It's not supposed to be happening like this.'

'How many weeks along is she?'

'Thirty-six.'

'Just the one baby?'

'Yeah.'

'Have there been any problems with the pregnancy?'

'No.' The man's face twisted. 'Not until now…' He put his arm around his wife's shoulders. 'It's okay, babe. We're here now. You're gonna be okay…'

He seemed to be trying to reassure himself as much as the woman, but for Jo there was relief to be found in knowing that this was a singleton pregnancy that was this close to full term. A high-risk situation like a very premature delivery or the imminent arrival of twins or triplets would have rung much louder alarm bells, but Jo still turned to the young doctor beside her.

'Page whoever's on call from Obstetrics, please, David. And let's get someone from Paediatrics down as well.' If this was going to turn into the fairly rare event of a birth in the emergency department Jo still needed to plan for any complications such as post-partum haemorrhage for the mother or a newborn with a respiratory arrest. They had two patients here.

It was also a relief to feel the rigidity beneath her hand beginning to soften. The woman's contraction, along with her groaning, was beginning to subside.

'I'm Jo,' she introduced herself, 'one of the doctors here. We're going to take good care of you and your baby. What's your name?'

'She's Susie,' her partner answered for her. 'She's my wife.'

'Is this your first baby?'

'Yeah…'

Still clinging to the passenger seat, Susie's breath came out in a sob. 'I think I'm bleeding. There's something horribly wrong, isn't there?' She turned her head to hide her face against her partner. 'Jack… I'm *scared*…'

Jack put both arms around her. They were both crying.

'You're not bleeding.' Jo had already checked what she could see of the towel Susie was sitting on. 'You're feeling wet because your waters have broken, which is perfectly normal at this stage of labour.' There was some staining in the fluid that could be meconium, which would suggest the baby was stressed, but Susie didn't need to know that. 'Let's get you inside before your next contraction and then we'll be able to see what's happening.'

Hanna was beside her again, with a wheelchair that she was using to carry a blanket, the equipment roll that contained things that might be needed for a birth, like clamps, scissors and a scalpel, pads and a suction bulb. She had also thought to grab a cylinder of Entonox but it quickly became apparent that providing Susie with inhaled pain relief, let alone trying to move her into a more desirable environment might not be possible. She was gasping, crying out and trying to speak all at the same time.

'It's coming... I can feel the head... Oh... *Oh*...'

There was a short period of controlled chaos as Susie was helped to turn onto her back, her upper body cradled against her husband as she lay on the back seat of the car and staff rushed to respond to orders for supplies like oxygen, an IV trolley and towels and to find out whether the specialist consults had arrived in the department yet.

Hanna used shears from the obstetrics kit she had unrolled to cut through clothing and they could both see that Susie was quite right—her baby's head was visible and about to be born. Jo's priority, as she knelt beside the car, was to try and control the speed with which it happened, by putting gentle pressure on the baby's head, to minimise trauma to both mother and baby.

As soon as the head had emerged, Jo used her finger to check for the position of the umbilical cord and found it around the baby's neck. Her careful attempt to bring it over the baby's head or even loosen it was unsuccessful.

'It's too tight,' she told Hanna. 'I'll have to clamp and cut it.'

Hanna handed her two clamps and then the sterile scissors to cut through the cord between them. Delivery of the baby had just become more urgent but, although Jo could feel that Susie was pushing, there was no progress to be seen in the movement of the baby's body.

'We're nearly there, Susie. Give me a really big push.'

Jo kept her voice calm but Hanna had picked up on the urgency as she held onto Susie's legs to support her.

'You're doing so well,' she told the young mother. 'One more big push, hon. Hard as you can. Push, push, *push*...'

In her peripheral vision, Jo caught the arrival of the obstetric consultant but there was no way she could hand over the management of this birth at this critical moment. She was holding the baby with both hands and she pushed gently downwards to free the first shoulder and then applied upward traction to free the second. The rest of the baby boy's body slid out rapidly and, at the same time, there was a loud, warbling cry from the infant that sparked an audible sigh of relief from the group of medical staff surrounding Jo and Hanna, a nod of approval from the obstetrician and the sight of both the first-time parents bursting into tears.

The baby was moving and clearly breathing well enough to cry so the priority was to keep him warm and get both mother and baby into the emergency department for a thorough assessment and the next Apgar score, which was due at five minutes after birth. Hanna handed Jo a warm, dry towel which she used to wrap around the infant, cradling him in her arms, and she got to her feet so that she could hand the baby to his mother as soon as she'd been helped into the wheelchair.

It had been a very long time since Jo had delivered a baby and, on that occasion, it had been put straight onto the mother's abdomen so it was even longer since she'd held one in her own arms. For just a heartbeat she looked down at the crumpled, angry little face of this tiny human that had just entered the world rather abruptly and it felt…heartbreaking.

Not in a bad way. It felt as if something had broken that had been filled with a liquid warmth that was now seeping, with the speed of light, right through Jo's body. The kind of warmth that came from the best of what life could ever offer. The kind of warmth that only really came from human connection.

From love…

Susie was in the wheelchair now, blankets around her shoulders and tears streaming down her face as she held her arms out for her baby.

'Here you go. He's just gorgeous.' Jo carefully transferred the bundle and had to blink away a tear or two of her own. 'This little guy's had a birthday you're never going to forget, hasn't he?'

She stayed where she was for a moment, peeling off her gloves, as Susie was wheeled into the department. She could see that her colleagues from both the obstetric and paediatric departments had already taken over the care of mother and baby so her own part in this drama was no longer essential and, well… Jo needed to take a quick breath before joining them to continue any involvement in the case.

Hanna rolled up the sterile cloth that had contained the scissors and clamps.

'Reckon this is one you're never going to forget either.' Her smile widened. 'Happy Birthday, Jo.'

Jo couldn't smile back at her friend. If anything, she

could feel her expression becoming quite sombre. It wasn't because she didn't want to think about her own birthday—she was looking forward to the planned celebration with Hanna after work, where they were going to try the tapas and sangria at the new Spanish restaurant in town.

No. It was because something much more important was happening. Jo could still feel that odd warmth that holding the baby had triggered and it felt as if a switch had been flicked, in her head as well as her heart.

'You know what?'

'What?' Hanna's eyebrows rose and then lowered into a concerned frown. 'Are you okay, Jo?'

'Never better.' Jo led the way back into the emergency department. 'I've just realised something.'

'Oh?'

Jo pulled in a deep breath as she turned her head. 'If I don't do it now, I never will because it'll be too late. It might be too late already but I won't know until I try, will I?'

'Oh, no…' Hanna stopped in her tracks before the automatic door could be triggered ahead of them. 'Delivering that baby has blown a fuse, hasn't it? You want one of your own?'

'I've always wanted one. One day. It's just never been the right time. And it never will be if I keep waiting for it to arrive. It's my birthday, Hanna. I'm forty-six.' Jo blew out a breath. How on earth had that apparently sneaked up on her? 'Forty. *Six*. Time isn't just running out…it's disappearing around the corner.'

'But…'

Was Hanna about to point out that Jo didn't even have a man in her life, let alone a partner to raise a child with? Jo didn't need to be reminded. It was also time to stop this snatched conversation and get back to work, but Hanna was looking worried now. As if she thought Jo might be completely losing the plot?

'There's something you don't know about me,' Jo told her. 'Something nobody knows.'

'Go on then… Tell me. I can keep a secret.'

But Jo shook her head. 'We can't talk about it here.'

'Just as well we're going out for dinner then, isn't it?' Hanna followed her inside.

Jo was already switching off from anything personal as she walked towards the resuscitation area that Susie and her baby had been taken to. She'd have to tell Hanna about it later because she'd already opened the bag that contained the cat, hadn't she? And when she started talking about it out loud it would become real and would end up changing her life.

But that was okay. Because that feeling was only getting stronger and it ramped up to a new level as she walked into Resus and saw Susie cradling her baby boy on the bed beside her.

The fuse *had* blown. The switch *had* been flicked. And Jo *had* meant what she'd said.

It really was now or never.

'*Whoa.*'

'It's all good, mate.' Cade Cameron threw the briefest of glances towards his junior crew partner, who was reaching to catch the water bottle that was sliding off his lap. 'I know what I'm doing.'

But his partner, Geoff, was grinning. 'I know. Word is that you've done a bit of rally car racing back in the day.'

Cade didn't look sideways again as the next twist of the hilly road demanded his full focus. 'Yeah…it's been one of my hobbies in the past. Off road driving too.'

Flickers of colour from the flashing beacons on the roof of the vehicle were lighting up the shadows of the pine forest they were driving through and reflecting on the wet tarmac beneath them. There wasn't much traffic on this road now that they were well out of the city so Cade didn't flick the siren again until they were behind a logging truck that obligingly slowed and pulled to the left as they reached a straighter stretch. Cade put his foot down then.

This was great. His first day in his new job and he was getting one of his favourite kinds of callout. Outdoors. Away from any main roads. Something that could well provide the kind of challenge an adrenaline junkie thrived on. Even the weather looked as if it was going to add another level to an unknown and potentially dangerous situation and that was fine by Cade.

Bring it on...

'Any more info coming through?'

Geoff scrolled through the information on screen. 'Twenty-three-year-old female. Slipped and fell while crossing a creek. Her leg's wedged between boulders up to her knee and she was in too much pain when they made an attempt to pull her free. They were worried that the leg could be fractured and they might be making things worse. She's conscious and cold.'

Cade was checking another screen that was providing his GPS, noting that he needed to slow down so that he didn't miss the upcoming turnoff. His thoughts, however, were mostly with a young woman who was in severe pain, possible losing blood and almost certainly very frightened. The sooner they got there, the better. It had already taken too long to get here from the central city.

'Who's on scene already?'

'There were three others on the tramp, all uni students. Two forestry guys who were working nearby heard someone yelling for help. They happen to be part of the local search and rescue team, knew that mobile phone reception can be dodgy out here and they texted someone who called emergency services. One of them will be waiting for us at the car park to show us the way and help carry any gear. It's about a fifteen to twenty-minute walk uphill to the scene. Fire service and police are on the way. ETA another five to ten minutes. Sounds like we might need their heavy gear and more manpower to shift a rock or two.'

Cade nodded. 'We'll see what we can do before they get here as long as it's safe for everybody. Might be a good workout for us. Any update on air rescue? We'll be well over forty minutes from the hospital if we factor in getting down that track.'

'They're still transporting a patient to hospital. Could be a while before they're clear.'

Cade turned into the parking area, making a mental note that it was big enough for a helicopter to land as long as the fire trucks and police vehicles stayed on the road. He also noted the steep set of wooden stairs that marked the start of the forest track. Shifting rocks wasn't the only workout they had ahead of them, with at least a fifteen-minute walk to reach the scene and having to carry a lot of gear, including a scoop stretcher, trauma pack, oxygen tank and life pack. There were fat raindrops hitting the windscreen as they came to a halt and he could see the grim expressions on the faces of the two men who were waiting for them.

'We know this area,' one of them told Cade as they prepared to set off up the track only a minute or two later, carrying a basket stretcher laden with gear. 'The girl's sitting in a creek that looks like nothing much but the water level can rise surprisingly fast with even a small amount of rain.' He turned up the collar of his raincoat. 'And this isn't a small amount.'

So Cade could add in a ticking clock to his assessment of environmental hazards before he even got to the scene. Yep…this was looking like a good challenge already. The urgency with which he got to the scene and gathered all the information he needed to determine just how serious this situation was—with both the condition of his patient and the environmental danger—made it feel as if time had sped up. Waiting for the air rescue helicopter to arrive, with the requested medical practitioner whose advanced skills he feared might be necessary if the only way to free this victim was by amputation of her trapped leg, made it feel as if time was going far too slowly.

And then, when the helicopter crew arrived on scene at the creek, for just an instant, it felt as if time completely stopped.

It wasn't that the emergency specialist he'd requested was a woman that surprised him so much. Or that she'd made it up that steep track so fast that she had to be easily as fit as he was. No…it was more that he'd never seen a face that was so instantly captivating. Intelligent. Passionate.

Quite possibly the most intriguing face Cade had ever laid eyes on.

Not that she was looking at him as she got closer, mind you. Her focus, as it should be, was on the young woman he was holding in his arms to keep her head well away from the rising water of this creek—a task that was becoming progressively more difficult as the force of the water behind him steadily increased. But then her gaze flicked up and Cade got the full effect of having that focus on *him* and, crikey...he could swear it felt like some sort of electrical shock.

'I'm Jo Bishop,' she told him. 'Trauma specialist. Talk to me...'

CHAPTER TWO

THE SOUND OF water rushing over rocks could well turn out to be a trigger that would raise Joanna Bishop's adrenaline levels for the rest of her life but, right now, it was no more than a background noise that had to be ignored in order to gather essential information. Like whether this young woman had been knocked unconscious when she fell, if any other visible or suspected injuries had been noted and if her vital signs had deteriorated during the time it had taken for the helicopter crew to arrive on scene.

'Blood pressure's dropping.' The paramedic confirmed the worry that the patient's condition was getting less stable. 'Systolic was under a hundred last time we were able to record it. Her radial pulse isn't palpable now.'

Which meant that her blood pressure was low enough to be dangerous. They needed to move fast. 'Blood loss?'

'Unknown. But she couldn't have been at the angle she was to her leg if it's not a major fracture so it's quite possibly compound. The water made it impossible to see if she's still bleeding.'

It did, because it was a huge volume of water and it was moving fast. The paramedic supporting this girl was a large man and his body was acting as an obstacle for water that was rushing past, in a wave that morphed into white foam as it coursed over the boulders downstream. Jo was grateful for the harness she was wearing and the fire officer who was holding the attached cable behind her in case the current made her lose her footing. Just behind them, the air rescue paramedics she had flown with were waiting for a signal to join her but, even though Jo had never met the man holding their patient, he was obviously going to be the person she needed to work with most closely. It would have been dangerous for the victim to try replacing him and Jo had the impression that he would have refused to move anyway. There was something very protective about his body language.

'I put a CAT on in case she was losing blood from an open fracture or laceration but she's becoming hypothermic, which could well be contributing to the decrease in blood pressure.'

It was a wonder that the paramedic wasn't hypothermic himself. It might have finally stopped raining so heavily but Jo was already aware of how cold her feet were from just a short time being immersed in this swiftly flowing water. This man had been here for a much longer time but he wasn't even wearing his heavy duty emergency services' raincoat because it was wrapped around the patient he was holding and his arms were bare beneath the short sleeves of his uniform shirt.

A part of Jo's brain noted the edge of an inked pattern below the hem of a sleeve in passing and added it to information her brain was automatically gathering because it was in assessment mode, but the tattoo, along with this man's dark olive skin and the black curls of hair currently plastered to his skull, were instantly filed into an irrelevant category.

'How long since you put the tourniquet on?'

'Thirty-three minutes.'

The watch on the man's wrist looked like something an elite soldier might wear and as if it could do a lot more than merely tell time, but it was helpful to know there was no need to think about loosening the Combat Application Tourniquet around the girl's thigh any time soon. Possibly not until they got her to hospital and even into Theatre. Jo could replace this item of the paramedic's gear with the same brand of tourniquet she had in the customised pouch in her own kit that was set up for amputation. The means of controlling both arterial and venous blood loss was tucked in amongst the scalpels and other surgical instruments like the Gigli saw—a flexible, serrated wire between two handles—that could be the best, perhaps only, device capable of a clean, precise cut through bone in a less than accessible space.

And maybe she didn't need the skills she knew her flight medic colleague could offer her by being the closest extra medic to this patient. She knew exactly how difficult it must have been to get an intravenous line in under these conditions, but there was a secure cannula in their patient's arm and someone in the knot of rescue workers nearby was holding up a bag of IV fluid.

'Good job getting the IV access before she was too shut down.' She caught his gaze again briefly to make sure he knew that she was impressed and not being patronising in any way. 'How much fluid has she had?'

'This is the second litre of saline. She's also had ten milligrams of morphine with good effect on pain levels.'

'GCS?'

'It was fifteen on arrival. She's responsive to voice but wasn't so oriented to time and place a few minutes ago.' He bent his head. 'Kayla? Open your eyes, sweetheart?'

Dark lashes, on a worryingly pale face, fluttered open and Jo could barely hear her voice. 'Where am I?'

'Still in the creek,' he told her. 'But we're going to get you out now. The cavalry's arrived.'

'But… I'm stuck…'

'We're going to unstick you.'

'How…?' The query was cut off as water suddenly surged under the paramedic's arm and washed right over Kayla's face. She coughed, choked and then cried out in pain as he tried to lift her a little higher, which must have put pressure on her leg.

'*No… Oh…that hurts…*'

Jo signalled to the helicopter crew that she needed her kit. Or, more precisely, the amputation pouch. Stat. Even in the few minutes she'd been standing in this creek the water level had risen noticeably. They needed to get more sedation on board for Kayla and get her out. Before she drowned. And, right now, it looked as if the only way they were going to achieve that was to do an above knee amputation.

Kayla was sobbing and her voice got loud enough to be very easy to hear. 'I don't want to die… Cade?'

'I'm here, darling.'

'Don't let me die… *Please* don't let me die…'

'I won't.'

'Promise…?'

'I promise.'

Uh-oh… Catching the surprised, swift glance of the trauma specialist made Cade realise that maybe he shouldn't have said that with such conviction. But it wasn't as though he hadn't meant it. He *wasn't* about to let Kayla die. Not if there was any way at all in the world he could prevent it, anyway.

And that meant staying right where he was, trying to protect Kayla from the full force of the creek's current and keeping her airway open as she was given enough sedation to lose consciousness and go limp in his arms. He was the only person in a position to monitor whether she was still breathing or had a pulse and, if either of those vital functions were lost, they'd have to get her somewhere they could try and resuscitate her in a matter of seconds.

'This won't take long.' There was a grim note in the doctor's voice and Cade could see that this woman was steeling herself to do something that went totally against her instincts. If she had the choice, she would be doing whatever she could to save the limb of this otherwise healthy young woman, not to be disabling her for the rest of her life by removing it. He could see the way she was gathering her courage as she picked up the scalpel after pouring disinfectant on bare skin. She would do this, and probably do it exceptionally well, if that was what it was going to take to save Kayla's life, but it was going to haunt her, wasn't it?

It would haunt everybody here.

'Wait…'

The glance he received this time was shocked.

'Let's give it one more try to shift this rock and pull her out.'

'*What?*' There was a flash of something like anger in that intense gaze. 'You mean you haven't tried everything you could already?'

'Of course we did. But…' Cade sucked in a breath. Was he about to anger this woman further by wasting time? It wasn't just loss of blood or the rising water that was putting Kayla in danger. She was getting progressively more hypothermic as well.

'*But…?*' The emphasis wasn't aggressive. She wanted to know what he had to say. Maybe she was hoping for a reprieve from having to go ahead with such a challenging procedure.

'I can feel the way her muscle tone's changed with the level of sedation she's under now.' Cade's words fell out rapidly. 'Maybe that could make a difference? What's the worst that can happen if there is a displaced fracture or partial amputation and we make it worse by dragging her out? She might lose her leg, but that's going to happen anyway, isn't it?'

She processed what he was saying in no more than a split second and then she turned and put the scalpel back into the kit the flight medic beside her was holding.

'One try.' She nodded. 'But it has to be fast.'

Cade nodded. They could do fast. There was already a sling around the top of the car-sized boulder with a rope attached that they'd used to try and move it earlier and he'd been sitting here long enough to get an idea of where the fulcrum point might be which was the best place to put long crowbars in and then try and lever it up. Who knew, maybe the increased pressure of water from this rising creek level would work in their favour as well? But would a group of emergency service personnel who'd never met him before today trust him to issue orders and give this a red-hot crack?

Apparently, the answer was yes. Cade had never shouted as many orders as loudly as this in such rapid succession and the last one was directed to where Dr Bishop was still standing beside the rock, ready to leap in at any moment and do the amputation if their patient's condition deteriorated.

'Move right back,' he told her. 'And I mean *right* back. If this rock moves, I don't know what direction it's going to go in and I certainly don't want you underneath it.'

She didn't hesitate to obey the command. And everyone else moved the instant Cade had counted down. Two men put their full weight on the crowbars as levers. Everyone who had been able to get close enough to grip a section of the rope started pulling. Another two people were waiting in case Cade needed extra muscle power to try and pull Kayla free.

And the rock shifted. Tilted. Its position in the creek bed didn't move but the gap between the rocks widened. Just enough for Cade to feel that Kayla's leg was not being crushed. Enough that he could pull her free, only needing the assistance of those behind him to help him keep his balance as he lifted her and then negotiated slippery stones and the froth of shallow rapids to get his precious burden safely to the bank of the creek.

He was as stiff as a board after sitting so still in that water for so long and his hands were so cold he couldn't have contributed to the task of stabilising Kayla enough to get her down to the helicopter, no matter how much he wanted to, but it didn't matter. There was more than enough medical expertise on hand. Geoff had a foil sheet ready to wrap over his shoulders and his own coat got taken off Kayla and handed back to him to provide another layer. It would have been sensible to get back to their ambulance and put the heating on full bore for the trip back into the city, but Cade wasn't about to walk away from a patient he'd been holding in his arms for rather a significant amount of time.

A young woman he'd promised that he wouldn't allow to die.

So he watched the swift but thorough assessment that Dr Jo Bishop gave Kayla and the expert way she realigned the badly broken bones in her lower leg and then splinted them safely before they carried Kayla down the track. Both the tibia and fibula were obviously fractured and severely displaced and although—miraculously— the broken bones hadn't punctured the skin and created an open wound, the foot looked as if it had been without a blood supply for some time. Too long, perhaps?

He followed the basket stretcher down the muddy track and found himself walking beside Jo.

'There's still a chance she might lose that foot, isn't there?'

She nodded. 'There were no limb baselines that I could see or feel. But you know what they say…' There was a tilt to the corner of her mouth as she looked up at Cade. 'Nobody's dead until they're warm and dead so maybe that can apply to a foot as well. How cold that water was might have been protective. *Oh…*'

The alarmed squeak was caused by the sudden slide in a muddy section of the track, but Cade was quick enough to catch her before she fell. Jo was clinging to his arm with both hands as he stopped so that she could regain her balance.

'Thanks.' The smile morphed into a grimace as she let go of his arm. 'I'd better stop talking and watch where I'm walking, hadn't I?'

Cade didn't say anything, maybe because his brain was too busy absorbing the feel of her holding his arm. It didn't matter how cold he was himself, it was impossible that he could have felt the body heat that seemed to have come through the thick waterproof fabric of his coat. But there it was. He could *still* feel it, in fact.

Like the way he'd been able to feel that jolt of electricity when he'd first caught her gaze.

There was something about this woman.

Something beyond simply intriguing.

Jo waited while the flight paramedics got Kayla secured into the back of the helicopter before she climbed on board and it was a moment that gave Cade an opportunity he couldn't pass up. He helped himself to a pen clipped into a pocket of her flight suit overalls and then picked up her hand. Every paramedic knew how useful gloves were for writing on when there was no paper available. Jo was too startled to take her hand away. Maybe she'd seen something in his face. Or was it an effect of that quick persuasive grin he'd offered? Anyway, the string of numbers took only a second or two to write.

'My number,' he told her. 'I'd love a follow up on this case.'

He held her gaze a moment longer. Long enough to let her know that it wasn't just the case that Cade would love to follow up on, but it wasn't long enough to get a gauge on whether she was remotely receptive—or available to be, for that matter—to the unspoken invitation. The rotors on the helicopter were gaining speed and she was being signalled from inside the clamshell doors.

It was only after she'd turned to run, ducking her head as she got beneath the rotors, that Cade realised he'd stolen her pen.

He was smiling as he clipped it into his own pocket. It would be rude not to return the item as soon as possible, wouldn't it?

'No...' Hanna's distinctive green eyes became very wide. 'He actually promised that he wouldn't let her die?'

'He did.'

Jo took an appreciative sip of the excellent glass of sangria she had in her hand, closing her eyes as she did so. This had undoubtedly been the most dramatic anniversary of her birthday ever. It had also been a very long day and she'd only just warmed up after standing in that freezing creek for so long. She and Hanna were late for their dinner but the restaurant had kindly held their table when they knew the reason why.

A long tress of bright auburn hair got flicked over Hanna's shoulder. 'Bit unprofessional to be making a promise he couldn't be sure that he'd be able to keep, don't you think?'

Jo still had her eyes closed. 'Oh, I don't know… If I was about to die I might rather go out thinking that the man who was holding me in his arms was going to make sure I stayed alive.'

'At least he didn't promise that she wouldn't lose her leg.'

'But she didn't in the end.' Jo opened her eyes, shelving the surprisingly pleasant thought of being held like that. 'And it was Cade's idea to have one more attempt to pull her out. I have to admit, I was impressed.'

'Cade…' Hanna wriggled her eyebrows. 'Sounds like a sexy cowboy. Did you exchange phone numbers as well as introductions?'

Another sip of sangria was a good cover for not encouraging Hanna along that train of thought. Jo knew how much she would enjoy knowing that Cade had, indeed, provided his phone number and that after she'd texted him, just before heading to the restaurant, to pass on the information that the surgery on Kayla's leg had been successful, he'd responded by saying he'd love to hear more. Over a coffee or drink some time, perhaps? That text was still unanswered. Because it had been a little disturbing how tempting it had been to respond?

'It was an emergency callout, not a blind date.' Jo's

tone was dismissive. 'For heaven's sake, he might be married with three kids.'

Highly unlikely, mind you. Jo might have only just met the man but instinct told her that he was very unlikely to be the type to cheat on any woman in his life. Snatches of the impressions she'd gathered were easy to retrieve. The solidness of him. The calm control of a tense situation as he'd directed that attempt to free Kayla. The tattoo. That watch… And something that she could sense in retrospect that was also purely instinctive. That Cade was a bit of a loner? A maverick?

'But if he wasn't?' Hanna's tone was teasing. She wasn't about to let this go.

'I still wouldn't be interested,' Jo said firmly. 'I'm over the effort it takes to get to know someone well enough, only to discover it's a dead end. Been there, done that way too many times, as you well know. Ooh…' It was a relief to be able to change the subject. 'Looks like our food's coming. Don't know about you but I'm *starving*. That helicopter callout made me miss lunch and then I totally forgot about it.' Jo lifted her glass and shifted cutlery to help make space as the first offerings of a smorgasbord of small bowls and platters were arranged on their table. 'This looks amazing…'

It was a delicious meal. For some time the two friends focused on sharing and tasting all the dishes. Tiny arancini balls, patatas bravas, chorizo with mushrooms in a tomato sauce, calamari and prawns. The food was good enough for Hanna to have totally forgotten to tease Jo about the impressive man she'd met today. It wasn't enough, however, for her to have forgotten about something else.

'So…what was it you were going to tell me about? Your big secret…?'

'I can't remember.' It was Jo's turn to tease Hanna. 'The surgery on that leg fracture today? The repair of the blood vessels was awesome. There's a big screen in Theatre and everyone can see what the surgeon sees through his magnifying glasses. Knowing how passionate you are about emergency medicine, I know you would've loved it.'

Hanna was giving her a long-suffering look.

'It was so satisfying to see that foot finally getting some colour back into it. Hopefully there's no lasting nerve damage and she'll get full function back...' Jo's words trailed off into a sigh. 'Okay...okay... I'll tell you.' She shrugged. 'It's no big deal, really. It's something that got popular for a while, that's all. Especially for single women in their mid to late thirties.'

Hanna was blinking. 'What? Online dating? Speed dating? Paying for an introductory service? One-night hook-ups?'

Jo shook her head. 'Freezing your eggs.'

Hanna's jaw dropped. 'You *did* that?' She looked slightly disconcerted. 'And there I was thinking we were soulmates who never had the slightest inclination to become parents.'

Jo shrugged. 'Seemed like a good idea at the time. I was over thirty-five and I knew how much my fertility would have already dropped. I thought if I hadn't found a partner by the time I was forty I'd seriously think about having a baby on my own.'

Hanna grimaced. 'Rather you than me.' She reached for the jug of sangria to refill their glasses.

'And then forty came and went,' Jo continued, 'and I was far too busy with my career and enjoying it too much to want to give it up and now...well...it might already be too late.'

'Hmm...' Hanna had picked up her phone and was already busy scrolling through whatever she was searching for online. 'Oh, my goodness. Did you know Janet Jackson had a baby when she was fifty? And here's a supermodel who had her first baby at forty-eight.' She was scrolling more quickly. 'It says it's more difficult to conceive naturally after forty-five but not impossible and you might need reproductive assistance but...' Hanna put down her phone. 'You're already halfway there, aren't you? You've got your eggs, which has to be the hardest part.'

'It was quite a big deal,' Jo admitted. 'I had to inject myself with hormones to stimulate as many eggs as possible and then it was a fairly invasive procedure to harvest them.'

'How many have you got in the freezer?'

'Six.'

'So all you need is a sperm donor.'

'Mmm...'

'Can I help you choose? Do you get a catalogue or something—with mug shots?' Hanna was grinning. 'Maybe it's an app these days and you can swipe right or left?'

'I have no idea. I expect a medical history and educational qualifications are deemed more important and I doubt they'd encourage people to go by looks to choose the father of their baby. It's probably not allowed, anyway. The donors are supposed to stay anonymous so they wouldn't want to be recognised by someone coming down the street pushing a pram, would they?'

'Yeah...and you're right about going by what someone looks like. I guess nobody wants to be accused of trying to create a designer baby.'

'Mind you, isn't that what you're doing when you

choose a partner in real life?' Jo was frowning. If she was really going to go ahead with this, perhaps it was time to start thinking seriously about it. 'You get attracted to someone for lots of reasons and what they look like is part of that initial attraction, isn't it?'

'Totally. You're not going to set up a questionnaire about a guy's medical history before you decide whether or not to fall in love with him.'

'There are things that would never show up on paper about someone.'

'Like what?' Hanna fished a slice of orange from her glass of sangria to taste.

'Like the qualities that make someone outstanding. Courage, for example. Or compassion. You might think someone's compassionate if there's evidence of their contributions to a charity or volunteer work, I guess, but you wouldn't really know how they felt about it, would you?'

Not like seeing someone who was prepared to sit in icy water to hold onto someone who was frightened for their life. Who would promise them that he wasn't going to let them die, even if it might turn out to be a white lie.

'So you'd want to meet the donor and interview them?'

'I'm quite sure that's not going to happen. Sperm banks probably have to guarantee anonymity.'

'So you haven't checked on the rules and regulations?'

'No…' Jo sighed again. 'I did think about it a few years ago but then it went into the "too hard" basket.'

'Until now.'

'Until now,' Jo agreed.

'Because it's now or never.' Hanna raised her glass. 'Here's to now. Happy birthday, Jo. And, you know what?'

'What?'

'While it's not something I know—or would ever want to know—anything about, my gift to you is that I'm going to help you find a baby daddy.'

Jo laughed. 'How, exactly?'

'We're going to make a list of exactly what you're looking for. Social networks are amazing things these days. Who knows? If you put it out there, something might just click. I heard a story a while back about some guy that went around in his camper van and made himself available to women who were just looking for a sperm donor.'

'No...' Jo shook her head. 'Really?'

But Hanna was busy smoothing out a clean napkin. She found a pen in her bag. 'Shoot,' she told Jo. 'What's the most important thing about the man whose sperm you want?'

Weirdly, the first thing Jo thought of was not a particular quality. It was more like a whole package of desirable traits. Wrapped up to look remarkably like Cade Cameron? She shook the image away.

'GSOH?' Hanna prompted.

'What's that?'

'Good sense of humour. You really haven't done the online dating thing at all, have you?'

Jo shook her head. 'Been too busy for that too. Have you?'

'Of course. But I gave it up a long time ago and we won't go into that tale of woe tonight. We're talking about you. Or, rather, what you want in the father of your baby.'

'Intelligence,' Jo decided. 'He doesn't have to have a PhD but if there's no way of having a conversation with them, I guess you'd have to look at what they do for a living.'

Hanna was nodding. 'You don't get to be a nuclear physicist or a brain surgeon without being reasonably clever.'

Or a critical care paramedic, Jo thought. She knew the years of training and experience that were behind that qualification were easily on a par with graduating from medical school.

'Resilience,' she added. 'The ability to face adversity and not throw in the towel.'

'Bit harder to judge.' But Hanna wrote it down. 'And what was it you said before? Ah, yeah...compassion. And courage.'

And there it was again. The memory of Cade sitting in that water. Protecting his patient. Oh...and that cheeky grin he'd given her when he'd stolen her pen and grabbed her hand to write his phone number on her glove. There was mischief there, which suggested a sense of humour. There was also a confidence that was also attractive.

Oh, help...that was what this was all about, wasn't it?

Jo was attracted to him.

Seriously attracted. And by a lot more than merely good looks.

Hanna had finished her sangria. She eyed the empty jug. 'Shall we get another one?'

'Is that wise?'

'I start my days off tomorrow. And you're heading off to speak at that emergency medicine conference in Melbourne, aren't you? What time's your flight?'

'Not till ten.'

'You can sleep in then. This list might take a while.' Hanna was grinning as she pushed back her chair. 'I'll

order the sangria on my way back from the loo. Oh…'
She turned back a moment later. 'Did you catch up with
the news that the ambulance bay baby got named after
you?'

'No way, really?'

'Yep. Someone told the parents that it was your birthday and they were thrilled. It's officially Joseph, but
they're calling him Joey. Cute, huh?'

Oddly, it was something way deeper than cute. Jo
found herself blinking back tears as Hanna disappeared
into the bathroom because she was back in that moment,
holding that newborn baby in her arms and feeling the
flood of that warmth. There was something else there
now that Jo recognised from long ago. Something she
had developed as a child when she'd identified something that her brothers could do but she couldn't. Like
riding a bike or surfing or winning academic prizes.

A certainty that this was what she wanted, along with
an absolute determination to make it happen. But this
time there was also a yearning that was so strong it was
almost painful. Having a baby might be totally different to any goal she'd ever set herself before, but it also
seemed more significant. Something her life would not
be complete without.

And…maybe…

Well, it wasn't totally beyond the realm of possibility, was it? Okay, maybe this was just in her imagination, thanks to experiencing a level of attraction she'd
almost forgotten existed, but perhaps it wasn't a coincidence that fate had dropped Cade Cameron into her life
on this particular day? That this was an opportunity she
might be unwise to ignore?

She had nothing to lose if it was a dead end.

And it might be fun to find out. Kind of like a birthday gift to herself.

Jo pulled out her phone. She didn't have much time before Hanna got back from the bathroom but she only had to find the last text message she'd received. The one suggesting that they meet for a coffee or drink.

She tapped 'reply'.

Saturday afternoon good for you?

Jo added a smiley face.

I think you might have my pen.

CHAPTER THREE

IT WAS SATURDAY AFTERNOON.

Cade Cameron could have been right on time for their arranged meeting place outside the main entrance to the Princess Margaret Hospital, which was quite a walk from the emergency department, but Joanna Bishop knew for a fact that he wasn't there waiting for her. A swift glance at the nearest clock revealed that she was a couple of minutes late to finish her shift, but all she needed to do was sign this prescription for her last patient and then it would only take another minute or two to change out of her scrubs. Perhaps Cade simply didn't like having to wait?

The ambulance bay entrance to the emergency department was probably the one he was most familiar with, having been on duty while Jo had been out of the country for a couple of days, but it hadn't occurred to her that he might come looking if she wasn't in the arranged place. She wouldn't have expected a paramedic to use an entrance that was inappropriate when he wasn't working either, so she was taken completely off guard by his arrival.

Not just by the somewhat dramatic entrance he was making either—a lone figure walking in as the double doors obediently slid open to admit him—looking as if he'd just stepped out of some blockbuster action movie for a break.

No... Jo was thrown off-balance because she hadn't expected him to look quite so...what...intimidating?

Drop dead gorgeous?

She'd known he was tall. She'd known he was dark. But, even given the focus she'd had on their trapped patient a couple of days ago and the challenging conditions the environment had presented, how on earth had she failed to notice just how devastatingly good looking this man was?

He was dark from head to toe. Black wavy hair that was long enough to be almost touching his shoulders. A black leather jacket that could be vintage RAF, with its sheepskin lining visible. Black jeans. Black boots. A black motorbike helmet under his arm.

A serious expression on his face.

'Dr Bishop?'

'Um...yes?'

'I do believe this is yours.' Cade reached inside his jacket and then presented Jo with a ballpoint pen.

Her lips twitched but she suppressed the smile. 'Thank you.'

Jo took the pen, her gaze locked on his. Cade had to be just as aware as she was that every single person currently in this department, including patients that weren't screened by curtains, was staring at them. Jo couldn't ignore what a juicy bit of breaking news it would provide for the hospital grapevine that the emergency department HOD was about to go on what could only be deemed a date with the hot new paramedic in town and the potential for embarrassment was also taking her off guard. What *had* she been thinking when she'd responded to that text invitation?

Of course he was aware. Of the risk of embarrassing her as well as their audience. She could see the gleam of both mischief and amusement in those very dark eyes of his.

'No worries.' An eyebrow quirked. 'Gotta go,' he said calmly. 'I'm meeting someone for a coffee date. Catch you later, maybe.'

'Mmm…' The sound was slightly strangled. He was making their rendezvous private, which was exactly how she wanted it to be. But it seemed to have just become a secret between the two of them. As if they were doing—or going to do—something more than a little bit naughty.

And heaven help her, but any regret about accepting that invitation had just evaporated to make room for a flash of the kind of anticipation that almost took her back to childhood—when something was different enough to be on a whole new level of exciting.

'Nice…'

Jo tucked her hair behind her ears, the spark in her eyes telling Cade that she was trying to decide whether his hum of approval was a sarcastic reference to her finally showing up to where he was leaning against one of the pillars that framed the hospital's main entrance. He held her gaze just a heartbeat longer. It wasn't just to make sure she knew he understood perfectly well that not finishing on time was part and parcel of the jobs they both did. No… The urge to hold that gaze was also there because he wanted to test what he'd suspected a short time ago when they were being watched so intently by everyone in ED—that they could communicate rather well without saying a word.

'Great outfit,' he added, even though he knew she

wasn't at all put out now. 'It's good that you're not wear-ing a skirt.'

He couldn't help another glance at those long, slim legs of hers, encased in faded denim that was tucked into knee high boots. Very nice…

'I don't do skirts.' Jo shrugged and then grinned at him. 'I was such a disappointment to my mother. I re-fused to wear dresses or play with dolls. She said it was cosmic punishment for finally getting the girl she wanted after having four sons, only to have her turn out to be a tomboy.' Her smile faded. 'Why it is good?'

'I've found what looks like the best place for us to have coffee,' Cade told her. 'And I thought you might be up for a ride there on my bike. I've got a spare hel-met and jacket.'

'As a specialist in prehospital emergency medicine, I'm sure you know as well as I do how dangerous mo-torbikes are.'

It was Cade's turn to grin back at her. He was liking a lot more than her outfit. And he could read her real answer in her eyes as clear as day.

'So…you're up for it, then.'

A statement, rather than a question. And it felt as if it was an effort for Jo to break the eye contact with him.

'Sure…why not? It's been a busy shift and I could do with blowing a few cobwebs away.'

The Triumph Scrambler motorbike was Cade's pride and joy, so it was gratifying to see the genuine apprecia-tion on Jo's face when she saw it.

'Very cool.' She nodded. 'Cross country?' Then her eyes widened. 'Twelve hundred CC?'

'I like a bit of grunt.' Cade raised an eyebrow. 'You know bikes?'

'I've got four brothers. How could I not know bikes? I rode one myself until I got a bit older and wiser.'

Somehow that didn't surprise Cade one bit. He could imagine this woman on the open road with the wind on her face, revelling in the freedom a bike could offer. He opened the shell case on the luggage rack and took out a leather jacket, old enough to be butter soft, holding it out for Jo to slide her arms into the sleeves. Weirdly, helping her to put an item of clothing on felt as intimate as it might be to help her take one off.

Oh, man...

He'd been looking forward to seeing Joanna Bishop again, but he certainly hadn't expected that being this close to her would feel *this* good. Even better, he was about to surprise her and he had a feeling that she might really enjoy something a bit out of the ordinary.

It was quite a tight squeeze, sandwiched between Cade's body on the front of the seat and the luggage box on the back rack, but Jo didn't mind a bit.

After a moment of feeling awkward as she put her arms around Cade's waist and felt the solid shape of his lower body against hers, she decided she might as well enjoy it. She was enjoying it so much she didn't even notice the direction that Cade was taking. She would have expected him to head for one of the trendy cafés up in the hill suburbs that gave fabulous views over the largest city in New Zealand's South Island, with its pretty harbour and the peninsula that sheltered it but, having started on the motorway that could have eventually taken them all the way to Invercargill at the bottom of the south island, Cade then turned towards the coast.

She was being abducted, Jo thought.

Whisked off to who knew where, with a man who was almost a complete stranger. For coffee…

Yeah, right… Jo actually laughed out loud as she felt the bike leaning sideways to accelerate around a bend.

'All good?' The wind whipped the words from Cade's mouth as he turned his head. 'We're almost there.'

Really? They were well past any picturesque beach-side cafés that Jo knew about. Sure enough, when Cade turned off the road, there was no hint that a good espresso machine might be nearby. Instead, they were in an almost deserted parking area surrounded by farm-land.

'Bit of a walk,' Cade said. 'But my research suggests that it's worth it.'

'Research?' Jo decided to keep the borrowed jacket on as the brisk sea breeze had a bite to it.

'I'm the new boy in town. I always start by looking for the more interesting corners to explore. You never know what treasures you're going to find.'

'So you make a habit of it?' Jo watched as Cade took a small backpack from the luggage case and hooked a strap over his arm. 'Being the new boy in town, I mean?'

He shrugged. 'Guess so. I never stay in one place too long.'

'Because you get bored?'

'Because I don't want to miss out on things that might be the best thing I've ever found. Like a place.' It felt as if Cade was standing very still as he spoke. As if he wanted to hold her gaze like this for as long as possible. 'Or a person…'

Oh, dear Lord. That look. The sound of his voice. The isolation of wherever it was they were, with clouds scud-ding over a vast sky above them and the smell of sea salt in the air was all adding up to something extraordinary.

Possibly the best thing ever?

'Where are we?'

'You don't know?'

'I grew up in the North Island. I've only been here for a couple of years.'

'So you're like me, a bit of a traveller?' Cade didn't wait for a response. 'I knew we had a lot in common, Jo Bishop. This is something new for both of us then. I like that.' He held out his hand. 'Watch out for this gravel road, it looks steep enough to be slippery down there.'

It felt like the most natural thing in the world to be holding his hand as they walked towards the sea. This was definitely something new for both of them. And Jo was liking it too. A lot.

'This is Tunnel Beach,' Cade told her. 'Apparently, back in the eighteen-seventies, some rich early settler dude decided he wanted a beach where his family could swim privately.'

'I can't see a beach. It looks as if we're walking towards the edge of a cliff.'

'That's the thing. They had a tunnel hand-carved down through the cliff. Seventy-two steps and we'll be there.'

'And there's a coffee shop?'

Cade laughed. 'I said I'd found the best *place* for coffee, not the best shop.'

A decent walk and a careful scramble down damp stone steps and Jo had to agree that this was the best place for coffee she'd ever seen. They were on soft white sand, a crescent of turquoise sea with waves being ridden by surfers, the beach framed by dramatic cliffs and massive sandstone boulders that were natural works of art. There was even a waterfall.

When they'd explored from one end of the beach to

the other, there was a sheltered spot in a sandstone cleft to sit in and watch the waves and it was a bonus that the narrowness of the gap meant their hips were touching when they both squeezed in. There was hot, strong coffee, just the way Jo liked it, from a Thermos that Cade had in the backpack and there were no awkward moments in a conversation that had started at the beginning of the walking track and was now flowing so freely it felt as if they'd known each other for ever.

'Did you know that Dunedin is built around seven hills? So is Rome. And Barcelona.'

'How on earth do you know that?'

'I told you, I do my research when I go somewhere new. There's lots of places that claim the seven hills thing. Edinburgh is another one, which is kind of appropriate because Dunedin is also considered the most Scottish city outside of Scotland.'

'I *did* know that. There's a statue of Robbie Burns in the centre of town in the Octagon. And I've heard people playing bagpipes there.'

Jo liked the way Cade had laughed when she told him how she'd competed so hard with her older brothers to get the attention of their father. How she'd had to do everything they did and try to do it better. How being told she couldn't do something because she was 'only' a girl made her all the more determined.

'I wouldn't let anyone call me Joanna. I wanted a boy's name because I wanted to be just like my brothers.'

'They went into medicine?'

'Two of them are surgeons, like Dad. One works in London and the other in New York. One's a firefighter and the last one works for NASA. He's a rocket scientist but don't ask me what he actually does because I don't understand any of it.'

'Somehow, I doubt that.' The look that Jo received was one of admiration. 'Impressive family.'

'Intimidating, I've been told. Maybe that's why we all suck at relationships. I've got two brothers who are divorced, one's been engaged twice but has never married and the last one seems determined to be a bachelor for the rest of his life.'

Cade's nod was approving. 'I can relate to that. Let me guess…is he the firefighter?'

'Yep.'

'And then there's you.' Cade's eyebrow lifted. 'Are you engaged, married or divorced?'

'None of the above. My poor mother's beginning to think she's never going to get a grandchild.' She shook her head. 'I suspect she's dreaming of a girl that actually wants to be girly.'

'I like tomboys,' Cade said. 'And being single is a good thing.'

Jo ignored the odd tingle at Cade's approval of tomboys. 'Why is being single a good thing?'

'Well, I doubt that we would be here, doing this, if either of us had family or relationship commitments out of our working hours.'

'That's true…'

Jo caught her bottom lip between her teeth. The burning question for her was *why* Cade was single? Putting aside his rugged, ultimately masculine physical attraction, she'd identified qualities in him during their first meeting that would make him irresistible to almost any woman whose path he'd crossed over the years. And he never stayed in one place for long? She wanted to know the reason for that as well. She'd suspected he might be a loner, but there was always a story behind a trait that no one was normally born with. But, despite the ease of the conversation between them, the questions seemed too personal to ask so she settled for something generic.

'Have you got siblings? A bunch of sisters, maybe?'

'No. No father either, but I have enough cousins and uncles to make up for that. I might be only part Pasifika but family's still…well…everything.'

Jo had to stifle her curiosity. She knew how important family was to people with Pacific Island or Maori heritage so, if Cade had such a big extended family, why did he not live closer to them? What had happened to drive him away? And did he not want a family and children of his own? If he did, then—like her—he was leaving it a bit late. He had crinkles of lines around his eyes and the kind of ease of being in his own skin that Jo associated with men mature enough to be well into their forties.

But Cade had every right to choose what he shared in the way of personal information. She already knew from their conversation during their walk towards the beach that he'd trained as a paramedic in Auckland and had later gone on to work on oil rigs and in the mines in Australia. He'd been overseas working with Médecins sans Frontières for a few years before coming back to New Zealand to do postgraduate training and become a critical care paramedic. His working history only added to the impression that he was a maverick. That he had compelling reasons that made him walk away from commitment of any kind?

It only added to the aura of this man as far as Jo was concerned. Quite apart from the crazy idea that he could be the perfect choice for a sperm donor, he was also the most compellingly attractive man she'd ever met in her life. The point of contact where their hips touched was generating a heat she could feel throughout her entire body, so it was rather ironic that she suddenly shivered. Just a subtle quiver but Cade clearly felt it instantly.

'Yeah…it's getting colder.' He was frowning as he scanned Jo's face. He reached out to pull the over-large borrowed jacket back from where it had slipped down her shoulder and, for a heartbeat, when his thumb brushed her chin, Jo could see a flash of something in his eyes.

As if he was thinking about kissing her…

Oh…help… Jo couldn't look away. And this time the shiver that ran through her body had nothing to do with how cold it was getting as the sun went down.

It was Cade who broke that eye contact, turning to screw the cap back onto the Thermos and put it in the backpack. 'Climbing back up those steps should warm us up.'

Jo handed him the plastic mug she'd been using. 'Thank you. That was great coffee.'

'I should have brought something to eat as well.' Cade wriggled out of the space and then held out his hand to help Jo to her feet. 'Let me make that up to you by taking you out to dinner.'

Jo got to her feet and let go of Cade's hand before he could guess the effect his touch might be having. Brushing sand off her clothes and tucking herself further into the warmth of this well-worn, soft leather jacket gave her time to blink away the surprise of both the reaction her body was having to his touch and the unexpected invitation.

A second invitation.

A date on top of a date.

Was Cade feeling the same way she was? That there was a curiously urgent need to find out as much as she could about him? To share as much about herself as he could possibly be interested in? That they had wasted too much time already because they should have met each other a long time ago?

It was unlikely. But not impossible. The way he was looking at her right now suggested that, at the very least, the level of attraction between them was on a similar level.

'Sounds like a plan,' she found herself saying, as if it was no big deal to have a date on top of another date. 'I should warn you, though, walking up hills makes me super hungry.'

'No worries. We can have an eating competition if you like.'

Jo laughed. 'You sound like one of my brothers. When he was about twelve years old.'

'I remember being twelve years old. It would have been fun to have had a little sister like you.' Jo could hear the grin in Cade's voice even though she wasn't looking at him. 'What's your favourite food?'

'I tried a new Spanish restaurant the other night which was fabulous. But I like everything. French, Italian, Chinese. Or hamburgers...' Jo was still deliberately keeping her gaze on where they were heading—towards the opening of the tunnel at the end of the beach—because she didn't quite have the courage to catch Cade's gaze again so soon. Because she knew that it wouldn't be anything like the kind of look a big brother and little sister might exchange.

The idea of asking Cade if he might consider being part of her plan to have a baby was absolutely the last thing on Jo's mind. She'd even forgotten all those burning questions about why he couldn't settle long term anywhere or with any*one*. She didn't want to ask him anything right now, to be honest.

She just wanted *him*…

She needed to pull in a steadying breath. 'I *love* a good hamburger.'

Hamburgers it was.

Gourmet burgers, mind you. Full of bacon and mushrooms and blue cheese and pulled beef. One of the best burgers Cade had ever tasted. Even better, the shop was so close to his apartment that it was a no-brainer to take them home rather than sit at outside tables on a chilly evening. They sat at the small table in his kitchen rather than anywhere more comfortable because the hamburgers were so juicy they dripped, which not only made them all the more delicious but gave Cade the pleasure of watching Jo have to lick her fingers or chase droplets with her tongue when they threatened to roll down her chin.

The kitchen was as sleek and modern as the rest of this apartment—the kind of living space Cade always rented because he didn't want a property that required maintenance. Or one that he might get attached to. He'd only been living here for the last week or so but this messy meal in the small, well-appointed kitchen was making him feel as though he had really settled in.

As if this might turn out to be his favourite apartment ever.

Because it felt so incredibly vibrant right now. Because he had one of the most beautiful, intriguing women he'd ever met bumping her face with a hamburger as if it was the best meal she'd ever tasted and he was watching her like a hawk because he didn't want to miss a single glimpse of her tongue chasing a drop of juice. Or licking her lips after a sip of the bottle of red wine that was rapidly diminishing thanks to Jo's decision to get a taxi home.

Cade didn't want her to go home, mind you.

Not any time soon.

Oddly, though, this was different to any time he'd brought a gorgeous woman home in more ways than one. Normally, he'd only have had one thing on his mind and they would have been in the bedroom some time ago but, dammit…he'd never met someone that he enjoyed talking to this much. Someone who seemed to be so at ease in his company that he felt as if he'd known her for ever. Maybe it had something to do with the fact that Jo had grown up with four older brothers and was a self-declared tomboy because he did feel as comfortable as he would if he was having a night out and a few beers with one of his best mates.

The conversation was as interesting as any he'd ever had with mates, or colleagues too. Only people with the same kind of passion for emergency medicine could have a discussion about a case they'd worked on together while they were enjoying a meal. Talking about how they would have managed the amputation if it had been necessary and about the microsurgery that Jo had watched to repair that badly fractured leg. And when they weren't talking about their work they were sharing snippets of their personal lives, like hobbies.

'What's your favourite way to burn off steam? Or stay fit?'

'I've just taken up fencing,' Jo told him.

'What, on farms? Like post and rail, or sheep netting fences?'

'No.' The peal of Jo's laughter was enchanting. '*Fencing*. With swords. You know, foils and sabres.'

'Wow…' He could imagine her wearing the skin-tight

outfits and the metallic vests that recorded the touch of the weapons. 'Now that's something I'd like to try.' He could almost see Jo lunging towards an opponent with a sword in one hand and the other arm in the air for balance and, heaven help him, it was the sexiest thing he could imagine any woman doing.

'Come along to a class some time. Newbies are always welcome.'

'I'd love that. What else do you like doing?'

'I also love dancing. Lindy hop—the really fast kind. Like they did in the 1930s? Now, that's a way to really keep fit. Want to try that too?'

'Nah… I'll pass on that one, thanks.' Cade was shaking his head. 'You don't do anything ordinary, do you?'

He got to his feet to find some paper towels because the serviettes that had come with the burgers were too damp to be useful any longer. He wiped his own face before turning to offer some to Jo, who was also on her feet, gathering up the wrappers their meal had come in. He was about to pass her a towel to get rid of the drip of sauce he could see at the corner of her mouth but, for some reason, his hand froze in mid-air.

Jo turned as if she could feel his gaze and then she also froze, the balled-up wrappers slipping from her hand to land silently on the table. Her lips parted so that the smear of sauce was even more visible but, instead of offering the towel, Cade found himself reaching out instead to collect it, very gently and very slowly, with the pad of his thumb. He did it without breaking the locked gaze they were sharing. And when he lifted his thumb to remove that tiny bit of sauce by putting it into his own mouth, licking it off and then taking it out as slowly as the way he'd touched Jo's lips, he saw the exact moment that desire exploded.

He saw the way her eyes darkened. The way the tip of her tongue came out to dampen her bottom lip. He could *feel* the astonishing electricity between them. There was no need to ask out loud for consent either, given the way Jo reached for him at the same time as his hand slid behind her neck and under her hair to cup the back of her head. And the way she rose up onto tiptoes so that he could find her lips with his own a nanosecond sooner than it might have otherwise happened.

Cade had never encountered a combination of softness, fierceness and heat quite like this. A conversation in the dance of pressure and the touch of tongues that was in a totally new language for him. A taste that was like liquid fire. The shock of her bare hands touching his skin under his tee shirt made it feel as if her fingers were leaving a trail like lava across the delicate skin above his hips. It actually did feel as if it was burning his nipples a moment later so he had to grab Jo's wrists. He had to try and slow things down or this was going to be over far, far too soon.

He held her gaze again as he lifted one of her hands to his mouth. He could still taste an echo of the meal they'd shared as he took a fingertip into his mouth but it was no more than a faint background to the taste of her skin. The flavour of this extraordinary woman. He was watching the way Jo's eyes drifted shut as she made a tiny sound of need. A sigh that suggested a depth of yearning he could relate to only too easily.

Okay…maybe this was going to be over too soon but they had the rest of the night, didn't they? He swept Jo up into his arms to carry her off to his bed.

They could go slower next time…

CHAPTER FOUR

'OH, MY GOD… What on earth's going on…?'

The expression on Hanna's face made Jo completely forget what information it was she had come to the central desk to chase up. Her head swerved to see the doors sliding open to admit a stretcher with the paramedics in attendance, but Hanna was right—this was by no means the usual way a patient was brought into the emergency department.

There was only one paramedic pushing the stretcher. The other was hanging off the edge of it by balancing on the frame. He was hanging onto the side bar to steady himself with one hand and the other seemed to be gripping the neck of the patient. Not only that, the paramedic was spattered with blood and grim-faced.

'Resus One…' Jo went ahead of the stretcher fast enough to grab gloves and be putting them on by the time it came through the doors of the high-tech resuscitation area. She reached for the protection of a mask and eye shield as the lead paramedic began a handover. There was—or had been—a lot of bleeding happening here.

'Thirty-eight-year-old male. Penetrating neck injury from an explosion in a factory. I've had direct pressure on a carotid artery bleed for…' he glanced at a military style watch '…coming up to four minutes.'

'Okay. Don't move. We'll give it at least ten minutes before releasing the pressure. Preferably twenty.' Jo could see the patient was conscious. And terrified. 'We've got you,' she told him. 'We're going to take good care of you.'

The trauma team was gathering around her. 'Let's see if we can get him on the bed—but only if it doesn't increase agitation and interfere with Cade's haemorrhage control. We're going to need bilateral wide bore IV access, oxygen on and I'd like a set of vital signs, stat, please.'

Of course it was Cade. The thought that only this man could repeatedly find such dramatic ways to attract her attention was no more than a fleeting background acknowledgement. Likewise, the visceral reaction to being this close to him for the first time since the most extraordinary first date of her life couldn't be prevented but could certainly be ignored for the time being.

'I didn't want to try and get IV access on the scene,' Cade told her. He was moving carefully with his patient during the transfer to the bed and keeping his gloved fingers buried in the wound on the side of the man's neck, despite the man's agitation and attempts to move away from pressure that was probably painful. 'Not when we were so close to ED. He's had significant blood loss. I'd estimate there was at least a litre on the factory floor and, while the first aiders had known to put pressure on the wound, they were using a folded towel and it probably soaked up another litre. There was projectile arterial bleeding again when the pad was lifted as we came through the door.'

So this patient had lost possibly thirty percent of his blood volume, which would put him in the second most severe degree of hypovolaemic shock. No wonder he was looking so pale and sweaty and was clearly breathing more rapidly than normal. The agitation was part of that as well and the sooner they had IV access to administer both pain relief and sedation, the better. Staff were moving fast around the bed now, cutting clothing clear and attaching monitoring equipment like ECG electrodes and a blood pressure cuff. Cade used his free hand to help get an oxygen mask in place, keeping up a running commentary to let his patient know what was happening around him and to reassure him. An IV trolley was being wheeled close on the other side of the bed and the airway doctor in the trauma team had a stethoscope on the man's chest already.

'Any other injuries? Was he KO'd?' Jo could see that the member of the trauma team tasked with circulation was frowning as he tried to find a vein that could be used for a wide bore cannula.

'No head injury or loss of consciousness. GCS was fourteen on arrival due to non-orientation to time or place. He's got increasingly agitated since.' Cade turned his head to make eye contact with his patient again. 'You're doing great, Bruce. Dr Bishop's right. We've got this, okay?'

Jo ordered some morphine and fentanyl to be drawn up. They could get some intramuscular medication on board to deal with the patient's pain and anxiety until they could get the IV access they needed.

'Any past medical history we should know about? Allergies?'

'No. Poor guy was just in the wrong place at the wrong time. Caught some shrapnel from the inside of a machine that spat the dummy.'

'Blood pressure's fifty-six over twenty-two,' a registrar reported. 'Heart rate one-twenty.'

Jo could see the rapid spikes of the ECG trace on the monitor's screen. She could also see that the oxygen saturation in Bruce's blood was low at ninety four percent. Their first priority was fluid resuscitation to maintain adequate perfusion for vital organs but that needed to be balanced against the risk of disrupting clots or increasing blood loss by raising the pressure. A degree of low blood pressure was preferable at this point in time. But not this low.

'Let's get some bloods off, please,' she ordered. 'I want a haemoglobin, electrolytes, group and cross-match.' She also wanted an arterial blood gas measurement as soon as possible and they'd need to get a catheter into their patient to monitor urine output. And it was taking too long to get IV access suitable for rapid infusion of fluids.

'I'm going to get a central venous line in.' She met Cade's gaze. 'Can you stay put until I'm scrubbed and we're set up? I'll go subclavian rather than external jugular so we won't get in your way. I'd prefer it to be closer to twenty minutes pressure on that wound before we test whether things are stable. I'd rather not risk switching you out for someone else before then or we might be back to square one.'

Cade ended up staying where he was long enough for both the central line and peripheral venous access to be put in place and a rapid infusion of a saline bolus to be started. The technology to monitor blood pressure internally was working and levels were already rising, thanks to the increased fluid volume. Packed red blood cells were being readied for infusion. Oxygen saturation was improving and the heart rate slowing a little as the patient's condition was stabilised and arrangements were made to take him to have a CT scan of his neck prior to being taken to Theatre.

Finally, it was time for Cade to release the pressure he'd been keeping on the carotid artery and for everybody to hold their breath, waiting to see if a spurt of blood would indicate that this crisis was not yet under complete control.

Jo breathed a sigh of relief along with everyone else in Resus when there was no sign of breakthrough bleeding but it was only after the bed was being wheeled out, surrounded by several members of the trauma team, to go to Radiology for the scan that she switched her focus, turning to where Cade was finishing his paperwork so that he could leave the patient's copy to go in the notes. His crew partner had already taken the stretcher away to clean it.

'You've been exposed to a lot of blood spatter,' she told him. 'Maybe I should take some blood and check your antibodies for HIV and hepatitis.'

'I'm vaccinated for Hep A and B. Unless something shows up in Bruce's bloodwork, I think I'm good.'

'You've got blood on your arms. Have you got any broken skin?'

'Not that I know of.'

'Let me check...' Most of the trauma team had gone already, either to CT with their patient or back to other positions in ED, but there was a nurse tidying up discarded packaging and a technician wiping down equipment. Not that there was anything unprofessional about Jo touching Cade's bare arms below his uniform sleeves to see if he had any obvious cuts or grazes that could present a hazard for blood borne diseases.

It just felt really, really personal.

Maybe that was because she could see the lower part

of Cade's tattoo and she knew perfectly well that the waves and swirls of the traditional Polynesian design covered his whole upper arm and extended onto both his back and his chest. And because, despite the gloves she was wearing, she could feel the heat of his skin and that took her straight back to Saturday night.

She'd never had a date like that in her life.

Ever.

She'd never talked so much about herself during the first part of their time together. Or eaten messy food, not caring that it was dripping all over her face. She'd definitely never even considered going to bed with someone on a first date, let alone losing count of how many times they'd had sex.

Okay, that wasn't quite true. She knew exactly how many times. Three. But only if you counted that first explosive release that was more about sheer lust than the delicious exploration and pleasure of the lovemaking that came later.

Jo didn't dare look up to meet Cade's gaze as she scanned the bare skin of his arms with such unprofessional thoughts flashing through the back of her mind, but she had to look up to check the rest of the unprotected skin on his face.

'Were you wearing a mask and eye shield?'

'Yes. We knew we were going to a serious blood loss incident. I took them off when I was confident I had things under control. I hate it when the plastic starts fogging up.'

'Hmm.' Jo knew she should impart a bit of professional advice about the use of PPE but Cade was smiling at her and…and she was losing her train of thought.

He'd texted her the day after that astonishing date.

Just a smiley face, but it had been enough to suggest that he was thinking about her. About the sex? And that thinking about either or both of those things was enough to make him happy…

She'd texted him and offered an invitation to join her in a fencing class because he'd said he'd like to try the sport, but he'd been working an unexpected night shift to cover a colleague whose wife had gone into labour. She hadn't texted him yesterday because she knew he'd be sleeping after the night shift so this was the first time they'd seen each other since Saturday. It was all very well sending a smiley face to suggest that Cade had been feeling good after his time with her. It was quite another thing to see the warmth that was lighting up his eyes in a silent message that no one else could possibly be aware of.

He looked as though he would be really happy to see her again—out of work hours. Somewhere private…

And heaven help her, but Jo was suddenly having trouble thinking about anything else herself.

'Um… I can't see any broken skin,' she murmured. 'I'd recommend you have a shower as soon as possible, though, and get out of that contaminated uniform.'

Oh…there was more than a gleam in those dark eyes now. There was a cheeky grin simmering in the background as Jo got the message that there was plenty more skin she would be welcome to inspect but, again, it was a secret communication.

'I'll do that,' was all he said aloud, as a nurse came in with a sterile pack in her arms that was probably a replacement central venous line kit. 'Thanks, Doc.'

'No worries. If you're back in later on your shift, come and find me. I'm sure you'll want to see the CT results on your patient. You saved a life today.'

* * *

It always felt good to know that you'd made a positive difference to someone's life, let alone saving it, whether or not it got acknowledged by others. It was even better, however, when it got noticed by someone like Joanna Bishop. Cade might have only been working in this city for a week or so but he was already getting a feel for the medical scene. He was rapidly learning which rest home he'd choose for his mother due to the high standard of care and which GP was notable for a less than acceptable standard. He'd met colleagues whose opinion and skills he could respect and staff in the emergency department that were on top of their game. None more so than the head of department, however, so winning Jo's respect for his work really meant something.

Winning her interest on a personal level was a completely unexpected bonus but the frequency with which Cade found himself thinking about Jo was a warning not to let it become too significant, which was why he hadn't texted her since Sunday evening, when he'd had to decline her invitation to try out a fencing class. It wasn't that he didn't want to see her again, it was simply that he was playing it cool. At some point, preferably as soon as possible, he needed to have the conversation that he always had with any women who'd shared any part of his life in the last ten years. The one where he made sure they were on the same page and that this was never going to be anything more than a friendship. Spending time with Jo could become a very enjoyable part of his life outside working hours when or if it suited them both but it had to stay casual.

Fun.

As much fun as the game of keeping it to themselves in a professional environment was turning out to be?

Yeah…especially when he suspected Jo was enjoying it as much as he was.

Okay, maybe he was leaning a little closer than he should have when she was showing him the CT scan results on the carotid artery injury later that day, having spotted him when he'd been on his way out of the department, but she was using the small screen of a tablet and he needed to be close enough to see properly.

'So you can see the shadow of the foreign body, with metallic density, here at the carotid sheath space.'

'Good grief… I'm kind of glad I didn't know it was there. I might have thought twice about how much pressure I put on his neck.'

'He'd be dead if you hadn't stopped the bleeding.' Jo scrolled into another file. 'They did CT angiography before he went to Theatre and they found multiple traumatic pseudoaneurysms of the left internal carotid artery.' Her head was bent as she peered at the screen. 'Look… Can you see that? There? And…there?'

'Yep. Hmm.' Oh, he was close enough to smell Jo's skin. And he knew exactly how soft that particular spot at the nape of her neck was. He also knew it was a very effective erogenous zone for Jo. Cade had to clear his throat before speaking again. 'I could imagine that that would have taken some fixing.'

'They used a shunt, blocked the external carotid artery, resected the pseudoaneurysm, removed the fragment of metal and then stitched everything up. Patient's doing well so far but he's in ICU for monitoring.'

'I might come back when I've finished my shift and see if I can visit him. I wonder if Kayla's still an inpatient. I could pop in and see how she's doing as well.'

'Let's check.' Jo accessed an inpatient data base on the hospital's intraweb. 'No,' she said moments later.

'Kayla got discharged over the weekend. But the discharge summary sounds positive. Good movement in her toes and any nerve damage causing lack of sensation may resolve in time. She's non-weightbearing until they review her in Outpatients when she comes in to get a more lightweight cast.' She tucked her hair behind her ear as she glanced up to smile at Cade. 'You have a bit of a talent for being involved in memorable cases, don't you? Kayla and now today's drama. Everyone's still talking about the way you rode in on that stretcher. I've heard the word "cowboy" a few times.'

Oh…he loved the way she tucked her hair behind her ears like that.

He loved her smile even more.

'I have always been a trauma magnet,' he admitted. 'And it's not the first time I've been called a cowboy but people seem to like working with me. Nothing like a challenge or two to keep a job interesting.' He leaned even closer and lowered his voice. 'I know how to make time out of work pretty interesting too, if you don't mind a bit of the Wild West.'

To outward appearances, it would seem that Dr Bishop was focused on what she was reading on screen. In reality, she made a humming sound that made it hard for Cade to stifle a grin.

'I owe you a dinner,' she murmured. 'How 'bout I text you my address?'

Jo's small Victorian terraced house in the central city couldn't have been more of a contrast to Cade's modern apartment even though they were no more than a few blocks apart. The rooms had high ceilings with elaborate plaster cornices and roses, bay windows at the front and gas fireplaces set inside carved wooden surrounds.

It was cold enough this evening to have the fires going and the real flickering flames added to the cosy ambience of the rooms.

The food Jo intended to offer for dinner was going to be rather different too. No messy, drippy hamburgers. Maybe she wanted Cade to see a different side to a woman who could appreciate street food. And, okay, maybe she hadn't had the time to make everything from scratch but the nearby upmarket delicatessen and butchery had the kind of elegant food she wanted to serve. She had a whole beef fillet and scalloped potatoes ready to go into the oven and green runner beans tied up in elegant little bundles with the edible string that chives provided.

Fortunately, she'd only just turned the oven on by the time Cade arrived, with a bottle of excellent red wine under his arm. Because while the décor and food might be very different from the Saturday evening they'd spent together last weekend, one thing was exactly the same.

That astonishingly fierce desire for each other. Sexual tension like nothing Jo had ever discovered. There was no way they were going to sit down and eat dinner any time soon. They couldn't even do more than taste the wine.

'I think you'll like this,' Cade said, handing her a glass. 'It's one of my favourites.'

Jo tasted the wine, made an appreciative sound and then looked up at Cade as she licked her lips, to find his gaze fixed on her mouth. She heard the way he released his breath in a silent whistle and it was as eloquent as if he'd said what was foremost in his mind. His action of taking the glass back from her hand and putting it down on the table beside his own was also a clear message of his intent but Jo didn't mind him taking charge like this.

For someone who'd always rebelled against being

told what to do, she actually liked it far more than she should have.

She was ready for the touch of Cade's hand on her neck, just lightly, on that sensitive spot on her nape before he slid his fingers up into her hair. It was instinctive to lean into that touch. To tip her head back, which also made her close her eyes. That way, she was ready to experience the shock of pleasure as his lips covered hers, simply through touch and taste. Hearing got added with that grunt of bliss that came from Cade as his tongue joined the party. And smell was there as a background, of course. This man had the most amazingly fresh masculine scent, but there was also a raw musky tone that was pure sex and utterly irresistible.

They stopped at the foot of the narrow staircase at the end of the hallway to kiss again. Shoes got kicked off and an item or two of clothing got discarded on the stairs before they reached Jo's bedroom and then she discovered that something else was different about tonight.

The sex was different.

Better.

Because, already, there was a familiarity that made things more comfortable and gave them both more confidence to initiate—and respond to—everything every sense, including sight, could offer them.

And as Jo lay in Cade's arms some time later, catching her breath, she realised that there was something she'd never found this early on in any relationship she'd had over so many years—a feeling of trust… Which was weird because that was something that had become harder and harder to find as the years, and failed relationships, had gone by. She'd barely met Cade but there seemed to be a connection here that was completely new.

And very, very different.

Perhaps that was because she'd made such a huge decision the day she'd met Cade. She might be planning to have a baby but, as she'd told Hanna, she'd given up long ago on finding a life partner. She might have seen Cade as a perfect donor but the reason they were here together, like this, was only because she'd thought it would be fun getting to know him better.

And…wow…she hadn't been wrong. It was so good that there was a tiny voice in the back of her head suggesting that she might have stumbled across what she'd been looking for for ever. That this could be the start of a relationship that could last the distance. For ever, even?

Jo needed to silence that voice. She might be aware of a level of trust between herself and Cade but she wasn't going to allow herself to go down that well-worn track when she knew the kind of heartbreak she would find at the end. And she needed to distract whatever was behind that voice before it could come up with even more persuasive suggestions.

She twisted away from Cade's arms. 'I'd better go and rescue our dinner.'

Like everything else about Joanna Bishop, the food she served was impressive.

'Man, you can cook,' Cade told her. 'This is like restaurant quality.'

'I have a confession to make.'

'Oh?'

'All I had to do was put it in the oven for the prescribed time and steam the beans. It was really made by the deli that I walk past when I'm coming home. I can't cook to save myself.'

Cade ate in silence for a minute but he was liking this a lot. Not just that a seemingly perfect woman had flaws like any normal person but that she was happy to be honest about them.

'Your turn,' Jo told him.

'My turn for what?'

'Confessing something.' Jo eyed him over the rim of her wine glass.

Cade grinned. 'I have to confess that... I like you,' he said.

'That's your confession?' She put her glass down.

'Yep.'

Jo laughed. 'Fair enough. Okay, I like you too but I'm sure there's something more interesting about you that I don't know.'

Cade shrugged. 'I'd rather talk about you. And how you tried to outdo those poor brothers of yours? I'm guessing that's how you ended up being a head of department at such a young age.'

'Young? How old do you think I am?'

Cade swallowed another piece of the melt-in-your-mouth fillet steak. ''Bout my age?'

'How old *are* you?' Jo was spearing beans with her fork.

'Thirty-seven.'

The fork dropped with a loud clatter. 'Oh, my God.' Jo sounded horrified. 'You're kidding.'

'Is it a problem?'

'You're not even forty.'

'That's generally how it works. You have to be thirty-seven first.' He grinned at her. 'You mean you've already hit the big Four-O?'

'Some time ago. Good grief...' Jo picked up her wine glass. 'I've become a cougar.'

'As in an older woman who preys on younger guys

for sex?' Cade laughed. 'As if. You don't even look forty but if you are, bring it on, I say.'

'I'm forty-six, Cade. *Nine* years older than you.'

'So what?' Cade shrugged. This was perfect. They could have the conversation he'd been intending to have without it seeming awkward at all. 'It's not as if this is anything serious.' He'd been there, done that. Never again. He didn't talk about it either, so it was a bit disturbing that he found himself wanting to tell Jo about it right now. To confess that he wasn't capable of falling in love again and…that sometimes it was a lonely way to live…

But Jo didn't need to know that and maybe he didn't want to tell her because he didn't want her to feel sorry for him. He cleared his throat.

'I told you I never stay in one place for long.' It was a well-honed protective mechanism. Never get too attached—to people or places—because it was so much easier to cope when they weren't there any longer. 'A year or two and I'll be moving on again—that's the way I roll. As I said, I like you, Jo, and age is just a number. It doesn't make the slightest difference. Not to me.' He held her gaze. 'But maybe it does for you? If you're looking for something more…significant?'

She shook her head. He could see something in her eyes that was familiar. A bit heart-wrenching. 'I think I gave up on the idea of significant a long time ago. I've had too many dead-end relationships. I've watched too many other marriages disintegrate, including my brothers'.'

Ah…that was what it was. Jo Bishop knew about the particular kind of loneliness that came from the knowledge you were treading a path through life alone. She was clearly quite capable of doing that very successfully but Cade was aware of a vulnerability that made him want to reassure her.

To look after her—to the best of his ability—at least for a while?

'There you go, then. No wonder we get on so well. We're good together.' He raised his glass. 'Maybe we should make the most of it while it lasts?'

'I'd like that.' Jo clinked her glass against his. 'I do have another confession, though.'

'What's that?' There was a sparkle in her eyes now that he'd seen somewhere before. Oh, no...she wasn't about to tell him that she was falling in love with him, was she?

She took a deep breath. 'I'm planning to have a baby,' she said.

Cade came very close to choking on the mouthful of wine that tried to go down the wrong way. He might have sworn a little under his breath as well. And then he shook his head.

'I've never met anyone like you,' he said. 'There's a proper confession for you.' He could feel one side of his mouth lifting into a crooked smile. 'Your mother will be delighted.'

Jo screwed up her nose. 'I'm not sure about that. She'll probably think it's irresponsible to actually plan to be a single mother.'

The odd tension Cade was experiencing dropped noticeably. Except...good grief...was this why she'd been so happy to jump into bed with him on their first date? Thank goodness he'd had a good personal supply of protection. The thought that Jo would use somebody like that didn't sit well, however. Had his instinct about her being trustworthy been misplaced? His tone was cautious when he spoke again.

'So…you're planning to get pregnant and not tell the father?'

'I think that's usually how it works for fertility clinics and donated sperm.' A flush of colour was appearing in Jo's cheeks. 'Oops…too much information.' She reached for her wine glass to drain the last mouthful.

Cade couldn't look away from her face. She really was blushing, which was kind of cute. He filed it away, with that hint of vulnerability he'd seen in her. The other side of the coin that was the extraordinarily confident, competent woman he'd been so attracted to.

He picked up the bottle of wine to refill her glass. 'Something else you might have to make the most of,' he said. 'You'll have a long stretch of going wine free soon.' He raised an eyebrow. 'Presumably soon?'

'I'm finally ready to get on with it.' Jo nodded. 'I decided last week. On my birthday. The day I met you, actually.'

'I didn't know.' Cade raised his glass in another toast. 'Happy belated birthday.'

'Thanks.'

'That's quite a present you've given yourself. It's a big decision.'

'Not a spur of the moment one, though. I had eggs frozen when I was in my late thirties. I didn't want to wake up one day and find I'd totally lost the opportunity to be a mother. It was in the wake of another disastrous relationship ending and I'd just become a consultant as well, so I knew it would be a few years before I could take time out from my career.' Jo let her breath out in a sigh. 'I have no idea why I'm telling you all this. Except that… I would like to spend more time with you, so I guess I thought it was only fair to tell you about what's going on in my life. Plus, you know… I was on a bit of a roll with those confessions.'

'I get it.' Cade looked down at his plate. There was still some of that delicious deli-bought food left, but somehow he'd lost his appetite. Something had gone very wrong with the conversation he'd been planning to have with Jo. The one where they confirmed that they were both on the same page about a no-strings, no-expectations friendship that included plenty of the best sex he'd ever had in his life?

Jo had followed his gaze. 'You've had enough?'

He nodded. 'It was great. I've just…had enough.'

'I didn't get any dessert, I'm sorry.'

'That's a good thing. And…' Cade glanced at his watch '…it's getting late anyway and I've got a five a.m. start for my day shift. I should probably head home.'

Jo was on her feet instantly. She shook her head when Cade went to pick up his plate, however.

'Don't touch a thing. I'll take care of it. My penance for not actually cooking for you.'

Cade pulled her into his arms so that he could kiss her. 'You have talents that I appreciate even more than being able to cook.' He kissed her again. 'You're an astonishing woman, Jo Bishop. Did I tell you that I've never met anyone like you?'

She was smiling up at him. 'You did.'

'And I admire you for going after something that you want. You'll be as amazing as a mother as everything else you do in life.'

There was a sparkle in her eyes that made him think that she might be about to cry so he kissed her again before reaching for his leather jacket that he'd draped over the back of a chair and started to walk towards the door.

'Let me know if there's anything I can do to help.'

It was an automatic thing to say by way of a farewell. Stealing another kiss on Jo's front doorstep as a final goodnight was just as automatic.

'Well…you *would* make the perfect father.'

Cade's heart actually skipped a beat despite the casual tone of her words, but then Jo's face creased into an apologetic sort of smile that was almost a visible cringe.

'Just kidding….'

Cade didn't say anything. He *couldn't* say anything. Jo wasn't to know that she'd stepped onto forbidden ground. That she'd blindsided him and that his fight or flight reflex was telling him to get the hell out of Dodge. He zipped up his jacket, jammed his helmet on and fired up his bike.

It could never be a joke. When he lifted a hand as he took off on his bike he knew the gesture might later be interpreted as a final farewell.

Okay, he already knew that Jo didn't deserve to be dropped like this, and he felt bad about that, but this was another of his well-honed protective mechanisms. Never going anywhere near that forbidden ground voluntarily had been the way he'd learned to cope in the first place.

And if something wasn't broken there was no need to fix it, was there?

CHAPTER FIVE

SHE'D BLOWN IT.

Time after time, over the next week or so, Jo watched Cade come into the emergency department. She might see him talking to Hanna as she triaged the patient being brought in and, more often than not, it was a run-of-the-mill type of situation that didn't need her involvement. An elderly person with exacerbation of their COPD due to an infection, perhaps, or an abdominal pain or minor injuries from an MVA. Cade's reputation as a 'trauma magnet' who got sent to the most serious cases might be getting dented but he didn't seem bothered. He looked happy in his work and was perfectly friendly when he smiled at Jo in passing or followed up on one of his cases.

Given that they'd been so careful to keep their mutual attraction a secret, not even Hanna had any idea what Jo was thinking or feeling when she saw Cade—or worse, when he was talking to her about a case and standing close enough to make her skin prickle. When she didn't dare meet his gaze directly because she had a bit of pride and she wasn't going to let him know that she was surprisingly badly hurt.

She would never want him to know that she'd fought back tears as she'd cleaned up the meal that neither of them had finished. That she'd come even closer to being undone when his scent had filled her nostrils as she'd straightened the rumpled linen on her bed. That looking out of the window at the street as she'd pulled the curtains that evening made it impossible to stop a single tear trickling down the side of her nose, as if she could see him leaving all over again, as if she was still standing on the doorstep. Watching him disappearing into the night, with a single dismissive wave of a gloved hand.

Knowing it was her own stupid fault for even joking about something that would send any committed bachelor running for the hills didn't help because she suspected Cade had known that, on some level, she hadn't really been joking at all.

This was the flip side of that connection that let them communicate without saying a word, wasn't it? The one that had made it so enjoyable to flirt secretly at work. Fortunately, Jo discovered it was possible to cut the line on that connection and, to outward appearances, at least, she wasn't bothered in the least. She could be just as friendly. Only yesterday, she'd sent Cade a link to an introductory session her fencing club was offering to anyone who might be interested. She'd received a smiley face in response.

Not that it made Jo smile this time. But it did give her enough of a shove in the right direction to realise that she could choose how to react to this. It didn't have to change anything. When the private disturbance had settled enough to not be messing with her head, she would simply move on and the first positive step into her future would be to make an appointment with that fertility clinic. Maybe fate had sent Cade Cameron crashing into her life to demonstrate that too much information on a sperm donor was not a good thing, after all.

She was almost at that point just a day or two later. She even had the contact details of the clinic in her phone so, when her pager went off to request a trauma specialist to go with the helicopter callout to a bad accident on a rural road, the thought that Cade might be at the other end of the flight was no problem. Jo pulled her flight suit over her scrubs, shoved her feet into the steel-capped boots she kept in her locker and ran for the lift that would take her up to the rooftop landing pad.

She hoped Cade *would* be there, for the sake of victims who might need a hero to keep them alive.

He knew it was going to be a nasty smash before they got anywhere near the scene or updates on the status of the victims. They wouldn't have dispatched a helicopter at the same time as a road vehicle unless the local fire and rescue or police personnel had advised how serious this multi-vehicle accident was. He just hoped that they wouldn't have requested the addition of a trauma specialist to the crew because he would rather not arrive to find Jo as the lead medic and he was sure she would rather not have to work with him.

He felt quite bad enough, having backed away from anything to do with her on a personal basis, and he knew damn well that he'd hurt her. It didn't seem to be getting any easier to get past that guilt as the days ticked past. If anything, he was increasingly missing what they'd discovered with each other. He knew that an opportunity had been lost to make the most of something that was rare enough to be like winning the lottery.

A lottery that you couldn't even buy tickets for.

Ironically, though, the more days that stacked up, the more out of reach any way to put things right was becoming. Cade could feel himself slipping back into a space where deeply personal communication—especially the kind that could happen when you didn't say anything aloud—was something best avoided. Which was easy when you were only with someone in a situation when something personal was the last thing on your mind.

Like when you arrived at a scene on a rural road now blocked off from normal traffic, by emergency vehicles in the direction Cade arrived from and a helicopter that had landed further up the road on the other side. There were crumpled cars in between, rescue workers in high-vis jackets crowded around the wrecked vehicles and the noise of pneumatic tools being used to gain access to their interiors, with metal popping and glass shattering. One car had a tarpaulin covering its windows.

The police officer wearing a scene commander vest told Cade that two vehicles had collided head on at high speed and a third had been collected by a car spinning onto the wrong side of the road. She confirmed that the covered vehicle had a deceased driver and passenger and that the people from the third vehicle had been triaged as being status three to four, which meant that their injuries were minor to moderate. Cade sent Geoff to reassess them. He went towards where the main drama was obviously focused on one vehicle.

Fire crews were in the process of peeling back the roof of this car and a man wearing a cervical collar and oxygen mask was in the driver's seat. A flight paramedic was in the back seat of the car, stabilising the man's neck, and they were both under a protective plastic sheet so he didn't see Cade approaching.

'Over there, mate,' a fire officer directed him. 'I reckon the doc needs some assistance.'

The 'doc'. Cade knew who it was as soon as he saw

the back of the figure crouched in long grass on the verge of the road. She had her stethoscope ear pieces in and the disc on the exposed chest of a patient who was lying on a helicopter stretcher with the bright orange spinal board that would have been used to extricate him from the vehicle still beneath him. IV access had already been secured and a bag of fluids was being held aloft by a police officer who looked relieved to see Cade's arrival. Cardiac monitoring was in place but, more tellingly, the patient was already intubated and hooked up to a portable ventilator, which told Cade that his condition was critical. Had Jo managed all that by herself or had her crew partner been assisting before he climbed into that wrecked car?

It wouldn't have surprised Cade at all if Jo had already achieved major life-saving interventions without expert assistance. He knew how good she was at her job. And it only took a split second to realise how wrong he'd been in assuming that Jo wouldn't want to work with him.

'I'm so glad it's you,' she told him. 'This lad was initially responsive to voice on arrival, but became unresponsive with increasing respiratory distress as soon as we lifted him out. Correct tube placement confirmed by capnography but I'm not happy that he's stable enough to load and go.'

She didn't look happy, Cade thought. He could see a mix of complete focus and real distress in her eyes and the need to support Jo was instantly right up there with the need to do whatever he could to help with this patient. He shrugged off the strap of his backpack to put it down in the long grass.

'I think there's decreased air entry on the left side,' Jo said, 'but it's so hard to hear with the background noise. Could you have a quick look at his chest from his feet, please?'

'Sure.' Cade knelt and then leaned on his elbows so that he could be at eye level with the chest he needed to assess. This was an effective way to spot serious injuries that could be invisible when you were looking from above at either the side or head of the patient.

It was a small chest. Jo had called him a 'lad' and he was clearly no more than a child. Nine or ten years old, perhaps. Cade pushed the thought away. Hard. He focused on what he could see. Bruising that was already appearing on pale skin and…yes…he could see that a part of the chest wall was not moving the way it should. Instead of going out with a breath being drawn like the surrounding ribs, it was being drawn in and then rising as the breath was expelled.

'Paradoxical movement left side,' he told Jo.

She nodded. 'Peak pressures are rising, which is consistent with pneumothorax, and we've got some surgical emphysema happening now as well.'

Cade positioned himself on the other side of the young boy. He could see the bubbles of air under the skin that Jo was referring to. It was quite possible that, within a short amount of time, they might be dealing with a cardiac arrest due to blood and/or air accumulating within the chest and preventing the lungs from functioning despite the mechanical assistance.

They were in real danger of losing this patient.

And it took an even bigger push to get rid of that thought. This was almost too hard… Harder than it had ever been, but this wasn't the moment to wonder why that was the case.

'Needle thoracotomy?' he asked.

Jo shook her head. 'It rarely facilitates lung expansion and it's not enough for a large volume of blood or air. I'm going to do a finger thoracotomy. Quick and effective. You happy to assist?' She was pulling an equipment roll out of her kit. 'I could get Tom out of the car but that needs to be a very controlled extrication. The guy's got severe neck pain and no movement in his hands or lower limbs. It was a mission for Tom to get him calm enough for the firies to be able to get started on the car.'

'I'm good,' Cade told her. 'What do you need first?'

'I need his left arm abducted and externally rotated. And then the lateral chest wall well disinfected with chlorhexidine spray.' Jo opened her sterile kit and then stripped off her gloves to put on a new pair.

Watching Jo work dispelled any doubts about her ability to work alone. It also gave Cade too much time to think about their patient, and it had to be because he was with Jo and she'd already ventured unknowingly into that forbidden space that he found his own protective barriers crumbling. Jo was fighting to save this boy's life. Cade was fighting his own battle and he had a horrible feeling that it could be a fight he might be losing.

Something wasn't right.

Not that Jo could afford to give it any head space but it was obvious that Cade was far from happy. She knew it didn't have anything to do with him having to work closely with her, however. He might not be deliberately trying to communicate silently with her—quite the opposite, probably—but she could sense that he was on the brink of being overwhelmed by something far more significant.

It didn't interfere with what she was doing. Creating an opening in the chest wall to deal with a life-threatening problem was a procedure she was more than simply familiar with and the steps were almost automatic. With one hand, she felt down the ribcage to locate the fifth intercostal space, keeping a finger to mark the mid-axillary line as she reached for a scalpel with her other hand. The small incision was only through the skin. She used small, curved artery forceps for blunt dissection through the intercostal muscles, over a rib and into the pleural space. Opening the forceps allowed the release of both a gush of air and blood and then Jo did a finger sweep, mindful of the hazard that the sharp edges of broken ribs could present, to ensure decompression.

'I can feel the lung expanding,' she told Cade. No matter how many times she performed this procedure, the relief that came with that feeling beneath her fingertip never got old.

They weren't about to lose this patient. Oddly, though, Jo didn't see a reflection of her own relief as Cade's gaze brushed hers and, again, she knew that this wasn't about her. She wanted to ask if he was okay, but they could both hear Tom calling for assistance. They were about to lift the adult male from the car.

'Go,' Jo told Cade. 'I'm good here.'

He couldn't get away fast enough, judging by how swiftly he jumped to his feet and turned and Jo could see him assisting Tom, moments later, as they carefully extracted the man with a potentially serious cervical injury from the wreckage. They had him immobilised with sandbags and strapping on a spinal board by the time she'd dressed the chest wound she had created and was happy with the vital signs she reviewed. A second air rescue chopper was landing so all they needed to do was transfer the man with the neck injury into the care of the other crew and they could get this boy back to her emergency department and into the care of appropriate specialists.

The patients with minor injuries could be left to Cade and his partner to treat and transport to hospital by road, if necessary. As the lead medic at this scene, Jo needed to ensure that Cade was aware of what was happening but, when she got close enough to speak to him, moments before she needed to get back on board the helicopter, it wasn't the other patients that were foremost on her mind.

'Are you okay?' she asked him.

'I'm fine.'

He clearly wasn't. He was pale. The muscles in his face looked set in grim lines and there was something in his eyes that Jo couldn't interpret but it seemed as dark as their colour.

'You don't look fine.' She didn't need to speak quietly because the helicopter's rotors were starting up. Tom was holding the clamshell door, waiting for her to get in so he could pull it shut, but Jo hesitated for just another heartbeat, her gaze fixed on Cade's face, the squeeze in her chest on his behalf painful enough to be stealing her breath.

'Drop it, Jo.' Cade's tone was a warning. He spun around so that she was facing his back. '*Dammit…*' He actually sounded as if he was in physical pain. 'Just leave me alone, will you?'

He strode away, leaving Jo momentarily stunned by the way she'd been pushed away so viciously. But then she turned away herself almost as swiftly. She was needed on board the helicopter and it was all too obvious that Cade neither needed nor wanted her in his life.

And that was fine by her.

CHAPTER SIX

MAYBE THIS WAS a bad idea.

It was late enough to have been dark for some time. Late enough for someone to have already had their dinner and be winding down for an evening that was chilly and more than a little damp. Cade had to wonder whether Dunedin was considered the most Scottish city outside of Scotland for its weather as well as its early settlers and architecture?

Whatever. Jo probably wouldn't be remotely interested in the large bag of rapidly cooling Thai takeaways he took out of the case on the back of his bike. She probably wasn't going to be remotely pleased to find him on her doorstep at all, but what else could he do in the way of a peace offering?

The answer to that came the moment that Joanna Bishop opened her door. He could apologise with absolute sincerity. He'd known just how far over the line he'd stepped the moment he'd turned his back on her, hours ago, at the scene of that MVA. The fact that defence mechanisms he'd relied on for so many years had suddenly disintegrated and left him feeling so vulnerable…okay, *afraid*…was no excuse to have treated Jo like that. Or like he had been treating her for the last week or more.

'I'm so sorry,' Cade said quietly. 'I don't have any excuse but I could explain if you want me to?'

Without a word, Jo led him into the house. She ignored the paper bags he put on the table. Her arms weren't completely folded but the way she was almost hugging herself was a protective gesture that made Cade feel even worse for the way he'd treated her.

'How is he?' Cade had to ask. 'The boy from the car crash? I didn't get a chance to ask anyone later.'

'He's alive. He's in ICU but considered stable now, rather than critical.'

Cade nodded slowly.

'His dad's been transferred to a specialist spinal injury unit but they think his cord injury is incomplete, which is good news. He could make a good recovery.' Jo was watching him carefully. 'It was a tough job for you today, wasn't it?'

Cade nodded again.

'Working on critically injured kids is always tough, I get that.'

Cade shook his head this time. 'I've always managed before, but yeah…it was beyond hard today but I had no right to blame you for any of it. Or take it out on you like that.'

'You *blamed* me?' Jo actually took a step backwards.

'No…that's not the right word.' Cade let his breath out in a sigh. 'Look…this isn't easy for me to talk about. Could we at least sit down?'

Silently, Jo pulled out a chair and sat down at the table, pushing the paper bags to one side. She had to be able to smell the food as well as he could but she was clearly no more interested in eating at the moment than Cade was. He also sat down, his heart sinking a bit when he remembered they were sitting in the same places when he'd had dinner here with Jo—the night things had started falling apart.

'It was what you said.' The words were hard to get out. 'That I would make a perfect father.'

Jo bit her lip. 'I'm sorry. It was a stupid thing to say.'

'You were joking.'

Jo opened her mouth as if she was about to say something else but then closed it again, pressing her lips together.

'You weren't to know,' Cade said. 'That, years ago, that was all I wanted to be. The perfect father.'

Jo's eyes widened. The rest of her went very still.

'I joined a shearing gang that my cousins were in when I left school. There was a girl in the gang—Nina—who worked as a rousie on the gang. Throwing fleeces? Anyway...long story short, we fell in love. Spent a few years travelling and then decided to settle down. Nina went into nursing training and I decided to become a paramedic. We got married—big family wedding—and then had an even bigger celebration when Nina got pregnant a year or so later. That was when I decided I was going to be the perfect father. And husband. I was already loving my work, we had a big family network and...well, life couldn't have been better.'

Jo still hadn't moved. She was waiting for what was obviously not going to be a happy ending to his story.

'There was an accident,' Cade continued quietly. 'Nina was seven months pregnant. Driving home on a rural road and a drunk driver went through a stop sign straight into the driver's side of the car. I doubt that she had any idea what hit her—at least I hope not.'

'Oh, my God...' Jo breathed. 'Cade, I'm so sorry...'

'It was the end of my world as I knew it.' Cade shrugged. 'I'd had my family torn away from me and

I couldn't handle any of it. Even being around my own family was too hard. That was when I joined MSF and worked overseas. The oil rigs were good too. Anything that kept me moving was good because I couldn't get attached. To anywhere. Or anyone. I'm not saying it stopped me having fun with people I liked being around.' Cade offered Jo a slightly tentative smile. 'But there were rules.'

'I knew that.' Jo nodded. 'You made it very clear that you never stayed long in one place. If I'm honest, I wasn't really joking, I *did* think you'd make a perfect father for the baby I want to have and that was partly because you'd move on. I'm really not looking for a partner. I just…' There was a wobble in her voice that went straight to Cade's heart. 'I just want to be a mum.'

Unspoken words were an undercurrent that pulled Cade away from a perspective that felt suddenly selfish. He needed to know what it was that he could feel but didn't understand.

'It means a lot to you, doesn't it?'

'So much.' She pressed her fingers against her lips for a moment. 'Too much maybe. Which might be why I kept putting off making a decision. What if…' The vulnerability in Jo's eyes was far more heartbreaking than any broken words. 'What if I fail at being a parent?'

Cade was genuinely astonished. This clever, courageous, compassionate woman doubted her ability to raise a child? 'How could you possibly do that?'

'I'm sure almost every parent does their best, but it doesn't always work out, does it? Sometimes…sometimes that child grows up to believe they're not good enough. Perhaps, deep down, they believe that they don't deserve to be loved.'

Wow… How had Cade not realised what had been

buried so deeply in Jo's heart? She'd practically spelled it out the first time they'd really talked.

I was such a disappointment to my mother... Unless I did something at least as well as, preferably better than, my brothers, my dad didn't even notice I existed...

Had he missed the significance of what seemed like something to joke about, because Jo herself had never realised how much it had affected her?

'You want to be the parent you never had,' he said softly. 'To get the kind of unconditional love that every child deserves to get.'

Jo was holding his gaze so he could see how his words touched a chord. It was her smile that was wobbly this time, as she broke that eye contact. 'I've got so much love bottled up inside me,' she whispered. 'But I've only just realised how much I need to give it to someone. And babies need lots of love.' .

'They do...' Cade's voice was also a whisper.

'We all do, really, don't we?' Jo was staring at her hands. 'Okay, we can learn to live without it if we have to but we know, deep down, that it's the thing we'd choose above everything else if we could.'

'Yeah...' The word was a sigh. 'You're not wrong. I can remember what it was like waiting for my kid to be born. How much I loved her before I'd even seen her as anything more than a blob on an ultrasound screen. Imagining what life was going to be like watching her grow up. We had a name all picked out. Aroha. Love...'

'No wonder you were avoiding me after what I said. That was what made it so hard at the accident today, wasn't it? Why you blamed me?'

Cade shook his head but then blew out a breath. 'I guess I'd been thinking more about the past because I couldn't help thinking about what it would be like to have a baby with you. And that made me think about what my kid might have been like. She'd be nearly ten years old now.'

Jo had her hand pressed against her mouth again, this time to stifle her gasp. 'The same age as that boy who nearly died today.'

'Yeah...' Cade had to swallow a rather large lump in his throat. 'It's not the first time it's happened. In the early days I'd see other people's babies and wonder if she'd smile like that or be falling over when she was learning to walk. I'd see little kids going off to school or I'd go to someone who'd broken their arm in the playground or something and it would cross my mind that she'd be about the same age by now but, you know, I got good at dealing with it. I thought I had it pegged. Until today. But I didn't and it was so hard to make sure it didn't affect how well I could do my job. The last straw was knowing that you could see right through any shield I thought I had and that made me feel more vulnerable than I think I ever have. So I attacked as a form of defence and you caught the flak and I'm really sorry.'

Jo covered his hands, which were making fists on the table, with her own. 'It's okay, Cade,' she said softly. 'Forget it. If it's any comfort, it didn't affect how professional you were at all. I'd work with you any time. I'm really sorry too. For saying something so stupid in the first place.'

'But that's the thing. What you said isn't that stupid. Yeah, I was kind of avoiding you but it was ticking along in my mind somewhere and after today, when I'd calmed down, I knew that it could actually work. For both of us.'

And now, after learning something that he suspected nobody else had ever known about Joanna Bishop— that she'd never known the kind of love that she so very much deserved to have—he was even more convinced that this was the right thing to do. It could be a priceless gift for them both.

'What…?' Jo's gaze was fixed on his face. She didn't understand.

'I'm not saying I could be a real father—any more than I could fall in love with anyone again.' Cade's head shake underlined his words. 'That part of me is broken. But… If anything, today's shown me how haunted I still am by the "what ifs". Maybe being a father from a distance would give me what would fill that hole in my life. I wouldn't have to wonder what my child would be like or what he or she would be doing at any age because I'd know. We'd keep in touch, wouldn't we? They'd know who their biological father was?'

'Absolutely,' Jo whispered.

'And… I really do think you're an amazing person. And I can't imagine how lucky your child is going to be to get all that love you've been saving up for far too long. On the other hand, I *can* imagine what a kid with a combination of our genes might turn out like. How awesome would they be?'

Jo was smiling but it was wobbly. 'They'd end up ruling the world.'

'They'd end up pretty special, that's for sure. Maybe the world needs someone like that.'

Cade could see the way Jo pulled in a very deep breath. 'This isn't something that either of us should rush into,' she said slowly. 'Especially you, after an overwhelming day.'

'Maybe I needed to get pushed that far. To see things I've been avoiding for ever. To find a more positive way to move on with my life. I've been stuck. I found something that seemed to work but I was hiding, wasn't I? I've been hiding for years and years.'

'So it won't hurt to hide a little bit longer, will it?' Jo squeezed his hands. 'Why don't we get to know each other better? Talk about it more. A whole lot more because there'll be a million things that need thinking about. Give it a month and then you can decide. Either way, I'll be ready to go back to the clinic by then. This is something I know I have to do. And thank you… You've made me feel like it's something I might even be good at doing.'

Cade had long since relaxed the fists his hands had made. He'd turned them over with that last squeeze of hers so that Jo's hands were lying on top of his and he found himself stroking the top of her hands with his thumbs. He was holding her gaze too, and they'd slipped so easily back into that silent kind of communication.

He'd never told anyone his story before because that had been part of his self-protection. But Jo had seen what was happening, even if she didn't understand why, and she'd cared enough to want to help. She'd listened to every word he'd said and it felt as if she understood everything now. That she knew him better than anyone else in his life.

And after hearing an admission about never feeling loved, that Jo hadn't even realised she was making, it felt as if Cade knew more about her than possibly anyone else in *her* life. They were complete opposites in a way, because he had lost the ability to give love and Jo had too much of it that she desperately needed to give, but that kind of made them opposite sides of the same coin, didn't it? Whatever the analogy, he'd never felt closer to another human being.

He'd never wanted to be this close to someone again.

Or to be even closer…? Not simply for the sex, but for the human touch. The connection. Feeling that someone genuinely understood something as visceral as the inability to love and could accept that about him. That they *cared*…

Somehow that silent communication had brought them both to their feet. Into each other's arms. Into a kiss that was erasing every bit of the tension that had been accumulating since they'd last been together like this.

'Come upstairs?' Jo's invitation was whispered when they finally broke the kiss.

Cade's lips were against her neck. 'The only thing I thought to bring was food. Do you have any condoms?'

Jo's huff of breath was a soft laugh. 'Do you know the odds of someone my age getting pregnant naturally? Almost non-existent, that's what. And I'm squeaky clean as far as anything else you might need protection from.'

Cade knew he was also safe and, if the odds of an unplanned pregnancy weren't almost non-existent, it didn't really matter, did it? Not when Cade was quite confident he wouldn't be changing his mind in a month's time.

And what better way to put things right? He could not only wipe out the tension of the last week and particularly today with the kind of communication they could share by making love, it could be like a new beginning as well. A foundation for a future that they might not be going to share in a traditional sense but it could very well be life-changing for both of them. That priceless gift of bringing a baby into the world might be a single thing but it could be given and received by both of them.

He took Jo's hand as they went upstairs.

Whoever had said there was no such thing as magic was definitely wrong.

CHAPTER SEVEN

THIS WAS COMPLETELY NEW.

Totally different.

And so much more exciting than anything—or any-one—that Jo Bishop had ever invited into her life before.

Had she had things the wrong way around, all along?

She'd always tried to find that perfect relationship—the one that could offer a future that would ensure she didn't miss out on any of the best things life had to offer—only to find they always trailed into dead ends or imploded into messy, hopefully never-to-be-repeated emotional disasters.

This time, she'd defined the future that she knew she wanted and had somehow stumbled into a perfect—for now, anyway—relationship. She and Cade were dating. Except they weren't because she would have never considered dating someone who was so much younger than her he was almost in a different generation. For heaven's sake, by the time Cade reached his fortieth birthday, she would almost be *fifty*.

No. This definitely *wasn't* dating. They were simply getting to know each other better. It just *felt* like dating. The kind of no-holds-barred dating that you might expect in a couple who'd fallen so madly in love with each other they were going to be married within weeks. Over-the-top dating in a way, because they were taking turns to choose where they went and what they did whenever they had any time off that coincided. There were interesting restaurants from all sorts of cuisines to try and so many places that Jo had never explored. Being midspring was a bonus. There were days of perfect weather, there were rhododendron and magnolia trees in full, glorious bloom and Cade, in particular, had a talent for choosing outings that were mini adventures, like that trip to Tunnel Beach had been.

There were echoes of those first hours together in more than the sense of new discovery and adventure. Jo could feel echoes of that urgency to learn as much as possible about Cade in the shortest amount of time. Because it still felt as if this could be what had been missing from her life? If so, Cade seemed to feel the same way.

This was different, however, because they both knew there was no possibility of a long-term relationship, let alone the prospect of getting married. Not in the near future. Not ever. And that was fine with both of them. Better than fine, because it provided a safe space in which they could both be completely honest with each other. There was also a perfectly legitimate reason to find out as much as possible about each other, despite the fact they had no intention of spending the rest of their lives together, because they were planning something just as important. Maybe even more important. They were planning to create a new human being that would be a mixture of their genes.

There was so much to talk about. They asked each other endless questions and talked about anything and everything. A lot of it was fun, like comparing likes and dislikes and personality quirks. Some of it was serious, like listing childhood illnesses and family history of any serious health concerns and some of it was difficult to talk about because it was very personal but it was also very necessary—like laying down ground rules. That was probably the most significant conversation that Jo and Cade shared and it happened on the first 'date' after Cade had opened up to Jo about his past. They were in the rhododendron dell on the hilly outskirts of Dunedin's botanical gardens. The scent of the gorgeous flowers, the warmth of a sunny afternoon and a private patch of grass to sit on together made for the perfect setting for perhaps the biggest question.

'How will it work?'

'You probably know more about that than I do.' One of Cade's eyebrows lifted. 'I'm guessing you make arrangements with the fertility clinic and then give me an appointment where I can rock up and...' his smile was cheeky '...make my contribution.'

'I didn't mean the mechanics of being a sperm donor. I meant...you know...later. You said you wanted to stay in touch. Do you want photos? Videos? Real contact—like spending time with him or her?'

Cade's smile had faded completely while Jo was speaking. She saw the way his eyes darkened and the tiny lines at their corners deepened. The movement of his head was a slow single shake.

'Not contact,' he said quietly. 'That's more than I would want. Too...close.'

Jo understood. He didn't want to get close enough for his child to steal his heart. To present a risk of the new life he had so carefully built for himself falling apart because of another overwhelming loss.

'But you'd like them to know who their biological father is?'

'When it's time. Aren't there laws around adoption

and, presumably, sperm or egg donation that mean some-one can trace their biological parents when they're eigh-teen?'

'I think so. But there's also DNA tracing now, which changes things. It's possible your child could turn up on your doorstep one day, with no warning. Would you be able to cope with that?'

'They'd be an adult. It feels like that would be very different to meeting a kid.' Cade closed his eyes for a long moment. 'Yeah...' he said, finally. 'I reckon I can cope with that.' He opened his eyes to meet Jo's gaze. 'But what will you tell them when they're young? When they start asking questions about why they don't have a daddy like other kids?'

'Traditional nuclear families are only one variety these days. Single parents, blended families, same-sex parents... Different is so normal I don't think they'll be anything more than curious—about who you are, not so much why you're not in their life.'

'What will you say?'

One of the large, pale purple blooms of the closest tree gave up holding onto an overladen branch. It sepa-rated into single trumpets that settled on the grass be-tween Cade and Jo. She picked one up, bringing it close to her nose to inhale the gentle scent.

'I'll say that their daddy was a very special friend who couldn't have his own family but really wanted to help me have someone to love *this* much...'

There was a moment's silence. Jo could almost hear Cade swallowing hard. She certainly heard him clear his throat.

'He'll ask "why?" Or she will.' Cade also picked a trumpet. He touched the darker, speckled part of the flower at its centre. 'I hope it's a girl. I'd like her to grow up to be as awesome as her mum.'

It was Jo's turn to swallow hard and clear the prickle behind her eyes. If only things were different, Cade would be exactly the person she would choose to not only father her child but to *be* their father. Her partner. Because he was the first person in her life who made her almost believe she *was* awesome when it had nothing to do with her professional skills. That she was special enough to deserve the kind of love she'd never been given.

But things weren't different and, in many ways, it was going to make this all a lot easier. She would be able to focus completely on being the best single mum possible, which would be quite enough to juggle along with her career. How much more complicated would it be to be trying to be the best lover or partner or wife at the same time?

'I'll tell her that you couldn't have a family because you're a hero. That you have to go to all sorts of dangerous places to save lives.' She offered Cade a smile. 'Like Superman.'

He gave a huff of laughter. 'Might work for a six-year-old but I can just imagine what a teenager would think of that.'

Jo shrugged. 'They'll be smart enough to know that relationships can be impossible for all sorts of reasons.'

'I wouldn't want them to think they were unwanted.'

'They won't. They'll be the most wanted baby ever.'

'I mean by me. I'd like them to know that their existence isn't an accident. That we planned this?'

Jo nodded slowly. 'Let's take photos,' she suggested. 'I'll frame some—in one of those multi-picture frames—and keep them on a wall where they'll be seen every day. They'll grow up to know your name and that you were my friend and when they ask questions about their daddy I'll be completely honest and it will be…' Jo had to pause and take a breath. 'Just the way things are, I guess. You will always have been part of their life in a way.'

'And when they ask where I am?'

'I'll probably be able to be completely honest about that as well and say I have no idea.' She dropped the now bruised petals in her hand. 'You will have long moved on by then. You could be anywhere in the world.'

There was a longer silence this time. Cade was clearly thinking about everything she'd said. Jo didn't realise she was holding her breath until she heard Cade release his in what sounded like a sigh of what…relief?

She certainly felt relieved. Cade was happy with the ground rules. They were a big step closer to making this happen.

'So…photos, huh?' Cade pulled his phone from his pocket. 'Somewhere where they're seen every day? We'd better make them good.' He wriggled closer to Jo and held the phone above them. 'Do you know, I've never taken a selfie?'

'Me neither.' Jo could see her face, and Cade's, on the screen of his phone. He was making a silly face and she was laughing as she heard the click of the first image being taken.

This was new.

Not completely new, because there were echoes of what he and Nina had found together all those years ago. Like the closeness that came with being able to be absolutely honest with another person—about absolutely everything, including things that had been hidden from anyone else in his life—even from his family because he didn't want them to be worried about him. It was cathartic to admit weird things, like that early habit of compulsively searching crowded places, in case there was a baby or child of about the right age and hopefully skin colour that gave him a moment of thinking...yes...that could have been my child. That could have been what my life would have looked like. Maybe it had been a version of poking at a wound to see if it was healing and when the need to poke had lessened and it only happened by accident he knew he was dealing with his loss. That he could live with what was missing.

He'd forgotten about the excitement of being able to share dreams for the future with someone else, though.

Not the same future exactly, of course, and that was what made it safe enough to enjoy that excitement and to take pleasure in being part of its creation. Cade would move on—sooner or later—to live the same life he'd been living for the last decade but he would take with him the satisfaction of knowing he had helped a remarkable woman achieve her dream of motherhood. He would have filled the gap in his life that had haunted him by being able to watch—to care, maybe to worry but no doubt also feel very proud—from a distance, as his child grew up. There was something rather nice about knowing that he would be part of the small person who would have Jo's total love, guidance and protection on their journey to adulthood. He would never be *too* close to either of them, however, and that way there was no threat to limiting where he went with the career he loved and the risk to his heart was perfectly manageable.

There was also something more than nice about knowing that his photo would be on the wall of the house they lived in. That he would be seen as a real person and that his child would know that he had been wanted by both his parents. To that end, Cade had put some effort into learning how to take a good selfie, but today's setting, about three weeks into the month they had allocated to get to know each other properly, was providing a distinct challenge.

They were on an exposed part of the Otago Peninsula's coastline, on a viewing platform that gave them a spectacular vantage point to watch the flight path of members of the royal northern albatross colony as they came into their only mainland breeding area in the world. The fierce wind, which helped chicks learn to fly later in the season, was not only uncomfortably cold—it was playing havoc with their hair as Cade tried to take a photograph with the lighthouse at the head of the peninsula just visible in the distance behind them and hopefully also with one of the magnificent seabirds showing off its three-metre wingspan.

'That's no good, you're missing an eye,' Cade told her as he checked the image. 'And my hair's starting to look like one of the nests those big birds are building.' He held the phone up to try again. 'Reckon it might be time to cut it off.'

'*No*…' Jo was laughing as she pulled her hair behind her ears and the wind instantly whipped it out again. 'Your hair is one of the things I love most about you.'

The wind, in combination with the laughter, seemed to swallow most of her words. The ones that he could hear the most clearly sounded like 'I love you…'

It should have been enough to sound the kind of alarm that had always signalled the end of any past relationship Cade had included in his life but…this was different, wasn't it? There was an agreed plan in place and a limited time that they were going to be together like this. They were getting to know each other and they were almost through the month that Jo had stipulated they needed before making a final agreement. He had no trouble putting a smile on his face as he tapped the screen to take a rapid volley of shots. Surely one of them would be a much better photo for that frame.

They re-joined their tour guide to hear about the breeding cycle of the albatross and see the nest building that was being done by the male birds and the courtship dances that were happening nearby.

'That's called a "sky-point",' the guide told them, 'when they lower the head and then swing their beak up sharply like that. And that's "sky-calling". They're showing off their wingspan by extending them and they throw in a "sky-point" and the loudest call they can make for good measure. Never fails to impress the girls.'

The noise was raucous. The wind was cold and, for most women, it would probably have presented a date from hell but Jo was clearly loving it. She was grinning at Cade as the guide was speaking. And then she elbowed him in his ribs as they moved on.

'I wouldn't advise it,' she told him. 'For any girls you might want to impress in the future.'

'Noted,' he said. But impressing unknown females in his future was the last thing on Cade's mind. He couldn't—or didn't want to—begin to imagine it. How on earth was he ever going to find someone that he enjoyed being with as much as Joanna Bishop?

He didn't want to think about it but he couldn't shake it out of his head when they were walking back to the car park. This month of being together as much as possible was going too fast. What would happen next? Would the plug be pulled straight away from their time of having adventures together like this? They'd been to every beach they could find within a reasonable travelling time, checked out museums and public gardens, the heritage attractions and art in the harbour settlement of Port Chalmers and enjoyed a performance by the city's champion bagpipe band in the Octagon, in the shadow of Robbie Burns' statue.

Would the interesting taste-fest of sharing meals at an eclectic variety of restaurants also have to stop? Okay, they'd probably tried most of the best already but he would be quite happy to go back to a lot of them and eat the same food. Like the Viking style sardines at a very cool Nordic gallery/restaurant combination and the best fried chicken he'd ever had at the Southern USA style eatery in the central city. They'd sampled Italian food, Asian fusion, Hungarian and there was always that amazing hamburger joint to go back to, along with the deli that was Jo's go-to for a meal at home.

And what about the best sex Cade had ever experienced? That probably had to stop even before Jo got pregnant. How quickly would that happen? And *then* what would happen? Would she want him to be involved with the birth? Did *he* want to be involved? And, if he didn't, where in the world would he go next? He didn't want to think about that either. Because, right now, he didn't want to *be* anywhere else in the world.

Cade had pulled out the big guns with it being his turn to organise this time together. Jo wasn't due to start her next shift until tomorrow afternoon and he was doing a night shift so he'd added a surprise on to the visit to the albatross colony.

'We're not going home,' he told Jo as he handed her a helmet to put on before they got back on his bike.

'What? Never...?' Jo's eyes were dancing.

'Not till tomorrow morning. After a sleep in. In a castle. New Zealand's *only* castle, no less.'

'Oh... I've heard about the castle. That's somewhere else I've never been.'

Cade jammed his helmet over his wayward and now probably tangled waves. 'Excellent. First times are always the best.'

That wasn't entirely true, Jo decided later that night.

Part of it was. Not knowing what to expect from visiting an albatross colony or exploring the wonderful castle and its gardens that was another popular landmark on the Otago Peninsula made a first time something extraordinary, it had to be admitted. But *this*...this feeling of lying in Cade's arms after they'd made love was getting better every time it happened and Jo had lost count of how many times that was now. Getting to know exactly what could take their intimacy to the next level, tease an arousal to new heights and deliver a climax that could leave them both beyond satisfied hadn't actually been a consideration when Jo had suggested getting to know each other well enough to make a well-considered choice about something as big as Cade becoming the father of her baby, but...wow...it was a bonus that she would remember for the rest of her life.

They were in a luxurious room in a lodge built on the seaward side of Larnach Castle, beside the historic stables. The brass bed ends were antique, the soft, warm duvet and pillows made the bed a nest that Jo had no intention of getting out of any time soon and, through the windows, she could see the stars of a clear night sky. She could hear the steady breathing from Cade, who was still holding her in his arms but had clearly slipped into sleep,

and she could smell the scent of him—of *them*—and…
she had never felt quite this contented and happy. Ever.

Jo shifted just a little. Enough so that she could touch
Cade's skin with her lips and taste him as well as be
aware of his scent. She shifted her hand carefully too,
spreading her fingers so that every fingertip could feel a
separate patch of skin on his chest that included smooth
skin, chest hair and a disc of a nipple that was harden-
ing instantly despite a touch that was no more than the
kiss of a feather. Tilting her head, Jo could see that Cade
was not asleep, after all. He was watching her with those
gorgeous dark eyes, the strong lines of his face softened
by the waves of his hair and a smile on his lips that was
so tender it broke her heart.

Dear Lord, she loved his face.

She loved *this*—being naked in his arms and feeling
his skin against hers.

How could Cade really believe that he wasn't capable of being in love with anyone again? That that part of
him was broken beyond repair? Jo could see it there—
his ability to love—so close to the surface in that smile
and the look in his eyes. She could feel it, even, with
just the memory of how his touch could make her feel.

But Cade wasn't aware of it. And if he had been
Jo knew he would not be here with her like this. He
wouldn't have offered to be a part of helping her achieve
her dream of becoming a mother, and she was beyond
grateful for that. She could also be grateful that the sex
had been the perfect end to a perfect day and it was
going to be pure bliss to drift into sleep knowing that
neither of them needed to set an alarm to rush into work
early in the morning.

She was going to miss having these adventures with
her cowboy Cade when he moved on. No…she was

going to miss *him*. In that split second, as her own lips curved in response to that smile on his face, Jo realised just how much she was going to miss him because it wasn't just this man's face or his lovemaking or his company in having adventures that she loved.

It was him.

And it wasn't just that she loved him in the way you could love a good friend. It felt as if she was *in* love with Cade. Jo found herself closing her eyes as the disturbing thought filled both her mind and her heart. So that Cade couldn't see it as he dipped his head to kiss her again. She did her best to dismiss it and, thankfully, that became so much easier as his lips touched hers and desire was rekindled.

Falling in love was not part of any plan to get to know each other better. There was a tacit agreement between them that it was forbidden, in fact, so it couldn't be allowed to happen.

Because it could change everything.

Maybe it already had…

CHAPTER EIGHT

CPAP.

Continuous Positive Airway Pressure.

A ventilation technique that could be beneficial in all sorts of clinical situations, like heart failure, chronic obstructive pulmonary disease, pneumonia, chest trauma including a flail segment, toxic inhalations of chemicals or smoke, obese patients, near drownings…the list could go on.

It should go on but Cade found himself simply staring at the screen of his laptop, his mind drifting away from this presentation he was supposed to be working on. His abstract and outline had been accepted for the programme of an international emergency medical conference next year in Europe. Prague, no less, which was a city he'd never been to. It could be where fate intended him to go next, given that he'd just received the final acceptance of his proposal to join what would be a very well-respected gathering of experts in pre-hospital medicine and the fact that the timing could be perfect. It might be better if he was gone from Dunedin well before Jo had her baby. Before it was obvious she was pregnant, even?

Except…something seemed to have changed, although Cade couldn't quite put his finger on what it was. Perhaps it was actually because nothing had changed? The end of the month deadline for confirming his decision had come and gone and he'd made it very clear he hadn't changed his mind about being a sperm donor for Jo, but nothing much had happened since to move things forward.

She'd been in touch with the fertility clinic in Auckland who had performed the egg collection and freezing process years ago and discovered that they were associated with another clinic in Dunedin so Jo could apparently have any further treatment without the need to travel. The first step would simply be an examination by blood test to check her hormone levels and an ultrasound to make sure no abnormalities had developed in her uterus since it was last checked, but Cade didn't know if that appointment had happened yet, or if it was even scheduled. He had no idea what the timeline might be for moving forward either, and that seemed odd because he knew how important this was to Jo and she had been very aware that time was running out, so surely the sooner they started, the better?

She was working an afternoon shift today so wouldn't be home until nearly midnight, but it was such a familiar action now to pick up his phone and drop a text message that it was becoming automatic. They texted each other at least a couple of times a day and more often if their schedules prevented them from spending any time together, as was happening this week.

Hey…how's your shift going?

Just sending a message into the ether was enough to made Cade feel as if he'd picked up the end of the thread that connected him to Jo. He wasn't so alone in his apartment now and he could flick his focus back to the task at hand. He started reading over the introduction to his presentation.

Single use disposable CPAP devices have become readily available, affordable tools that provide one of the most effective interventions in out-of-hospital treatment to assist respiratory effort and oxygenation in patients with acute exacerbation of a wide spectrum of cardiovascular or respiratory conditions.

Cade copied and pasted the list of conditions and situations he'd just compiled and then made a note with a question mark to flag that its inclusion needed more thought.

Evidence from recent studies raises the question of whether it is now a failure in duty of care for any emergency medical service to not have these devices available for every skill level and their use a part of their standard operating procedures: SOPs.

The beep of his phone pulled Cade instantly away from his note.

So far so good. Just had three guys in who had a bit of a disagreement at the pub. Total of fourteen stab wounds to assess.

OMG. Sounds messy.

Mostly superficial. One deeper wound that reached a kidney but no surgery advised. Lots of stitching up lacs. Gave Security a bit of fun keeping a lid on things.

Cade was frowning. The thought of Jo being anywhere near drunk, violent men angered him to the point where he had to unclench a fist to respond to the message.

Be careful.

Will do.

She added a thumbs-up emoji.

Still on for tomorrow?

Cade had said he wanted to come and watch one of her fencing classes. Maybe even give the sport a go himself.

En garde! came the response.

Who knew there was an emoji of someone with a sword and a mesh mask?

Cade put his phone down and turned to his laptop screen again but he found himself unable to focus on what he'd just written. What had become a normal kind of conversation with Jo didn't sound normal any longer, did it? What was going on? He picked up his phone again.

Any word? On a start date?

It took a while for his phone to beep again. No doubt Jo had another patient to see. Or was she avoiding the subject?

No. When Cade was finally thinking about his presentation again, another message came through.

Have spoken to clinic. Will fill you in tomorrow.

It was Cade's turn to send a thumbs-up. He couldn't push for any more information and…it was a start, of sorts, at least. Had the clinic given Jo the green light? And, if so, what was being planned?

The diagram on his screen that he was designing to help explain how CPAP could push fluid back out of the lungs and into the bloodstream by changing alveolar/hydrostatic pressure dynamics failed to recapture his immediate interest. Instead, Cade opened a new browsing window and looked up assisted reproduction clinics in both Auckland and Dunedin. There were different tabs to open that offered all the information he didn't want to push Jo to provide. He sat back and clicked what was a very user-friendly web page. He went to the treatment tab and then chose a sub tab for freezing—sperm, eggs and embryos.

He skimmed over statistics on the age-related decline in fertility and the reasons why women might choose to have eggs frozen, to discover that it seemed a straightforward process to use the eggs. They could be thawed, after an indefinite storage period, by quickly warming them to thirty-seven degrees Celsius. When the cryoprotective liquid was removed and they'd had a bit of time to recover, they could then be injected with a single sperm and the formation of an embryo would be monitored in a laboratory before implantation, usually at an extended blastocyst stage at day five. A pregnancy blood test would be performed nine days later.

Cade's interest was well and truly caught now. He'd had no idea of how advanced technology had become in assisted reproduction. A special IVF culture had been developed, containing a growth factor that occurs naturally in the uterus, to provide better embryo development and chances for a successful implantation. Embryos could be frozen and used later if another attempt was needed—even embryos that had been created from a previously frozen egg. That made it possible to take a biopsy from the embryo's outer cells, freeze it while the cells were analysed for any chromosomal or genetic abnormalities and then thaw and implant it when the results were in.

Would Jo want to do that? Cade went searching again to look for more personal information and found a forum where women could ask questions and support each other through the process. He found a lot of advice that ranged from taking prenatal vitamins to avoiding using plastic water bottles because of BPAs. There were strict guidelines about avoiding salt, caffeine and red meat before a transfer, perfume and stress during and sex or hot baths afterwards. There were superstitions that might seem silly but following them had become like a talisman for good luck. And there was one in particular that made Cade smile.

He'd have to tell Jo about it, he decided, in case she wasn't reading this kind of stuff online. No…he could do better than that. He scribbled a note onto a scrap of paper. He'd go shopping tomorrow, after work. Before he met Jo at the fencing studio.

It was getting worse.

That spiral of sensation that Jo could feel, deep in her belly, when she merely caught a glimpse of Cade Cameron. It was more than the stirring of physical desire because it created a warmth that rippled through her body and that felt more like…relief? Sheer joy that she was in this man's company again?

Oh, man…

There was no getting away from the fact that she'd fallen head over heels in love with Cade.

And it was doing her head in.

He couldn't see her. Or, rather, he wouldn't be able to tell which of the club members, paired off and practising techniques, was her because they were all wearing their protective gear. The jackets and breeches, the steel mesh masks and Kevlar neck bibs, the glove on the sword hand, the chest protector.

Jo could see Cade, though. He was talking to the head instructor, who seemed to be explaining the positions and moves that people were making and the footwork they were using. Feints and parries, ripostes and lunges. Jo wanted to improve her footwork to enable her to better control the distance between herself and an opponent as she stayed within the limits of the allowed width of the 'strip'. The fact that she was being watched—and that the instructor might have pointed her out to Cade—should have made her able to focus more clearly and do her best to impress him but it was unfortunately having the opposite effect.

She couldn't concentrate well enough because she was so aware of Cade being here. Of how she felt about him and of the growing tension of not only debating whether or not to tell him how she felt but whether she could go ahead with the plan of him being the father of her baby. This was her fault, wasn't it? She'd wanted to know her donor but she'd allowed it to go too far. Too deep. She could keep her feelings secret, of course, and Cade would move on and out of her life, probably before her baby was born. But could she live with carrying and then raising a child that would remind her every day that she'd found the love of her life but it was impossible for them to be together? It wasn't just the age difference. Cade had made it very clear that it was the last thing that he would ever want.

It would be far easier to have a baby and be aware

only of the information that was made available by the sperm bank. To have no personal connection with the father at all.

'Sorry…' Jo shook her head at her partner, one of the more senior members of the club. 'I nearly tripped over myself. Can I try that again?'

'Sure. Try and keep your lead foot pointing forward and your back foot perpendicular. And maybe lean forward a bit more?'

Jo tried. She did better the next time but, if this had been a competition, her partner would be wiping the floor with her. She couldn't help sideways glances towards Cade. Or the track her mind insisted on returning to.

She couldn't pull the plug on the plan simply for her own future peace of mind. Cade wanted this as well. Not as much as she did, perhaps, but it was still important to him. It would allow him to be a father in the only way he could deal with it—from a distance. He couldn't be so involved that it would open old wounds and remind him of the pain of losing the love of *his* life and the baby they'd almost had.

Telling him how she felt might do that too.

She couldn't tell him.

She *had* to tell him. Because this was the most honest relationship Jo had ever had with anyone. She felt as if she was increasingly living a lie and it didn't sit well at all. Cade deserved better.

'Sorry…' Jo had to apologise again as she failed to put up any kind of defence that her partner had to get through. She was fencing like a complete beginner. 'I must be tired, I think. Or brain dead.'

'No worries. Let's call it quits. Class is nearly over, anyway.'

Jo pulled off her mask as they made their way to the edge of the space. Cade was waiting for her and, because he didn't know anything about fencing, he was looking beyond impressed. She could see admiration and respect in his eyes and something that looked a lot like pride and that was enough to break her heart. He was *proud* of her?

He wouldn't be if he knew the truth.

That she had broken what was probably the most important rule.

'I won't be long.' Jo softened her brusque greeting with a smile. 'I'll just get changed.'

'Take your time,' Cade said. 'I'm loving this. I think I want to sign up.'

'Great…' The instructor slapped him on the back. 'Let me check when we've got a new introductory course starting.'

They picked up hamburgers and took them back to Jo's place but she really wasn't hungry tonight. The odd glances she was getting from Cade told her that he was aware of the tension, but then it became obvious that he thought he knew what was causing it.

'Was it bad news from the clinic?'

'What do you mean?'

'You said you'd fill me in on what they told you. But I'm getting the feeling that you don't really want to talk about it. Is there something wrong?'

'No…' Jo shook her head. 'I've got an appointment booked for next week for the check-up. If I'm given the all-clear, I'd only have to wait until my next cycle starts to begin treatment.' She tried to sound upbeat—as excited as she wanted to be about this. 'I'd take medication to optimise uterus lining development, have a mid-cycle ultrasound to assess how it's going and then they'll boost hormones, along with making sure I get all the supplements needed to maximise the chances of the treatment being successful.' Was forcing herself to sound positive helping, in a 'fake-it-till-you-make-it' kind of way? 'The embryo gets transferred about six days after starting the progesterone.'

'I've been reading a bit about it,' Cade admitted. 'I was supposed to be working on a presentation I'm giving for a conference in Prague next year, but I fell down a search rabbit hole and discovered all sorts of things I didn't know. They've made some great advances in the field, haven't they? Like the growth factor they put in the culture when the egg is sitting in the dish for fertilisation and development. Sounds like it improves the chances, especially for older women or someone who's had failed IVF cycles or miscarriages previously. I even read all the messages on a support group page. Oh…that reminds me. I've got something for you.'

Cade put his hand in one of the pockets of his leather jacket hanging over the back of the chair and came out with a small parcel.

'What is it?'

'Open it and find out.'

Jo had to look away from the gleam in Cade's eyes. She had the feeling that he got a lot more pleasure out of giving gifts than he would in receiving them himself and that fitted right in with the character of this amazingly generous, caring man. And it only made her love him even more.

She opened the parcel to find a pair of the softest, fuzziest socks she'd ever felt.

'They're a good luck charm,' Cade told her. 'For Implantation Day. Kind of silly, but it was something I read about in the support group. Apparently, there's a principle in Chinese medicine that claims a "cold" uterus is a cause of infertility. Socks keep it warm and make it more likely that the embryo will stick.'

'Oh…' Jo had to look away from the hope she could see in his eyes now. He really wanted this to work, didn't he? For her. And for himself?

'They're great.' She put the socks down on the table beside her. She knew she should say something else but the words were stuck in a huge lump in her throat. Maybe if she ate something it would get rid of it. She picked up one of the oven-baked potato wedges they'd ordered with their hamburgers. Then she looked at the sour cream dip and actually felt a wave of nausea that made her drop the wedge to lie on the plate beside her barely tasted hamburger. By the time she lifted her gaze back to Cade, the silence between them had grown enough to be an elephant in the room.

'What is it, Jo?' Cade asked quietly. 'What's wrong?'

The last thing Cade had expected to see was Jo's eyes filling with tears. But he'd known there was something wrong, hadn't he? He'd been sensing that for some time. Weeks, even. Ever since one of their best times together, when they'd gone to the albatross colony and stayed the night at Larnach Castle.

What he really hadn't expected was the way it was making him feel. The inescapable evidence that Jo was a very long way from being happy gave him a catch in his chest that was starting to squeeze like a vice around his heart. That quiver in her voice made it even worse.

'I can't do this,' she whispered.

Cade said nothing. He could only wait for the information that would help him understand. Had Jo decided she didn't want the kind of disruption to her career—and her life—that being a single parent would represent? He would have to respect that, given that he would never choose to allow a child, or anyone else, to become the centre of his own universe, but it was surprising how fast his heart was sinking.

'I thought I could,' Jo continued. 'I thought if I just hid it and you didn't know anything about it, I could carry on and I could have your baby and it wouldn't make any difference to how much I loved her.' Her inward breath was a hiccup. 'Or him…'

Cade was genuinely bewildered now. 'What wouldn't make a difference?' he asked slowly.

'Me being in love with you…'

Oh, *no*…

Okay. *This* was the last thing Cade had expected. He'd been so confident that they were on exactly the same page about relationships and commitment. That neither of them was looking for a significant other in their life. That he knew Jo had gone through her life with the appalling belief that she didn't deserve to be truly loved made this so much worse. How could he have let this get this far without seeing this coming?

'I'm sorry.' Jo was courageously holding his gaze. 'I wasn't going to tell you, but it's been getting harder and harder not to be honest with you. Because…well… because of how I feel about you, I guess. I could never deliberately deceive you.'

The tears in Jo's eyes were spilling out now and rolling slowly down her face. That vice around Cade's heart ramped up the pressure to the point of real pain. He reached out to brush a tear away and, without thinking, he found himself getting to his feet and pulling Jo into his arms.

'I'm sorry too,' he said quietly. 'If I was ever capable of falling in love or wanting to be with someone long term, it would be you. But...' he had to close his eyes against the pain he knew he was causing '... I can't and I'm sorry. I never wanted to hurt you.'

'I know. It's okay. This isn't your fault.' She looked up at him and was doing her best to smile even. 'My bad...'

Cade kissed the top of her head. He should let go of Jo. Say nice things about how special she was and how they would always be friends and then get the hell out of here and as far away as possible. As he'd always done when the women in his life had stepped this far over that boundary line. But his arms refused to obey the command to loosen their grip and...he needed another minute or two to soak in the scent of her hair and the feel of her shape against his body. He was going to miss this so much, but it had always had a time limit and he'd known it was rapidly approaching. He'd just assumed it would all stop in conjunction with the treatment that Jo had wanted so much.

'I was so right when I said you'd make the perfect father,' Jo said softly. 'You still would. But I don't think I could live with just a part of you and not all of you, if that makes sense.'

It did. And he wouldn't want to live with contact for the next twenty years or so as their child grew up, with the reminder that would bring that someone had been, albeit unintentionally, hurt. Children were very good at picking up on emotional stuff like that. His kid might have grown up to hate him because he'd hurt their mother. He might have had an angry adult track him down one day just to tell him what a bastard he was.

'I get it,' he murmured. 'And I know we should just pull the plug before this gets any harder for either of us.

Tell me to go and I will, I promise. But...' he pressed his lips against her hair again '...oh, God, Jo... I'm going to miss this. Miss *you*.'

She had her head buried against his chest, which muffled her voice. 'Me too...' She looked up again and he'd never seen her look quite this vulnerable. This... sad. 'Maybe we could just have tonight? One last time?'

How on earth could he say no? Not just to put off the separation in their lives that this change signalled. This could be the last gift he could ever give her. A chance to apologise, even, for his contribution to this having happened. He could do his best to use his touch and, later, his words in the aftermath of intimacy to convince her that she really did deserve to be loved.

Sadly, as they had both known all along, it just couldn't be by him.

CHAPTER NINE

UNLESS THEY WERE bringing in an expected, critically ill patient who needed to get into Resus as soon as possible because they were under CPR, perhaps, or about to bleed to death like the man Cade had brought in with the carotid artery injury, it was emergency department protocol for ambulance officers to wait by the central desk with the stretcher for the triage nurse to tell them where to go.

Hanna was on duty again today and she had a welcoming smile as Cade and Geoff brought their first patient in. With it being the first day of a four-days-on, four-days-off cycle it felt like a long time since he'd been in here. Longer than it normally did, that was for sure. The whole of the last week had dragged noticeably, to be honest, and he knew the reason why.

He was missing Jo.

He hadn't seen her since that last night together. The last night they would ever have together, which had, unexpectedly, hit him a lot harder than any friendship he'd had to walk away from before. If he'd seen her at work in the first couple of days it might have made it easier to navigate the new space they were in but their shifts hadn't even overlapped since then, which wasn't unheard of, but this time it seemed as if Dr Bishop had simply vanished and it was becoming concerning considering how upset she'd been that night.

Cade knew that Hanna was the closest friend Jo had but he wasn't sure he should ask her what was going on. Or how much she might know about his relationship with Jo. It had been a bit of a game to make sure nobody would guess what was going on between them when they were together at work. Maybe Jo had kept it a secret on a personal level as well, like he had? When she'd told him about why becoming a mother was so important to her, he'd had the distinct feeling that it was something she'd never shared with anyone else.

He certainly couldn't say anything to Hanna while he had a patient lying on a stretcher beside him, anyway.

'This is Shona Braydon,' he told her. 'Fifty-seven-year-old, Type One diabetic. Her grandchildren have been off school this week with a gastric bug that's apparently doing the rounds. Shona became unwell and started vomiting today and her daughter called an ambulance when she recognised the signs of hypoglycaemia. Shona was sweating, shaky and very confused. We started a glucose infusion fifteen minutes ago but her BGL was still low on our last check. She's also tachycardic and experiencing transient atrial fibrillation.'

Hanna's glance went straight to the cardiac monitor hooked to the end of the stretcher. The rhythm on the screen was still clearly irregular but she had a reassuring smile for his patient.

'Hi, Shona. You poor old thing, catching this latest bug. My name's Hanna and we're going to get you sorted out, okay?'

'Thank you, dear...'

Hanna shifted her gaze to Cade. 'Room Two's free,' she told him. She had another smile for Shona. 'A private room for you,' she said. 'We only do that for our special patients.'

And the ones who needed isolation to avoid infecting others who might be vulnerable enough for a gastric illness to be a serious complication. Having handed over Shona's care to one of the junior doctors on duty, Cade parked the empty stretcher and stopped to help himself to the hand sanitiser on the desk beside Hanna a few minutes later. He'd been wearing gloves and a mask with this latest case so he wasn't worried about having picked up the bug—using the sanitiser was more of an excuse to pause enough to have a good look around at what was happening in the department.

'Looking for someone?' Hanna asked. 'I think I saw your crew partner heading for the loo.'

'Thanks.' Cade rubbed his hands together to spread the gel. 'It's not norovirus or something going around at the moment, is it?' If it was, they'd need to take extra precautions, especially with any calls to rest homes or other institutions.

Hanna shook her head. 'Just a twenty-four-hour thing. Mainly kids getting it. We have had a few staff away, though.'

'Ah…' Cade let his gaze roam the department again. 'Is that why I haven't seen Jo Bishop for a while?' He knew he might be stepping over that private boundary so he thought fast. 'There was a patient I brought in a week or more ago that I was hoping to follow up on.'

Hanna's quick glance made Cade wonder if she knew more than she was letting on. She was Jo's closest friend, after all. Was it presumptuous to think she'd told him things about her life that she wouldn't have told Hanna? Or anyone else?

'She could have had a mild dose last week. She did

take a couple of days off, but she said she thought it was a sour cream dip or something that had made her feel sick.'

The thought of Jo being unwell gave Cade a knot in his stomach. If he'd known about that he would have been there. Taking her some chicken soup or just making sure she was looking after herself. But what if it was actually something she would not have wanted him to know about? Like a broken heart? Because she hadn't let on that she wasn't well when Cade had texted her a day or two after the plug had been pulled on their private arrangement. Her response to his query of whether she was okay had simply been All good. With a smiley face to confirm it.

'You'll probably see her today, anyway.' Yeah…there was a gleam in Hanna's gaze that suggested she was aware that he'd had something going on with Jo. 'She's around somewhere. Ah…there she is.'

And there she was, pulling a curtain back into place as she came out of one of the cubicles. She didn't see Cade straight away so he had a moment to observe that she was looking a bit pale. A bit…subdued? Whatever it was, it gave him a kick in the guts to go with that knot of concern in his stomach. When she looked up and spotted him, her smile and nod of acknowledgement chased the impression away. She looked the way she always did at work. Focused, in control and ultimately professional.

It would have been completely convincing to anyone who didn't know her so well. But Cade did know Jo that well and he knew how courageous she was. How well she'd learned to hide any personal disappointments.

A dollop of guilt got mixed in with the other emotions that Cade was keeping a very careful lid on. This was all his fault. He'd been the one to flirt with Jo in the first place, when he'd written his number on her glove and given her 'that' look when he'd said he would be interested in following up on Kayla's treatment for her badly broken leg.

He'd deliberately made a thing about returning her pen with an over-the-top performance that was intended to let her know that whatever might happen between them would stay completely between them, if privacy was an issue for her. He'd wanted her to know that she could trust him. He'd hoped that she would also like him.

And she had. Enough to choose him as a preferred father for the baby she wanted so much. Enough to give him a glimpse into a life that had shaped her determination and success but also undermined her confidence in how amazing a woman she really was. What Jo needed was someone who would love her so much that they would happily spend the rest of their life convincing her of that. If only things were different, he would have been that man.

They weren't different, of course, but that didn't mean that he had to stop caring about her, did it? He ignored the fact that Hanna was watching him as he stepped close enough to where Jo was bringing up some information on a computer screen to speak to her quietly.

'Hanna thinks I'm asking about a patient,' he said. 'But what I'm doing is asking about *you*... She said you'd been sick?'

Jo kept her gaze on the screen as she clicked tabs to locate and open a digital patient file.

'I'm fine,' she told him.

There was relief to be found in the genuine warmth of the quick sideways glance Cade received. She didn't hate him, anyway...

'I did have a bit of a bug or something,' Jo added. 'But I'm over it now.'

Another heartbeat of eye contact and he found that their ability to communicate silently hadn't vanished due to the new distance between them. Jo was telling him that she was over how she'd felt about him now. Or would be in the very near future.

'I had to cancel an appointment for that check-up,' she added, turning her gaze back to the screen. 'But I've rescheduled it for the end of this week. I've decided it's time to get things moving.'

That was exactly the way he would have expected Jo to deal with a challenge in her life. To find a solution and make it happen. It was even more of a relief than knowing she didn't hate him for having offered to play a part and then agreeing that it would be better for both of them if it never happened. Cade held that eye contact for as long as he could.

'Hasn't put you off, then?' he murmured. 'I'm glad to hear that.'

'It's made me more determined to get on with it, if anything.' Jo threw him a bright smile. Any observer, like Hanna, would surely think there was nothing personal or heavy about their discussion but Jo lowered her voice anyway. 'At least I know that getting to know my donor is not the best idea I've ever had.'

She was taking the blame herself? Absolving him? Cade wasn't sure he deserved that, but this wasn't the time or place to do anything more than they already had to set their new boundaries and make it clear that anything that had happened between them privately was not going to affect a professional relationship. He didn't want to leave their exchange on a negative note but he could see Geoff walking back into the department and towards the stretcher tucked in against the central desk.

'Best of luck.' Cade returned Jo's smile. He even nodded, as though he'd received the update on a patient he had been seeking. 'I'll look forward to news. And…' He was turning away but he caught her gaze for an extra heartbeat. He wanted to say that her idea might not have been the wisest but that getting to know her so well was something he would never regret. There were no words, however, and real life was pulling them apart. Geoff was beginning to look around the department to see where his crew partner had got to. It was time for Cade to take the first step into his new reality—a world where it would be safer—and kinder—if it did not contain Jo Bishop in anything other than a professional role. His words trailed into almost a sigh.

'…and take care.'

The ambience of the private fertility clinic was one of discreet optimism laced with a confidence that inspired hope. There was a beautiful sculpture of a mother and baby in the entranceway and there was no waiting for Jo's appointment to talk to the clinic's senior specialist.

'I've spoken to our colleagues in Auckland,' she told Jo. 'And we've arranged the transfer of your eggs. As I said when we spoke on the phone, all we need to do is make sure we've got all our ducks in a row and we can get started—possibly on your next cycle. Do you know when Day One of your last cycle was?'

'Um…yes…' Jo told her the date.

The doctor hesitated in marking a calendar. 'You're not sure?'

'I'm sure. It was just a bit slow to get started and a bit lighter than usual.'

'We'll see what's going on with your hormone levels. Let's get your blood test done now, and the ultrasound examination, and then we'll talk through the next steps in more detail.'

The phlebotomist was efficient and the procedure of collecting the blood samples completely painless. Jo was given a gown to change into and then shown into a warm, dimly lit room to meet the ultrasound technician and get settled on the bed.

'Have you had a transvaginal ultrasound done before?'

'Yes. Several times. I had eggs collected and frozen a while ago.'

'Great—' the technician beamed '—you'll know all about inserting the probe yourself, then.' She opened a condom package and slipped the protection over the ultrasound probe.

Oh…help. Would she ever be able to see one of those little packets being ripped open without thinking of that first night she'd had in Cade Cameron's bed? In his arms? On their *first* date? Or what about the second, when she hadn't had one available and she'd had unprotected sex for the first time in her life because, right from the start, that extraordinary trust had been there on both sides? Jo pushed the thoughts away. She was not going to lie here thinking about how much she was missing Cade in her life. This was about moving forward. About achieving what it was that had made it okay to get that close to Cade in the first place—bringing a baby into the world. *Her* baby. Her future.

The technician took control of the probe once it was positioned and then she peered at her screen as various shapes and blobs appeared and faded as she searched for recognisable landmarks. She angled her screen as if it was a normal thing to do to make the images clearer, but Jo went very still. She knew the screen was being angled so that she wouldn't see what was on it. Because the technician had seen something of concern?

Oh, God…was she going to find out that there was actually no chance she was ever going to have this baby she wanted so much because there was something wrong with her uterus? Like a visible mass that could turn out to be cancer and mean she needed a total hysterectomy?

'What's wrong?' she asked. 'Can you see something?'

'Nothing's wrong. I just… I might just see if one of the doctors is free.' She removed the probe and turned her screen off. 'Be right back.' Her smile was reassuring. 'It's nothing to worry about, I promise.'

Yeah…right… You didn't rush off in the first moments of an examination to find a medical opinion on what you were seeing unless something was very obviously not right. The carefully calm expression on the specialist's face when she came in to pick up the probe and turn the screen back on was another giveaway. So was the silence. Jo wasn't going to ask again, however. She was too nervous.

The specialist turned the screen so that Jo could see it.

'Is that…? No… It couldn't possibly be…'

'It is.' The specialist was smiling. 'You're pregnant, Jo. About ten weeks, I'd say, but we'll do some measurements and get a more accurate date for you.'

'But…'

'You did say your last period was lighter than usual. What about the one before that?'

'I…don't remember…' Jo was trying to count back through the weeks. Had she actually conceived that night that she'd assured Cade the odds of her getting pregnant at her age were almost non-existent?

It hadn't been a sour cream dip that was a bit off that had made her feel sick that last night she'd had with Cade. It hadn't been the tummy bug that was going around either. And it hadn't been just that she was missing Cade so much that she'd been feeling so tired and flat and not hungry.

Non-existent odds.

And here she was, almost through the first trimester of a pregnancy.

This was amazing. Unbelievable. For the stunned moment before it hit her, Jo had never felt so happy in her life. And then, suddenly, she'd never felt so afraid.

She had just lost control of how this was supposed to happen. She wasn't ready. This new reality was too enormous to take in. Too good to be true? What if… what if her fear that she would fail at being a parent— like her parents had—was justified? It wasn't as if she would ever have Cade by her side again to make her believe, even for a moment, that she was actually awesome. She would have to cope with her entire life completely changing and would be doing it totally alone.

Jo could feel tears gathering and then rolling down the sides of her face. The technician handed her some tissues. The specialist was blinking quite hard herself.

'I've heard of happy stories like this,' she told Jo. 'But I've never had a front row seat before.'

She thought Jo was crying from joy and she was. As terrifying as this was, there was still definitely joy in that mix of the overwhelming flood of emotions but it was all too much to take in, let alone process, just yet. And there was something new making Jo's heart sink too fast to catch.

This would be worse for Cade than the fact that she'd fallen in love with him.

And, like how she felt about him, there was no way she couldn't tell him that he was going to become a father.

He'd had a bad feeling about this ever since he'd got the text from Jo asking if he could come to her place this evening because she needed to talk to him. This wasn't part of Plan B, which was where he stepped back from any involvement in Jo's private life because he needed to protect her from being hurt any more than she already had been.

And, yeah…he needed to protect himself as well. It had been unexpectedly difficult to step back and he'd found himself thinking about Jo far too much. When he ate anything, for example, it would bring back memories of all the different cuisines they'd tried together. If it was something new, he'd be wondering if Jo would like it as much as he did. If he was tempted by an old favourite, like one of those gourmet hamburgers, the memories— like seeing Jo enjoying her meal so much she didn't care that she had to chase droplets of juice before they could run down her chin—were obviously going to be too raw. Cade had given up eating hamburgers.

He didn't go to bed until he was so tired that he knew he would fall asleep the moment his head hit the pillow because, if he lay awake, he would be far too aware of the empty space beside him. He knew he could easily find someone to fill that space for a bit of fun that wasn't going to go anywhere but he didn't have the slightest inclination to flirt with any of the women he was meeting. On the plus side, staying up late made him way more productive. He'd finished that presentation for the conference in Prague next year. He had been planning to give it a final read-through and polish to email it through this evening, actually, so he'd almost sent a message back to Jo to say that it wasn't convenient to go and see her.

Instead, here he was, on her doorstep. With no take-away food, or wine, or anything else to offer other than his presence. Because he'd had a bad feeling about that message. Jo had been as aware as he had been that the brief conversation in the emergency department the other day had been a farewell. The closing of the door that had provided an entry into each other's private life. Jo wouldn't be opening that door again if she didn't have a very good reason.

It was Friday today. He hadn't forgotten that Jo had told him she had rescheduled her appointment with the fertility clinic. Had she had some bad news? Had she changed her mind about asking for his help as a sperm donor because there was no suitable alternative available? No...that was ridiculous. It was more likely to be that she'd been told she could never carry a child for some reason and perhaps he was the only person she knew would understand how devastating that kind of news would be.

Cade's heart sank even further on seeing Jo's face when she opened the real-life door of her house to invite him in. He'd never seen her look like this. Or to be clearly summoning her courage to say anything. She took him into her living room, which might well have been a conscious choice because they'd never spent time together in here, they'd only used the kitchen and bedroom on his previous visits. This was a lovely room, lined with overstuffed bookshelves and with a gas fire providing the light and heat of real flames.

The silence grew when they were both sitting in old armchairs on either side of the fire.

'Can I get you a drink? Coffee or something?'

'No, I'm good, thanks.' Cade bit his lip, stopping himself from asking Jo what was wrong. What if she burst into tears like she had the last time he'd done that? He'd have to take her in his arms and comfort her and he knew where they'd end up. Exactly where they'd ended up last time. In her bed. That Cade could already feel the pull of wanting to provide that sort of comfort again was a warning he wasn't going to ignore. He was too involved, here. Jo didn't need him. She'd always coped on her own and she'd need to do that again in the very near future. The best thing he could do was to encourage her to do just that.

Or maybe she didn't need his encouragement. She was taking a deep breath. 'I'm sorry to summon you like I did but there's something I have to tell you and I thought it would be better for it to be completely private.'

Cade nodded. He was watching Jo's face but she was looking at the flickering flames of the small fire.

'I had the appointment at the clinic this afternoon,' she said. 'Blood tests and an ultrasound.'

He nodded again. 'That's good news. Did they give you an idea of when you can start treatment?'

'I'm not going to start treatment,' Jo said quietly. 'I can't.'

Cade closed his eyes for a long moment. So he'd been right. Jo had developed an abnormality that would prevent her being able to get pregnant. His heart was breaking for her as he opened his eyes again to find that Jo was the one watching him carefully now.

'I'm pregnant, Cade,' she said.

There was an odd buzzing sound in Cade's ears which was possibly why he'd misheard what Jo had said.

'Sorry…what did you just say?'

She was taking another deliberate breath. And she spoke slowly and very clearly. 'I'm pregnant. Just over ten weeks.'

The buzzing sound had gone but now there was some kind of mental fog rolling in that made it impossible to do the maths. A gestation was counted from the first day of a woman's last menstrual cycle, wasn't it? Which meant that you had to subtract a couple of weeks to come up with a conception date?

'I'm sorry,' Jo whispered, her gaze sliding away from his. 'I really did believe that the odds of conceiving naturally at my age were almost non-existent but that must have been when it happened. That first night you stayed here with me and I didn't have any condoms in the house.'

'Not your fault,' Cade muttered. 'Everyone has to take accountability for their own protection.' He'd thought about it at the time, hadn't he? He'd dismissed both the likelihood of it happening and that it could be a disaster if it did because, after all, he was planning to father a baby for Jo when he'd gone through the time period she had deemed necessary to be sure. 'It's not as though that was the only time.'

'I had no idea that I was pregnant. I was still getting my period, although it was lighter than normal. I thought that I'd picked up a dose of mild food poisoning from that sour cream dip we'd had that night. I was pretty sure you hadn't eaten any of it, so I didn't say anything at the time.'

Cade finally met Jo's gaze again. 'How do you feel about it?'

'I'm not sure,' she admitted. 'I'm all over the shop, to be honest. Part of me thinks it's some kind of miracle. I'm over the moon but I feel really guilty as well. As if

I did it deliberately to someone who had no idea it was a possibility.'

'Well…' Cade managed to find a wry smile. 'That last bit's true.'

'And we'd both agreed that it wouldn't be a good idea to go through with the donor bit, given my feelings for you but…' Jo was holding his gaze and she looked as fierce as he'd ever seen her look '… I can do this. I'm already getting over it. I think we can end up being simply friends. That we can go back to the plan and you can be a father at a distance. That part doesn't have to change at all.'

This time, Cade shook his head. 'But it already has.'

'How? The end result would have been the same, wouldn't it? I'd be pregnant and we wouldn't be spending so much time with each other. You'd be totally free to get on with your life anywhere in the world. It's just happened in a different way. Without a laboratory and procedures to go through. And I'm suddenly a lot further along the track too, I guess, but that's a good thing in a way. The risk of something going wrong in the first trimester would have been scary.'

Cade had stopped taking in her words by the time Jo had finished speaking.

'It is different,' he insisted. 'I was prepared for being part of a medical procedure. A legal agreement, even, but…but we made a baby the normal way. The way…'

Oh, God…the way he and Nina had made *their* baby. By making love.

Shaking his head again wasn't going to help his thoughts fall into a space where he could deal with them. He had to move. He got to his feet without being aware of sending any instructions to his legs.

The expression on Jo's face as she looked up told

him that she'd guessed what he'd been thinking. That she knew she had caused him pain by reminding him of what had shattered his life so completely all those years ago. She didn't want to hurt him any more than he'd ever wanted to hurt her.

'It's okay,' he said. 'Or it will be. It's a bit of a shock, that's all. I don't know how I feel about it. I need some time to think.'

Jo was on her feet now. She had her arms wrapped around her body and was she carefully keeping herself out of touching distance from him?

'I know…and I'm sorry. But it wasn't something I could tell you by a text message or phone call. I can keep this as private as you want it to be.'

'Thanks…'

'And it will be okay.' The tilt of Jo's lips was poignant. 'Maybe miracles don't happen unless they're meant to?'

The hope in her eyes almost took his breath away but it was the way Jo's arms loosened to leave her hands resting on her belly that pushed this a bit further than Cade could deal with right now.

'I can see myself out,' he told her. 'We'll talk soon…'

Cade would have no idea that Jo was upstairs, in the darkness of her bedroom, watching him ride away on his bike.

Or that he was taking a good chunk of her heart with him because she understood exactly how he felt right now. Blindsided. Afraid of how this could affect the future. Having memories come at him from all sides to remind him that he'd been right to protect himself from anything like this being able to happen again. She could understand all too well why Cade was so afraid to let love back into his life because this was so, *so* huge.

She wanted to protect him herself but she couldn't change this reality. And she didn't want to change anything now. Again, she found her hand resting on her belly and the gesture had become a kind of touchstone in the last few hours. She had someone else to protect now. She already loved this baby who was safely cocooned in her womb and she knew it was enough to stand up to the fear she'd had herself, that she would fail as a parent.

There was one thing she certainly wouldn't fail in providing. This baby would grow up to know how much it was loved and that it deserved to be loved that much. Cade had understood that she wanted to be the parent she'd never had herself and, while Jo knew it wasn't going to be easy, she also knew that she *could* do this. She had more than enough love to make it work. And Cade had given her more than he realised.

He'd made her believe, on more than one occasion, that she deserved to be loved herself.

That she was, indeed, awesome.

If—or rather when—things got tough, she could hang onto that. As tightly as she needed to. Times like now, in fact, as she had to admit she hadn't been telling the truth when she'd told Cade that she was already getting over being in love with him.

CHAPTER TEN

'CANCEL… CANCEL. STAND BY, PLEASE…'

Cade picked up the dashboard microphone. 'Roger that.' He glanced sideways at his partner, one eyebrow raised. It had to be something major coming through to bump an elderly person who had probably fractured their hip further down the queue.

The radio link to Control crackled back into life. 'Code One… Go to twenty-six Montgomery Crescent, repeat—two-six, Montgomery Crescent. Two-year-old boy found at bottom of swimming pool. Unresponsive.'

Cade swore under his breath, hit the switches to activate the beacons and siren and put his foot down. His sideways glance this time was not to take in the grim expression on Geoff's face but to check that the sat nav was providing directions to the address.

'Next right,' Geoff said. 'And then first left. It's only two blocks away.'

Cade changed the siren sound as they reached the intersection, but he slowed the ambulance for only a few seconds.

'Clear left,' Geoff said.

They could see a woman on the street, frantically waving, as soon as they turned into Montgomery Crescent. Cade turned off the siren but the beacons were still flashing as he backed swiftly down a wide driveway and they grabbed the gear they needed. The bars of the metal pool fence and the wide-open gate made it easy to see exactly where they needed to go. A man was kneeling beside a tiny, still figure. He raised his mouth from the child's face and began pushing on the small chest. His hair and clothes were soaked and dripping. A woman crouched beside him, holding her head in her hands as she made distressed sounds.

'How long?' Cade asked the woman who'd been waiting for them on the road. 'How long was he missing for before he was found?'

'Only a minute.' She looked terrified. 'His dad was cleaning the pool and he just came inside to get a bucket.'

She was following Cade and Geoff as they walked swiftly to the scene. It was tempting to run but they were trained not to. It wasn't simply that they could trip and damage equipment or themselves, rushing into a scene created a frame of mind that was not conducive to dealing effectively with a life-or-death situation.

'He saw Toby as soon as he went back and we saw him dive straight in the pool. He knew to start CPR.'

'That's great.' Cade was beside the boy's father now. 'You're doing a great job. My name's Cade. Let me help you…'

'I'm not sure I'm doing it right…' The boy's father was moving back to let the crew close to his son. He was young, probably only in his late twenties. 'It's a long time since I did that first aid course.'

Any CPR was better than none, but Cade could see the ominous blue colour of cyanosis on the child's lips and fingers and he knew even before he began his assessment that he was going to find him not breathing and probably without a pulse. Geoff was already setting up the defibrillator and had the pouch open to take out the pads he needed to stick on the boy's chest. Cade kept up the CPR until Geoff had applied the pads and then unzipped the backpack he'd carried from the ambulance and took out an airway roll and a bag mask as they paused just long enough to see what was happening on the screen.

The boy's father had his arms around the woman who was still crouched on the ground sobbing.

'You're Toby's mum?' Cade asked gently.

'Y-yes…' It was the man who responded, through chattering teeth. There was enough of a wind to be a concern for anyone who'd been immersed in cold water.

Cade turned to the second woman. 'Could you maybe find some blankets in the house? Geoff will give you a foil sheet to put round Toby's dad as well.'

Geoff nodded acknowledgement of Cade's suggestion but his gaze was fixed on the screen of the monitor. 'Looks like normal sinus rhythm,' he relayed.

Cade put his fingers on the child's neck again but he was already shaking his head. 'There's no pulse,' he said. 'Could be PEA.'

Pulseless electrical activity, where the heart was still receiving signals to contract but there was either no response or it was too weak to be able to generate a pulse or provide circulation. It was also not a shockable rhythm.

'Carry on with compressions,' he told Geoff. 'I'm going to intubate.'

Getting an airway secured was the first priority. Ventilating the toddler to get him breathing again was the next and the most effective way to do that if the lungs were full of water was to have the airway secured with an endotracheal tube. Compressions to keep his blood circulating were just as important and getting IV access for the drugs needed for resuscitation was another priority. The ABCs. Airway, breathing and circulation. The foundation of a first response in any emergency. They had protocols to follow so it was easy to be completely focused. To know exactly what needed to be done and not think of anything else.

'Let's have continuous end-tidal CO_2 monitoring and the pulse oximeter on,' Cade directed.

'Do you want me to call for a back-up crew to assist with transport?'

There was probably already one on the way because it was standard procedure when they might have to transport a patient under CPR but Cade gave a single nod. 'I hope we'll be on the road before they get here,' he said. 'I'll get IV access and then we'll load and go.'

Placing the endotracheal tube and checking it was in the correct place had been simple. Getting IV access in veins that were not only tiny but now completely flattened by no discernible blood pressure was not going to be simple. Or even possible, given the urgency with which they needed to get this small patient to definitive care in an emergency department.

'I'm going to put a needle into a bone in Toby's leg,' he warned the parents, now huddled inside blankets as they watched on in horror. 'It looks awful but he won't feel a thing, I promise. And it means we can give him any medications he needs.'

He had to cut open the leg of the jeans Toby was wearing, extend his leg and paint disinfectant on the skin below his kneecap. With clean gloves on, he used one hand to locate the patella and stabilise the joint. With his other hand, he picked up the insertion device that looked like a small gun, having already loaded the intraosseous needle. He was aiming for the flat side of the tibia, just below the patella. When he felt the needle touch the bone, he pressed the trigger to start drilling, ready to stop the instant he felt the 'pop' of the needle entering the space within the bone. It took only seconds to put the stabilising dressing patch on and attach the extension that gave them a port to run fluid into as part of the resuscitation and a means of getting drugs into circulation at least twice as fast as peripheral intravenous access in a patient with unrecordable blood pressure.

Cade used that port for drug administration a very short time later, whilst they were en route to the hospital and Toby's heart rate dropped to a bradycardia of only forty beats per minute. The adrenaline he injected raised the rate to well over a hundred beats per minute and lifted the blood pressure enough for Cade to be able to feel both a carotid and femoral pulse. It was only then— with the glimmer of hope that this little boy might be one of the lucky few that survived a near-drowning, perhaps even with no neurological damage—that Cade's focus slipped just enough, for just long enough, to feel a shaft of what Toby's parents were going through.

He could feel some of that fear that they were about to lose their precious child. The guilt that they should have been able to protect him and the potential yawning void of not being able to watch him grow up. And, in the split second before he pushed his own feelings aside to focus again on only what he had to do as this boy's emergency medical care provider, Cade realised that he was feeling this so acutely because he was going to become a father himself.

And he couldn't avoid the risk of loss by taking himself away and watching his child grow up from a distance because it was already there. *His* child—his and

Jo's—was already in existence and his need to protect it was also already there. Imprinted into his cells, perhaps, because he knew the pain that loss could bring?

Toby was still unconscious as they stopped in the ambulance bay and Geoff expertly backed up to the ledge. Then he jumped out to pull open the back doors of the vehicle. Having called through the critical status of their patient as they were travelling under lights and siren, there was a team waiting for them, headed by Joanna Bishop. Cade knew she'd had warning of what to expect but he also saw how tense the muscles in her face looked. Was this too close for comfort, in the wake of having only just discovered her own pregnancy? Was she over the shock and already in love with the baby she wanted so much? Surely that would make it even harder to deal with a case like this?

She wasn't showing any signs of stress that others might have noticed, however. She led the team into Resus, where others were waiting for them, including an anaesthetist and a paediatric critical care consultant that Cade recognised, asking rapid questions as they moved.

How long had he been under water?

Was there any evidence of head or neck trauma?

How long had his rhythm been PEA?

How long had he been receiving chest compressions until a palpable pulse was found?

Exactly what drugs and dosages had he received?

What were the current vital signs? SpO2? Fraction of inspired oxygen?

Toby was still being ventilated but he'd lost the dreadful shade of cyanosis on his lips and fingers and Cade noted that his skin felt slightly warm to the touch for the first time as he helped lift the toddler onto the bed. Jo and the other consultants ordered the remaining wet clothes to be removed and his temperature checked again. They wanted an arterial blood gas measurement, a blood glucose level, a nasogastric tube inserted, a urinary catheter and a chest X-ray. They discussed ventilator settings and the heart rhythm and rate as they switched Toby over to the hospital equipment for monitoring.

It was the controlled chaos of an expert team with a lot to do to save a young life. A nurse was with Toby's parents on one side of the room. Toby's father still had a foil sheet and a blanket draped around his shoulders but his mother looked as if she was too scared to cry any more. It was good that they were being allowed to watch everything being done for their son. Nobody asked Cade or Geoff to leave the room and Cade was quietly finishing his paperwork in the corner, listening and watching what was going on at the same time and keeping his fingers crossed that another urgent call would not come their way too soon. He was still there when Jo stepped back to talk to Toby's parents.

'We're going to keep him asleep for a while so that we can watch his breathing and organ function very carefully and make any adjustments needed.'

'How long…?'

'Possibly a few days but we'll know more tomorrow. Some of the blood tests he's having will let us know whether he's suffered a brain injury from lack of oxygen and he'll have other tests in the next few days. He'll be going up to the paediatric intensive care unit from here, as soon as he's stable, and you can stay with him there.'

'Is…?' Toby's mother was clinging to her husband's hand. 'Is he going to make it?'

'He has a lot of things in his favour,' Jo told them. 'You found him quickly and started CPR and the ambulance crew were not only on the scene almost immediately but got him in here fast and he had a spontaneous pulse again by then. The shorter those time frames are, the more we can hope for the best outcome.'

It was time that Cade left. He tore off the copy of his paperwork that he needed to leave to go in the patient file and signalled Geoff, who began rolling the stretcher out of the area. He was caught by Toby's parents as he went past them, though, and he felt their fear hit him again, but there was something else in the blast of their emotion. Hope. And gratitude.

'We can never thank you enough,' Toby's father told him. 'You have no idea how much it means to us…'

Except he did. And, over the man's shoulder, Cade caught Jo's gaze and it was one of *those* moments. She understood the impact that this case would have had on him even if he hadn't just received the shock news that he was going to become a father again himself. It felt like he was successful in letting her know that he was okay. About more than this case. He was ready to accept the responsibility of becoming a father.

Embrace it, even if he might not be capable of the kind of emotional involvement he might have once been able to offer.

It was Jo's idea that they went for a walk the next time their shifts gave them a window of free time that overlapped. After several emotional days, she was ready for a blast of fresh air and suggested that they went back to Tunnel Beach—the place they'd been when it had actually been a first date.

Before Jo had realised the huge age gap they had.

Before she'd scared him away by telling him that

he'd make the perfect father for the baby she was planning to have.

Before they'd made an agreement that had changed everything.

The edges of the shock of what had so unexpectedly happened was continuing to wear off and Jo suspected that Cade was getting his head around the news as well. She'd had a feeling that he might be ready to talk about it after she'd seen him in the emergency department when he'd brought in the toddler who'd come so close to drowning. He was certainly happy to accept her invitation to go for the walk but he refused to take Jo on his motorbike. They went in Jo's car, which was a low-slung sporty BMW roadster.

'You're going to need a new car,' was the first thing Cade said as he folded his tall frame to get into the passenger seat. 'This isn't going to be very practical for a baby seat, let alone the pram and everything else you'll be carting everywhere.'

'Mmm...' Jo threw him a deadpan glance. Did he really think she hadn't already thought of that, along with a million other things that could be important? 'Just as well I gave up riding my own bike, isn't it?'

He was silent as they drove away from the central city.

'How's your week been?' Jo asked. 'You've just finished your night shifts, yes?'

'Yep. It's been good. I've been out and about in my time off, getting to know the city a bit better. There are some really lovely suburbs. I love being up on top of the hills, like in Maori Hill with the spectacular views or over in St Clair right by the beach, but I think I love the peninsula best. Have you ever been to Glenfalloch?'

'Don't think so. It sounds like a good Scottish name.'

'It's a woodland garden that's been around for about fifty years. I was told I'd come at the best time of year to see it and it wasn't crowded when I went on a week-day. There's a restaurant as well. They do a lot of weddings there.'

Jo laughed. 'Probably why it's never been on my radar.'

Cade didn't seem amused. 'It's worth seeing,' he said quietly. 'And a great place to wander around when you've got a lot to think about.'

Like the fact that he was well on the way to becoming a father? Jo was more than sympathetic in that Cade was no doubt dealing with traumatic memories of the last time he'd been preparing to become a father but she was the one who would be facing the most change in her life, wasn't she? Cade might well be gone by the time she was due to give birth. Off doing exciting things with a rescue service or on an oil rig or maybe in some war torn, impoverished corner of the globe.

And she was fine with that, she really was. Jo's confidence in her ability to cope with whatever the future had in store for her was growing each day.

'How's Toby?' The abrupt change in the conversation made Jo blink. 'Have they woken him up properly yet?'

'Yes. He's going to be discharged, in fact. I did message you about the biomarkers of neuronal damage being within acceptable parameters and the results from the electroencephalogram?'

'You did. Thanks. Caught me at a busy time so I couldn't respond.'

'And you got the one about the MRI yesterday?' Come to think of it, Cade was much less likely to answer text messages promptly than he had before they had ended their 'getting to know each other' period, even though the subjects had only been professional since then.

'I did. That's why I thought they might have woken him up by now.'

'He's a lucky little boy,' Jo said. 'Fifty percent of children who survive after needing CPR at the scene of a drowning go on to have lifelong disabilities.' She took the turning that led to the Tunnel Beach car park and, despite how low slung her car was, she could feel a stiff sea breeze buffeting the vehicle. It was going to be cold outside. And she couldn't read Cade's mood but it was obviously going to be a very different experience to the first time they'd come here, when it had been so easy to talk to each other.

When they'd held hands to scramble down to the beach and wedged themselves into the gap in the rock to shelter from the wind and there'd been laughter and attraction and an inevitability to the way they'd ended up in each other's arms on the same night. She'd already been on the slippery slope to falling in love with Cade back then, hadn't she? If she'd realised that, would she have backed off before anything had happened?

Perhaps she should have but, if she was honest with herself, she probably wouldn't have. The pull had been irresistible and it was still there. But Jo had already accepted that it was just going to be a background hum in her life. It would be easier to ignore it now that she had her pregnancy to focus on and plans for the future to make. It would be even easier in the long term when Cade was too far away to spend time with him like this. To be close enough to have to curb a desire to touch him or to be searching his face to try and read what he was thinking. And she didn't want to forget it, anyway. She wanted to remember how special Cade had made her feel, but maybe that would also be easier when distance and time had softened the intensity of feelings that were still too close to the surface.

'It looks cold out there,' Cade said. 'And that's quite a wind.'

'Maybe we could both do with blowing some cobwebs away?'

Jo pushed the door open and climbed out of the car. It slammed shut behind her as the wind caught it and her hair flicked over her face so she couldn't even see Cade getting out of his side of the car.

'Jo?'

She tried to tuck her hair behind her ears. Cade was right in front of her now.

'I've had a lot of time to think.' He had raised his voice because the wind was snatching his words away. 'And I've changed my mind.'

Jo's breath caught in her throat. What had he changed his mind about? Had he discovered that he was capable of falling in love? That he'd discovered he felt the same way about her as she did about him? It felt as if Jo's whole world was balancing on a cliff top, not unlike the real ones so close to them on this wild bit of coastline.

'I want to be a part of our baby's life,' Cade said. 'I'm not going to go somewhere else. I want to be a *real* father and take the kind of responsibility that a real father should take. I…' He reached out to hold Jo's shoulders as if he was worried she might be about to turn away. 'I want to marry you, Jo.'

The ground didn't feel stable beneath her feet. It was crumbling, sending her over that cliff, and there were rocks to crash on at the bottom.

'Why?' she heard herself ask. 'Because of the baby?'

A line appeared as Cade's brow furrowed. 'Of course.'

'So, if I wasn't pregnant with your child, you *wouldn't* want to marry me?'

The line deepened. Cade was genuinely puzzled, wasn't he? 'You know the answer to that, Jo. You know why…'

Oh… God… What could be worse than bringing up a child who would remind her every day of the man she'd fallen in love with so hard she would never really get over it?

Marrying him, that was what. Living with him. Knowing that he could never, ever feel anything like the way she would always feel. Knowing that the baby had been worth staying around for but she hadn't been…

She stepped back, away from the touch of his hands on her shoulders.

'No,' she said. And then she said it again with more emphasis. '*No*. Forget it, Cade. That's the worst idea ever. I'm not about to marry a man who doesn't love me.' She wrapped her arms around herself. It was just the icy wind or the salt it carried that was bringing tears to her eyes. 'You're right. It's too cold.' She turned to pull open the door to her car. 'I don't think I want to walk.'

The silence in the car when Cade got back in would have made the prospect of the drive back to the city very unwelcome except for the crooked smile he offered Jo.

'I'm sorry,' he said quietly. 'It *was* a bad idea. I wasn't thinking straight.'

Jo simply nodded and started the engine of her car. How easy was that for Cade? It hadn't even been a remotely genuine consideration, had it?

'But we can still be friends?'

'Sure.' But Jo didn't turn to meet the gaze she could feel on her skin. She was looking straight ahead of her in the direction that she was heading.

This was a curveball and she needed time to think about how she was going to handle Cade being more of a part of her future than she had expected. Time to deal with what felt like a damaging blow to the confidence she'd managed to gather about facing single parenthood. About really getting over being in love with Cade. Time to pick up the pieces of her soul from the metaphorical rocks she'd found at the bottom of that cliff.

Had she really thought, for even an instant, that Cade had fallen in love with her? Of course she hadn't. Not really...

But, if that was true, why had it hurt so much to land on those rocks?

CHAPTER ELEVEN

IF CADE WASN'T going to provide the distance Jo knew she might need to keep her heart intact and restore her confidence, she would just have to create it herself by establishing boundaries to keep herself as safe as possible.

It didn't seem to be getting any easier, however, as one week and then another slipped by and suddenly she couldn't zip her jeans up over the neat little round bump of her belly. It was a good thing she wore scrubs while she was at work because no one would guess her secret and there was only one person she had needed to tell so far. It had been far too long since she and Hanna had been out for a meal so her best friend was delighted to spend some time with her.

Amazingly, Hanna had made it easy by guessing the big news that Jo wanted to share, possibly because she'd chosen a soda water for her pre-dinner drink and not her usual glass of wine. Hanna had also assumed that Jo had simply thawed her eggs and become pregnant independently and, for now—until she felt safe enough to cope—it was easier not to correct the assumption.

'Why didn't you tell me? I wanted to help you choose the donor.'

'I think you were out of town that week. That trip to

Australia? And we've both been so busy. We've hardly seen each other since my birthday.'

'That's true.' Hanna was too distracted to pursue the dateline. 'Was it hard? To choose?'

Jo could, at least, be completely honest about that. 'Not at all. He stood out from anyone else by a country mile.'

'What's he like?'

'Tall. Healthy. High achiever. Adventurous. Ticks all the boxes.'

'What about getting to know him for all those other boxes that didn't show up on the forms?'

'I decided that wasn't a good idea.' This was also true—she was just leaving out the fact that she'd decided it in retrospect. 'Imagine the complications that could create.'

Like falling in love with someone who was unavailable for the kind of relationship that was enough to overcome obstacles and last for ever? Like having him decide that he wanted to be part of his child's life right from the start, as far as parental responsibilities went? She wanted to tell Hanna about the new issues she was facing but...she couldn't. It wouldn't be fair on Cade. As far as she knew, she was the only person who knew about the tragedy of him losing his family. He had trusted her with a glimpse into a life, and past, that he preferred to keep very private and Jo would have respected that kind of trust from anyone.

Neither was it simply that she needed to be confident about the framework she and Cade were in the process of trying to create that would allow him to be more involved in his baby's life but give her a dignified space to get over being in love with him. And it wasn't just that, either. Even if she did get over being in love with him, she would always care about him enough to want to protect him.

It was a combination of all those things but it also went deeper than any of them. He'd given her the most amazing gift by fathering her child and, in doing so, he'd made himself vulnerable. He must have known he was risking his heart by getting close to something that he'd lost before, with devastating effect—his own child—but she could understand that void of wondering what it would be like to be a parent all too well. She'd been only too willing to let him experience that from a safe distance so, even though it was an alarming change, she couldn't—and wouldn't—deny him the chance to be a father.

Hanna was shaking her head sadly, now. 'You didn't even tell me when you were waiting to find out if it had worked.'

'If something's not very likely, sometimes it's better to assume it's not going to work and save disappointment.' Jo was being deliberately vague. 'I'm telling you now that I'm safely through my first trimester but I'd rather other people don't know yet.'

'Really? How long do you think you can keep it a secret?'

'Long enough, I hope. Another month or two, anyway. I can follow protocols and stay well away from X-rays or infections like shingles.'

'And soft cheese. And sushi. You can't eat that stuff any longer.'

Jo laughed. 'There you go. That's one of the reasons I don't want anyone else to know. I know people would mean well but I don't want the whole world to be telling me how I need to live my life. I've waited so long to do this. I want to do it my way. I'm not even going to tell my mother.'

'I get it.' Hanna held her hands up in a gesture of surrender. 'Sorry. I won't say anything else. It's not as though I know anything from personal experience, anyway. Everyone knows I have no interest in babies or pregnancy. I'll make an exception for yours though, Jo. This one's special.'

Jo sighed. 'That's another reason I'm not ready to go public. Can you imagine what the gossip will be like with me getting pregnant at my age?'

Hanna bit her lip. 'That's true. I'm glad you've told me, though. Let me know if I can help. Do you want company when you go for your antenatal appointments? Like your scans? How far along are you?'

'It's all good.' Jo dodged the question of how far along she was already. 'It's hard enough scheduling appointments in my own shifts without factoring in someone else's. And…you know… I like being independent.'

That hadn't stopped her inviting Cade to come to her next scan but that was different. That was for him far more than it was for herself. The courage he was showing in taking this step in his life was huge, given that he'd told Jo how much he'd already loved his first baby when she'd been no more than a blob on an ultrasound screen. He was putting trust in his ability to cope, in the universe to not let history repeat itself and in Jo, that she was going to allow him close enough to make it happen.

She might not have any influence on Cade's strength or what fate might have in store, but she could at least make sure she didn't break the trust he had in her. You didn't do that to people you loved. She knew how hard it had to be for him to take this step. And even though at the moment it felt like he was only doing it out of a sense of responsibility, surely he wouldn't be able to help falling in love with his child once he or she had arrived safely in the world?

He hadn't expected this to be so nerve racking.

It wasn't as though he hadn't been here before, in an ultrasound suite waiting with a pregnant woman to get the first glimpse of his own child. And maybe that was why Cade's heart was beating so fast. Why he was holding himself so rigidly. Because he knew the impact of seeing those tiny limbs. A miniature heart that was beating. The smudged features of a small face that would suddenly make this developing child a real person who was going to need all the love and protection of loving parents.

Cade didn't want to feel that slam of emotion. He wasn't ready. He knew it was going to come at some level, because he'd felt the stirrings of it for little Toby who wasn't even his own child, but he still needed some form of protection. Until this miracle baby had, at least, entered the world safely and he'd got past the point where his life had crashed and burned last time he'd been in this position. It was difficult, however. Cade found himself standing, his muscles as tense as if they were poised for flight if necessary. He was far enough away from Jo that, if she reached out her hand, she wouldn't be able to touch him and he was keeping his gaze firmly on the shifting shapes on the screen, rather than risk any of the kind of silent communication that eye contact with Jo seemed to spark.

Not that she was looking at him. Jo also had her gaze fixed to the screen, which was understandable. At this stage of her pregnancy it was possible to see details like fingers and toes, perhaps even facial expressions and to possibly discover the gender of the baby, but Cade had found a new safety net. He could focus on what the technician was doing, as she moved cursors and clicked on points to make measurements and screen for any anomalies. He could watch the clinical data that was being collected as the limbs and spine, the brain, kidneys and heart were examined and measurements recorded.

Cade could see that Jo was as tense as he was, by the way the hand he could see at her side was clenched, but he knew the reasons were very different from his own. Jo had no barriers that could prevent her wanting and loving this child as much as every child deserved to be wanted and loved. Her anxiety was all about how healthy her baby was. Cade's heart gave a painful squeeze when he saw her swipe away a tear of relief when the technician told her that, while a doctor would double-check her findings, she was happy with everything she'd seen. There was a wobble in her voice as well.

'Can you tell whether it's a girl or a boy?'

'Are you sure you want to know?'

Cade couldn't avoid catching her glance as Jo turned her head, her eyebrows raised, asking how he felt about it. The muscles in his jaw might be bunched but he managed what he hoped was a smile that threw the decision back to her. He added a shrug for good measure. He didn't care. It was only the health of the baby that mattered.

'Yes,' Jo said. 'I'd like to know, please.'

'It's just a bit early to be a hundred percent sure,' the technician said, moving her transducer again over the skin of Jo's now obviously rounded belly. 'But I did get a good look earlier. And…there…that's a good angle too. Those legs can't be hiding anything significant, so I'd put good money on Team Pink.'

Oh...*man*...

A girl.

A daughter.

He could hear his own voice in the back of his head from a time when the plan of fathering a baby for Jo had been a very different proposition.

I hope it's a girl. I'd like her to grow up to be as awesome as her mum...

He'd planned to take Jo out to dinner after this appointment. He had some properties shortlisted and wanted to show her the brochures and get her opinion. He'd hoped she might come with him to view the houses, especially the lovely old villa he'd found on the peninsula, not far from those woodland gardens, with an amazing view of the harbour.

Instead, he found himself fishing the phone he'd put on silent out of his pocket, as if he'd felt it vibrating to signal a call. He was pretending to read a non-existent message as the technician was using soft paper towels to wipe the gel off Jo's skin.

'Sorry,' he said to her. 'But I'm going to have to go. They're desperate for someone to fill a gap on night shift.'

'No worries.' Jo was pulling up the elastic band of her skirt to cover her belly. 'Thanks for coming, Cade. We'll talk soon, yes?'

'Sure thing.' Cade was already heading for the door.

Heading towards an escape that would give him time to settle the chaos in his head. And his heart. Time to pull the remnants of the defence he needed around himself and shore it up so that it could last the distance. He needed distraction. Maybe a blast of wind in his face from taking his bike out on the open road would do the trick. Because freedom could also be safety, couldn't it?

* * *

Jo felt the baby move for the first time about a week after that ultrasound appointment. A tiny ripple of sensation in her belly that was earlier than she'd expected but was unmistakably the movement of those miniature limbs.

Her first thought was to share the news with Cade. To call him. Or hope that he would come into the department with a patient so she could tell him face to face. To find a private space and let him put his own hand on her belly, perhaps, in the hope that he would be able to feel it himself?

Her next thought was a panicked U-turn as she imagined his hand on her belly, knowing that he was only touching her to feel the baby. It was bad enough having him show her pictures of houses he was thinking of buying, knowing that he was only staying in the city because of his need to embrace the responsibilities of fatherhood. She was gradually getting used to the idea of having Cade as no more than a friend and co-parent in the future but it was too soon to think she could cope with him touching her and not have her heart break into even more pieces.

It was, however, time to tell people at work. Not that she'd have to scale back her time on duty or anything, but they'd need time to organise a locum to cover her maternity leave. When the extra pager Jo wore on duty buzzed to let her know a call was coming in for an air rescue that required a doctor on board, her first thought then was that she would have to give up the extra risk that this part of her job presented. Maybe she should step back now, in fact.

Even when she picked up the phone to learn that this was an MCI—a multiple casualty incident, with a crash involving a camper van and a group of cyclists in a gorge not far out of the city and that every resource the emergency services had was being mobilised, Jo was still on the point of telling them she would send someone else from the emergency department. But then she heard that there were children involved and she knew she had to go. This would be the last time. She wouldn't put herself or the baby in any danger but she needed to be there. She needed to do whatever she could to help.

The road was unsealed. It was narrow enough to present a huge logistical challenge to get large emergency vehicles like a fire engine close enough to the scene to be able to do their job which, in this case, might involve getting steel cables attached to a camper van that had tipped over the side of the gulley road after trying—and failing—to avoid a collision with a group of cyclists as it rounded a downhill hairpin bend.

There was a family trapped in that camper van with only a rocky outcrop and a tree that was now on a sharp lean acting as an obstacle to it rolling further towards the bottom of the gully and the river, which wasn't a huge distance but could potentially turn a minor injury into something life-threatening. Nobody could get near it until it was stabilised and there was a terrified family trapped inside. It had been Cade who'd scrambled down, at a safe distance, to try and assess the situation and the first impression was not great. A man was in the driving seat, his head tipped back and his eyes closed.

'Hello…can anyone hear me?'

A woman's face appeared around the unconscious driver's body. There was a trickle of blood on her cheek from a cut on her forehead.

'Me… I can hear you. Help…' She gave a strangled sob. 'I'm too scared to try and get out because I can feel

the van move. And I think my foot's stuck, anyway…
Please…*help*…'

'That's what we're here for, sweetheart. And don't
move for the moment. Stay as still as you can. My name's
Cade. What's yours?'

'Jules.'

'Okay, Jules. I can't get any closer just yet but we're
working on making it safe to get you all out as quickly
as possible. I need you to tell me everything you can
for the moment.'

He quickly discovered that the man in the driver's seat
was her husband. He was unconscious but breathing and
did not appear to be bleeding heavily. Jules thought she
might have broken her arm but she was more concerned
about the three children who'd been riding in the back.
She could just see her two children aged six and four
and a toddler of eighteen months who were huddled in
a mess of bedding against the back door, amongst the
debris of items that had been dislodged as the van had
rolled sideways and possibly glass from the smashed
back window. With her foot trapped under bent metal,
she was distressed that she couldn't get to her children
but Cade was actually happy to hear them crying loudly
in the background because it meant that they were conscious and breathing.

'Try not to panic, sweetheart,' he told her. 'Keep talking to the kids. Keep them as still as you possibly can.
I'm going back up to the road to let everyone know
what's going on but I'll be back very, very soon and then
I'm going to stay with you until we get you out, okay?'

He needed to pass on all the information he'd gained
to the scene commander from the fire service. He also
needed to see what extra resources were needed and
bring a kit back down with him. As soon as it was safe,

he had to get close enough to the van driver to assess him properly and start treatment before they extricated him.

Geoff was working in the triage area that had been established to assess and treat the cyclists involved in the accident but, luckily, none of them seemed to be seriously injured. There was another ambulance arriving on scene already and he could see the helicopter he'd requested hovering as they came into their landing area, which had to be further up the road, far enough away to not be creating a problem with dust and stones being thrown up from the unsealed road.

For just a split second, Cade was taken back to the first day he'd met Jo, when she'd flown in with the helicopter crew to work with him in that icy river. That first, utterly captivating glimpse of the intelligence and passion he could see in her eyes was something Cade was never going to forget. Pushing the flash of memory aside came with a feeling of relief that those days were over for Jo. There was no way a pregnant woman would be allowed to jump into a helicopter to take part in any dangerous rescue missions. And thank goodness for that...

He skirted a pile of mangled bicycles.

'Any change in the status of patients?' he asked Geoff.

'No. All status three and four, but most of them are going to need transport. We've got fractures, lacerations and one woman with neck pain and paraesthesia in her hands. We're just getting her on a back board and into a collar. She'll be the priority for transport.'

Cade nodded and kept going. He could see the fire chief directing the deployment of cables and other officers were setting up cutting gear that might be needed to access the interior of the camper van. Beyond the fire truck, he could see that the helicopter had landed and the crew were getting out and loading the equipment they needed onto a stretcher. At that distance, with their flight suits and helmets on, it was impossible to recognise anyone but…there was a smaller figure amongst them who seemed to be working with a determination and focus that sent a chill down Cade's spine.

He shook it off. No… It *couldn't* be…

By the time he'd rapidly relayed what information he had about the number of victims in the camper van, where they were and what condition they were in as far as he could tell, the helicopter crew had covered the distance between their landing point and when Cade turned his head again they were more than close enough to recognise someone he knew. Like Tom. And the woman walking beside him.

That chill that he'd felt moments ago was still there but it was becoming something very different as it spread. By the time he'd pulled in a breath it was a heat filling his chest that was a powerful mix of utter disbelief and…and *anger*…

Fury, even.

His eyes were narrowing as he took a step closer to Joanna Bishop. He lowered his voice, instinctively keeping what he was saying between only the two of them, but it had the effect of making his words even more vehement.

'What the *hell* do you think *you're* doing here?'

CHAPTER TWELVE

THIS WAS A moment like no other.

Jo had never experienced a 'sliding doors' kind of moment when it was easy to recognise a decision that had changed the whole course of her life, but this was how she'd met Cade Cameron, wasn't it? She'd climbed out of a helicopter and walked into his life and, by the time they'd worked together in that tense situation when it seemed likely that they'd have to amputate a young woman's leg in order to save her life, she had known that this meeting was significant.

The flashback was instantaneous and took only a heartbeat of time. Jo could hear the engine noise of the helicopter diminishing behind her as it was shut down. She could hear the pneumatic gear from the fire service being set up and tested and the shouts of officers as they worked on getting the unstable vehicle safe to approach. She could see a pile of damaged bicycles and paramedics working with at least half a dozen people who were sitting or lying on blankets that had been laid on the ground.

That was where she needed to be and where she would be in a matter of seconds. What felt like an unfair attack from Cade wasn't about to slow her down but, even as she kept walking, Jo was momentarily caught by that flashback. And she must have slowed a little because Tom was well ahead of her within a few steps. Or had Tom heard the outrage in Cade's voice and sped up to avoid being caught in what was clearly a very personal exchange?

What felt like the opening salvo of a confrontation was the jarring note in what was almost a recreation of the first time they'd met, with Jo stepping out of a helicopter to walk into Cade's professional arena. It wouldn't be happening at all if she'd made a different choice the day they'd met and had gone through a different set of doors. She'd known that an invitation from Cade had been hanging there that day, just waiting for her to decide whether or not she wanted to accept it. She'd seen the admiration in his eyes. She'd known perfectly well that he was interested in more than an update on their patient when he'd written his phone number on her glove.

But this…this couldn't be more different. There was nothing like admiration in his eyes right now. Cade was so *angry* with her. It looked as if she was the last person he wanted to see. That she couldn't possibly do anything that could earn his approval, let alone his admiration. If he'd looked remotely like that the first time they'd met she would never have sent that text message to accept that invitation. They would never have got to 'know each other' so well, with all the emotional, and now physical, repercussions.

There were echoes there of the way Jo's parents had looked at her all too often as she'd been growing up. Her father annoyed that he was being disturbed, with any approval or affection so closely guarded it was almost impossible to get within touching distance. Her mother disappointed, yet again, because she wasn't behaving in an acceptable manner.

There was another layer over that too, with a flash of remembering the way Cade had pushed her away when they'd worked together at the scene of that horrific car crash when they'd had to fight to save the life of that young boy. Another sliding doors moment, perhaps, because she'd been quite prepared to walk away from any kind of relationship with Cade at that point? Until she'd learned that there was a very good reason why he'd been so upset.

And suddenly Jo knew exactly why he was reacting like this now. Because she was pregnant. With his child. It wasn't that he cared that she might be putting herself in danger, was it? It was because there was something— some*one*—far more important at stake.

And, just as suddenly, Cade wasn't the only person who was angry because maybe that was Jo's only defence against having her heart broken that little bit more. Did he really think that she was about to put this precious baby she was carrying into danger? She was trusting him by letting him close enough to be the father he wanted to be to this child, but where was *his* trust? It made no difference that she'd known it would be wise to step back from this part of her job because of her pregnancy. Or maybe it did. Maybe she was feeling guilty that she'd followed her instincts of needing to help and she was angry with herself as well as Cade. Or maybe she was automatically tapping into the mode where she'd always had to fight for the things she wanted, or needed, for herself even when she knew she was losing the battle. When she simply wasn't good enough…

Whatever…

'I'm doing exactly the same thing here that you are, I expect,' she snapped. 'My *job*…'

Cade was still right beside Jo as she reached the treatment area for the cyclists, where Tom was standing in front of a whiteboard that was keeping track of patients, their status and their injuries, talking to a fire officer who was wearing a vest designating him as the scene commander. Cade stooped to pick up a paramedic kit from where equipment and supplies were being stored and then turned away to head to the edge of road where she could see the cluster of rescue personnel focused on what was happening below them.

'Stay here,' Cade ordered Jo. 'Do *not*, under any circumstances, come anywhere near where we're working on the camper van.'

He still looked furious as he slung the strap of the pack over one shoulder and strode away but Jo could feel her own anger dissipating into a fleeting acknowledgement of something else. Sadness that she was being ordered around like someone who'd failed to do what was expected of her? Or perhaps it was a poignancy that her baby had something she would never have herself, a person who loved her enough to do whatever it took to protect her?

Again, whatever...

This wasn't the time to unpick any stray emotions. As she'd told Cade, Jo was here to do her job and that was the only thing she was going to focus on. There would, undoubtedly, be way too much time to think about any personal issues later.

The anger wouldn't go away.

Cade might have been able to shut down any personal considerations the moment he'd climbed back down the slope to where steel cables were now preventing the van from sliding or even rolling any further, but that knot of emotion was still there in his gut and it wasn't acceptable.

He had a job to do here and he couldn't allow a distraction that might interfere with his focus on the first patient. The driver of the van had regained consciousness by the time he got close enough to assess him thoroughly but his confusion and combativeness suggested that he had a significant head injury and it would make the task of extricating him a danger to everybody involved, including the patient. It wasn't going to be possible to get to his wife or the children in the back until he was out and that added to the urgency.

It should have made it easy to completely forget the shock of seeing Jo on scene, but that knot in his stomach wouldn't go away. It wasn't interfering as Cade sorted his assessment and treatment priorities but he could feel it as a background niggle that he knew he'd have to deal with later.

In the meantime, sedation was needed, which meant IV access was a priority. A C collar was called for because the mechanism of injury could well have caused cervical spine trauma. Oxygen was on this list and further interventions to secure the man's airway could well be necessary. An extrication device that fitted like a vest and immobilised the spine, neck and head would have to be used to lift the patient from the vehicle. A baseline set of vital signs would let him know what the most urgent action was going to be. Cade tried to catch a flailing arm and wrist to check both the heart rate and rhythm and get at least a rough gauge of blood pressure as he watched and listened to assess respiratory effort.

'Take it easy, mate. I'm just trying to help. Try not to move just yet.'

Jules was trying to calm her husband from where she

was still trapped in the passenger seat. 'Stay still, Pete. It's okay…we're going to be okay…'

Pete's knuckles narrowly missed Cade's chin. 'I need another medic down here,' he told the nearest fire officer. 'Stat.'

'Sure thing. Want us to bring the doctor down as well?'

'*No*…' Cade's response was emphatic. 'Dr Bishop is not to come down here. Send another HEMS crew member, please.'

Okay…so maybe that niggle wasn't quite far enough in the background but, good grief…how could she be taking a risk like this? Even being a passenger in a helicopter was bad enough. Surely Jo, of all people, knew how fragile life could be. For anyone, but especially for vulnerable children or an unborn baby…

It was Tom who joined him to work in the cramped and difficult space that the front seat of the van provided. The look he flicked Cade made him wonder if something had been said about Jo not being allowed to work down here with him but Tom made no comment. He was already completely focused on what was clearly going to be a challenging job ahead of them.

Accident scenes that involved a lot of emergency services personnel were a bit like a nightmare version of an emergency department for Jo. They were centred around the same injuries and sometimes medical events that she was well used to dealing with in a hospital setting but the environment and resources were far more chaotic out in the field and you couldn't summon backup or push a cardiac arrest button knowing that more staff and equipment would arrive in seconds.

It was the reason Jo had always loved this part of her

job, but today it seemed noisier and more challenging than it ever had before. Stressful, that was the word for it. It didn't help that there was still no sign of what was likely to be the most seriously injured patient in this incident being extricated from his vehicle so he could be stabilised and taken to that nicely controlled emergency department that was waiting for him.

'What's happening down the bank?' she asked the scene commander as he stepped back to let two ambulance officers steer a stretcher towards a waiting ambulance.

'They're still working on getting the guy out. Shouldn't be too much longer. How's it going here?'

'Under control. We've pretty much sorted all the cyclists. That patient going now has a probable fracture/dislocation of his ankle. The others have some cuts and bruises but they're all okay to transport themselves and they want to stay here and sort out the bikes.'

'What about that woman with the neck injury?'

'She was the first to go by ambulance—about ten minutes ago. I don't think it was a serious injury. The tingling in her hands disappeared as soon as she stopped hyperventilating but she'll get properly checked out at hospital.'

Jo wanted to go and look over the edge of the road to see what was happening but she could still hear Cade ordering her not to go near that part of the scene under any circumstances. Being so busy with the injured cyclists had meant she hadn't had an opportunity to think about how angry he'd been that she was here but there was nothing to distract her now. Except that she was also aware of something else that was adding to her stress levels. As usual with a HEMS callout, she hadn't taken the time to go to the bathroom before rushing up to the rooftop helipad but it wasn't usually a problem because the adrenaline that came with this kind of work could shut down the need for as long as an emergency took.

She'd never had a baby pressing on her bladder before, though, had she?

Cade's baby.

Her own anger had long since evaporated. Right now she had the kind of squeeze on her heart that she'd had when she'd first heard Cade's tragic story. The kind of squeeze that had only become more painful the more she'd fallen in love with him. He was just trying to protect himself, wasn't he? And if it was so hard he had to use anger as a shield now, would he even be able to keep those barriers in place at all when he was able to hold his baby in his own arms?

'You think it'll be a few minutes before they bring up the driver?'

'Yep. They were just starting to get him into that jacket thing they use. He'll have to be secured to the scoop stretcher and then brought up the bank. We'll be able to get to the woman and children then, so it'll get busy again.'

'I'm going up the road for a minute or so,' Jo told him. 'Nature's calling.'

The scene commander gave her a thumbs-up sign. 'No worries. Don't go far away, will you? You might be needed soon.'

'I won't.'

Jo had no intention of going any further than she needed to in order to find a private spot. There was plenty of vegetation and large rocks on the slope between the road and the river and it wasn't so steep further up the road towards where the helicopter had landed. There was nothing else she needed to do at the moment and she'd be back in plenty of time to help Tom and the other paramedics still on scene to treat and load the van driver.

She took extra care to watch her footing so that she didn't slip as she climbed a short distance down from the edge of the road and then searched for a sheltered space behind rocks or a bush. If she couldn't see anyone else, they wouldn't be able to see her, would they? A minute or two later, she was zipping up her flight suit again, feeling much less stressed, and she closed her eyes to let out a long breath.

That was when she heard it.

An odd noise.

It sounded like…what…a lamb bleating? It made Jo take a few more steps down the slope, anyway, to see what it was and she found herself much closer to the river. And, yes…it did look like a lamb. A small, white shape near the water's edge. Except… Jo took another step, trying to focus. Trying to make sense of the movement she could see. It wasn't a lamb, she realised. It was a very small child, wearing just a nappy and a white singlet. Her head swerving, Jo realised she could see the back of the camper van now that she was away from the shelter of the bushes and rocks. She could see the smashed window in the van's back door. Was that where the baby had come from? Why had nobody noticed? Would they hear her if she shouted loudly enough?

Another blink to check on the child and she found it was standing up. Wobbling on small, chubby legs. Heading straight for the edge of the river. It was less than twenty metres away from where Jo was, but it was too far. And anyone near the van who heard her shouting would be even further away. The river might not be huge but she could see that there was a decent current. More than enough to snatch a baby and wash it away.

There was a much steeper slope before the ground levelled off near the river but Jo couldn't take the time to search for a safer route. She did her best to avoid injuring herself by sitting down on her bottom and pushing herself into a slide so that she didn't fall. She held her breath as she started moving and sent up a silent plea that she would get there in time.

The twist in the tail of this rescue mission was completely unexpected.

Every pair of hands that could get close enough to the camper van had been utilised to get access to the injured driver and get him out safely. Cocooned in a cervical collar, the extrication device that wrapped around his body and warm blankets beneath the straps of a basket stretcher, he was being passed from handhold to handhold by the rescue workers positioned on the steep slope between the van and the road where the helicopter was waiting to transport him to hospital.

The most difficult aspect of this rescue had been successfully completed as far as Cade and the others were aware. Tom was heading up with the stretcher. He and the rest of his HEMS crew could take over. Cade was now focused on getting Jules and her children out. The young mother did have a fractured wrist, which Cade swiftly splinted. He couldn't tell if her ankle was broken or only sprained, but her foot wasn't badly trapped after all and he'd been able to ease it out of her shoe to get her free. She refused to climb out of the van before her children, however, reaching through the gap between the front seats.

'Hayley? Come here, darling. It's okay…we're going to get out now.'

The young girl squeezed through the gap and Cade

lifted her out to pass her into the arms of a waiting fire officer.

'Does anything hurt, sweetheart?' he asked.

She shook her head but burst into tears. 'I want Mummy…'

'I'm coming,' Jules called. 'Jamie? Where's Danny?'

'He's asleep. Under the duvet.'

'How old is Danny?' Cade was leaning into the van, one knee on the driver's seat.

'Fifteen months. He's our baby.' Jules was twisting her body, trying to see into the back. 'Can you get in through the back door?'

'There's a tree blocking it.' Did he need to get the firies to use their cutting gear on the rear of the van? They were talking about a baby here. A silent baby.

'Where is he, Jamie?' There was an edge of panic in Jules' voice. 'I can't see.'

Cade could see into the back. He could see Jamie sitting in the nest of crumpled bedding. He could see the duvet covered lump beside the small boy that had to be the sleeping baby, but something didn't feel right. Cade could actually feel the hairs on the back of his neck rising as he put his arms through the gap and pulled at a corner of the duvet he could reach. One good tug and he uncovered the lump.

'Oh, my God,' Jules said. 'That's a pillow… Where's *Danny*?'

Cade's gaze flicked up to the smashed window in the back door. Had the baby been thrown clear? Was he lying badly injured and hidden in the undergrowth? He was out of the van before he'd taken his next breath. Behind it as he instructed the rest of the team to get Jules and Jamie out. He could see more now. All the way down to the river, which wasn't that far away. His gaze snagged on a white blob at the water's edge but then swerved sideways. The bright orange of a flight suit was far more eye-catching.

He knew who it was, of course. And he knew he was seeing the moment just after Jo must have fallen because he could see the speed with which her body was moving—straight towards the rocks that bordered the river.

'*No…*'

Maybe a cloud happened to block the sun at precisely that point in time. Or maybe he had just imagined it, but Cade was always going to remember the way the entire world seemed to have dimmed as he began to run.

It wasn't the first time Jo had been thankful for the steel-capped boots she always wore with her flight suit for a HEMS callout. She used her foot to slow and then break her slide well before she reached the bottom of the slope. She was on her feet a heartbeat later and had the baby in her arms before she'd even pulled in a new breath.

Almost in the same moment, she found she was herself in someone's arms.

But it wasn't simply someone. It was Cade. There were others right behind him. People who took a baby who seemed miraculously unharmed, leaving Cade to help Jo back up to the road.

Except he didn't move straight away. Instead, Jo could feel the grip of his arms tighten around her.

'Are you sure you're okay? I saw you fall…'

'I'm fine.' Although Jo could feel that she was trembling. 'I wasn't falling, I was sliding. I *had* to, Cade… I had to get to the baby before he went into the river.'

'I know…'

'I'm sorry…'

'What for?'

'Being here. I *could* have fallen.' Jo could feel tears rolling down her face as the fright kicked in. She'd done something that could have been catastrophic. Her next words were no more than a whisper. 'I could have hurt our baby.'

Cade's baby. She could have repeated a history that would have destroyed this man she loved so much. It would have destroyed her. Cade had every right to be even more angry with her than he had been when he'd seen her arrive. But he didn't seem angry as he cradled her body in his arms. He certainly didn't sound angry when he spoke, his lips close to her ear.

'I could have lost *you*…and, right now, that's all I can think about.'

Jo blinked. That didn't make sense. The baby was more important than anything else. It was the only reason Cade intended to stay in her life, wasn't it? The only reason he'd asked her to marry him?

'I was wrong.' Cade's voice was a low growl that seemed to be answering a question Jo hadn't asked aloud. 'I guess it's true that you don't know what you've got till it's gone, and when I saw you falling I knew…'

Good grief…it sounded as if Cade's words were being choked by tears.

'I knew what it would be like if you *were* gone and… and it felt like it would be the end of the world. I love you, Jo.' There was amazement in his voice. 'I didn't think I could ever feel that again but… I do. I love you. I think I always have.'

Yeah…that heartbreaking catch in his voice conveyed a depth of emotion that was utterly compelling. The kind of emotion that stole your breath and squeezed your heart so hard it hurt. The kind Jo had been feeling herself ever since she'd fallen in love with Cade.

'Me too,' was all that she could whisper.

Cade's radio crackled into life and almost drowned her words but she knew that she'd been heard. She could see it in his eyes.

'You guys okay down there? Need any help?'

Cade cleared his throat and pushed the button to respond. 'We're on our way. We're all good.'

He caught Jo's gaze and, for the first time in weeks, they had one of those silent conversations that could happen in a heartbeat.

Are we good?

Yes... So good...

We can't talk now.

No. We've got a job to finish.

We'll talk later, though.

Oh, we absolutely will.

They began the scramble back to road level, with Cade keeping a tight hold on Jo's hand. He didn't catch her gaze again until they were about to step back into their professional roles. Tom was already in the helicopter with their patient and the rotors were picking up speed. Geoff and another ambulance crew were caring for the rest of the rescued family, who would be able to be transported by road. It was time to put the finishing touches on this mission.

So it was merely another blink of an eye that they shared. Just a graze of eye contact, but it was more than enough for Jo.

I do love you. Cade looked as stunned by the revelation as she was feeling. *More than I could ever tell you.*

You just did, Cade. Jo could feel her lips tilting into a misty smile. *You just did.*

EPILOGUE

A month later...

HE WAS THE luckiest man on earth.

He was being given, quite literally, a new life. On more than one level.

The ability to feel love was an unexpected gift. And yes, that came with risk and he still had moments when fear could edge its way in, but it was worth it because, without taking that risk, you could never feel like this. Like you had found the very best of what life could offer. That simply living each day was so much more meaningful and that your future was so much more exciting because you had someone to share it with.

If you were really lucky, the person you loved felt the same way about you, and if you were as lucky as Cade Cameron that person was an extraordinary woman who had admitted that she had so much love to give. Love that she'd bottled up because she'd never had someone who loved her back. But now she did and she was choosing to give all that love to *him*. And their child, of course, but for now it was mostly just for him and he was going to make the most of every minute.

Would he be pushing his luck if he asked the question that was, once again, burning a hole in his brain? It had been pushed aside in the last weeks because life had got so busy, what with work and going public with their relationship and Jo's pregnancy. With moving in together and house hunting and antenatal appointments. And with using every possible free moment to just be together and get used to this miracle of loving and being loved. He couldn't ask for any more than that, anyway. Could he?

'There you go…' It might be too dark to see the smile on Jo's face but he could hear it in her voice. 'I knew she'd wake up as soon as I started to go to sleep. Did you feel that?'

Of course he had. Cade had his hand resting gently on the increasingly rounded bump of Jo's belly, his fingers splayed, and he'd felt the ripple of movement beneath them as a sensation that had been picked up by every cell in his own body.

'Hey, Bump…' He stroked Jo's skin, knowing that the baby must be able to feel his touch. 'How're you doing in there?'

Jo laid her hand on top of his and kept it there as the baby moved again. A distinct kick, this time.

'I've got an idea.' Cade grinned. 'Kick once for "yes" and don't kick for "no", okay?'

Jo laughed. 'Yeah…right… Good luck with that.'

Cade wasn't deterred. 'What did you think of the house we looked at today, Bump? The one with the view of the harbour and that big garden with the swing. Did you like it? Do you think we should buy it?'

They both felt the contact of the baby's foot against their hands.

'I guess that's settled.' Cade grinned. He leaned sideways to kiss Jo. 'Unless you disagree?'

'It *was* a lovely house.' Jo was smiling again. 'A real family home.'

There was a note in her voice that made him kiss her again. 'That's what we need. Because we're going to be a *real* family.'

'Mmm…'

'If we bought it now, we could be all moved in and settled in a couple of months, well before Bump's birthday.'

'As long as we didn't make the settlement date for when you're in Europe. You'll be away for a week for that conference. Have you booked your tickets yet?'

'I was going to talk to you about that.' Cade was smiling. 'I was hoping you might like to come with me. You've never been to Prague, have you?'

'No. But I had Hanna telling me that it was on the top of her bucket list today. She's hoping to go to that conference herself. She reckoned she could kill two birds with one stone—some professional development plus an adventure.'

'Adventures are good.' Cade still had his hand on Jo's belly, although it felt as if Bump had gone back to sleep. 'We're good at adventures. You should come.'

'But… I wouldn't be allowed to fly by then, would I?'

'You can fly up to thirty-six weeks, if there are no complications. There's plenty of time.'

Jo had woven her fingers through Cade's. 'It could be our first family holiday. Sort of.'

Cade took a deep breath. 'It could be our honeymoon.'

He held his breath in the silence that followed his words.

'Are you…are you asking me to marry you?'

'Yes. But not because we're having a baby together. Because I love you. The way you always have and always will deserve to be loved.' He pressed his lips against Jo's hair. 'The way I will love you as long as I have breath in my body.' He had to clear the sudden lump in his throat. 'Will you? Will you marry me?'

Jo sounded as if she had a lump in her own throat. 'I was really hoping you'd ask me again,' she said softly. 'Ever since what was probably the last helicopter mission I'll ever go on. When I knew that you loved me as much as I love you.'

'Is that a "yes"?'

Jo was smiling through tears now. '*Yes…*'

The kick against their hands surprised them both into laughter and Cade had to blink back his own tears.

'I guess that makes it unanimous.'

Yep…there was no doubt about it.

He was the luckiest man on earth.

* * * * *

CORNISH REUNION
WITH THE
HEART DOCTOR

LOUISA GEORGE

MILLS & BOON

CHAPTER ONE

'OKAY, EVERYTHING'S QUIET. Fairly sure I'm up to date.' Lexi Fisher removed her stethoscope from around her neck and dropped it into her work bag.

So long. Farewell. I won't be needing you where I'm going.

'Dr Fisher! Hush your mouth! Don't you know it's bad luck to say the...' charge nurse Chantelle grinned as she looked up from her pile of paperwork at the nurses' station in the general paediatrics Peter Pan ward and mouthed *quiet* '...word. You've probably jinxed us to a night shift from hell.'

'Oops. Sorry.' Lexi twirled round, barely able to breathe for the excitement rippling through her. 'But... drum roll. That's me finished for the week. Seven days. Seven whole days without work. And how sad is it that I'm this excited?'

'Not sad at all. I don't remember you ever taking a holiday and I've been here almost eighteen months. I hope you have lots of fun, Lexi. You deserve it.'

'Oh, I will. I see cocktails and beach walks in my future. And probably rain, knowing Cornwall, but I won't care. It's holiday rain. Far better than walking to work rain. Or horizontal day off rain. Don't ask me to send you a postcard. I'll be too busy doing...' Lexi closed her eyes and imagined the quirky fishing village she'd seen online, the beautiful beaches and gorgeous sunsets. And the loaded e-reader she'd packed, full of her favourite authors' summer releases. 'Nothing. At. All.'

'Really? Nothing? Come on, Lexi. Sun, sea, sand and…sexy surfers?' Chantelle winked suggestively. 'How about a holiday romance? It's been a while, right?'

Four and a half years. Not that she was counting. 'Trust me, the only other two "S's" I'll be participating in are sleeping…and smiling hard at my friend's wedding.'

'A week's a long time for a wedding.' Chantelle's eyebrows rose in question.

'The wedding's tomorrow, but a group of us are staying on for the rest of the week. It's so overdue. I haven't seen some of these guys since we graduated, back in the Dark Ages—'

'Dr Fisher! Dr Fisher…thank goodness you're still here.' One of the younger nurses came screeching round the corner. Younger? Lexi sighed as she looked at the woman's swinging shiny ponytail and youthful energy. Who was she kidding? Everyone was younger than her these days. At forty-three she was probably old enough to be this nurse's mother. *As if that could ever happen.* 'Can you come, please? Baby Ahmadi's oxygen sats have dropped and he's struggling a bit.'

All thoughts of her impending holiday and her poor parenting prognosis slid from Lexi's mind. 'I'll be right there.'

'No way.' Always protective of her colleagues, Chantelle held up her hand but threw Lexi an *I told you so* look. 'You'll have to ask Dr Kowalski. Lexi's signing off. She hasn't had a holiday for…'

'Hey, I know the drill. I said the quiet word, now I have to deal. I just left Dr Kowalski with a patient in

ER and she'll be tied up there for a while. It's okay. It's fine. Honestly.'

As she put her bag back down on the chair, Lexi checked her watch. Her old friend Jono's train was due to arrive in half an hour. She'd planned her timetable to perfection: collect him from the airport, drive down to Cornwall and snatch a few hours' sleep before Emma and Mark's big day.

Things were inevitably going to be delayed now. Ah, well. Jono was a medic too. They'd trained together back in the day. He knew the score. He'd understand.

Would he? Surely. It had been over five years since she'd seen him in person; he could have changed. She smiled, remembering the emails they'd sent back and forth during and after her divorce. What had started with a quick check-in from him because he'd heard about her marriage split had become a lifeline that had helped her get through it. Somehow, the anonymity of writing rather than talking had given her a safe space to vent her feelings and he'd always replied with tales of his *interesting* love life and adventures in the Australian Outback as a flying doctor. Sure, he'd always been part of her friendship circle, but now she counted him as one of her closest friends—on paper anyway.

And he'd always been reassuringly the same; she had never known a man less bothered about rules or timings. God, she couldn't wait to see him. See them all. A holiday reunion!

But first…she retrieved her stethoscope from her bag. It was still warm.

Two hours later Lexi steered her Mini into the train station car park, jumped out and ran into the waiting room. Where was he?

No grinning, tall, miscreant doctor. No one at all except for an old guy swishing an industrial floor cleaner along the tiled floor.

She checked her phone. Had Jono received her texts about being late? Where was he? Had he left without her? She'd expected him to be standing waiting for her near the exit.

She wandered along a dimly lit platform and there… lying curled up on his side on a metal bench, with one of those wide-brimmed Australian Akubra hats over his face and a large rucksack on the floor, was a shape that resembled Jono Neale. If Jono Neale had taken up weights and grown a scruff of dark beard.

Her heart began to pound.

Would he be angry she was late? Would things be awkward between them after five years? Between all of them tomorrow?

They'd graduated from medical school twelve years ago; no doubt they'd all changed and grown up since then. They were different people…well, she certainly was. She'd been to hell and back since those heady days of study and nightclubs and freedom, and even though she'd had regular catch-ups with some of them, like tomorrow's bride Emma and the rest of the bridesmaids… who knew how she'd get on with the others?

'Hey.' She prodded his arm gently and whispered, 'Jono. Hey. Wake up.'

An arm lifted. The hat was removed as he turned onto his back muttering something that sounded a lot like, 'Can we have a quickie?'

She couldn't help but laugh and tut and eye-roll and smile. Because… Jono. Bad boy and chancer extraordinaire. An older, sun-kissed Jono now, with smatterings of red dust in hair that was longer than he used to wear it. But Jono nevertheless. Her heart settled. He hadn't changed at all.

'You can't shock me, Jono Neale.' She prodded him again. 'I've got more dirt on you than five years in the Outback will ever match.'

'Lexi? Dr Lexi Fisher? Is that really you?' An eye opened. Then the other. He smiled. A broad, happy grin that instantly wiped away any of her anxiety about meeting up with him again.

He was still heart-throb-gorgeous...half the women at med school had lusted after him, and a good chunk of the men too. Not her, though. Not least because Jono was eight years her junior, but also because she'd been infatuated with—and subsequently married to—Ross as soon as they'd finished university.

Jono jerked upright and enveloped her in a huge, warm hug. He was tall and broad and so familiar. And he clung on, and so did she because it really was so good to see him. Her chest heated. Good old Jono. He felt good, strong, safe, familiar and yet new. She'd forgotten what a good hugger he was.

Eventually he let go, held her at arm's length and looked her up and down. 'Sorry, you caught me napping. I was fast asleep. Dreaming about...'

'No! Stop!' Laughing, she put her hands over her ears, knowing he was playing her. Either he hadn't been asleep or the quickie reference had been meant to shock her. It hadn't. She'd stopped being shocked by his antics years ago.

'Aw. You cut me off. I was just getting to the good bit.'

'Way too much information. I can't believe you're thinking about sex after a twenty-four-hour flight.' Whereas she never thought about it at all these days.

'More like forty hours. I don't even know what day

it is. I flew from Kununurra to Darwin, to Sydney to Dubai, to Heathrow. Then the train up to Oxford.'

'And I kept you waiting. I'm so sorry. I should have picked you up at Heathrow or something and saved you the train trip. But I got caught up with an eight-month-old with RSV. Sats had dropped to eighty-nine.'

'Poor kid.' His accent had a tinge of Aussie in it, his sentences inflecting upwards at the end. 'But I'm betting you sorted them out.'

'For now. A preemie too. Went a bit floppy so I had to stay around to get those oxygen levels back up and make sure he was stable.'

'Of course. I got your text so I had a cup of tea, then caught up on some sleep so I can be your wide-awake wingman on the drive down.'

The man was a doctor, he'd been trained to sleep any time anywhere because, when on call, you never knew how much sleep you'd be able to get. But tea?

'You drank tea? Not beer? Wine? Whisky?' She looked behind him. 'Who are you and what have you done with my old mate, Jono?'

'Yup. Tea. What do they say, a change is as good as a rest?' He looked very pleased with himself. 'I'm going to be your sober wingman. It's a five-hour journey to Cornwall and it's late. I want us to get there in one piece.'

'Is this…is this you being responsible?' She gaped in disbelief.

He shrugged and grinned. 'I know, right? Who'd have thought?'

Who indeed? She pointed to his rucksack. 'Come on, then. We can squeeze your bag onto the back seat.'

'No room in the boot?' He looked at her the way a parent would look at a disappointing child, but his tone was teasing. 'Lexi Fisher, did you pack your whole wardrobe for a week's trip to St Quintin?'

'It's a Mini. No room at all. But it's either squeeze in with me or you wait until the train down to Cornwall in the morning. Which will mean you'll miss the wedding. And as a groomsman I'm not sure you want to do that.'

'Mark would kill me. Not to mention Emma. Looks like I'm stuck with you then.' He pecked a quick kiss on her cheek then led the way outside. She followed him, walking quickly to keep up with his long strides. The man was far more refreshed and awake than anyone should be after a long flight and a sleep. In fact, he was looking better than she'd ever seen him. He'd certainly filled out, developed muscles and a tidy backside, and a sharp jawline she didn't remember being quite so acute.

Her gaze slid to that backside again. Or…cute.

What? She snapped her gaze away from the denim. Had she really just thought Jonathan Neale was cute? No way. She'd known him since he was eighteen and she was twenty-six, and always thought of him like a younger brother. After dithering about her career choices and making a couple of course swerves she'd decided to study medicine later than most and found herself significantly older than a lot of the other students. But they'd always included her in their plans and she'd made firm and lasting friendships.

No way could she think anything other than *Jono is my friend. He's been there for me through everything.*

Cute? Something a lot like panic resonated in her chest. Yep, she definitely needed a holiday. *Sun, sea and sexy surfers…* Even a holiday romance.

But not with Jono.

Does Jono surf?

Stop it.

Having deposited his rucksack in the back, he folded himself into the passenger seat, filling her car with a scent of Australian heat, travel and something that flung her mind back to when they'd lived in a shared house in their fourth year. Memories tangled with scents and her heart lifted. They'd had a lot of fun back then.

Then they were off. As she drove, he tried to stretch his legs out, then drew them back, his knees bent up to touch the dashboard. He played round with the seat levers, pushing back as far as the mechanism allowed. 'This is the most uncomfortable car I've ever been in.'

'Because you're six feet two. For Hobbit me it's perfect. Look.' She wafted her left arm in the air. 'Look at all this space I have. So much space. I could fit three of me in here. Maybe only a half of you would fit neatly.'

He'd always been tall and characterful, but since when had he filled the spaces he inhabited?

'Never change, Lexi.' He smiled but the corners of his mouth dipped down as she yawned. 'You're tired. Right. I'm going to ask you lots of embarrassing questions to keep you awake.'

She chuckled. 'Not sure I like the sound of that.'

'I do. One.' He ticked it off on his finger. 'What have you been up to since we last messaged?'

'Work.' She shrugged and thought sadly that work had, indeed, been the only thing in her life for the last few years. 'Yes. Work.'

'That's it?' His tone was incredulous.

'Yes. I like work.'

'Me too. But seriously? It's not my everything. Anything else? Trips? Hook-ups?'

Uh-oh. 'What?' She dared a glance at his face. Yes, he was grinning at her embarrassment. 'No. I'm too old for all that.'

'Oh, yeah.' He laughed. 'Way too old for going on trips.'

'No. Idiot.' She rolled her eyes. 'For hook-ups.'

'Ancient. You're forty what?'

'Forty-three and I *feel* ancient. And I'm going to look ancient tomorrow compared to all you spring chickens.'

'Rubbish. What's a few years between us? We've all caught up with you now. Anyway, you look amazing, and you've got more energy than all of us put together. Apparently, you kick-box and run half marathons for charity in your spare time. You're a regular wonder woman. Unless your emails were made up just to make me feel inadequate?'

'As if anyone could ever do that with an ego the size of yours.' She laughed. 'I exercise to exorcise my demons. If I stay still too long, I remember all the crap in my life.'

'But you got rid of him.' He shot her a look she couldn't read.

It felt different sharing things face to face rather than over email. She could see his reactions for one. And she didn't have time to consider her replies. 'I did. Well... let's be honest, he left me. But things had been bad between us for a while.' And it had hurt so much at the time, but she was definitely over him. 'I feel great about it now.'

'I can tell.' There was something in Jono's tone that made her turn to look at him. She caught his gaze. Even in the amber glow from the motorway lights his eyes glittered. Had they always been quite so blue? And clear? And warm? She'd never noticed before. He grinned. 'So...not even *thinking* about dating anyone?'

'No. Not since Ross.' Why did this feel suddenly too personal? The man knew all her secrets. Something weird rattled through her chest. She swallowed and searched for a question of her own. 'Are you excited about the big move back to England?'

He nodded and if he thought her abrupt change of subject was odd, he didn't mention it. 'Absolutely. Feels a bit strange coming full circle back to Oxford where we all studied, but it's the right time.'

'Oh? Why now? Did you run out of women in Australia?'

'Cheeky.' He gave her a side-smile. 'I didn't even get to Tasmania. That's a whole island I've yet to explore.'

'And yet here you are.'

'It was time to renew the work visa and I just...' His expression flattened into something uncharacteristically serious. 'I guess I ran out of reasons to stay there.'

'Homesick?'

'Kind of. Dad's been ill, and I know he hasn't exactly been father of the year, but I'm all he's got so I thought it better to be around in case he needed me...anything,' he added quickly.

Talking about his dad had always been difficult for Jono. Their relationship had deteriorated in his teens and they'd drifted apart. So this reason for his return was surprising.

'What's happened? You should have said. I'd have gone to visit him. Wherever he is. Not that I've even met him, and it would be weird to have a complete stranger turning up, but I'm sure I could have done something to help.' It was the least she could have done after all the support Jono had given her.

'Really, it's fine. I wouldn't have known much at all, but his GP tracked me down as Dad's next of kin. Apparently, he's finally settled near the army barracks in Abingdon. I haven't told him I'm coming home, but the cardiologist vacancy came up at the right time and I jumped. It's about time me and Dad talked.' He grimaced. 'That's going to be interesting.'

'What's the medical issue?'

'Apparently, he had a myocardial infarction a few years ago. Never told me. He's also got type two diabetes and high blood pressure. And then last month he was diagnosed with heart failure.' Jono blinked.

'Ironic that you're a cardiologist then.'

'Yeah. I'm probably going to need a few big drinks after I've met up with him. It's been so long I'm not sure what we'll have to say to each other.'

She laughed in sympathy. 'Absolutely count me in for that. It's about time I gave you support—you've been doing it so long for me.'

'A drinking partner is always welcome. Oh, and thanks for the offer of your spare room until I get myself sorted.'

'No worries. It's just sitting there empty.' The nursery. That was what they'd planned all those years ago, before the endless rounds of failed IVF attempts. Before Ross had upped and left with a woman who could provide him with the child he'd so desperately wanted. But Jono coming back had finally given her the impetus to paint over the soft pastels. 'It'll be fun to have some company. Although I don't want any of your shenanigans like when we were at uni.'

'Shenanigans? Me?' His eyes widened and he put his hand to his heart as if shocked.

'Yes. You. The sock on the door handle to let everyone know you were…ahem…' she faux cleared her throat '…entertaining a guest.'

He grinned. 'I went through a lot of socks.'

'No, you didn't.' She laughed. 'You just wanted to.'

'I'm surprised you even noticed. Didn't you move in with Ross halfway through our fourth year?'

'Term three. Big mistake in retrospect.'

'I know. I never said anything, because it was your choice and you seemed so happy.' His nostrils flared as if remembering something distasteful. 'But I always thought it was a bad idea. There was something about him I didn't trust.'

'Really?' Had all her friends thought that? 'I wish you'd said something at the time.'

'What? And get my head bitten off? You were totally in love with the guy.'

'Yeah—and look where that got me. Turns out you were right about him in the end. Now I'm not sure I can trust my own judgement about these things. It's just easier not to date or think about dating.' An idea struck her. 'Hey, maybe you should vet any potential boyfriends in the future. You can be totally honest with me. I promise I won't bite your head off. Not that I see any romance in my future. But you know…just in case.' Having been reminded how empty her life was, apart from work, she was starting to warm to the idea of sun, sea and something to spice up her life.

'Sure. If you see anyone who takes your fancy this week let me know and I'll suss him out.'

'Excellent.' She couldn't help smiling at the thought of Jono going all macho around any guys who might want to ask her out. 'A proper wingman.'

'At your service, ma'am.' He leaned his head back against the seat and looked out of the window. She followed suit, staring at the long road ahead. The motorway was quiet; the huge overhead lights flashed by as they ate up the miles.

Eventually he sighed. 'Ah. The M4. Something familiar at last. I've spent the last five years getting to know a new place for six months and then moving on, rinse and repeat.'

'You should be used to it. Didn't you do that your whole life growing up?'

'Every couple of years, yes. Thanks to being an army brat. But it gets old.'

She struggled to hide her surprise. She'd imagined this new job in Oxford would be temporary, same as every other thing he did. 'Not thinking of settling down? *You?*'

'Not exactly.' He shrugged. 'But who knows?'

'I don't believe it for a minute.'

'Never say never.' A pause. 'I am so glad to be back and to see the old gang.'

She could feel his eyes on her, and she turned to look at him again. 'I wonder if everyone else is the same or if they've changed. I'm always wary of reunions because there's so much comparison going on. Who's achieved the most. Who's got the cleverest kids.' She felt a pang in her heart. 'I don't think I'll be winning that one.'

His smile was sympathetic and his eyes softened. 'You had a rough time of it.'

'I'm sorry I blurted it all out to you in my long emails. But writing it down seemed to help.'

'Hey…' He squeezed her knee. 'I'm glad you did. That's what friends are for.'

She'd been fine about it all recently, but something about having him here, the one person she'd shared everything with, and this tender gesture suddenly made her feel wobbly. Pressing her lips together, she nodded and focused back on the road, not wanting to revisit her past and spoil the journey. 'It's going to be a fun week. That's all I'm after right now.'

'Me too. Before the job starts and I have to be serious again. Let's make sure we have the best week.' He winked, all teasing.

'Totally.' She smiled.

If she could stop thinking he was cute.

Maybe she did need to start looking for a date. Someone cuter than Jono. Someone who could take her weirdly treacherous mind off her old friend's nice backside.

Then there was this...*weird* feeling she'd had when he'd wrapped her in a hug. And again, when she'd glanced over and caught him smiling. And right now...

Sure, she'd always known he was good-looking. But he'd matured into something even better. A smattering of grey at the temples. Crinkles at the sides of his eyes. And that look in his gaze that was calmer, settled, less restless. But still lots of fun. A woman could lose herself in those eyes.

Oh, God.

It was the worst thing she could realise and so inconvenient given she was spending a week with him. And he was coming to live with her until he found accommodation in Oxford...

Yikes.

Because Jono Neale wasn't just cute. He was smoking hot.

CHAPTER TWO

AFTER THEY'D STOPPED to fill the car up with petrol and fill Lexi up with caffeine, they pulled back onto the winding road towards the sleepy fishing village of St Quintin on Cornwall's north coast. Despite his best efforts, Jono was struggling to stay awake. He shuffled in his seat and blinked rapidly, opened the window for some fresh air and inhaled.

Beside him Lexi was gripping the steering wheel, staring ahead as if she was in a trance.

She looked tired. Still pretty…very pretty in fact, but her brown eyes were edged with the shadows of someone who'd worked too hard for too long. She'd let her hair grow out to her shoulders from the no-nonsense short cut she'd had through medical school and wispy layers softened her features. Her smile was the same, though. Warm and friendly and honest. With a touch of tease.

She'd been through a lot over the years, and he'd felt so bad he'd been across the world when she needed friends around her. Work and the virus that cut off all travel for months, and issues with time zones had meant he'd only been able to bolster her through online messaging and emails. So now he was here he was going to make sure she smiled again. A lot.

'How are we doing? Do you want me to take over the driving?' It was the fifth time of asking.

'Not after forty zillion hours of travel. Besides, my maps app says we'll be there in twenty minutes.' She held up her takeaway coffee cup. 'This is helping, but I do feel a bit wired. Put some music on?' She swapped her coffee cup for her phone, picking it up from the cup holders in between their seats, and flipped it to him. 'Something loud.'

He was mid-scroll when a movement outside the car made him look up. Seemingly out of nowhere, a large shadow slid in from his left peripheral vision. 'Watch it!'

'What?' Lexi screamed at the same time he slammed the dash with his hand. 'No!'

The car lurched forward. Brakes screeched.

Thud.

They were flung forward, then back.

It took a second for reality to hammer home; they'd hit something. Then adrenalin surged and he jumped out of the car.

His gut lurched at the sight of a body on the road, illuminated by the car headlights. A few feet away a bent bicycle lay on its side, the front wheel still spinning. Jono dashed to the body just as it began to move. A teenager…best guess at around fifteen, but who knew these days…slowly sat up with a groan.

Jono put a hand on the kid's shoulder. 'Hey, stay still. We need to check you haven't hurt yourself.'

'It's okay. I'm fine.' The boy shook his head, a hand shielding his eyes from the car headlights. 'I'm sorry. So sorry.'

Talking, moving all limbs. *Good signs.*

Behind him Lexi's voice wavered. 'What did I hit? What did I hit? Is it a deer? Please don't tell me it's a person.'

His heart squeezed. She was always such a softie. It made her a good paediatrician, but it must have hurt to carry all that emotional load around. 'It's okay. The bike's a goner, but our friend here says he's okay.'

He didn't have a helmet on though, which meant there could be all manner of issues. Jono peered closer at the boy. 'Did you hit your head?'

'No. I put my arm out to stop the fall.' The kid cradled his left wrist. 'It hurts like hell.'

'Good reflexes, though. I'm impressed. It could have been a lot worse. I'm Jono. This is Lexi. What's your name?'

'Tyler.'

'Well, hey, Tyler.' Jono flicked on his phone's torch app and shone it onto the ground, checking for any dangers, then, satisfied there weren't any, knelt in front of the boy and looked at the swelling wrist. 'If you're ever going to pull out in front of a car, always make sure the occupants are doctors. This is your lucky day.'

The kid looked down at his misshapen hand. 'Don't feel very lucky.'

'Trust me, hurting your arm is far preferable to your head.' Having scooped her hair back into a ponytail, Lexi was now next to him and examining the boy's arm. She scrunched up her nose. 'Looks like you might have broken it, though.'

'No.' Tyler shook his head and grimaced. 'I was supposed to be starting a new job tomorrow. That's not going to happen now.'

'As long as you're not using your hands, you'll be okay.'

'Serving food at a wedding.' Tyler's mouth formed a typical teenager sulking pout.

Still assessing for any other internal or non-obvious injuries, Jono kept the lad talking. 'Wild guess here, but is it at the Royal Hotel? St Quintin?'

'How did you know?'

Lexi smiled. 'Because that's where we're heading.'

'Oh, great.' The kid's shoulders slumped even more. 'Now I've probably ruined it for you.'

'No, you haven't.' She flashed Tyler a knockout smile. 'Fairly sure they can manage without one server. If they're that stuck for staff, I'll serve it myself.'

'Yeah, but they'll give me grief. Both my sisters work there, and my auntie owns the hotel. It was my first proper job. And now I've really messed up.'

'Without lights or a helmet and pulling onto a main road without looking, I'd say so.' Jono tried to make his voice teasing while trying to make the safety point, but clearly it didn't work because Lexi squeezed his shoulder. 'We can get to that later, Jono. Let's get Tyler sorted out first.' She fixed the boy with her gaze. 'Hey, accidents happen. I'm sure your auntie will understand.'

But Tyler hung his head. 'This isn't the first time I've messed up.'

'Believe me, I've lost count of the times I've messed up. We all do it.' Jono knew from experience how much it sucked to be a kid who couldn't catch a break, particularly with relatives. Specifically, fathers. 'But if you've got work tomorrow, why are you out so late?'

'Really? *You* have to ask that?' Lexi looked up at him and grinned. Okay, so yeah...he might have been known to have worked hard and played harder. Easy when you're fifteen, not so easy twenty years later.

She clearly still thought of him as a kid brother. But she'd changed, so why did she assume he hadn't?

'Hey, I'm a responsible adult now.' He winked at Tyler. 'I could tell you a story or two, though. What were you doing?'

'Just chilling at my friend's house and we lost track of time. He lent me his bike to get home.' As Tyler spoke a waft of stale beer filled the air.

Jono leaned in. 'Have you been drinking?'

'Just a couple. Maybe three.'

'What the hell?' But Jono tried to control his reaction. Probably failed. It was easy to see the foolishness when you were the wrong side of thirty-five, but he'd spent a good amount of his youth making these same mistakes.

'So.' Lexi flashed them both a combative look. Jono felt the warning as well as seeing it. 'You've learnt a lot of lessons tonight. The wrist is going to need an X-ray. Is there a hospital near here?'

Tyler looked up the road, back to where they'd come from. 'Fifteen minutes, maybe twenty.'

'Then we'd better take him.' Lexi stood up. 'By the time an ambulance gets here we might as well have driven there anyway.'

'Okay, you're the boss.' Jono looked at Tyler and raised his eyebrows, receiving a similar look in return.

She gave them both a satisfied grin. 'Don't either of you forget it.'

The emergency department was mercifully quiet for a Friday night. After they'd given details to the receptionist, they took a seat in the waiting room.

Tyler's sulking hadn't let up. 'My mum's going to kill me.'

'No, she won't. She'll be relieved you're alive. Although she might also be angry that you didn't look before you pulled out, or wear a helmet and cycled after drinking.' Now he was sure the kid didn't have any injuries other than a busted wrist, Jono had decided it was time he had some truths told to him. 'If she's anything like my mum, though, she'll leave the telling off until you're feeling better. But my guess is you won't be doing any of that again.'

'No way.' Tyler shook his head.

'Right, give me her number. I'll call and explain, then you can do some heavy apologising.' Lexi took the boy's phone and made the call.

Jono was impressed at the way she handled the mum with compassion and yet honesty. Finishing off with, 'It's really no trouble at all. And please go easy on him. He made a mistake, we all do. But I'm fairly certain he won't make the same one again.' She paused, her mouth turning upwards as she listened, then she finished on a smile. 'I'll tell him. Don't worry.'

Tyler looked up at her with dark eyes. 'Is she angry?'

Lexi handed the phone back. 'More worried than anything. She's on her way. She says don't be scared, she understands. She loves you.'

Tyler's expression morphed into one of reverence. 'Thank you, Lexi. I can't believe how you turned that around for me. I thought she was going to kill me.'

'She loves you.' Jono wanted that reinforced. Because it mattered that, as a kid, you knew your parents loved you unconditionally. 'Just think before you do things.'

'I will. And thanks for the help.'

'No problem.' Lexi smiled and ruffled Tyler's hair as if he were five not fifteen. 'Now stay out of trouble.'

As they wandered through the hospital towards the exit, exhaustion bit at Jono's brain. 'Well, that's our good deed of the day.'

'We couldn't have left him to wait for an ambulance or travel in it on his own. I just kept thinking, what if he was my son? I mean, I know that's never going to happen, but I'd be so glad someone helped him.' Something flickered behind Lexi eyes, but it disappeared as quickly as it had arrived. Had she pushed the pain away? Was that what she did now? Pretended it didn't hurt. Because he could see right through that.

He wished he'd been there to carry that hurt for her and hoped their emailing back and forth had helped, even though they'd got a little intense at times. It had gone from the odd check-in message to writing more details, then secret-sharing. Lexi had shared her despair at her husband's affair and her desolation at her infertility, and even Jono had admitted things he'd probably never have told another soul. Mainly about his woeful love life. But having that connection had helped him too. Being thousands of miles away from friends and family and not being able to travel had made him feel disconnected, and he'd relished having someone to 'talk' to. Rambled on, more like...

She'd been devastated not to be able to have kids. Which was a bloody shame, because she'd have made a fantastic mum. Working as a paediatrician every day while going through failing rounds of IVF must have been torture.

She smiled brightly. 'Although I'd hoped I wouldn't be stepping into a hospital so soon after I've left one for my holiday.'

'Fingers crossed that's the first and last time.'

She wagged a finger. 'And no drunk cycling.'

'Note to self.'

'Yes, well, we all know that young adults make stupid decisions, right?' She chuckled. Even though she was clearly exhausted, her eyes sparkled. All he could see was the beautiful woman she'd become this side of her difficult divorce. She really was something.

Plus the way she'd dealt with Tyler had been far more compassionate than anyone else would have been or expected. She genuinely cared about people.

And he had to admit she was right—he had made a few stupid decisions in his life too. 'You talking about me? Of course you're talking about me. What did I do that was so bad?'

She rolled her eyes. 'Where do I start? Sowed cress seeds in the university library computer keyboard so they unwittingly grew their own mini garden.'

'Hey, study snacks on tap! And I replaced the keyboard. But I take your point.'

'Put food colouring in the quad fountain…' Her eyes grew wide. 'Please don't tell me you've got something planned for the wedding.'

He laughed. 'No. I did send some ideas for the stag weekend though. Did you go to the hen night?'

She shook her head. 'Working, sadly. It would have been good to catch up before the wedding.'

'We can wow them tomorrow.' He checked his watch as they walked through the automatic doors to a warm summer's night. 'It's pretty late.'

'Or early, depending on which way you're looking at it.' The sky was an eerie shade of bronze and pale yellow and she stopped and raised her head to look upwards and smiled. 'Wow, Jono. Just look at that sky. It's beautiful.'

'I hope it means we're in for good weather.' Just as he'd have done years ago, he wrapped an arm round her shoulders and she leaned her head back against his chest—stopped, straightened and tugged her hair from its band, then leaned back against him again and exhaled.

A scent of fresh shampoo and something like vanilla ice cream wound round him. There was something else there too, something that smelt pretty damned fine. A sort of welcome home with a twist of the exotic.

It was so good to be here with someone who knew him, who'd shared things with him, who he didn't have to explain things to and who he could reminisce with. That hadn't happened often to him much in his life.

Her gorgeous, happy smile at the train station had been the best thing he'd seen in a while. Good old Lexi. *Never change.*

His chest heated. Which was weird. But jet lag did strange things to a body. He shrugged it off. 'Well, that added a few more hours to our journey. I'm bushed. I cannot wait for my bed.'

He felt her stiffen. Then she was striding towards the car. He chased to catch up. 'Hey, Lexi. Are you okay?'

'Just tired. Shaken up, to be honest, and still wired, but okay. Let's get go—' She stopped as she reached her car. The front passenger side was dented and scraped. 'Oh, I didn't even think to look at it before. I'm going to need a panel beater too.'

'We'll sort it out later. We've got all week.'

'At least we won't have to drive to the wedding venue, seeing as we're staying at it. That's something. Imagine driving up to a wedding in that.' She cringed.

'I never told you about how we arrived at your wedding, did I?'

'No!' She looked horrified and scared and intrigued and a little excited. She rolled her eyes and zapped the car remote to unlock the doors. 'What did you do?'

'Ha! Got you. Nothing. Absolutely nothing. But you are far too easy to wind up.' Laughing, he reached for the door handle then pulled back quickly as his muscles screamed in pain.

She frowned as she watched him. 'Are you okay?'

'Sure.' It felt as if he'd done an intense arm day at the gym.

She was by his side in a second. 'I braked hard—are your shoulder and chest okay from the seatbelt? Whip-lash?'

He ran a hand over his left shoulder, checking. Cricked his neck from side to side. 'I didn't notice. Yes. Fine.' As if he'd admit any pain to her anyway.

'We need to check.' She followed the track of his hand, her palm gently pressing against his shirt, look-ing up at him with dark soft eyes filled with concern. How had he never noticed how pretty they were? Not just regular brown. A rich warm chocolate brown.

She pressed fingertips into his pec. 'Here?'

'It's fine.'

But please don't move your hand.

What?

Weird.

She pressed again, her gaze still locked with his, as-sessing him the way she'd been trained. But he wasn't thinking about any of that.

'Here? Jono?'

Something white-hot streaked through him and it was nothing to do with a seatbelt bruise or pain. It was her touch on his skin.

Lexi. This is *Lexi Fisher.* He'd known her half his life.

They were firmly in the friend zone. Nothing more. He was her wingman. He was going to find her a decent bloke who would make her happy. Which meant he was definitely out of the picture.

There was no picture.

Freaked out by his body's response to her, he stepped back. 'It's fine. Honestly. Let's get going. This jet lag has really caught me up.'

Either that or his brain was playing tricks on him. Because how many times had he touched Lexi's skin over the years? Hundreds, possibly thousands… Squeezing into the back of a taxi on a night out, brushing against each other in the shared kitchen, in the lab, at the dinner table…countless times of silly, stupid, playful, friendly touches. And never had they made his skin react like that. Like…

He wasn't even going there.

A good night's sleep would sort him out.

Right?

CHAPTER THREE

THE MORNING WAS a whirlwind of happiness and joyful reunions, and Lexi desperately trying to hide the shadows under her eyes with lashings of concealer as she sat in the hotel suite with the other three bridesmaids and Emma—who looked stunning in her silk sheath wedding dress—and Emma's mum. It was quite a squeeze and a lot of excited hormones.

'It is so good to see you, Lexi.' Preeti, who had also shared the fourth-year house, sat down next to her, her very pregnant belly filling out the champagne-coloured dress. 'It's been so long. It was such a shame you didn't make the last two get-togethers and missed Sally's wedding.'

Because she'd been entrenched in misery and hadn't wanted to spoil things for the others. But she was so much better now. 'Work always seems to get in the way these days; you know what it's like with hospital staffing levels. But I'm so glad I made it this time.'

She really was. Despite what she'd envisaged, she didn't feel older than them like she used to...well, not so much. Although after little sleep she did envy their brightness and lack of eye bags. But they didn't all have perfect lives and impeccably behaved children. They had messy, chaotic families and were trying to juggle work and personal lives and they were all just about muddling through, like she was.

Preeti looked down at her bump and sighed. 'Bad timing for me, though. I wish I'd known about being a bridesmaid before I got pregnant. Then I would have delayed this little one until next year, or at least until the end of this year, and had one of those cute, neat bumps instead of waddling round like a whale. Poor Emma, having me on her wedding photos.'

'What? No. You look amazing, Preeti.' Preeti had been able to time her two other pregnancies around the football premiership dates, so her husband Bhavesh would still be able to get to all his team's matches, and her work schedule. *Lucky thing.* Lexi would have given anything for a pregnancy any time over the last fifteen years, and would have fitted her life, not just her schedule, around it. 'Being pregnant really suits you. You're glowing.'

'Thanks, but I'm not. I'm a hot mess. It gets so much harder as you get older, right? What did they used to call it? A geriatric pregnancy. And I'm only thirty-six. Charming! Some of the other pregnant mums at the clinic are well into their forties— Oh. God.' Preeti's hand went to her mouth. 'I'm so sorry. I just realised… you…and Ross and his… Oh, *shoot.* I'm putting my foot in it even more. Aren't I?'

Lexi's heart thumped but she fought to steady it. It was in the past. Even though her unsuccessful IVF journey hadn't been a secret, it was the first time she'd faced everyone altogether since Ross had left. Only Jono truly knew what she'd been through. She'd kept the others a little at arm's length because she knew they'd all want to jump in and offer support and she wouldn't have been able to handle their concern. She hadn't wanted to talk about it. Couldn't, in fact, without breaking down. Writing had been her salvation because she'd been able to do it without judgement and without seeing people's reactions and, probably, pity.

Now, though, she was stronger. 'Ross and his pregnant secretary? Is that what you mean?'

'Yes.' Preeti's cheeks pinked up and she patted Lexi's knee. 'But don't worry, he wasn't invited, so you won't see them. I'm so sorry, I won't mention it again.'

'Please don't walk on eggshells around me. I'm totally fine about it. Honestly. I'm glad he's gone. And as for babies, well, it's just not meant to be for me. But I'm thrilled for you. Another brother or sister for Jay and the twins.' As she spoke Lexi realised the whole room had fallen silent. She looked up and saw eight pairs of eyes looking at her and made sure to hide the pang of wistfulness in her tone. She dug very deep for a smile to reassure them. Because even though she hadn't always confided everything in them she knew they cared about her and she didn't want to spoil this lovely day. 'Hey, where's the fizz? Isn't it time we toasted our beautiful bride?'

The drinks were passed around and Lexi recovered her embarrassment. In a lull of cheers and clinking of glasses she asked the bride, 'So, who else is going to be here?'

Emma beamed as she fastened a white gold necklace with a simple diamond heart around her neck. 'The old gang from one-seventeen…you wonderful ladies, the guys who played rugby with Mark, and Bhavesh, of course. Cheng's coming back from Singapore, and I'm so glad Jono managed to get back for it. Man, he's looking good these days.' Emma fanned herself with her hand and her eyes sparkled.

'Emma! You're getting married in…an hour,' her mum chastised. Then winked. 'But yes, he's looking great. Australia was good for him.'

'Is he dating anyone?' For some reason Preeti turned to look at Lexi.

She shrugged. 'I don't think so. He didn't actually say.'

Emma's eyes widened. 'You were in a car with him for five whole hours and you didn't ask? Girl, you need to up your game.'

Lexi laughed, hoping her fluttery feelings from last night wouldn't return. 'I don't want to *game* with Jono. He's like a brother.'

'No, he isn't.' Preeti giggled and then her eyes narrowed fleetingly. 'Oh, well, maybe to you.'

Because I'm so old?

But Lexi just breezed over any innuendo. 'He didn't mention anything. We were busy catching up about other things. Then the accident took up a lot of time and talking opportunity.'

'What accident?' Emma whirled round. 'What happened?'

Lexi filled them in on Tyler's drunk cycling and the crash, but decided not to mention the weird static that had zipped over her body when she'd touched Jono's chest or the exact place her thoughts had strayed when he'd mentioned going to bed.

'Should have just brought the poor kid here.' Preeti laughed. 'We have, what…? Two orthopaedic surgeons, a paediatrician, an ER specialist, an obstetrician, three GPs and a very sexy cardiologist. We're covered for any and all emergencies.'

'Oh, I think I might have heart issues. I may need assistance from the sexy cardiologist.' Grinning, Emma's mum clutched her heart, then sighed at their shocked faces. 'Oh, come on. You're never too old.'

Really?

Lexi looked at the older woman, so bright-eyed and enthusiastic and game. Lexi hadn't been game for years. Maybe Jono was right. Maybe this week she could dip her toe back into the dating pool and hopefully pick someone suitable…or, she grinned to herself, someone suitably *unsuitable*.

She had her trusty wingman to vet them, after all.

The white canopy overhead was a welcome relief from the July sun and Jono was glad it wasn't raining. Although a bit of inclement weather might have helped clear his foggy brain.

The wedding was taking place in the grounds of the hotel, overlooking a small cove, a private beach and the sea. The green lawn, the blue water and the white of the chairs set out for the guests dazzled him. It was like being in a dream where all the edges were blurred, and a far cry from the never-ending dust and ghost gums and other eucalypts in the Australian desert. The difference was jarring. The jet lag was unsettling, and he was second-guessing himself.

Had he made a mistake coming back?

The email about his father had made him reassess everything.

It was the right thing to do. Even if his father wouldn't think so. That was a bridge Jono would have to cross as soon as he got back to Oxford.

The celebrant was droning on and if they didn't get the chance to actually move soon he was going to fall asleep. Forcing himself to stay awake, he cast his gaze around the group.

All eyes were on the bride. And sure, Emma did look stunning, but for some strange reason Jono's gaze kept returning to Lexi.

Her long dark hair was pinned up in a messy bun, with strands escaping and framing her face. She was wearing a below-the-knee silk dress with tiny straps, in a colour that reminded him of an intense Australian oaked chardonnay, and high heeled sandals in a matching colour.

She'd been pretty at her own wedding, when they'd all been guests, happy she'd found a man she loved, and of course every bride looked stunning on their wedding day. But today there was something different about her.

His mind wandered to last night and her fingertips on his chest. His body prickled. It had been…good.

He squished the memory. Then realised people were starting to move and clap. He'd missed the bride and groom kiss.

Had he actually fallen asleep?

Dreaming about Lexi touching him?

Before he knew what was happening, Bhavesh gestured to him to stand up and the wedding party was peeling out from the aisles, each groomsman paired up with a bridesmaid.

'We're the odd non-couple couple so we get to walk back down the aisle together,' Lexi had told him, laughing and rolling her eyes, when they'd met at the church earlier. Having missed out on yesterday's rehearsal, she'd managed to catch up on the etiquette and plans and filled him in.

She held her bouquet in her left hand as they followed the bride and groom down the makeshift aisle. He offered her his arm, the way the other groomsmen had to their bridesmaid. Smiling, she slipped her arm into his and whispered, 'That was nice. It's a perfect venue for a wedding.'

'It took a bit longer than I expected, but the celebrant seemed to enjoy the sound of his own voice.'

'Give a man a microphone…' She chuckled. Her eyes lit up and her smile was full and wide and warm.

He felt wired and his edges were still blurring, but she was in full focus. 'How can you look so fresh after so little sleep?'

'Make-up hides a multitude of sins.' She winked and patted her cheek. 'How are you holding up?'

'I don't even know which hemisphere I'm in. I keep looking for spiders and snakes under the seats. People must think I'm crazy.'

'Nothing different there.' They'd stopped walking now so the photographer could take some shots. She spoke out of the side of her mouth. 'To be honest, I feel a bit weird at weddings these days.'

'Me too. Is that because of Ross?'

'Yes. I won't be making that mistake again. I'm going to take a leaf out of the Jonathan Neale book and avoid being the main attraction at a wedding ever again.'

He looked at the way Emma was gazing at Mark with adoration and love and a shared happiness, and knew he'd never had that. Part of him wanted it. A lot of him.

Which was a surprise because he'd always thought he was like his father, flitting from one woman to the next and never looking back. But yes, he wanted more than that. 'Actually, I think it would be cool. I see myself having all of it one day. The whole shebang.'

'Not you too?' Her head whipped round and she frowned, something like disappointment flickering through her gaze. 'I thought you were a confirmed bachelor.'

'People change. I'd like for at least one of the Neale men to be a decent human being. Faithful husband, you know. Good father, if that ever happened.'

She winced. 'I never pegged you as the settling type.'

'I never pegged you as being cynical about weddings. But then, I guess you have cause.'

'I do.' Then she laughed, even though what she'd been through had been so distressing. 'See what I did there? *I do*...at a wedding. I'm so funny.'

'Are you though?' he teased, taking her lead and laughing along because underneath her smile he could see the pain she was still hiding.

'Yes. Very.' Her eyes glittered. 'So, do you have anyone in mind to do the whole shebang thing with? Is there already a special someone you haven't told me about?'

'No and no. But I'm knocking on a bit, and I need to start looking.'

'Do not talk to me about being old.' She slid her arm from his and he remembered her quip about everyone comparing themselves at events like this.

'You look better than every single one of the women here.'

Her eyes narrowed. 'What do you want?'

'A beautiful woman on my arm.' He grinned and realised he really did mean that. 'That strange feeling I have at weddings? It's weird, it's a lot like hope. Or want. Or something.'

'You want to have a wedding?' She gaped.

'No. I want that feeling. That I'm...done with the awkward dating and constant moving. That I've stopped chasing and I'm living how things are going to be for the rest of my life.' Normally, he'd never say these kinds of things, not to anyone. But Lexi probably knew him better than he knew himself. At least, he'd blabbed on so much about things in those emails and messages she probably thought he needed professional help. 'Yes. That's it. I want to stop and just be.'

'Being married doesn't mean you stop, Jono. In fact, you have to work very hard and sometimes you fail…' She glanced around the wedding party, her eyes settling on Emma and Mark. 'Let's not talk about that here.'

'I'm sorry you were hurt, Lexi. The guy's a jerk.'

'I know.' Her eyes glistened now and for a moment he thought she was going to cry. But instead she smiled and looked down at her dress. 'Hey, if you get married, can I be your bridesmaid? I like getting all glammed up, makes a change from hospital scrubs.'

He allowed his gaze to graze over her, just for a moment. The dress clung to her body. She'd lost weight—no doubt from all that stress-relieving exercise, but her curves still filled her dress in all the right places. She had a body most women would die for. And she was funny, clever, bright. Warm. Ross had made a huge mistake in leaving her.

Ugh. Hello? Jono dragged his gaze back to her face. Ogling his friend? Who was the jerk now? 'It suits you. Yes, you can be my bridesmaid. Actually, how about my best man woman?'

'Excellent. So, how about I be your wingman this week too? If you see any women you want to get to know, let me suss them out for you.'

'Deal.' He stuck out his hand.

She slid hers into his grip and shook. 'Deal.'

But it didn't settle well. More skin on skin with her had heat flooding through him. He glanced at her, to find her looking up at him, her expression mirroring his panic. He dropped his hand. She wiped hers down her dress. Looked away.

What the hell? What was going on?

Luckily, their attention was distracted by Preeti, who was beckoning Lexi over for more photographs.

Lexi laughed and looked relieved. 'I'm so in demand. Got to dash.'

He watched her join her friends and confirmed that yes, she was stand-out compared to the others. She just was. Fact. Objective observation.

And sexy as hell.

So, it wasn't jet lag. He'd spent too much of his life enjoying the chase that it appeared to have rubbed off on his friendships too. That was going to stop, right now. There was no way he was going to jeopardise his relationship with Lexi by letting a fresh case of lust get in the way. No way. She was worth more than he could give her. Geez, she was worth everything and he wanted to keep her in his life.

'Hey, Dr Neale. Is that you?' A voice from behind had him turning round.

'Tyler! How are you doing?'

'Good, thanks. The pain's not too bad.' The teenager grinned and held up his plaster casted hand. He held a brown paper bag in the other. 'Thought it was James Bond or someone. I didn't recognise you in the penguin suit.'

Jono made a gun with his fingers. 'Licensed to thrill.'

'Mate, you're way too old for all that,' Tyler quipped then glanced around. 'Is your wife here?'

Wife? He'd been thinking about one and now...? Lexi. His wife?

A sudden pang snagged his heart. A lifetime with Lexi?

Whoa. No. Nope. Niet. No. They were friends. That was all.

He laughed. 'Firstly, thirty-five isn't old. The guy who plays James Bond is over fifty. And secondly, I don't have a wife.'

'Thirty-five, fifty-five…all the same to me.' Tyler's happy expression turned to embarrassment. 'And sorry, I mean Lexi. Um… Dr Fisher.'

'Sure. I just saw her go into the reception room for photos with the bride and bridesmaids. Come with me. But beware of happy wedding shrieks and antics.'

'Women, huh?' Tyler gave him a weary old man shrug he could only have inherited from his father.

'Yeah. Women.'

Although wandering over to her while he was in this state of mind might not have been a great idea. What he needed was space from Lexi and all the weird feelings whirling round his chest. Fat chance of that at an intimate wedding, where relationships were the order of the day.

Lexi looked up to see Jono and Tyler ambling across the terrazzo floor. Her heart did a little skip and her cheeks heated. After the zip of electricity with Jono a few minutes ago she'd decided it would be best not to look at him. But how could she not? The man was in full wedding morning suit. He'd been hot yesterday in his travel clothes and a hint of stubble, but well-groomed he was gloriously, sexily beautiful. It was taking all of her strength not to touch him again.

She had it bad, but refused to allow herself to be derailed by it and focused on the boy. 'Hey, Tyler. How's things?'

'Great.' Tyler beamed up at her and offered her a brown paper bag. 'These are for you. To say thank you for all your help. You…' his cheeks turned beetroot red '…you…um… You look great.'

'That's really lovely. Thank you. It's amazing what a bit of make-up can hide.' She looked in the bag and found a box of chocolates. So kind. 'Glad to see you're looking a lot better too.'

'Yeah.' He glanced down at his feet, suddenly shy.

'And how's the job thing going? Did you get into trouble?'

'A bit.' He rolled his eyes.

'Did they find anyone else to serve the food?'

'Yeah. I asked Charlie, my mate. He's over there.' He pointed to a scrawny kid straightening the cutlery on the top table. 'He's happy.'

'Phew. That means I don't have to do it. Didn't want to spill on my dress.' She smiled at the top of his head. Fifteen, full of hormones. 'But I guess it means you're not earning anything.'

'My auntie said I can update the hotel website until I have two arms to serve food.' The red had now reached the tips of his ears. 'Yeah. So…thanks again. Got to go.'

'Okay. See you around.' She watched as the boy dashed away. No way would she want to be his age and so tongue-twisted again, or to relive what she'd already been through. There was some benefit to being older.

'Someone's got an admirer.' Jono stepped closer. 'I think he's got a crush on you.'

'Don't be silly.'

'Just being your wingman. A quiet word, though.' He leaned in, so close his scent filled the air. Grass and smoke and spice. It made her belly heat. 'He's a bit young for you.'

She looked up at him with a sudden crushing in her chest. *Aren't they all?* 'He gave me chocolates. He'll make some girl very happy if he keeps up with the presents and the good manners.'

'And stops the drunk cycling.' Jono grimaced. 'I didn't get anything from him but cheek. He said I was old.'

'Sucks, huh?'

'Hey, Jono. Did you enjoy the service? Or did I detect a yawn or two?' Emma glided over and teased him. 'Jet lag getting to you?'

'It was a wonderful service. Congratulations.' Jono grinned and pressed a kiss to the bride's cheek while flashing a conspiratorial smile towards Lexi. 'Who knew wedding ceremonies could last so long?'

'Oh, yes. Be prepared for that,' Lexi whispered and nudged him.

But she clearly didn't say it quietly enough, because Emma's eyes grew large. 'Oh? Planning a wedding, Jono? Tell me everything. I want all the gossip.'

'Me? No.' He shook his head, his smile turning into undisguised panic. 'No wedding plans.'

'Yet?' Emma's head tilted to one side as she looked at him.

He shrugged casually. 'I'd have to find someone who's daft enough to marry me first.'

'I'll ask all the single women here to form an orderly line. But first, come have your photo taken with the rest of the groomsmen.' Emma looped her arm into his and steered him towards the photographer, but not before Lexi heard the bride ask, 'Marriage, Jono? I can't wait. And what about having kids? Are they in the plan too?'

Lexi craned her neck to catch his answer, but she couldn't hear his words, just saw him nodding and smiling and then the two of them laughing. No doubt discussing exactly how many children he was hoping to have.

Her heart squeezed tight. Judging by the way he'd interacted with Tyler, Jono would make a wonderful father. Which meant if he was looking for a mother for his children Lexi would be definitely and totally out of the picture.

She mentally shook herself. How had she gone from looking forward to seeing him to being upset she couldn't bear his children in a matter of hours?

Needing to clear her head, she wandered out onto the stone patio and looked down the grassy slope that led to the sea. The evening was calm and still, the fading light casting a golden glow over the village in the distance. She inhaled salt-scented air and closed her eyes, tiredness from her late night now catching up with her.

'Taking time out from the madness?' Jono's voice behind her made her jump.

Don't look at him. Don't look at him.

If she didn't look at him, maybe she wouldn't feel all these complicated things, especially now she knew his long-term goals, which could not possibly include her if kids were a deal-breaker. 'Just taking a minute to watch the sunset.'

'It's beautiful here. I didn't expect Cornwall to be so pretty.'

'It's gorgeous.' She peered over the wall down to the beach. 'I'm going to swim down there tomorrow, and I heard there are some lovely walks on the cliffs.'

'Doesn't sound like a relaxing holiday to me.' He rested his palms on the stone wall and looked out.

'I'm an active relaxer. I don't like to sit around all day.'

'Let's organise a game of beach volleyball and a swim. Tomorrow, after breakfast.'

She did not want to think about Jono in beachwear,

but she could hardly refuse. She was spending the week with him, then God knew how long at her house. She was bound to see him in many states of dress and undress. Possibly with a woman on his arm, in his bed. No, make that *definitely* with a woman because she knew the old Jono far too well.

Had he really changed so much? Or was this reaction just a flash of jealousy inside her rearing its head?

She swallowed. Cleared her throat. 'Beach volleyball sounds fun. Make sure you invite all the single women, so I can wingman them.'

'Wingman them?' He guffawed. 'Not a verb.'

'Whatever. I'll see if I can find the perfect woman for you.' She turned to look at him.

Big mistake.

His gaze caught on hers for a second longer than necessary. 'I'm not looking for perfect, Lexi. Just someone who will accept me for who I am. Not perfect at all.'

Then he was gone.

CHAPTER FOUR

THE VIEW FROM the top of the cliff was stunning. To Lexi's right, the white buildings of quaint St Quintin village flanked narrow streets that led down to a tiny marina, fish market and stone pier. Directly below her the beautiful, centuries-old hotel built of cream-coloured stone stood proudly on its promontory.

To the left was nothing but rolling green fields then the sharp cliff edge, atop buttery rocks and a sheer drop. The sea, calm and deepest turquoise blue, was tens of metres below, giving onto the golden sands of the Royal Hotel's private cove. The sun was burning off a veil of wispy clouds, with the promise of a sunny day ahead. It was pretty special.

Obviously she wasn't the only person to think that because, further over to her left, two middle-aged guys were unfolding something that looked like sails and a sort of contraption…hang-gliders or paragliders, she didn't know the difference. But the bright red and yellow fabric jarred with the vibrant green grass.

The helmeted men looked over and nodded at her. She waved back then inhaled deeply, mainly because the run up the steep hill had sapped most of her morning-after-the-late-night-before energy. Her body had strained against the effort of the steep path—and, far from fighting it, she welcomed the burn and the ache because it made her feel stronger and alive.

Peace. Quiet. Space.

Just what she needed to get her head straight. Overnight, she'd wrestled the wayward feelings about Jono under control and put it all down to sentimentality and, perhaps, a bit of loneliness.

How could she be lonely when every waking hour was spent at work, with people?

But she had to admit she did miss having someone with her at the end of the day. Or to run ideas through with. *And sex.*

No, not sex…physical contact. A touch, a kiss, a hug.

She sat down and hugged her knees to her chest.

Jono is not my antidote to loneliness.

But he was her crush.

Ugh. That was it. Nailed.

Geez, she felt about the same age as Tyler.

Way down below, tiny figures sauntered across the sand, wafted beach towels in the air, then sat down. One of them—she couldn't make out exactly who, but a woman, jumped back up and waved at her.

Then suddenly the whole group were waving, smiling, mouths opening and closing. Her friends. She stood and cupped her hands around her mouth. 'I can't hear you!'

One of them darted towards the sea and then ran back, using both arms to beckon her down. *Come for a swim.* She tiptoed to the cliff edge. Whoa. Were those men really going to jump off here? It was a long way down. 'Okay, I'm coming!'

So much for space and quiet.

Luckily, Lexi had put her bikini on underneath her

running gear, so she worked her way down the steep path and onto the beach.

'Wow, you must have had an early start!' Preeti patted her beach towel for Lexi to sit down next to her. She was wearing a one-piece navy swimsuit that accentuated her baby bump.

Lexi removed her socks and trainers and stretched. 'A good dose of fresh air and a decent run usually wakes me up in the morning.'

Preeti frowned at her. 'Girl, nothing gets between me and my morning coffee and a scroll through social media. Not even my kids.'

'Oh, I do that too.' Lexi glanced round at the others. No sign of the bride and groom, but some of the other bridesmaids and guests were here. And Jono, kicking a football to Bhavesh and Cheng and some other guys she didn't know. He gave her a wave.

She waved back to them all, but her eyes slid back to him. His hair was tousled as if he'd just showered or swum. His top half was T-shirt-free and tanned. And what she'd imagined was under yesterday's suit was a whole lot better in reality.

Don't look. At least, don't stare.

But she couldn't help it. He had toned shoulder muscles, defined pecs any man would die for and a six-pack...

Stop looking.

Preeti nudged her, her gaze fixed on the six-pack too. 'Damn, I married the wrong guy.'

'Aww. No. Bhavesh is a darling and adores you and the kids.'

'I know. I'm only joking. I love him to pieces and would never swap.' She batted her eyelashes over to her gorgeous husband then looked back at Jono. 'But

I'd definitely put down the coffee and social media for that every morning.'

'I guess.' Lexi felt duty bound to join in. And anyway, there it was. Objective proof that Jono was hot. She sighed. She was just having a normal female reaction. It would go. Crushes wore off. Heck, she wasn't still mad about Robbie Williams like she had been at school. 'Well, maybe I'd just put down the social media. Coffee's too precious.' *Liar.* 'I've offered to be his wingman. So if you happen to meet any suitable women, let me know so I can vet them.'

'*His* wingman?' Preeti threw her a look she couldn't read. 'Don't you think it should be the other way round, and you should be issuing a warning to any woman who gets close to him? Keep away from this man. Heartbreaker and serial non-committer. Look, but don't touch.'

'He said he was ready to settle down so maybe he's changed.' He'd told her he had so why wouldn't she believe him? 'I know I'm not the same person I was at medical school.'

But she had to admit that in her current crush state the thought of Jono committing made her envious of the woman he eventually fell in love with.

She lay back on the towel and looked skywards. Above them the two hang-gliders swooped and dipped like huge red and yellow birds. 'That looks amazing. So free.'

'Nope. Not for me, thanks. Not when the only way is down.' Preeti stood up and brushed sand from her bum. 'Right. It's far too hot. I'm heading in for a swim.'

'Great idea. I'll come with you.'

Preeti's eyes narrowed. 'Don't come in on my account. You don't need to babysit me.'

Lexi dragged her eyes away from Jono, where they

seemed to want to rest far too frequently. 'Actually, I need to cool off.'

'That gorgeous body getting to you too?' Preeti fanned her hand in front of her face and wiggled her eyebrows.

'No.' Was it that obvious? 'I'm still hot from the run.'

'Yeah. Right.' Her friend ran ankle-deep into the water and screamed. 'It's freezing!'

Lexi followed. 'Be careful, the sign says there's a sharp drop-off.'

'I'm fine. Honestly. I used to swim for Bedfordshire in swimming comps.'

Lexi shook her head. 'And I'm a doctor. I'm programmed to think of worst-case scenarios.'

'It's good for my back if I just lie back and float. And the baby loves it. He's kicking like a footballer.' Preeti rolled her eyes. 'Just like his dad. Bhavesh's already bought him season tickets. The poor child hasn't even been born yet.'

'Proud dad, though.'

'Oh, yes. He just loves having them around. He's already called my mum four times to make sure the others are okay while we're here. He's worse at worrying than I am.'

Lexi had managed not to think about Ross again, but listening to Preeti made her gut tighten. He'd been hell-bent on being a dad too. And she'd let him down. Let them both down. Stupid bloody infertility. She shivered involuntarily.

Stupid bloody Ross. Because once he'd had a chance to escape her, he'd taken it. So much for their wedding vows and all the promises.

She lay back in the water too and tried to push him out of her head, but the only other option was thinking about Jono, because—it appeared—she only had a two-track mind where men were concerned.

And she wasn't going to have a relationship with either of them.

After a few minutes of tortured thoughts about Jono and Ross, Preeti swam over. 'Hey, you look frozen. Go back to the beach.'

But there was only Jono on the sand now; the rest of the gang had dispersed. Bhavesh was at the far end of the beach exploring what looked like caves, so there was no one to keep an eye on Preeti. 'I'm fine. I'll stay with you.'

'Your teeth are chattering. Go. Use my towel. I'll use Bhavesh's.'

'Seriously, I'm fine.'

'Go!' Preeti splashed water at Lexi. 'Your lips are blue. It's because you don't have an ounce of fat on you. I've got baby to keep me warm. I mean it. Go.'

Lexi had to admit she was starting to shake. The water was very cold and the sweat she'd burnt up was now well and truly doused. 'Okay. If you're sure. I'll keep an eye on you from there.' She swam back to the beach and walked over to Preeti's towel, but unfortunately Jono was sitting next to it. She dripped over him and made him move up so she could sit down. 'Hey, there. Shift up a bit, please.'

'Here. You look frozen.' He handed her his towel and she wrapped herself in it.

'The water is bracing.' She rubbed her arms to get some warmth in them, acutely aware that he was watching her, and not sure whether the erupting goosebumps were because of the cold water or the fact his eyes were on her.

This was nuts. He was her *friend*. Friends didn't think like this about each other.

'So.' He took the towel and rubbed her back. 'I've been wingmanning for you.'

She laughed. 'You said it wasn't a verb.'

He groaned. 'Do you want the lowdown on eligible guys or not?'

She tried not to think about his hands running strokes down her spine. 'Okay. Hit me.'

'Lucas, the guy in the green shorts...' he gesticulated to the huddle of guys wandering back towards the hotel '...is an old school friend of Mark's. Nice guy. Big teeth. Balding.' He grimaced.

'Looks aren't important.' She dragged her eyes away from Jono's chest and up to his face. Bad move. She couldn't stop thinking about how gorgeous he was.

'Really big teeth.' He raised one eyebrow. 'Accountant. Lives in Newcastle. Could be an issue. Big commute to work.'

'I could relocate.'

'Don't, Lexi.' Jono stopped rubbing and shifted to face her, his knees pressing up against hers. This close she could see the flecks of amber in his eyes, the long slow graze of his eyelashes on his cheeks when he blinked. The slightly crooked tooth that made his smile imperfectly perfect.

Her heart thumped as heat rushed through her. 'Don't what?'

'Give up things for someone else. You did enough of that with Ross.'

Sometimes she wished she hadn't told Jono everything. It meant she couldn't hide behind pretence. It also meant there were no secrets between them. Except for that infuriating crush... 'It's about compromise, Jono. But okay. Someone who lives closer. What about the dark-haired guy?'

Focusing on someone else would make her focus less on Jono. *Please.*

'Josh?' He shook his head sadly. 'Gay.'

'That's a shame for me then. He's lovely.'

'Because looks aren't important, right?' His eyes glittered as he laughed.

'What about blue shorts man?'

'Ash.' Jono shrugged. 'Ashley something.'

'What's wrong with him?'

'Nothing. I guess. He's probably great. Not the best footballer. But passable. Lives in Swindon.'

'Oh? We're practically neighbours then.' Which was a lot better than sharing a house. She gulped at the thought of spending more time with Jono when he looked like a freaking god. 'Okay. Ash it is. Introduce me later. I'm looking forward to meeting him,' she lied, as she hugged her legs and rested her chin on her knees. Hoping that if she locked her arms round her knees she wouldn't be tempted to touch Jono. 'This is fun.'

He snagged her gaze, his blue eyes capturing her attention. 'Just be careful, Lexi. You don't know these men.'

'Is the whole point?' She bugged her eyes at him. 'Getting to know them is the fun bit, right? You always liked the chase, you said.'

His mouth set in a line. 'Just be careful.'

'Again, not the point. I don't want to be careful. I want to have fun.' Lexi scanned the water for Preeti. Out there, *deep* out there, their friend was frantically waving.

'Oh, God.' Lexi jumped up, heart hammering. She should have been watching out for her friend, not ogling Jono. 'Look! Is she okay? Is she waving? Or is that an SOS?'

'I can't tell. She's a long way out.' Jono jumped up too and ran to the water.

Lexi ran past him, back into the freezing sea. 'It's okay, Preet! Don't panic.'

But as they got closer Preeti screamed, 'No! No!'

Swallowing more water than she intended, Lexi thrashed through the waves to her friend, who had swum over to meet them halfway. 'It's okay, we're here. It's okay.'

Preeti grimaced. 'I'm fine. I told you I could swim. But look. Over there. One of the hang-gliders has crashed onto the rocks. He needs help. Quick.'

Lexi followed Preeti's pointed finger to the far right of the cove and saw a mangled mess of sail and metal crumpled on a rocky outcrop. Her gut knotted. 'Oh, my God. I didn't hear a thing.'

'Because the wind's blowing offshore. Quick.' Preeti started to kick towards the beach. 'You go to them. I can't run, but I'll call an ambulance and phone up to the hotel for a first aid kit and some extra pairs of hands.'

Jono was ahead of them and called back, 'I think he's going to need more than a few bandages.'

When she reached them Jono was already on his knees on the jagged rocks talking to the injured man. 'Hey. It's okay. It's okay.' It wasn't okay; it was a mess. The guy was groaning, his leg looked bent out of shape and his face was just blood and sand. On the plus side he was wearing a helmet and goggles, but that was the only plus she could see right now. 'We're going to help you. The ambulance is on its way.'

No reply.

Jono felt for a carotid pulse. 'Weak. How far did he fall?'

Lexi knelt next to him and tried to stabilise the guy's neck. 'I don't know. I wasn't watching.'

Because she'd been far too busy looking at Jonathan Neale.

CHAPTER FIVE

THE GUY WAS badly injured. Obvious open fractures on left tibia and fibula and right ankle. Bruising on his ribs, which possibly meant internal bleeding. Jono tested the man's reactions to stimulus. His eyes flickered open when Jono squeezed his fingernail bed and he groaned again. 'Glasgow coma score's eight.' Not good. He held the towel against their patient's left leg to stem the gush of blood. 'Looks like he might have ripped an artery too.'

A figure tore down the beach.

'Dad! Dad!' It was Tyler. 'Dad...'

No. Jono's gut turned over. Before the boy got too close, he held up his palm. Realised it was covered in Tyler's father's blood and wiped it on his board shorts. 'Hey, mate. How about you go to that lady over there. Her name's Preeti and she's a doctor too. She'll talk you through what's happening.'

But Tyler ran to Lexi instead and grabbed her shoulder. 'Save him. Like you did me. Help him.'

'I'm trying to, mate. I'm making sure to keep his neck nice and stable.' Lexi blinked up at Tyler. 'I promise I'll come talk to you later.'

'You have to save him.' His voice carried a desperation Jono felt.

Lexi looked deep into the boy's eyes and Jono could

see emotion welling up within her. She breathed out a long sigh. 'I'm going to try my best, okay? But truth is, Tyler, he's in a bad way.'

The boy grabbed her arm, desperation in his eyes. 'But I know you can do it, Lexi. You can do this.'

'Hey, please don't grab me. I'm protecting his neck in case it's hurt, and any slight slip could be bad, okay?'

'We need to let Lexi do her job.' Jono tried to verbally steer Tyler away from Lexi as he pressed the heel of his hand onto the bleeding leg. 'What's his name?'

'Dad's? It's Dean.'

'Okay. Thanks. Hey, Dean. We're going to get you to hospital as soon as we can.' No response. 'We need you to hold on. Tyler's here. Fight for him, okay? Fight for your son.'

A thought flickered through his head; would Jono's father have ever fought for his son? Maybe, if he'd ever taken the time to get to know him properly.

He shook it off. Now wasn't the time to think of his own life when someone else's was in danger. What they needed was equipment. Oxygen. Fluids. A tourniquet. X-ray and scanning machines. A chest drain. An operating theatre. Blood supplies.

Jono was only wearing beach shorts and Lexi...hell, Lexi was only in that sexy red bikini...the one he'd been trying hard not to look at all morning. He swallowed, then scanned Tyler. 'Quick, give me your belt.'

The boy struggled to slide the belt off with one arm in a plaster cast but eventually he handed it to Jono, who fastened it three inches proximal to the wound and pulled it tight. It would help stem the bleeding for a while but it wasn't ideal and if it didn't stop soon Dean would be in a lot of trouble.

Out of the corner of his eye he saw Bhavesh jogging

towards them and he turned to Tyler. 'Look, see that guy there? He's an ER doctor. He's going to help us stabilise your dad.'

'We're going to do our best, Tyler. I promise you.' Lexi's voice was wobbly and he got it. It was one thing to be a doctor, another to be a breathing, living human with feelings for the people she was helping. Tyler had somehow become a friend and she would be hating that she couldn't magically fix things for him.

Jono leaned in to talk to their patient, all the while assessing for any change in status. Truth was, he was deteriorating by the second. 'Hey, Dean. It's okay, mate. We've got more doctors here than the ER department. We'll get you sorted, just stay with us, okay?'

The sound of sirens suddenly filled the air, but they couldn't relax now. Even with this number of doctors dealing with the situation it was still a race against time. Preeti was on the phone, ferrying messages back and forth to the paramedics and admitting hospital about their classification one emergency. Bhavesh was co-ordinating care with the limited equipment they had.

Cheng had taken over from Lexi, managing Dean's back and neck. Emma had put two lines she'd had in her doctor's bag into their patient's arms, ready for fluids. A helicopter had been dispatched.

And then, finally, the paramedics arrived, along with the other hang-glider, who turned out to be Tyler's uncle and the hotel owner. A real family affair.

While Lexi was on the phone to Tyler's mum for the second time in twenty-four hours Jono put his hands on the kid's shoulders. 'Do you want me to go with you to the hospital?'

'I don't know. I don't know what to do, Jono.' Then, to

his surprise, Tyler turned and sobbed into Jono's chest. 'He can't die. He's my dad.'

Hell.

Jono wrapped his arms around the boy and held on. A surge of pressure filled his chest, accompanied by an unbearable sense of responsibility. Not just to Tyler but to the boy's dad…and inexplicably to his own. What would it be like to have such respect…love even, between father and son?

He had no idea. But he knew he'd done the right thing by coming back.

He held on to Tyler while the team worked with the paramedics on Dean. And while they stabilised him enough to transport him to hospital.

Eventually, as the helicopter rose into the air, a woman around Jono's age, maybe a bit older—around Lexi's age?—not that there was that much difference, despite what she seemed to think—darted across the sand towards them. 'Tyler! Tyler! Dean!'

'Mum…' The kid's voice was tangled and raw as he peeled himself off Jono.

Her eyes darted to the rising helicopter. 'How is he…?'

'He's holding on. They're taking him to the Royal Cornwall Hospital in Truro. I'm Lexi, I called you earlier. And the other night.'

'Okay. Right. Thanks. Thank you so much. I'm Anna.' Tyler's mum looked disoriented. Shocked. And then it dawned on her. 'Oh. Yes. *Dr* Lexi. Tyler won't stop talking about you.'

'He's a good kid.' Lexi smiled. 'You'd better get off to the hospital; I told them you'd meet them there. If you don't understand any of the gobbledegook medical language just call me and I'll interpret. You'll have my number on your phone.'

Jono patted Tyler's back. 'You want me to come with you?'

The boy looked over at Anna, then his back straightened. He blinked fast. 'No. Thanks for the offer but I need to look after my mum.'

Poor kid, acting all grown-up to protect his mother when inside he was probably crumbling. Jono knew exactly how that felt. 'Sure thing, mate. Good move.'

After seeing them off Jono turned round and found Lexi had gone. Was she okay? Shaken up? Did she need... him?

Why the hell would she need him?

What a ridiculous idea. And yet he couldn't shake it off. Was it because he needed her right now— needed to debrief with his friend?

Or something else altogether?

That Tyler thing... Truth was, it had rattled him. Fathers and sons were a difficult territory at times and navigating them wasn't easy. But Tyler adored his father, that was plain.

How did that feel?

He found her washing her hands in the hotel's outdoor shower facilities. She was shivering. That itsy-bitsy red bikini wasn't covering much of her skin and the chopper downdraught had blown sand everywhere. The towel she'd previously wrapped round her shoulders was covered in blood and unusable. He dashed over to the little pile of things they'd left on the beach then ran back and wrapped a towel around her shoulders. 'Here, you look frozen.'

'I'm okay. Thanks.' She smiled up at him, her expression a mixture of sadness and gratitude. His heart did a weird dance.

He smiled back as he washed his hands too. 'Doctors on holiday, eh? It's always a drama.'

'Because we can't walk away or rely on anyone else. We're duty-bound to act.'

'That is one accident-prone family.' It was a poor attempt at dark humour but it made Lexi smile.

'Right about that. I hope Dean makes it.'

'Me too. You okay?' The sadness in her eyes had eased out the gratitude.

'Not really.' She tugged the towel across her shoulders. 'I'm a medical professional and I should be totally unemotional dealing with this…heck, I deal with emergencies all the time…but I felt so out of my depth with no equipment. And there was that connection too, you know? With Tyler. Made everything seem so intense.'

'It's always worse when we know the patient. You want to go back inside—grab a hot drink to warm you up?'

'No, I'm a bit shaky.' She showed him her trembling hands. 'I think I need to walk off some of the adrenalin first.'

'Come on, then.' He tugged her hand and they walked along the shallows, kicking through the water. The sun was high in the clear blue sky. A few people were now sunbathing on the little beach as if nothing dramatic had just happened a few yards away. 'We did our best, Lexi. It's up to the ER team now. At least they have better equipment than we had.'

'I just couldn't bear the way Tyler looked at me. As if I was going to wave some kind of magic wand.'

He nudged her. 'You're his hero.'

'I don't want to be anyone's hero. It's too much pressure, especially in cases like Dean's. We didn't know the extent of his internal injuries. I couldn't make any promises.' She shivered but still managed a smile.

Hot damn, she was so beautiful in that tiny bikini and with her ponytail all dishevelled. She was... He forced any ideas other than that she was his friend to the back of his mind. She'd hate it if she thought he saw her as something sexual, even sensuous, a *chase*. He shouldn't be having those thoughts.

Her head tilted to one side. 'I was really impressed with the way you dealt with Tyler.'

'Yeah, he's a good kid. I see myself in him.'

'The better parts.' She winked. 'You're a good role model. *Now.* I might not have said that a few years ago.'

'Me neither.' He laughed. 'Thank God I've grown up.'

Her pride in him was a real power punch to his gut. But there was something weird going on here too. All his life he'd kept his emotions tightly bundled up and deep inside—except with those emails he'd written to Lexi about his life in Australia, about the women he dated, and just general stuff. Chatting with a friend— a good friend. Confiding his frustrations about times when things went wrong at work, or an argument with a girlfriend.

But how was it that this was all spilling over with Lexi face to face? They'd never been so close before the messaging...and sure, he'd assumed they'd have a tighter connection, but not this kind of connection. Noticing things like her pretty mouth, the gentle tone of her voice.

That bikini?

That she was so freaking sexy?

Was it just him? What was she thinking? Was that electrical touch last night a blip? His imagination? Jet lag? Was it mutual?

But, on top of all that, he couldn't stop telling her things; it was as if he'd been programmed to share stuff with her—sharing parts of his life, emotions he'd never shared with other friends or even women he'd dated.

She carried on chatting, clearly oblivious to what was going on inside him. 'It was good that Tyler felt he could be honest about the way he was feeling, Jono. There's a real trust there.'

'I like him. But do you know what? Through all of that I was imagining what I'd feel like at Tyler's age if my dad had been hurt, and I came up with nothing.'

'Oh, Jono.' She stopped walking and touched his cheek with her fingertips. Fleetingly, but it sent spirals of warmth through him. 'I'm sure you'd have been desperate to have him better.'

'I would now. And for my mum's sake, yes. I didn't ever want anything to hurt her, even though he broke her heart when he had those affairs.' He scanned Lexi's face, making sure he wasn't triggering her sadness over her broken marriage, but she just looked concerned for him. 'I'm ashamed to say I may not have cared that much about what happened to my dad when I was sixteen.'

A frown wrinkled her forehead. 'What's changed? Why this sudden need to connect with him? You didn't really mention him in your emails.'

'Pretty much everyone I know has kids now and I watch them, see how doting they are with their babies, how much *love* there is. Like Bhavesh with Preeti's pregnancy. Third time for them and he's still so careful with her. Always talking about the twins and Jay. And I wonder what I did wrong, or where we went so wrong that my dad never did that. Why he preferred being a hands-off parent and then, after they divorced, a distant one. We have no relationship, have never had one, even though

I wanted desperately to see him when I was younger. I need to know why he's like that. And then maybe, if I can understand him, I can understand me. Why I can't commit to a relationship or settle down. Why I'm always moving on.'

'Don't blame yourself about your father's poor parenting. You didn't do anything wrong.' She gave him a soft smile.

'I did plenty, Lexi. Not when I was young, of course. But I was a thorn in his side whenever I did see him in my teens.'

'No more than any other kid, I imagine.'

'I guess I just wanted his attention and did anything I could to get it. Good or bad. Mainly bad.'

She laughed. 'But that was your job. That's what teenagers are meant to be like.'

'I bet you weren't. You were top in class at medical school. A bit of a nerd, to be honest.' He play-nudged her.

'Fairly sure I gave my parents enough cause to worry. I didn't even decide my career path until I was in my late twenties. Before that I worked all kinds of jobs, including being cabin crew and working in a pharmacy, then changing university courses from physiotherapy to medicine. I didn't know what I wanted or what I was doing for so long.'

'I'd never have guessed that. You were always so... mature.'

She grimaced. 'You mean old, right?'

'Experienced.' He grinned. Then the idea of an experienced Lexi settled in his chest. His belly. Then lower.

What would she be like in bed?

He couldn't go there. Refused to let his mind journey to that place.

'My mum and dad were probably hugely relieved I

eventually settled down and stuck with something.' Her smile faded. 'Not sure they're thinking that now, with my failed marriage and no grandchildren.'

'Ah, Lexi. I hate it when you say things like that. It's not your fault your ex was a douche bag. Or that your body doesn't always toe the line. Anyone would be proud of you. You're the best paediatrician I know. You care. You're dedicated.'

'All work and no play, though.' She looked up at him and grimaced. 'But you're going to sort that out for me, Wingman Neale.'

He didn't know how to respond to that. He didn't want her getting into bed with Ashley from Swindon. Or anyone else, for that matter. He wanted to take his wingman offer back, but that wouldn't be fair.

He tilted her chin so he could look her in the eyes. 'You are brilliant.'

For a moment their gazes locked and his body rippled with static again, as if jolts of lightning were crashing through him. And this time he was damned sure she felt it too because her pupils flared wide. Her cheeks bloomed two red patches in her pale skin. And did she… did she lean towards him? As in…lean in for a kiss?

Or had that been him?

He didn't know. Couldn't reconcile the way his body was reacting.

Friend zone. Friend zone. Friend zone.

Warning bells rang loud in his head.

But they had definitely moved closer. Her face was so close he could see the sweet bow of her top lip in full focus. The blushed red colour. The way her tongue darted out and wet her bottom lip before she said, 'I am far from brilliant. But I'll accept adept and professional.'

And sexy as hell.

She shook out of his hold and rubbed her arms. She was jittery and her breathing was shallow. Her smile was hesitant and her laughter sounded false. 'Anyway, I'm glad you've decided to contact your dad.'

'He's probably going to throw me out of the house. Or not let me in, in the first place.'

'Then he doesn't deserve you.' Her eyes blazed. 'He needs to know what a great son he has, what he's missed out on for all these years. Because you're a good man, Jono. A really good man.'

Wow.

And that was the final straw. She was so ardent and vibrant and gunning for him. He wanted to wrap her in his arms and kiss her.

No.

He couldn't. *They* couldn't.

But he was going crazy here. Her mouth. Her...everything.

Then she stepped away.

And his mind went into a whirl of missed opportunities and regrets. He reached out and touched her arm. Because he just couldn't stop himself. 'Lexi?'

'Jono.' She whirled round, her gaze catching his again. He saw it then. The need and desire. The same heat—yes, and confusion—that slammed through him.

She shook her head. 'I... We...'

He tried to read what was going through her mind, which was wild because he thought he knew her. But this was different. Things were different and he didn't know what to do with any of it.

'Lexi.' He tugged her towards him, unable to stop himself but trying to.

But before he knew what was happening her mouth slid across his.

CHAPTER SIX

IT HAPPENED SO FAST.

One minute they'd been talking and laughing and then things had got serious and she'd looked up at him and something in his gaze had reached deep inside her and the connection between them had coiled tight.

The urge to hold him, to kiss him even, had been so powerful it had almost overwhelmed her. And she'd tried. God knew, she'd tried to keep her emotions under control, but before she understood what she was doing she'd reached for him.

She registered his initial shock, then felt the sigh against her mouth. Heard the groan in his throat as he cupped her face and pulled her against him, his bare chest flat against her exposed skin. He was warm and soft and yet hard and hot, and she didn't know whether it was a dream or if she wanted it to be a dream or to be real.

She wanted it to be real.

His mouth opened and he deepened the kiss, pressing himself against her. She felt his arousal, the way he responded to her, and a corresponding ache settled deep between her legs. He tasted like everything she'd imagined. Heat and sun, excitement. Danger. And something that was quintessentially Jono. Spice. Sweet. She wound her arms round his neck and held him close, unable to remember the last time she'd kissed anyone. Had forgotten how good it felt.

And boy, did it feel good. His kiss burnt her soul and scorched her body. His hands explored her, fingers on her ribs, dancing so tantalising close to her breasts it made her curl against him. She ran her palms down his back and pulled him even closer, unable to get enough of him. His tongue slid into her mouth and she moaned, hot and hungry for more. Sexual need, so bright and hot it made her feel dizzy, rippled through her, pooling low. Who knew she could feel like this again? Had she ever felt like this? So alive? So turned on? Who knew Jono could kiss like this?

Her friend.

There. The warning siren was there. Blatant. Loud. And she listened. Felt it shiver through her as if the sun had abruptly disappeared behind a dark cloud, warning of an encroaching storm.

If this went wrong she'd lose everything they'd developed over the last few years: the trust, the caring, the respect. If they dated and he betrayed her the way Ross had…? If it went the way her marriage had, despite the vows and promises…

But she was way ahead of herself; there were no promises being made here. Long-term with him would be impossible. She was just crazy in lust with someone unattainable and totally unsuitable.

It was just a kiss.

She valued him as a confidant. If she had a thing with Jono, then who could she confide in? Sure, she had Preeti and Emma and the girls at work, but no one knew her the way he did.

She tugged away and wiped her mouth on the back

of her hand, not wanting to meet his gaze but forcing herself to. Had he wanted it the way she had? Was he repulsed? Shocked?

Shocked. Yes. Dazed. His deep blue eyes were hot with lust, edged with confusion. He clearly didn't know what the hell was happening either. He didn't say a word, just stared at her.

And she didn't know what to say to him. Had she ruined everything?

Probably. Because that was what she did. She ruined things. She hadn't held up her side of the marriage deal with Ross. She'd been unable to produce the child they'd wanted. She'd broken it all.

She pulled her gaze away to look at the sand at her feet. Felt as if she was retreating inside herself and she couldn't stop it, rushing behind the veil of heat and danger to somewhere safe and closed off. Where emotions couldn't reach her.

She put her hand to her mouth and realised, if she was withdrawing from him now, just exactly what a threat that kiss was to their friendship.

Was it already too late? Could they take it back? 'Oh, God. Jono, I'm sorry. I'm really sorry. I shouldn't have done that. I don't know why I did.'

He looked down at the sand too, and then back at her, searching her face. 'Don't apologise. It was a good kiss. Better than good.'

'Yes.' It was one hell of a kiss. 'But…no. This is stupid. One episode of emotion—which is weird anyway, because I'm a trained doctor and I work with sick and hurt people every day—and I'm all over the place. You're my friend, Jono. My friend. That is worth more to me than a kiss.'

But ever since he'd come back she'd felt off-balance,

her world bending out of shape. There was something about him that brought up so many emotions: memories of the difficult times she'd shared with him in the past and now something else, something new and delicious and tempting and so wrong.

Yet she was still stuck on the taste of him and she was shaking…had gone way beyond trembling. It wasn't anything to do with being cold; it was the ramifications of what they'd just done and the sensuous excitement the kiss had inflamed inside her. Her knees were almost knocking together and her teeth were on the verge of chattering.

He ran the heel of his hand across his forehead. 'I wasn't… I didn't expect that.'

'Me neither. I just… I don't know.'

'When did you…? I mean…have you…? Did…?' He closed his eyes. 'I don't know what I'm saying. Sorry.'

'I… Me too.' How was it that she couldn't tell him about the weird feelings inside her?

This man had read her emails about her failed relationship, her inability to get pregnant, about needing to have sex planned on a rota to maximise fertility times. And how it had become so routine and even…boring. She doubted sex with Jono would ever be boring. Life with him was always such fun.

He knew about her tests and the results. He knew about her rage. He knew about the days off sick she'd had to take because she'd been too depressed to get out of bed and the time she'd got so self-pity drunk she'd trashed her bedroom and thrown all of Ross's clothes out of the window onto the muddy garden below.

She'd written thousands of words to him and now she couldn't find a single one to say. Eventually she managed a very lame, 'Can we forget it happened?'

'You can, maybe.' He blinked, still obviously in shock. 'But I don't know how I'm going to forget that.'

Her eyes pricked with tears. She pressed her lips together. She just wanted to stop shaking. To have thoughts that made sense, instead of this insane need to kiss him all over again, because, he was right, it had been more than good. It had been the best kiss. The feel of him in her arms, the raw taste of him…

She needed space.

She took more steps away. 'I'm going to go back to the hotel.'

A sharp nod. Then he fell into step. 'I'll come with you.'

'No.' The last thing she needed was him by her side. 'No. Please. Please don't.'

'But—'

'Please, Jono. I'm trying to process. I need to be on my own.' Then she stumbled on—trying to save some dignity as her feet sank into the sand and made her footsteps off-balance as if she was drunk on lust and on danger and regret—back to the hotel.

The kiss had been the undoing of it all.

Who would have thought that one simple thing like that, something he'd done countless hundreds, probably thousands, of times in his life with other women, could damage a relationship so quickly?

But it had been two days and she'd avoided him. Or at least that was the impression he had, because every time he turned up in the group she skidded to the periphery and sought out her other friends.

Did he even count as one now?

But tonight the group had all squeezed into a tiny trattoria, and by some quirky hand of fate they'd been seated next to each other. Which was torture. But also pretty damned great, because she was wearing a burnt orange sundress with the tiniest straps he'd ever seen. The fabric skimmed her body. Her skin had a fresh blush on it from sunbathing, her nose a little burnt. Her eyelashes had a slick of mascara which accentuated her lovely eyes and her lips had a coating of gloss which made him want to glide his tongue over and taste.

They were friends.

They were friends and it was disrespectful to want her like this. He'd spent two days pouring metaphorical cold water over his libido and it hadn't helped. But he owed it to her to stop acting like Tyler and to man up and make preserving their friendship his priority.

It was time to clear the air. He smiled at her. Not forced. He was genuinely pleased to see her. 'Hey, Lexi.'

'Hey.' In contrast she gave him a sharp, tight smile as she gripped the stem of her wine glass.

'How's things?'

'Great.' She nodded, barely making eye contact. Her gaze darted towards Preeti, as if seeking refuge. But Preeti was chatting to a blonde woman, Helen, he hadn't known before the wedding. Bhavesh and Cheng were showing each other photos on their phones. Ashley and Josh were talking football. And the other couple at the far end of the table—Emma's sister and one of the other bridesmaids, Sarah—were deep in conversation. Lexi finally turned to look at him. 'It's been a lovely couple of days.'

'How so?'

She shrugged sunburnt shoulders. 'Running, exploring the village, reading. You?'

'Went fishing yesterday with the boys. Caught some sea bass. It was this big.' He stretched his arms as wide as he could in the tight space and winked. The fish had been so small they'd thrown it back. 'Apparently, fishing's better up here on the north side because the sea's so choppy. I almost threw up. Cheng did. Gross, but the fish liked it.'

'Great,' she said without enthusiasm, even though he knew on a better day she'd have laughed or rolled her eyes or…just something more invested than this. 'I bet you're missing the Australian climate.'

'The sun's hot enough here, thanks. It gets way too hot down there.'

'Yes. It was warm today.' Her voice sounded almost mechanical. 'Emma and Mark had a good send-off last night, right? I bet they're glad they've left us here. No more medical dramas for them in honeymoon Hawaii. Here's hoping, anyway.'

'Yeah. No. Yes.' This was awful. Small talk as if they were two distant colleagues at a stuffy conference, not previously good friends. 'Did you get my text about Dean?'

'Yes.' Her shoulders dipped and she seemed to relax a little. 'It's such good news that he's out of intensive care so quickly. Although his recovery is going to take quite a while.'

'But he's on the up, that's good.' And yet she hadn't replied to the text. Seemed they couldn't even write to each other now.

'That poor family have been through a lot these past few days but, even so, Anna's made arrangements to get my car fixed. The panel beater in the village is her brother and he picked it up last night. Should be ready in time for our return journey to Oxford.'

'Great.' All squeezed into the tiny car, not knowing what to say to each other? Or how to act? He'd had enough of this. He didn't want to do small talk. They needed to move on. How were they going to live together if this was the way they communicated?

He turned to face her and to block out Ash on his other side and Preeti across the table. 'This is too freaking awkward, Lexi. Talking about the weather and being too polite is rubbish. It's not us. Can we start over?'

'I...' She closed her eyes briefly and he could see the struggle there. She clearly felt as awkward and confused as he did.

'Can we?' He leaned a little closer to speak so no one else could hear. 'Just forget about the other day? We were both emotional. It was...just one of those things.'

One of those things he'd like to do again. Especially now he was close enough to smell the scent of sunscreen on her skin, mixed with her own fresh flowery perfume. He leaned back.

She exhaled heavily and her eyes widened. 'Yes, please. I didn't know what to say to you. The last thing I ever want to do is ruin our friendship. But I don't know how to handle things.'

'So you have been avoiding me?'

'Is it that obvious?' She groaned and winced.

'To me. No one else would have noticed.'

'I'm sorry about everything.' Finally a proper smile—warm and genuine and filled with relief. 'I was starting to think we'd never get back on an even footing. Let's promise never to go there again.'

'Okay.' It was only then that he realised how much he'd wanted her to grab him and kiss him right here, say it had been amazing and that she wanted to do it again.

But then, his dating track record wasn't exactly a rule book on stability and commitment: two things she deserved after Ross had betrayed her and destroyed not just their marriage but her confidence. Plus, she was saying no and he had to respect that.

She wrinkled her nose. 'And I know I said you could be my wingman but I've decided I'm not ready for anything at all. Not even something silly and temporary or fun with you. And anyway, I'm *so* much older than you.'

She thought he just wanted a fling? Would a fling get this attraction out of their systems?

'Sure, when you're eighteen and twenty-six there's a little age mismatch, but now it's really not important. It doesn't matter. Wouldn't matter if we…were thinking of having a rerun.'

Hot need flared in her eyes. She blinked. Swallowed. 'Which we're not. But my age does matter to me, Jono. I've done the whole marriage thing and it turned out badly. We're not looking for the same things.'

'Like what?'

She glanced down at her hands. 'Marriage. Kids…'

'I—' He was about to contradict her about that. Sure, he wanted stability and a partner somewhere along the track but who, when and where he hadn't planned out. It wasn't something you just planned, right?

Lexi couldn't have kids, he knew that already, so the picture of any kind of future with her would be different to a future with another woman. But why was he even thinking about this when they'd only had one kiss and she clearly didn't want another?

But when it came to Lexi he was clearly just confused. Every part of him strained for her touch; he ached for a rerun of that kiss.

She jumped in to the gap in conversation he'd been supposed to fill. 'Besides, it's all a moot point because we're never doing that again. Okay?' She patted his hand in a very platonic way. 'You are my friend and I value that too much to risk losing it.'

He pulled his hand away. More because he was afraid he'd grasp hers than anything else. And she was right. They had something rare and open and fresh in their friendship and if things went pear-shaped between them, if their kiss had turned to sex and then to a relationship and then they'd fallen out, he wouldn't have her on his team. And he'd miss her. 'Okay. Yes. You're right.'

Didn't stop the tug towards her, though. Or the need to kiss her again.

'Right. See Helen over there?' She indicated the blonde woman. 'I've just been in the bathroom with her and she was swiping on one of those dating apps. And I had a thought that—'

'Join a dating app? Too late.' He laughed. 'Didn't I tell you about that in my emails? I've been there. Done *all* of that.'

'No, I wasn't talking about the apps. Trust me, I remember your stories.' She rolled her eyes. 'No, I was thinking… Helen. She's pretty. Single. Intelligent. Clearly looking for a partner. Lives and works in Oxford. Perfect for you.'

'Except I don't feel attracted to her.'

Her eyebrows raised. 'Looks aren't important, remember.'

'It's not about looks. I just have a feeling.'

'You haven't even spoken to her.'

'She's not my type.'

'Which is?' Lexi opened her palms, inviting him to explain.

You. He swallowed a mouthful of his craft beer and another. Until the urge to say that had gone. It didn't sit right with him, after that kiss, that she *wingmanned* him and vice versa. 'You know what? I think I'm going to just aim for simple for the rest of this week. Fishing, mates, refreshing walks... Can we just drop the wingman thing?'

She frowned. 'But Jono, you won't find that happy family future you're planning if you don't get out there and play the field. Don't blame me if you get to my age and regret you didn't date Helen.'

'Trust me, I've played, I've dated. And I have plenty of regrets. I've also rushed into too many things and not taken relationships seriously enough. So I'm going to leave it until I'm settled in the new job.'

'Wow. You've been doing a lot of thinking. Sounds like an excellent plan.' She gave him a smile that anyone else would have believed to be genuine but he knew different. 'That means I can wingman you all the more when we're living together.'

'No. Really. Drop it, Lexi. Please.' Tension spiralled through him. Right now, the only woman he wanted was Lexi and she didn't want him. 'I do not want you to find me a girlfriend and definitely not a wife.'

She blinked at him, fast. As if shocked by his words, hurt almost.

And damn, that felt bad.

Then he looked round the room and realised Bhavesh and Cheng were staring at him. He dredged up a smile and held up his now empty glass. 'So, whose round is it?'

'Yours!' A chorus of replies and a mixture of strange looks.

'Right. Leave it with me.' He climbed out of his seat, edged the opposite way from Lexi and sought refuge at the bar.

But when he looked back she was still staring at him and he could not read her. Not at all.

CHAPTER SEVEN

IT WAS LATE and she'd drunk too much wine to try and settle the panicky and sexy thoughts about Jono running through her, but Lexi still couldn't sleep. She tugged the covers over herself, then pushed them away, unsure as to whether she was too hot or too cold.

Pre-menopause?

Ugh. God, no. Surely she was too young for that?

Jono would have a field day ribbing her about it. And she would definitely, officially, be too old for him.

They'd decided they were going to be friends again, but it didn't feel like they were, especially after he'd growled at her when she'd suggested a date with Helen.

And yes, she should have answered his text, perhaps that would have helped move things along, but she'd taken one look at his name on her phone and she'd retreated inside herself. Which was the coward's way out and now she was paying for it because she didn't know where they stood.

A sharp knock at her door made her jump. With a pounding heart she jumped out of bed and peered through the little peephole.

Jono? A rush of excitement ripped through her. Her already thumping heart skipped a few beats. What did he want?

Was this…? Did he want…?

Heat pooled deep in her belly and between her legs. What else could he want, coming to her hotel room so late?

Things had been too awkward in the pub and she'd been grateful when he'd gone to buy drinks and she'd quickly swapped seats with Bhavesh so she could chat to Preeti. But they hadn't really fixed things.

He'd mentioned a rerun. Was this…?

Her cheeks flushed as she opened the door. 'Jono? This is a surprise.'

'I know it's late. I'm sorry, I just needed to see you.'

He gave her a tight smile that told her booty call wasn't on his agenda and she didn't know whether to be relieved or disappointed. Because he was doing the right thing. They were doing the right thing, but she could still remember his taste and, regardless of what they'd agreed, she ached to savour it again.

'Oh? Why?'

'I didn't want you to get up in the morning and find I've gone. I wanted you to know what's happened. For some reason you're not answering my texts, so I'm not sure if there's a problem and you're not receiving them. I know reception's a bit dodgy round here.' He stepped into the room. Once again his presence seemed to fill the space.

'Yes, I am getting them. I should have replied, I'm sorry. I didn't know what to say to you.' She put her hand on his arm. 'What's happened? Is it Dean? Has he deteriorated?'

'I don't know. I don't think so.' He swallowed and his eyes clouded with pain. 'It's my dad. He's been rushed into hospital with acute heart failure. It's not looking good. I'm getting the first train out in the morning. There's one from Truro at five-twenty.'

She looked more closely at him; beneath the sun-kissed complexion he was drawn and tired. Suddenly all the awkwardness fell away, because at the core of their connection was care and affection and nothing else mattered if he was hurting or upset. 'I'll come with you. Don't take the train, I'll drive you.'

'Your car's in the garage.'

'Oh. Yes. So I'll get the train too. You can't do this on your own, Jono. We can work out something with the car. Let me come with you.'

'Actually, I think this is something I need to do by myself.' His expression was almost haunted. But she understood his need to face his father alone, especially if there wasn't much time left. Another person would only get in the way.

'Oh, Jono, I'm so sorry. What did his specialist say?'

'His heart's straining with all the fluid. They've given him high dose diuretics and beta blockers and, of course, he's on oxygen and pain relief. They're trying to stabilise him.'

She nodded. 'I'm so sorry.'

'I just hope I have the chance to make things up with him before…' His words trailed off into the unspoken words about death.

He didn't have anything to make up, but she wasn't going to argue that with him now. It wasn't the right time. 'I'm sure you will.'

'I should have gone to see him on Sunday, after the wedding, instead of staying here. I didn't realise he'd gone downhill and instead of visiting him I played in Cornwall.' He gave a rueful laugh.

'You didn't know he was sick.'

'I just thought I had more time.' He shrugged, a hand scuffing across his hair. He looked at her, his eyes sad and serious and so unlike the Jono she knew. 'I just need…'

A hug? A kiss? The embers inside her flickered back into life. And it was so inappropriate but she wanted to hold him. To comfort him in a very un-platonic kind of way. 'Yes?'

'The spare key,' he clarified. 'To your house? So I've got somewhere to sleep once I've seen him tomorrow.'

'Oh. Yes. Right. Take this one.' She fumbled in her bag, slid a key from her key ring and gave it to him. How could she have been thinking about anything other than making sure he was okay?

He took it and nodded his thanks. 'So this is where my holiday ends. Even if everything settles down with Dad, I won't come back. Doesn't seem much point.'

'There's only a few more days left anyway. I'll be back in Oxford by the weekend. I'm so sorry things are so complicated that I can't even hug you right now.'

He frowned. 'Yes, you can. We're still friends, right?'

'Of course we are.'

But we'll never be the same again.

That was what she'd been trying to avoid all along. And yet here they were, struggling to find their way back to how things had been. Where she was organised and calm, he was chaos. Where she planned, he was spontaneous. They were completely incompatible in personality…or maybe they complemented each other, like magnets drawn to their opposing force. He never made promises he couldn't keep. Despite his many sexual exploits, he always made sure his date was on the same page as him regarding relationship goals, or lack of. He was loyal to those he cared for. He didn't ask her to change, he liked her for who she was. That was why they couldn't ruin this. She wouldn't have her *person*. The friend who was on her side.

Hoping that a good old hug could bring them back to that happy train station reunion in Oxford only a few nights ago, before things had become far too complicated, and that they could restart their old friendship again, she held her arms open and he walked into them.

He wrapped his arms around her and held her tightly, inhaling and then exhaling deeply against her cheek.

He was a good hugger, all right. Too good. She felt the heat of him against her, the solid weight of him in her embrace, and she felt as if she fitted there. As if this was *her* place. As if he were her guy.

Unbidden and inappropriate sexual need rose inside her, filling her, making her want to press all of her against all of him. But she really, really couldn't do that.

Despite her earlier indignation, he was right about the wingman thing. While the memory of that kiss hovered over them she couldn't think straight. And thinking about him with another woman just plain hurt her chest. Another woman fitting so perfectly against him...

She'd get over it, of course. But she couldn't be the one to set him up with a date.

She pulled away and watched as he pressed his lips together into a thin line, his nostrils flaring, his breathing ragged as if he was trying hard to hold it all together. And for a moment she wondered if it was an I-don't-want-to-be-hands-off kind of hold it all together, or a my-dad's-very-sick kind. Either way, she couldn't press all of herself against all of him.

Instead, she put her palm to his cheek and his eyes flickered open. 'I don't know what to say, Jono.'

'Good luck? Don't mess it up?' He gave her a wry smile, as if everyone expected him to mess everything up.

'You don't need luck. And you will not mess anything up.' She stood on tiptoe and pressed a kiss to his cheek. 'Let me know how you go. Keep in touch.'

'Haven't I always?' He turned to go, but then turned back and cupped her cheek.

For a moment they stood there, staring into each other's eyes, held by an invisible cord of want and confusion and need.

Despite what they'd agreed, the electricity crackled around them and it would have been so easy to walk straight back into his arms and place her mouth over his. But it would definitely not be the right time. It never would be.

It was late, they were tired, he was all over the place emotionally. And clearly so was she. So this time she drew on every ounce of strength she had, looked deep into his eyes and smiled. 'Goodbye, Jono.'

He looked as if he was struggling too. His eyes flickered closed again.

When he opened them there was renewed determination there. 'Yup. See you in a few days, Lexi.'

'Thought you were in Australia.' Colonel Gordon Neale was propped up in the hospital bed attached to a drip stand and oxygen tubing. Far from the well-groomed, fastidious man Jono remembered from his mother's funeral—the last time he'd had any in-person contact with his father—he looked diminished, unshaven, frail, his hands trembling. Every breath was a struggle. His skin was thin and papery and bruised with cannulas sticking out of the backs of both hands. Jono knew how much his dad would hate that, and hate to be seen like that. Weak wasn't in his vocabulary.

Having put the grapes and bottled water he'd brought onto the overbed table, Jono pulled up a plastic chair to the side of the bed and folded himself into it, thinking briefly of Lexi and her tiny car. Thinking of Lexi and that hug. The way he hadn't wanted to leave her but had forced his legs to carry him back to his hotel room. The way she'd offered to cut her holiday short just to come back to be with him. The way she'd looked at him as if desperate for things between them to be better.

Should he have agreed to her coming with him? No. He didn't want an audience for this. But, all the same, he could have done with the support.

'I came back to see *you*... Dad.' It had been so long that he'd used the word as a name it felt strange in his mouth. It would probably feel more comfortable to call him Gordon rather than Dad. All the tensions from half a lifetime ago knotted in Jono's gut again. How? Why? He was a different person now. He would not, could not feel let down by this man again.

And yet...old habits had taken root inside him.

'Heard... I was dying?' His dad shook his head wearily and paused between each word.

'I heard you were sick.' Jono wasn't ready to admit out loud that his father could soon die.

'You're a heart specialist?'

'Yes.' How did his father know that? 'I've got a job here actually, in the hospital. Start Monday.'

'Can you fix this?' Jono's dad tapped his heart and shrugged, seemingly resigned to his fate.

Was he? Did he know how serious his condition was? It wasn't Jono's job to tell him.

'Be the relative,' Derek, the cardiologist consultant, had said. *'Let me deal with the medicine.'*

But, even so, Jono had sneaked a look at his dad's charts and knew that without this swift admission to hospital, and making use of everything they had available, his father wouldn't have made it. And the surprise of it all was that his throat had clogged up with emotion. He hadn't expected to feel this much for a man who'd cut him off years ago.

'We're using the best medicine available. Are you comfortable?'

'I have tubes in just about everywhere. This…' His father pointed at the oxygen tubing in his nose. 'And these…' He flicked a hand towards the IV cannulas. 'Don't see why they can't just let me stay at home.'

'Because you need looking after until they can get your heart condition back under control.'

'No, I don't.' He might have been weak but the steel was still there in his eyes. Any chance for an argument.

'Heart failure's a cruel illness, Dad, and there's no magic bullet. But we can definitely make you feel better. We just need you to stay here to let everything settle down.' Jono inhaled a deep breath through his ragged throat and then let it out slowly. 'I'm sorry.'

Sorry for everything. For acting out as a teenager. For not insisting we stay in contact. For not seeking you out earlier. For not forging a tighter bond—any kind of bond. For not being able to save you now.

But then it had been his father who'd loosened the ties, and eventually cut them. The last time they'd been together was at Jono's mum's funeral: a broken, grief-stricken eighteen-year-old standing next to a father he'd barely seen for seven years. The odd phone call had followed, then…nothing. They were strangers now, with no knowledge of each other's lives. How could two people bound by blood be so emotionally distant?

The air stilled and Jono searched for something else to say, but he couldn't think of anything. He waited for his dad to fill the silence. And waited.

Eventually, his father caught his gaze and held it, looking at him as if he were a puzzle he needed to work out. There was nothing else there, nothing Jono was looking for anyway. No affection or regret. Then, 'I'm tired. I need to sleep.'

'That's okay.' Jono tried to make his tone light, tried to ignore the heart squeeze that almost whipped his breath away. 'I can stay while you doze, it's fine.'

The stare hardened. 'No.'

'Okay, I get it. It's exhausting, being a patient. I'll let you get some rest and come back later.'

Shaking his head, his father lay back against the pillow and closed his eyes. End of conversation. That was it? They hadn't seen each other for years and this was how it ended? 'Dad?'

He recognised the frustration in his own tone and tried to work out exactly why he'd come all this way when he'd known all along this would be the response. But at least he'd tried. A heavy weight crushed his chest. He couldn't find words.

But he was starting his job on Monday. He had every right to be in the hospital then. And on the cardiology ward. His father would damned well be seeing him.

Jono thought about adding something more but couldn't think of a single thing that would appeal to his father's parental instincts—if he had any at all—so he gave him a nod and then left, after giving the charge nurse strict instructions to inform him immediately if his father's condition changed in any way.

He strode outside into the fresh summer's day, the bright light almost blinding him, and looked up and down the street. Where to go? What to do now?

Having no plan, he wandered from the hospital down to the river and walked along the bank. Boats bobbed about on the water, a rowing boat glided by, the cox shouting orders as the mixed crew heaved the oars. Families dotted the grass, sitting on picnic rugs, kids playing, parents chatting. Happy families. The ache in his chest sharpened. Bhavesh and Preeti. Emma and Mark. All the people he knew were pairing off to form little units of their own. And here he was, trying to heal a rift with the one remaining member of his family…and failing.

He knew Oxford well, and there were probably many friends still here he could catch up with, but he didn't know them well enough to descend on them while his chest hurt this much.

Lexi.

Lexi would understand. It occurred to him that over the last few years there'd been this undeniable pull to her whenever he'd needed to chat, to share a joke…just to share his life.

He found her number on his phone and called.

No reply.

He walked for a while along streets that were familiar but different. Some shops housed the same businesses, but some were changed. His favourite Indian restaurant was now a pizza joint. The off-licence near his old rental house had closed down. Seemed Oxford had moved along just as he had. Had it been a stupid idea to come back here? He couldn't seem to bridge the gap between then and now. Maybe he should have just stayed in Australia, kept on moving.

He called her back.

Nothing.

He was about to leave a voice message, but wasn't sure what to say. Maybe she wouldn't understand. Maybe she wouldn't want to hear from him. He hesitated, then decided on, 'Hey. Just calling for a catch-up. Don't worry. See you at the weekend.'

He'd been there when she'd needed him most and she'd made his life better when he was thousands of miles away in a foreign country.

And now...now he needed her, and things had been tipped sideways into territory he couldn't navigate.

Looked like the kiss had ruined it all.

CHAPTER EIGHT

LEXI LET HERSELF into her little cottage in Old Marston village and plonked her suitcase onto the hall floor, glad to be home but half wishing her holiday had lasted another two weeks. With all the excitement of the accidents and the wedding and the kiss, she didn't feel quite as relaxed as she'd hoped to be.

But enough time had elapsed between seeing Jono and now, she'd got her head around the brief and out of character crush she'd had on him. It was gone. 'Jono? Jono, I'm back.'

No reply. She wandered through the house, calling and searching for him, but he wasn't there. Nor outside in her little courtyard garden. But he'd clearly been there because things had been moved around—not in a messy way, just out of their usual place. There were clothes hanging in the spare room wardrobe. His scent in the bathroom. A toothbrush. It all felt strangely cosy and a little terrifying.

Did she really want to be so up close and personal with him?

Ahem. Duh. Yes.

But no.

After unpacking she hopped into the shower and washed off the grime from her five-hour journey. As she was getting out she heard the front door rattle. Hot damn. He was back.

Anticipation, concern and excitement rushed through her.

Living with someone again was going to take some getting used to. Living with Jono…well, the jury was out on that. Not because of the kiss, but because she'd lived on her own for so long.

Okay. Because of the kiss too.

She hurriedly dried and dressed and found him downstairs emptying shopping bags into cupboards. Man, he looked good in a battered old grey T-shirt and soft jersey navy drawstring shorts. He was tanned and tall and all domesticated, deep in concentration, searching, she assumed, where to put the jar of chocolate spread in his hand. Her heart did a weird little hiccup.

Oops. Despite all her hopes that her attraction to him would fade, it appeared it hadn't. 'Top shelf. Next to the muesli.'

'Whoa.' He whirled round and stared at her. 'You made me jump. You're back early.'

'Ah, you know what it's like… When your holiday's finished you might as well just go straight home instead of hanging around waiting until the last moment of check-out time. How's it going?'

'Good. I was just out getting provisions.' He smiled and her heart settled. After all the awkwardness they'd had in Cornwall she'd worried things would be the same here. But maybe the distance and the space had been enough to clear the air.

'Excellent. Good to see you're making yourself at home. And…' She admired the stretch of his arm muscles as he reached for the top shelf. The way his T-shirt untucked itself from his shorts' waistband, giving her a tantalising glimpse of more exposed sun-kissed skin and the arrow of muscles around his hips, the line of dark hair just below his belly button.

Her skin prickled. He was far too hot to be here with her in this kitchen. He was staying how long? Would she survive, or die of sexual frustration by the time he'd found another place to live? She swallowed and tried to drag her eyes away. But, to her shame, just couldn't. '…house trained.'

'Indeed. You've got a great little place here. Right, there's hot chicken with pesto sauce, roasted veg salad and bread. I bought enough for two.' He held up a bottle of wine and a French bread stick. And that was impetus enough for her to sway her gaze back up to his face.

'Expecting company?' She really hoped he wasn't. Was he sticking to the *no dating until I'm settled* plan? And yet if he did have a date it would hopefully indicate to her traitorous body to cease and desist with the hot flushes every time he was close by.

He grinned and put the bread stick on the counter. 'Yes, you idiot, I meant you.'

Relief flooded through her. 'I knew that. I was just pulling your leg.'

'How was the drive back?'

She grabbed the packets of cheese and olives spilling out of his bag and put them in the fridge. 'Uneventful.'

'No bikes coming out of nowhere?'

She smiled at the memory and was dazzled by how much had happened since that journey south. 'I can laugh about it now. But, no. Thankfully, no bikes. How's your dad?'

Jono's smile flatlined. In fact his whole body seemed to slump. 'Grumpy. Basically, no change to twenty years ago. I went to see him as soon as I got back from Cornwall. We didn't exactly hit it off. He was shocked to see me and didn't seem too happy about it. I went back the next day and he pretended to be asleep. Yesterday, he was having an X-ray when I visited so I didn't see him, but the charge nurse said he was no better, no worse. I'm so bloody frustrated with him. How can he be like this right now? Now, when he needs…family?'

'You didn't expect him to be any different?'

'No.' He stared at the counter. 'But a guy can hope, right?'

She was shocked, though unsurprised, about the way his father was behaving, but cheered that Jono hadn't given up. She wanted to go and give the old man a piece of her mind, but he was sick and there were years, decades, of a vacuum between father and son. It wasn't for her to meddle, no matter how much she wanted to protect Jono.

But she wanted so much to help him too. 'Have you got anything planned this afternoon?'

He shrugged. 'Not much. Why?'

'Fancy a walk?' Being outside would also feel less claustrophobic than she was in here, with him so close. Why hadn't she bought a mansion instead of buying Ross out of this cosy two-up, two-down stone cottage? Because this was all she could afford after the divorce.

'Okay.' Jono nodded with a genuine smile. 'Where to?'

'Some old haunts.'

'Really?' Although his eyes lit up with what she could only describe as enthusiasm. 'You live here, Lexi. It'll be boring for you.'

She doubted anything would be boring with Jono in tow. 'Actually, no. I'm so busy with work I never go to that part of the city. I could do with stretching my legs after that drive.'

'Okay. Let's pack a picnic.'

Half an hour later they wandered towards Christ Church college, stopping every few steps to talk about a party or event they'd attended here and there around Oxford. It was lovely to wander these streets with an old friend, just like old times. If old times had been filled with thoughts of how sexy Jonathan Neale was and her body had ached to touch him.

He was laughing about a prank they'd played on another friend when he turned to her and smiled. To anyone else it would have meant nothing but happiness, but the way his mouth curved and his eyes were lit up with mischievousness and a shared history and intimacy, something inside her just cracked open. And with that came the panic. She couldn't keep having these reactions to him. She just couldn't. It was a betrayal of everything they'd agreed on.

She decided to focus on work. 'How did it feel being back in the old hospital?'

He grinned. 'Other than my dad being there? Great, actually. Most things are reassuringly in the same place, even some of the same staff. So I won't need much orientation when I start on Monday. Should we go in together?'

'I cycle.'

He laughed. 'We could get a tandem. Now, there's a thought.'

'Absolutely no way am I getting on a tandem with you, or anyone. I'm a professional, respected doctor. That would totally ruin any credibility.'

'Okay, then. Tandem is out.' He nudged her. 'In that case I should probably get a bike too.'

She had visions of them cycling along the river path to work every morning like a married couple. And the panic intensified. Too cosy. Too couply. Too everything. 'I'd hang fire with that idea too, Jono. You don't know where you're going to end up living. You might have to drive in.'

'Want to get rid of me already? We haven't managed one night under the same roof. That is, if you're still happy to have me here?'

Happy? She didn't know if that was how she felt. Truth was, she was still all over the place, blindsided by her attraction to him. And wondering how she would last the next few days or weeks, or even months, with him in the room next to her. 'You can stay as long as you want. I just don't want you to waste your money on a bike if you don't need one. But if you're keen, there's always someone selling one. Look on the local social media pages.'

'I will.' He stopped walking and turned to her, suddenly serious. 'So, we're good? You and me?'

Her heart squeezed. 'Yes, we're good, Jono. Of course we're good. You're one of my closest friends. I'd hate that things were weird.'

'No one wants weird.' He pulled a face and his gaze slid to something behind her. 'Hey, that's new. Fancy an ice cream?'

She turned to see a gelato shop. After pretending that things were good between them and, in fact, lying because he was still hot and she was still noticing, she hoped the ice would cool down her raging libido. 'Sure.'

Having bought their ice creams they wandered along St Aldates, Christchurch college's familiar and imposing Tom Tower in the distance. In between licks Jono asked, 'What did I miss down in Cornwall?'

'Nothing much. We had plenty of fresh air and walks. Preeti, Helen and I had some amazing cream teas in the cute cafés along the main street. The boys went fishing again. I finished two books. It was so lovely just to relax and unwind.'

'Two? Man, you read as ardently as you do everything else.'

'Ardently? No one's ever said that about me before.'

He nodded. 'Yes, absolutely. With intention. Focus. You decide on a course of action then you stick to it.'

I wish. Because deciding not to want him and then actually not wanting him wasn't happening. 'I like setting rules and boundaries and goals. And you like—'

'Breaking them. I know.' He licked his salted caramel gelato. 'This is delicious. Want a taste?'

He held it out to her and she sucked the peak, their eyes meeting as she held her cookies and cream flavoured one to his lips and watched as he licked round the base with a long, slow movement of his tongue and devilment in his eyes. The man was nothing but a flirt. But it did the trick of seducing her back to wondering just what else he could do with that tongue. How good he would taste now…a mix of salted caramel and sexy spice.

With force, she drew her gaze back to the ice cream. 'We have very different techniques.'

'I have lots of techniques, Lexi.' He leaned closer. 'It's what keeps the women interested.'

'Oh, yeah?' She nodded and pulled an *I don't believe you*, face.

'Oh, yes,' he whispered, his eyes meeting hers for just a fraction too long. But long enough to make her insides turn to liquid heat. Then he dragged his gaze away and laughed. This was such a typical Jono thing she tried not to take it seriously. The guy was smooth and charming and funny…with every woman.

She rolled her eyes and shook her head, pretending he'd had no effect on her at all. 'You are such a tart.'

'I know. It's in my DNA.' He winked and laughed, even though she knew he was referring to his father's many affairs. 'Talking of. How was Ashley from Swindon?'

'Nice. Kind. Funny. Not a tart at all.' She dug at him.

The light in his eyes dimmed a little. 'Did you have any…alone time?'

Interesting. He'd agreed not to have a rerun of the kiss, but she remembered he'd suggested one, back in that Italian restaurant. He'd absolutely agreed not to pursue anything with her, but…did he still want to? Was he still attracted to her? But heck, she'd initiated the kiss— had he ever been attracted to her? Really? Or had the kiss just been a hot-blooded response on his part?

Ugh. It was all so confusing. 'Can you remember what I told you, Jono? In Cornwall?'

'Yes. That I'm a good man. Worth kissing…even if only once.'

'Nope.' She felt the creep of heat in her cheeks, shook her head. 'Not that. Try again.'

He laughed. 'You told me that you're not ready for dating. Because of what Ross put you through.'

'Yes. And four days later I'm still not ready. He hurt me and I thought I'd got over it, but I can't help protecting myself from all risks. Ashley would be a risk.'

'Hey, come on. Swindon's not *that* bad. Neither is accountancy or whatever it is that he does.'

'IT. Or something.' She chuckled as she raked through

her memory, because truthfully she'd paid the man very little attention. 'But no, no alone time with Ashley.'

'Good.'

'What does that mean?'

'It means you're sticking to your decision-making.' Having wolfed down his gelato, he wrapped an arm round her neck and landed a very cold and very platonic kiss on her forehead. 'Never change, Lexi Fisher.'

She didn't know how to take that. It wasn't the first time he'd said it, but now it just made her sound boring and old. But did he mean that?

She'd started to realise she coloured other people's words with her own slant and her own prejudices about being old. He didn't mean old and boring, he meant that he liked her the way she was. And that had to be one of the nicest things anyone had ever said to her.

Having been told by the ticket office they could visit for free because they were alumni, they wandered into the college quad. Lexi pointed towards the fountain and statue of Mercury in the centre of the lawns. The water had been turned off but there was still some in the pool. She peered down at the lily pads. 'Looks like the dye has gone.'

'Of course it has. I made sure of it. And it was a very long time ago.' He stopped walking and inhaled, hands on his hips, looked around at the honey-coloured stone buildings. 'I just want to see if any of it has changed.'

'It's reassuringly the same, I think. Remember when we were here? Running around, late for class or escaping for a pint. It feels like yesterday and yet so long ago. Weird how the mind plays tricks.' The university was closed for summer break, but it wouldn't be long before the students poured back in. 'I envy them their life ahead of them.'

He eyed her curiously. 'What would you do differently?'

'I don't know. Because if I hadn't married Ross I wouldn't be here, eating gelato, having just had a lovely holiday with friends. It's been a mixed life, really. Lots of ups and downs. But it got me to here. And I'm proud of who I am and where I'm at. Sure, there are things I'd have loved…like kids and everything, but I think I can manage without them. I have to. And I'm okay with that. I love my work and I get to see lots of babies and children every day. Better still, I take their pain away. Can't want more than that, right?'

He smiled at her. 'I know how hard it's been for you to get to this point. But I'm so glad you've worked through it.'

'Me too. No point yearning for something I can't have.' There was a lesson there. 'What about you? Any regrets? Anything you'd have done differently?'

'I'd like to say I'd have taken life more seriously, but I'm glad I didn't. I'm glad I went to Australia on a whim. I'm glad I've had a lot of fun. I had a difficult start but it's been a good life. Mostly. I have friends. I've fallen in and out of love.'

'Lust,' she corrected him.

'Probably lust, yes. There's been a lot of that.' He playfully wiggled his eyebrows at her, then grew serious again. 'But I wonder if my dad would be able to say that he's had a good life. He's all alone now with no loved ones around him at the very end. It's sad. Because that's what's important, right? The people you love. The love you give.'

And she could see Jono had a lot to give. What would he be like as a lover? She imagined he'd be a lot of fun.

But as a partner? She couldn't imagine. She knew him too well...and yet not at all. Because this Jono was different from the one she'd studied with, and even the one she'd exchanged emails with.

This Jono had serious moments, was giving consideration to a future, was concerned about his father. Sure, she'd known he was a good man, but hadn't realised, or had chosen to ignore, that the core of him was decent and honest and caring.

'What's the matter?'

His voice startled her and she realised she'd been lost in her thoughts. A blush crept up her neck. Dreaming about how Jono would be in bed should *not* happen when she was with Jono in real life. Not in bed. Nowhere near a bed. Never near a bed. 'Oh, nothing. Just thinking...you know.'

'Enough of being serious.' He raised a palm. 'We have barely two more days of freedom, then we're back at work. Let's go do something we're probably going to regret.'

Uh-oh. She had a list of things she wanted to do and then probably regret, and it started and ended with him. 'Like what?'

'Take a boat out on the river.'

'What? I was expecting you to say let's get drunk or something. Punt? That is such a touristy thing to do. I haven't been in one since my student days and even then it was under duress.'

'Exactly. No one living in Oxford would be seen dead doing it, but it's actually fun. Let's play tourists. Come on.'

'Okay, but you can do the hard work, because I'm letting you stay rent free.'

They strolled through the meadow with its avenues of

lime and poplar trees, past Merton Field and the Botanic Gardens, reminiscing and giggling as they went. Paid for the boat and chose the one that looked the most stable. 'Right.' Lexi stepped into it, cushions tucked under her arms and picnic bag in her hand. She shrieked as it wobbled. 'Hold it steady while I climb in.'

'It's a flat-bottomed boat, Lexi. It won't tip over.' He raised his eyebrows and pushed his hands towards her as if to push her in. Then he stepped in, shifting his weight heavily from one foot to the other to rock the boat.

'Stop that right now, Jono Neale.' She giggled and took her seat at the front of the boat while Jono picked up the long punting pole and pushed off.

She leaned back against the plastic cushion and watched him strain as he pushed the pole down into the water, then rhythmically pick it up, rinse and repeat. 'This is the life.'

'Your life, maybe. But my arm's soaked already.' Grinning, he flicked his hand at her, but he was too far away for any drips to touch her.

'Your technique's all wrong, that's why.'

'My technique is fine, Lexi. Look.' He dipped the pole in then pulled it out. 'Ta-dah! We moved. *We are sailing...*' he started to sing. Badly.

'No, you idiot.' But he looked so proud and silly and just damned gorgeous standing there with the pole she couldn't help laughing. 'You're putting the pole in at the wrong angle. And you take it out too soon. You're supposed to go hand over hand all the way up the pole.'

He stared at her. 'Wow, you really paid attention to the man's instructions.'

'Of course.'

'That's why you were always top of the class. You actually pay attention.'

'Someone has to. Or we'd still be back at the boat-house. Use the pole as a rudder. We need to go left.' She laughed again as he dipped the pole back into the water and the boat edged to the right. 'No, the other left, Jono.'

'Okay. Okay.' Still laughing, he stopped punting and let the pole drag in the water behind them. 'You do it then.'

'No way. We agreed you'd do all the heavy lifting here.'

'Not if you're going to criticise.'

'I'm helping you improve.'

His eyebrows rose. 'Honey, I don't need to improve.'

'And I don't need to hear that. You have a one-track mind, Jono Neale. I really do need to find you a date. How soon can you settle into your job? A day? Two?'

'Got anyone in mind?'

'Not anyone I work with. But I'll have a chat with Charge Nurse Chantelle first thing Monday. We need to get you a girlfriend.' The memory of that kiss pulsed through her, hitting her full in the chest. Jono was her friend, her person. The one she shared everything with. She wasn't sure she could share him with someone else. And maybe he didn't need to improve his sexual prowess, but his punting was woeful.

They were on a collision course with the riverbank. Wet weeping willow branches trailed over her hair and face like spiders' webs. She flicked them off. 'Ugh. Gross. Right, let me do it. I can't watch any more.'

'Okay.' He shrugged and held up a hand. 'You asked for it. Don't blame me when you can't move your sore muscles tomorrow.'

She clambered up and stepped towards him at the same time that he closed in on her. With not enough space to not touch, they brushed against each other.

'Here.' He held out the pole. Everything swayed. 'Grab this. Quick.'

'The boat wobbled—' she giggled '—you said it wouldn't wobble.'

'Stay still.' He grabbed her waist and slid towards her, then faced her while holding her steady in one place. His knee connected with hers, his thigh, his hip, their faces so close they were almost touching. And even though it should have taken a nanosecond to squeeze past each other, she froze. She could see the stubble of his unshaven jaw, the different hues of brown in his hair: gold, sand, russet and, to her surprise, some grey she hadn't noticed before. Not enough to make him silver fox worthy, but enough to hammer home that he was maturing too. She wasn't the only one.

And here was the thing: Jono didn't make her feel younger, or older. Or more mature or more anything, except more like herself. The self she'd lost somewhere along the way in the mire of infertility and divorce and work. The self who'd forgotten how to laugh and not take herself too seriously. It wasn't an age thing—it was an attitude thing.

She loved his attitude to life, enjoyed it. Pure and simple.

Bones and muscles and flesh and heat. Hard and soft. Smooth and rough. Jono's body tight up against hers. Not wanting to move in case the boat rocked some more and…not wanting to move in case he let go of her. He was so strong and solid all up against her. So there. So Jono. So much of a man.

Heat burst through her. *Also inappropriate.*

How on earth could she feel sexy standing up on a wobbling boat? But he was still laughing and she could see the light and the danger in his eyes and right now he was just about the sexiest thing she had ever seen.

He edged one leg past her and the boat lurched sideways. She grasped his wrist. 'Whoa. Now you're making it wobble more.'

'I am not making it wobble, Lexi. It just *is* wobbling. If you stopped laughing that might help. One of us needs to sit down.'

She reached out and took hold of the pole with her free hand. 'I can't let go of you or I'll fall in.'

'No, you won't. I've got you. You're fine.'

She was not fine. She was too aware of him. She needed to let go. With regret and relief she managed to prise her fingers from his arm and edged to the back of the boat, using the pole as a stabiliser.

He sat down in the seat she'd just vacated and watched her punting action. 'Wrong angle, my friend.'

'It is not the wrong angle.' Water was dribbling down her arm. 'Ugh. It's cold.'

'I know. Exhibit A.' He held up the soaked sleeve of his black cotton jacket. 'So where's the expertise now? How come you're getting just as wet as I did?'

'Punting's actually quite hard.' She was still giggling so hard her belly hurt as she bent her knees to push the pole deep into the water. 'But awesome. Look, I can steer.'

'I know. You're doing great, really.' He leaned back and closed his eyes. 'Wake me up when we get there.'

'Charming.'

'Always.' He winked and bowed his head. Then closed his eyes again.

'Hey, you're not allowed to sleep while I'm working.' More giggles burst from her throat because this was turning out to be a lot more fun than she'd first imagined. In fact, she could have fallen into the water right now and she'd have been fine, she could swim. She'd just get wet and nothing would matter at all.

How long since she'd felt like this? Ever? Never. She'd spent her married years calculating ovulation dates, living with tension every time her period arrived, wishing and hoping and thinking everything would be all right as soon as she was pregnant. It hadn't been living, it had been surviving, delaying any kind of joy until she'd achieved the unachievable.

But here, with Jono, she was herself.

After a few moments his eyes flickered open and he rubbed his stomach. 'I'm starving. Where are the snacks?'

'In the bag, but can't you wait until we reach dry land?'

He peered across the twenty or so metres from one bank to the other and winked. 'I don't know if I can wait that long.'

'Five minutes? Oh, yes, you can, my man. I don't want you snaffling all the rations. No one eats unless we both eat.'

He groaned. 'Then hurry up with your punting and let's get ashore, me hearty.'

'I'm trying my hardest.' She laughed, pushing the pole in faster and harder, getting soaked in the process and not giving a damn.

This is, hands down, the best date I've ever been on. What the hell?

Panic rippled through her. Had she said that out loud? She stole a look at his face. But he was still lying there like some sort of reclining god, eyes closed.

The laughter stalled in her throat as reality flooded her chest like a cold damp squib.

This was not a date. And he was not her man.

CHAPTER NINE

THEY FOUND A quiet place to stop to eat the picnic and disembarked. After munching on chicken and salad sandwiches and juicy peaches Lexi lay down on the picnic rug and stared up at the brilliant blue sky, relieved Jono hadn't been able to read her thoughts. This was not a date. She sighed. 'This is the perfect end to my holiday.'

'Hey. This isn't the end. We have one more day.'

'But you know what tomorrow's going to be like. Holiday washing to do, sorting out stuff for work.'

'Sharpening your pencils. Finding your gonk.'

Confused, she sat up. 'Gonk?'

'You know, those little plastic trolls with sticky-up neon hair. Purple. Pink. Blue. Everyone had one when I was a kid. Mine had blue hair.'

'I never had a gonk or a troll.'

'Aww. You poor neglected child.' He stroked the back of his hand down her cheek.

'I know. The emotional trauma.' Then she wondered if she'd said the wrong thing, because even though Jono's father hadn't ever hurt him he'd apparently cut him off emotionally from a young age. Her parents had always been so supportive—lack of gonk provision not withstanding—she couldn't imagine not having them on her side.

But he was just laughing and shaking his head. 'Now I know what to get you for Christmas. Do they even sell gonks these days?'

'I have no idea.' She lay back down and tried to ignore the rise of heat at his touch. Mentally ran through her to-do list, reminding herself that Jono Neale was definitely not on it. 'Packing my lunches for the next five days.'

'Five days? You don't get food in the canteen?'

'I eat on the run, usually when I'm doing paperwork. We don't get a lot of breaks...' The place where he'd touched her cheek still simmered from his fingers. Her whole body simmered, craving more. 'Going through my inbox and sorting out the important stuff. A word of warning—we get a lot of emails from management.'

'I'm used to it. Some people get clicky with the reply-all button.'

'This is next level emailing.'

He shook his head. 'Work talk is forbidden.'

'But I'm just—'

'Lexi Fisher.' His hand covered her mouth. 'Do not torture me with work. That's for tomorrow. Let me have one more day's peace.'

She giggled under his hand and tried to wiggle free. He'd rolled close to her, his face inches above hers. His eyes were shining with laughter, his face a perfect picture of fun.

He laughed and she felt the weight of his body against hers. The pressure of his thighs. His heat. The breeze of his breath when he laughed.

And for a moment, when their eyes met and held, she thought about reaching for him and pulling him down for a kiss. She imagined another day, in another life when she might have lain her head on his lap and read a book, or chatted, or kissed him. There'd be a lot of kissing.

But instead of kissing him she smiled and struggled to sit up. 'How about we open that wine?'

'Sure.' He nodded and jumped back, as if he too had realised the folly of them being so close. 'You grab the glasses and I'll pop the cork.'

He was reaching for the bubbles bottle when his phone rang. He pulled it out of his shorts' pocket and looked at the screen. The colour drained from his face. 'It's the hospital.'

His dad. It had to be about his dad. She nodded, all joy leeching out of her too. 'Quick. Take it.'

He scrambled up and wandered along the riverbank as he spoke to the caller. She watched his shoulders straighten, as if steeling himself for bad news. The paced steps. Back and forth. Back and forth.

Hoping it wasn't bad news, she held her breath, waiting and watching.

When he slipped the phone back into his pocket he stood for a moment, staring at the water, while she packed the picnic away. Not wanting to spook him or crowd him, she edged closer but not too close. Keeping her voice gentle, the way she did with concerned parents and scared children, she said, 'What is it?'

He turned to look at her but she couldn't read his expression. 'My dad.'

'Oh, Jono. Is he…?' *Dead?*

He obviously understood what she was alluding to but he shook his head, his features filling with hope. 'He wants to see me.'

'Okay. That has to be good news, right?'

A hesitant nod. 'It's the first time he's shown any interest.'

And it was the first time she'd ever seen that light in his eyes when he spoke about his father. Hope. She just prayed this wasn't going to end up hurting him in the long run. 'He wants you to go there now?'

'Yes.'

But she'd seen this kind of thing play out before. It could be an overwhelming and loving reunion; it could be disinterest; it could be selfish self-flagellation on his dad's part. Any of those and Jono would need emotional support. She zipped the cool bag closed. 'Then let's get the hell out of here.'

Lexi stayed by his side as they rushed down the hospital corridors. She hadn't questioned, just acted. But when they reached the ward she stopped, her hand on the small of his back like a gentle act of kindness, a comfort. She smiled softly and he saw genuine affection and care in her expression as she said, 'Do you want me to come in with you?'

Did he? No. But having someone else there might help. 'I don't really want to saddle you with my grumpy father, but yes please.'

'Sometimes you just need a buffer. I'm right here.'

The mixed-up emotions swirling in his chest—hope mixed with anxiety—slowed with her words. Just knowing she was there gave him courage enough to face his dad one more time. He went to push open the ward door but heard her say, 'Jono. Wait.'

When he turned she was looking up at him, arms outstretched. 'Come here.'

He slipped his arms round her waist and held her. He hadn't had to say anything about how he was feeling about his father. She seemed to understand. Or understood enough not to ask. 'Cheers, mate.'

She winked. 'Okay. It'll be fine. Whatever happens, you'll be fine.'

And he knew to trust her on that, because she'd been through enough emotional upheaval and she'd come out whole.

Once on the ward he could see his dad's condition hadn't deteriorated as he'd imagined. In fact, his colour was much better, his breathing—although still laboured—was easier. His eyes were less cloudy and he was sitting up, dressed in tartan pyjamas, in a wingback chair by his bed.

Some people lived with heart failure for years, others weren't so lucky. He just hoped his dad fell into the former category and that this positive response to the new drugs would last.

Jono hovered at the side of the bed. 'Hey, Dad.'

'Jonathan.' His father's eyes flickered open then strayed to Lexi. 'And…?'

Jono wrapped an arm round her waist. Call him territorial and possessive, but his father had charm form. 'This is my friend, Lexi. We were just out punting on the river when we got the call from the charge nurse to come see you.'

'Lexi.' Immediately, his father's normally gruff voice seemed to mellow, and was it Jono's imagination or was his dad smiling at her? Typical Gordon Neale, the charmer.

'Hi, Colonel Neale. Nice to meet you.' Smiling politely, Lexi sat down at the far end of the bed, leaving the chair close to his father for Jono to sit in.

His chest heaved with the pain of watching his father suffer, but soothing everything was the knowledge that he had her by his side. She'd been funny and relaxed today; he'd never seen her look more beautiful than when she'd been giggling on the boat.

'Lexi. Nice name.' Gordon nodded and closed his eyes. 'I had a good woman once. I messed that up.'

'I know.' But Jono wasn't going to attack his father with reminders of his many indiscretions or marital affairs. It was clear enough that he knew he'd acted badly. If he wanted to seek solace or forgiveness it was for him to ask for it, not for Jono to offer it.

'You wanted to see me, Dad?'

A slow nod.

'What about?'

'I'm not feeling too well.'

'I know, Dad.'

Silence stretched. Jono waited. He'd seen the way these scenarios played out many times between long-lost relatives. It was rarely the fairy tale ending that everyone wanted. His father had asked to see him; that was one step. Did he have something particular he wanted to say? Or maybe he just wanted company.

Jono's eyes slid to the name card above the bed. *Gordon Neale.* No status or rank. In hospital everyone was treated equally; what your job was or who you were had no bearing on the way you were cared for. He wondered how his dad felt about that.

Eventually his father spoke again. 'What do you do?'

'I'm a doctor.' Confused, Jono glanced quickly at Lexi, who shook her head, concern written over her pretty face. Then he peered more closely at his father. Maybe he was cyanotic, oxygen not reaching his brain, because he knew his only child was a doctor.

'No.' Gordon frowned and growled, a dim echo of the indomitable man he'd once been. 'Spare time? Sport? Still playing tennis?'

'I haven't played tennis since high school. I played

five-a-side football at uni. I surfed and hiked a lot in Australia. I play a bit of golf—'

'I was a great…football player.' Even though Gordon cut him off, his words were interspersed with ragged breaths.

'I know. Captain of the regiment's team, right?' Jono remembered the day, when they were living in family barracks in Germany, his father had come home drunk, crowing about the goals he'd scored. How he'd been man of the match for the last three games. How much the team needed him. And he also remembered that, in comparison, Colonel Neale had never once asked how Jono's tennis matches had gone. It wasn't that his father had been neglectful so much as disinterested and self-absorbed.

Pride simmered in his father's dull blue gaze. 'You don't get to play for the regiment if you're…not good.'

'Yeah. I guess.'

'Left-footed or right-footed?'

'Left.' A father should know that. A father should have shown some interest in his son's life. 'What did you really want to talk about, Dad?'

His father shrugged. 'I just wanted to see you. To let you know it's okay for you…to visit.'

'Great. That's good.' No *I'm sorry*. No *Let's try to be better*. Definitely no *I love you*.

Raw emotion filled Jono's throat. But what had he expected? Gordon Neale was not an emotional man… No, strike that. He'd shown a smattering of anger before the eventual divorce, if Jono's mother complained about his drinking or late nights, and a decent amount of charm with the women, he'd laughed with his mates, he'd adored being the centre of attention. He wasn't an affectionate man, at least not to his family.

'I've…um…got to…go.' Gordon dragged a walking frame from next to his chair and shakily stood.

'Go where?' Jono frowned and jumped up. What was he missing here?

'To pee.' His father's hands gripped the frame so tightly his knuckles were white. 'Doctor's orders. They've stopped all that measuring fluids nonsense and now I've got to go to the actual toilet. Or they won't let me home.'

Ah, yes. Jono put his hand on his father's back to help steady him. 'Let me walk with you.'

'No!' It was more growl than a word. 'I can manage.'

Jono cursed silently. He shouldn't have insinuated his dad couldn't do something, even though he was clearly struggling. Any sign of weakness was unforgivable. 'I can get a nursing assistant to help if you prefer—'

'There's never one around. I'm fine.' Gordon wearily shook his head and took a step forward. 'Bloody diuretics. I might as well set up home in the bathroom.'

Suitably rebuffed, Jono scraped his chair closer to Lexi and they watched in silence as Gordon slowly inched towards the bathroom, his whole body trembling with the effort.

Lexi reached over and squeezed Jono's hand. 'How are you holding up?'

He shrugged, his attention momentarily distracted as he watched his father close the bathroom door. 'I didn't know what to expect, to be honest. I certainly didn't think it was going to be small talk about my left or right foot.'

'You know how it is.' She crinkled her nose. 'People don't know what to say when they're nearing the end of their lives. Everything's either too important or not important at all. He acknowledged he did wrong by your mum; maybe that was his olive branch. It may be the best he has.'

'I guess. I don't know if we're ever going to break through.'

'Maybe you won't. We don't always get a resolution to things. Life is messy.'

He turned and smiled at her, taking in her freckled nose and large brown eyes. 'Oh, wise one. I wish you didn't know that.'

'It's okay. And this isn't about me. It would be wonderful if you did heal that rift with him, but I don't want you to expect that to happen. Your relationship with him is complicated.'

'You can say that again. Complicated by a complete lack of communication for the best part of twenty years.'

'Maybe you could use his interest in sport as a way of forging a connection. Does he support a particular team? Perhaps you could find some memorabilia or something to take him. It would give you both a focus that isn't just on you two. That's the kind of approach we get parents to adopt with teenagers when communication has broken down.'

'You want me to be the adult?' He couldn't help but laugh at the irony of that, although she was right. What he needed to do was stop waiting for his father to take the lead. He should just be the successful, professional, capable adult Lexi kept telling him he was.

Man, she was good for his ego.

'Just be yourself, Jono. He'll either see the true you or he won't. If he doesn't then at least you know you've tried. That's what we all want, in the end, right? To know that we've shown up and done our best in whatever situation is thrown at us. Be the better person. Be kind. Turn up, day after day.' She squeezed his arm.

Jono looked at the closed bathroom door. 'He's been a long time.'

'Everything takes longer when you're weak.' She raised her eyebrows.

They sat for a few minutes, waiting.

And waiting.

And waiting.

Jono looked at his watch. 'This is ridiculous, he's been twenty minutes. I'm going to knock on the door and see if he's okay.'

She nodded, although she didn't seem as concerned as he felt. Maybe he was overreacting, but something told him he wasn't. He stood and took a deep breath, imagining what his father's reaction might be to Jono hammering on the bathroom door. 'Okay.'

He knocked hard three times. No answer. 'Dad? Dad, are you okay?'

Lexi came over. 'Has he answered you?'

'No. And I don't think he's being bloody-minded.'

'Okay. There's a way to open these doors without a key. Here.' She calmly slid out a coin and wiggled it in the lock. Her movements were assured and steady. He needed that from her right now.

She pulled the door open.

Jono inhaled sharply as he surveyed the scene. Something tightened round his chest like a vice. They'd run out of time. 'No. Dad.'

Emotions tumbled through him.

His father was slumped face down on the floor, the Zimmer frame upended and a pool of blood oozing from underneath him. Jono knelt and felt for a pulse. Exhaled when he found one. But what the hell…? 'He's alive. He's alive. Lexi, get help.'

'I've pressed the alarm button.' Her hand was warm

and reassuring on his back but she knew the drill. 'I'll go hurry up the team.' Then she disappeared out into the ward.

Jono stroked his father's cheek. 'Dad, can you hear me? Dad?'

A flicker of eyelids. Then a croak, 'Jon...?'

'Thank God. Yes. It's me. Your son.' His voice cracking at that simple word, Jono did a quick assessment. Heartbeat was erratic but what he'd expect for someone with heart failure. Breathing rapid. Lips blue-tinged. 'What happened?'

'Dizzy.'

'Okay.' All the possible reasons why his father might be dizzy ran through Jono's mind. A reaction to the tablets? Too high a dose? Blood pressure? Low? High? A cardiac event? Had he thrown off an embolism? Stroke? A vasovagal collapse? 'Lexi's gone to get help. We'll get you back to your bed and then we can work out what's going on. Do you remember falling over?'

Where was the blood coming from? Lexi was right; despite being a trained doctor, giving care to someone you knew was hard.

'Dizzy.'

'So you were dizzy before the fall? And now? Are you still dizzy?'

'Don't know.'

'Does anywhere hurt?'

'Everywhere.'

Jono looked at the seep of blood on his dad's pyjamas. Where was it coming from? 'Look, Dad, can I roll you over and just make sure you haven't damaged anything in the fall?'

'The team's on its way.' Lexi's voice had him turning to look at her, standing in the doorway, breathless from rushing, her cheeks pinked up. He was beyond glad she was here.

'There's no room for more than one person.' But he watched her wedge herself into the room, determination shining in her eyes. 'Okay. Can you give me a hand to sit him up?'

'Of course.' She knelt at Gordon's other side and together they managed to sit him up.

'Wheelchair right here, if we can get him up.' One of the nurses placed the wheelchair in the open doorway and somehow they shuffled his father into it.

Then Jono was able to investigate where the blood was coming from. He almost laughed with relief, if it wasn't for the fact he needed to speak to the cardiac team and between them work out the cause of the fall. 'His cannula's ripped out of his vein. That's all.'

'It bloody hurts.' His father grimaced and Jono noted his breathing was getting worse. 'I need the portable oxygen before we move him and the team are going to want an ECG and bloods taking.'

Lexi's voice soothed his fraying grip on control. 'The team's here. Let them sort it out. You're the relative, remember?'

'Right.' He looked over and saw his dad's cardiac team rushing over. 'But I'm staying here until we know what's happening.'

'And I'll stay with you.' Lexi slid her hand into his, a lifeline that he gripped.

He might have paced. He might have snapped at the nurse when the ECG paper ran out. He might have silently prayed not to lose his father before they had time to reconnect. And he wasn't a praying man.

But eventually the ECG and other vitals came back

with nothing unexpected or out of the ordinary. Maybe it was just a dizzy spell after all.

But now he knew the answer to how he'd feel if his dad was hurt: useless, panicky and determined to bridge the chasm between them before it was too late. Whether Gordon wanted him to or not, Jono was not going to look back and regret not trying.

It was late when they finally left the ward, despite Gordon's remonstrations that he was fine and to go home.

As they wandered down the hospital corridor Lexi breathed out a long sigh. 'Well, wow, I'm wired now. I'm so glad there's nothing serious going on, on top of his heart condition.'

'I'm so glad you were here to help.' He stopped and turned to her, wanting desperately to hold her. Hell, they hugged all the time these days, but right now he wasn't sure if he'd ever let go. She'd become his rock; she steadied him.

'You'd do the same for me, right? That's what friends are for.' She grinned. 'Hey, we've still got that bottle of wine. Let's go open it. That is, unless there's something else you'd rather do?'

He had lots of ideas but they'd made a promise. *Friends.*

'Excellent idea.' Just being with her, just him and Lexi, would be enough.

CHAPTER TEN

'How was the trip? Did you get lots of relaxing me-time?' Chantelle asked Lexi at the end of the Monday morning rush of locating patients and doing catch-up ward rounds, fitted around on-call duties. 'Sorry I haven't had a chance to ask before, it's mayhem in here today. But you're looking rested and tanned so I'm guessing you had a good time.'

'It was great, thanks.' Lexi wasn't sure how much to say without giving herself away about Jono. She had a bad feeling that she couldn't hide her expressions too well from her colleague. 'The first half of the week was full of wedding and post-wedding excitement, plus we had a medical emergency that involved a hang-glider versus rocks.'

'Ouch.' Chantelle looked up from the computer monitor at the nurses' station and winced. 'Nasty.'

'It was. Luckily for him, we had our own medical team on hand.' She tried not to think about the after-math of that particular adventure: the *kiss*. 'The rest of the week was pure bliss of sunbathing, reading and eating far too many cream teas.'

Chantelle's gaze slid over Lexi's body in admiration. 'And yet you haven't put on an ounce, lucky duck. And the sexy surfers—how did that go?'

'I saw some from a distance when I was out running.' Lexi laughed and sat down next to Chantelle and tapped the keyboard on the free computer. 'That was about as close as I got.'

'No holiday romance?'

'None whatsoever.' *Liar.* But it hadn't been a romance, had it? It had been a kiss and they were over it. Done and dusted. Forgotten—or at least put aside. They'd had a nice easy chat over wine last night and nothing remotely sexual had happened. Nothing mentioned. Nothing tried. She'd been on her best behaviour, even though it had almost killed her to lie in bed knowing he was in the next room. 'Although I do have a souvenir.'

'Ooh?' Chantelle's eyes lit up. 'What is it? A stick of rock? Cornish pasty? Fudge? Please tell me it's clotted cream fudge.'

Any of the above would have been easier. A stick of rock wouldn't walk around topless after a shower, with honed muscles and broad expanses of skin on show. A Cornish pasty wouldn't have brushed past her this morning in the too-small-for-two kitchen—which had resulted in her fingers accidentally trailing over aforementioned bare torso as she'd reached for the kettle—when she was bleary-eyed and uncoordinated and trying to get her coffee fix. Of all her friends, why did he have to be the best-looking, the funniest, the most sexy? 'His name is Dr Jonathan Neale and he's the new cardiologist here at the hospital. He's staying at my place for a few weeks until he finds somewhere of his own to live.'

'And...?' Her colleague grinned as if she'd been the one eating all the clotted cream.

Lexi knew exactly what Chantelle was asking but wasn't going to be reeled in by it. 'And *what*?'

Chantelle bugged her eyes. 'What's he *like*?'

'Jono? Oh, you know. Male. Mid-thirties.' *Gorgeous. Great kisser.* 'I've known him for years.'

'Single? Married? What? Come on, girl. Details.'

Lexi couldn't help giggling at Chantelle's enthusiasm. 'Just relocated from Australia. Single.'

'And ready to mingle? Is he good-looking? Do you—'

'No, to whatever it is you're going to ask.' Lexi rolled her eyes. 'I'll tell you what, I'll bring him in to meet you. Actually, I have a favour. He's been living overseas for the last five years and needs to meet some new people. Should we have a ward get-together? Do you know any single women?'

'Er...you?' Chantelle's pointed finger drew an invisible line down Lexi's body.

'Not me. Really, not me.'

'Oh.' Chantelle pulled a face. 'Is he awful? Do you need him to move out? Smelly feet? Doesn't clean up? Aha. I've got two stinky teenage boys, I hear you.'

'No. Not at all. His feet are fine and he's the tidiest man I've ever known. Probably because he's only got a rucksack full of possessions.' But his delicious scent did linger in every room, and was it bad that she inhaled deeply every time she smelt it? 'I promised him I'd find him a date.'

'Why?'

So I don't fall prey to his charms. 'He's my oldest friend and he's...well, he was saying he'd like to get married and have kids and everything. I said I'd help find him the perfect woman.' And hopefully seeing him settled and happy would put a stop to this ache she had for him.

'We can all help. Excellent. I need a project, seeing as you're refusing to comply.' Chantelle rubbed her hands together in glee. 'Let's have a *Find Jono a Date* party. But of course we won't tell him it's that.'

Lexi laughed but cringed inside. 'Poor Jono.'

'Great idea! Let's throw a welcoming me party.' A deep voice with a slight Australian twang came from behind her.

Oops. Lexi rolled her bottom lip between her teeth. 'He's standing right there, isn't he?'

'Someone's behind you and, trust me, I am more than happy to help him do anything he wants,' Chantelle stage-whispered, then stood up and stuck her hand out. 'Hello there. I'm Chantelle, charge nurse here on Peter Pan. And you are…?'

'Hi. Jonathan Neale. Lexi's friend. Or you may know me as *Poor Jono*.'

Ugh.

Lexi turned round and took him in, searching his face for any hurt she might have caused. But there he was, grinning his usual grin, and once again she was hit with a rush of heat, a flash of electricity, her belly humming with anticipation. Although there was a touch of embarrassment in the mix too, because absolutely nothing about Jono begged for sympathy. He was all man: rugged and tall and broad and he oozed a sensuality that should come with a government health warning.

She gave him what she hoped was an *I was only joking* smile. 'Hey. Have you got lost? This is Paediatrics. Cardiology is floor five.'

'I know. I thought I'd come to see you. I'm just taking a lunch break.'

'What a coincidence.' Chantelle beamed. 'So is Lexi.'

'No.' Lexi frowned at her colleague. The thought of spending more time with Jono was wonderful and very tempting, but she couldn't allow her attraction to him to spill into her work arena. Sure, bump into him around the hospital, even cycle to work with him, but cosy lunches in her day job? It was too much distraction. Too much Jono. She needed one area of her life that wasn't dominated by her seesawing emotions. 'I've got discharges to sort out. Mountains of paperwork and a full inbox. I'm also on call. I can't just waltz off for a lunch break.'

'Why not? Ease your way back into the chaos. I'll get everything ready for the discharges. You need to eat. Everyone needs to eat, right…um…' Chantelle's gaze slid over his name badge, but Lexi was sure it was just an excuse to sneak another look at him close up '…Jonathan?'

'Everyone calls me Jono. I'm going to have to get the name badge changed.'

'Jono. Yes. Sorry.' For a fifty-odd-year-old woman Chantelle was clearly taken in by a good-looking man. She flapped a hand towards Lexi. 'Please take her away, feed her and bring her back in…thirty minutes.'

'No, I really—' Lexi's bleeper flashed and relief spread through her. 'Ah. No. See? Got to go. Accident and Emergency calling.'

'But—' Jono frowned.

'Sorry. See you later.' As she grabbed her bag and headed towards the door she just had enough time to hear him say, 'See you on Saturday then, Chantelle. Shall we say seven-thirty? Our place. Please invite your friends. Casual. Bring drinks. We'll just throw something on the barbie.'

Our place? Barbecue?

But he had every right to invite people over; it was his home too, however temporary. And after calling him *poor Jono* she couldn't refuse him a party. But…she couldn't work out why she felt so flustered. Was it because she was going to have to share him?

No. Sharing him was a good thing. She needed to not have him in her space all the time. Her body couldn't cope with craving his touch and his kiss so intensely.

Was it possible to die of lust?

But her escape didn't last long. After dealing with her asthmatic patient and their very concerned parents she was speed-walking through Accident and Emergency when she heard Jono's deep voice coming from another cubicle, discussing a patient's atrial fibrillation.

So as not to bump into him again, she whipped around and changed her route across the department, but suddenly he was in front of her. Hot damn. There were too many doors in this place. He was in her space here too. She couldn't get away from his lovely eyes and smart mouth. That body wrapped in a crisp white work shirt that accentuated his muscles and his suntan, and sand-coloured chinos that hugged a very nice backside and strong, long legs. A perfect package that stoked her attraction towards him.

She ground to a halt, her gaze grazing his chest, mouth, eyes. His smile hit her square in the solar plexus. 'Hey.'

'Hi Lexi.' His eyes twinkled. 'This is fun. There are so many doors in this renovated version of the department, it's like a rabbit warren. I'm hoping one time I'll open a door and walk straight into Narnia.'

'You'd need a wardrobe for that.' She chuckled. 'Only you would find this maze of a place funny. It's supposed to be an improvement but I'm not convinced. Finding your feet okay?'

'Shadowing on call.' He shrugged and raised his eyes

over towards one of the cardiology specialty registrars staring at an X-ray. 'I can do it with my eyes closed. Orientation overkill if you ask me; I just want to jump right in.'

'I bet you do. I'd be frustrated too.' She grinned. 'Have you seen your dad today?'

'Yes. There have been no complications from the fall, and no further incidents. In fact, he's looking a lot better. Derek says that because they can't find any reason for the dizzy spell they're going to work towards discharge, which is a huge step compared to how he was when he was admitted. To be honest, I wasn't sure he was going to make it.'

'That's great news.' Her heart lifted.

But he frowned. 'Yes and no, because it'll mean he's getting better, but I won't be able to keep my eye on him or get regular updates on his welfare or health when he's at home.'

She really wanted to slip her arms around him and hug away that frown before stomping up to the ward and giving old Gordon a piece of her mind. But she did neither and just flashed Jono what she hoped was a rallying smile. She couldn't take away his hurt but she could be there for him. 'You could offer to go round to see him.'

He shrugged. 'I don't have his address.'

'It's in his notes, right?'

He snorted. 'Whoa. Lexi Fisher, you know as well as I do that I can't go looking. It's unprofessional and unethical.'

'Then you'll have to ask him outright for it. Be up-front.'

His eyebrows rose. 'Sure. That'll be easy.'

'You've got nothing to lose, right? And Jono…' She

touched his arm. 'I didn't mean it…before… I was just playing along with Chantelle.'

He looked at her suspiciously. 'Mean what?'

'Poor Jono.'

He exhaled. 'Trust me, I've been called a lot worse.'

Probably from his dad, so now she felt doubly worse. What could she do to cheer him up? 'Hey, I know, let's have a party-planning meeting tonight.'

'Excellent. I have ideas.'

Of course he did. Jono was the party king. She grimaced. 'Why does that make me nervous?'

'Aww, come on. Don't ever be nervous around me.' He winked at her, back to his teasing self. 'I don't bite.'

No. But now she really, really wanted him to.

Images of his mouth on her throat, on her lips, on her…everywhere filled her head. Heat burst inside her. 'Right. Yes. Okay. Party…'

'Tonight. My turn to make dinner. Don't be late.' And then he grinned, as if he knew exactly the kind of effect he was having on her.

CHAPTER ELEVEN

THEY HADN'T PLANNED for rain.

And certainly not for a summer storm that meant they'd all be huddled up in the cottage. Except for Jono, who'd spent most of the party trying to cook sausages on a barbecue that sizzled more because of the rain hitting the grill than from the heat it generated. But it was a good way to dampen his ever-growing attraction to his housemate.

He wasn't sure if she felt it too, but this forced proximity—work and home—was hard. Like being in the tiny Mini, he felt squished out of shape, because all he wanted to do was touch her, kiss her, rub her feet at the end of a long day. Share the shower he heard her take every morning after her early run, or crawl under her covers and hold her in bed.

Living here was driving him wild; he hadn't realised he had so much self-control and it was getting harder by the day, but he didn't want to move out either, because... Lexi.

Still damp from tidying up the patio, they waved the last departing guest off and he turned to her. 'I think we can call that a roaring success, right?'

'I think so, yes. Even though we had soggy sausages and the drinks were diluted with raindrops, I think everyone enjoyed themselves.' Her smile shone...her eyes shone. She looked amazing in a baggy blue jumper she'd pulled on top of a pretty pink sundress that skimmed her toned thighs, before they'd dragged the food table back inside when it became clear the rain was not going to stop. Probably ever.

Her hair was damp, her skin was dewy. He had no doubt that any minute now she was going to say something about how terrible she looked, because that was the self-deprecating thing she did, but she was quite possibly the most beautiful woman he'd ever seen.

'Look at me.' She laughed and ran her hands over her hair, plastering the wet tendrils to her scalp. 'I must look awful.'

'Never. You look beautiful.' His smile stretched from the centre of his heart. He didn't know if he was allowed to say that, under the terms of their pact, but he couldn't help telling her.

She rolled her eyes but there was light and fun and heat in her expression. 'You have to say that because you don't want to be homeless.'

'True, being homeless in the rain isn't very attractive. But I'm not saying it because I need the room, I'm saying it because it's true.'

'Yeah, yeah.' She waved her hand at him. 'I'm a beautiful drowned rat.'

'Well, when I suggested a barbecue I'd forgotten about the British weather.'

He closed the front door and wandered into the kitchen to start on the clearing up. Truth was, he was always up for a party but the minute she'd walked down the stairs in that dress, with her bare skin showing, he'd wanted to put up a *Party Cancelled* sign and convince her to go straight to bed. Where he would have very slowly removed the dress and kissed every inch of her before making love to her all night.

Which was a problem. He couldn't live here and think like this, wanting her all the damned time.

What if they took a step towards each other...another kiss? Made love? And he blew it? What if he just couldn't settle down? The stakes were high here. He and Lexi were linked by a long history. What if he was more like his dad than he wanted to admit...and he just ruined everything?

'I didn't want to rain on your parade...pardon the pun, but the weather isn't something we can rely on to play ball.' She followed him, picking up a dirty platter and two wine glasses along the way. 'You've obviously had a lot of experience with a barbecue.'

'In Australia it's almost a religion. We should think about getting one of those big gas barbecues. You don't get the smoky taste, which is a shame, but they cook well in all weather.'

We? We? And we are talking about the weather. Small talk.

And yet it was cosy, comfortable. Normal. He knew her well enough that their conversation flitted seamlessly from one thing to another. He liked how in sync they were and that he could almost predict what she was going to say or think about one subject or another.

'And...' Lexi ran the tap and put the dishes into the sink then turned to him. 'You were a definite hit. I'd say you've not just made friends, but got yourself a few adoring fans too.'

'Hey, anyone bearing food is popular. You have a lot of colleagues and they are all lovely and very welcoming.' But even though this had been fun, what he'd craved—unusually for him—other than spending the evening in bed with Lexi, was a quiet night in with her. Like they'd had last night and the night before, just the two of them, a bottle of wine and conversation. She was a stabilising force to his party personality, and he liked who he was when he was with her.

She stopped scrubbing the platter and glanced up at him. 'Becky was very attentive.'

'Which one was Becky? Chantelle had a lot of friends.'

'Paediatric house officer. Swishy blonde ponytail.'

Nope. Didn't register. In truth, he'd only had eyes for Lexi, watching her caring for their guests, laughing at some joke, coy glances at him when she thought he wasn't looking. The slight tremble of anticipation of their first guest arriving. Was the house tidy? Had they got enough food? Always thinking of others.

When he shook his head, she rolled her eyes. 'Green dress. Silver sandals.'

'Ah. Yes. She's nice. Very young.'

'Oh? Only a couple of years younger than you. Which makes her a decade younger than me.'

There she was, throwing up the barriers again. As if something as insignificant as a few years' difference would stop him thinking she was beautiful. He tried to hide his grin. 'Lexi Fisher, are you jealous of Becky from Paeds?'

'No!' Her cheeks bloomed pink. 'I'm just wingmanning.'

She was still working on that? Had the last few days of living together not changed anything? It had for him. He knew he liked her—wanted to hold her, kiss her again. Even though he understood all her reasons why they shouldn't, and had a few of his own—seeing his father again after so many years was a constant reminder of just how badly he could mess everything up between himself and Lexi—he couldn't stop the tug towards her, the tightening connection. Couldn't ignore the way his body responded to her. 'We said we weren't doing that. In fact, I asked you not to.'

A faux innocent smile on her face, she said, 'Chantelle and I just thought you needed a gentle push.'

'Trust me, I can work out who I will and won't date when it's time for me to get out there again. Right now I'm working on me. And Dad, of course.'

'It was a genius plan to offer to drive him home on discharge.'

'You gave me the idea to think outside the box and my suggestion might have taken him by surprise but he couldn't refuse, given the medics and the nursing staff were all there watching. All going well, on Friday afternoon he's going home. Thanks for letting me borrow the car too.'

'Anything to help.' She picked up the tea towel and started to dry the dishes, but he grabbed the linen from her.

'I can do that.'

Laughing, she leant back against the sink. 'Leave it all to drip dry. I'll put them away tomorrow.'

'No way. My mum always made sure everything was cleared away at night. She said every morning was the gift of a new start and you had to make the most of it, not begin by clearing up yesterday's mess.'

'That's actually quite profound. It's like suggesting you don't let the past interfere with your present.' Lexi frowned and thought for a moment. 'I do that all the time.'

'In what way?' This was the kind of conversation he

loved having with her. It was honest and vulnerable and authentic. Just like she was.

'Oh, you know. I guard my heart very carefully. I know I shouldn't, but I do. I'm trying to let go and just have fun.' She quickly blinked and said, 'You never talk about her. Your mum.'

He noted the deft subject change but didn't comment, because she'd let something slip, and he'd already discerned this, but it was good that she recognised that she was guarding her heart. So, was the reality more that she was scared to date him, rather than didn't want to?

Or was he reading too much into it? Did she think he'd run? Move away? Keep moving, the way he had his whole life?

Did he want to? He craved stability, but he'd never created it before, always running from one job to another, never letting himself sink into a place, never putting down roots. Why would Oxford be any different? Because she was here?

But she didn't want him.

Because his dad was close by?

Ditto.

His chest ached. He rubbed at it, but the pain lingered. That same pain had fuelled his desire to be as far away as possible from his father and yet still craving his attention and affection. Had fed his hedonistic tendencies and been the foundation for him never getting close to anyone again. Love hurt. End of. Wanting to be loved by someone who just couldn't love you hurt more.

'Oh, I'm sorry, Jono. Did I overstep?' Lexi's voice brought him back to the present. 'I know how much you loved your mum, and I didn't want to bring back any painful memories.'

'No. Not at all.' He hadn't been thinking about his

mum, but Lexi was right, he didn't speak about his past unless prompted, and rarely about his mother because the memory still hurt. Not just losing her, but everything about that time was all wrapped up in the emotions he'd had about his father too. 'Like you, I prefer to keep the past in the past.'

'Yes, I get that, absolutely. It's okay. Forget I mentioned it.'

He shrugged. 'It's okay.'

She took the dish towel from his hands and hung it to dry on the oven door. Then she peered outside into the small back garden. 'It's stopped raining. Might have known it'd clear up just as everyone leaves.'

She opened the door wider, stepped outside and inhaled.

A warm breeze blew into the kitchen, ruffling the reminder lists and takeaway menus on the fridge door, pinned in place by a magnet that said *I love St Quintin*.

The place where it had started and ended. But if he went back in time right to that moment before they'd kissed, would he have stopped? No. There was absolutely nothing that he'd change about that moment.

He watched as her chest swelled on an inhale and the way her eyelids fluttered closed on the out breath. He took in the messy hair and the mascara run down her cheek. The patches of damp on her clothes. The fall and rise of her breasts as she inhaled and exhaled. And, as always when he was with her, his heart thumped harder, his blood pumped stronger. 'Lexi, are you okay?'

She turned and smiled, her face lit by the automatic light outside the back door. Her expression was serene. Calm. Simply beautiful. 'I love the way the garden smells just after it rains. It's so fresh and earthy. Come and sniff.'

'You make it sound so attractive.' He laughed, but went outside and copied her, inhaling deeply. 'Petrichor.'

Her eyes narrowed as she looked at him. 'What?'

'That's the name of the smell. Petrichor. Ozone and plant oils and rain.'

'I'd forgotten there was a specific name for it. Petrichor. I like it.' She grinned. 'I also love this time of night when everyone else is asleep. Sometimes I come out here and just sit in the darkness and breathe.'

'I remember you telling me that in your emails. You saw a fox once.'

'I did, just over there.' She pointed towards the end of the garden. 'I accidentally left the back gate open and it wandered in as if it owned the place. I saw a badger one evening too. They're huge. I ran inside and locked the door as if it was going to attack me. That's the problem with living alone and having a wild imagination.'

She giggled and it suited her. A lot. She'd been laughing a lot more these last few days. And, what with the stuff about his dad and starting this new job, he'd been the serious one for once. Go figure.

'You'd be absolutely rubbish in Australia then. You can't just sit down without checking your seat or the ground or anything overhanging for man-eating wildlife.' Laughing, he darted back into the kitchen, grabbed the dishtowel again, wiped down two sun loungers. Then, after pretending to check underneath for monsters, he indicated for her to sit. 'It's been a busy day. You sit down, I'll grab the wine.'

She craned her neck to turn to him. 'You know, Jono Neale, you could grow on me.'

'Steady now. Don't go overboard on the compliments.'

You've grown on me.

Too much. And he was toeing the 'friends' line because they'd agreed it was the right course of action. She was terrified they'd ruin the good thing they had going. And she was probably right. He wasn't the right man for her because she needed certainty and reliability and he wanted it but had no track record of staying. No blueprint for a decent, honest relationship: hence the work he needed to do. He couldn't offer anything to anyone until he'd worked out all that crap.

But what would he do if she moved on with another guy? If he had to sit on the sidelines and watch her fall in love? Pretend it was all okay with him, because he was being the good friend?

No, he didn't like that thought at all.

He poured two glasses of wine and took them back outside, along with a blanket that he covered her shoulders with and cushions to sit on. Then they sat next to each other on the patio, staring into the darkness of her walled cottage garden and listening to the night-time sounds. A rustle of leaves, an owl hooting. Something moving about in the hedgerow.

She shivered and pulled the blanket more tightly around her. 'It's chilly.'

'You want to go inside?'

'No, I'm fine right here. I don't mind the chill, it makes me feel alive.' She pulled her feet up onto the chair and twisted to lean over to his lounger and back against his chest. He wrapped his arm around her shoulders, his cheek against her head. And it felt so perfect, so damned right, that he couldn't help but answer the question she'd asked him earlier. The one thing he'd never talked about, but now seemed a good time. He knew anything he said would be kept sacred and secret by Lexi.

'My mum was lovely.'

Lexi's head turned slightly and he saw a question there.

He smiled to reassure her. 'It's fine. I want you to know about her.'

'Thank you.' She nodded and settled back against him.

'She was thoughtful and funny and pretty...and, yes, every kid says that about their mum, but mine was all of those things. She made sure to tell me how proud of me she was and made a big fuss of any achievements. I think she was trying to make up for my dad's lack of interest. But she was lonely too. When I was young we moved every few years and while the army had a lot of support for the families, groups weren't mum's thing. She was shy and quiet and didn't make friends easily. She found it hard to break into the cliques, and hated being in the spotlight.'

He felt Lexi's soft chuckle against his ribcage. 'And you're her child? I don't believe it.'

'I know, right? Which probably means I'm more like my dad than I care to be.' That thought sat heavily in his gut.

'We inherit things from both parents, Jono. Plus traits from ancestors and we have our own uniqueness too.'

'I guess. She was certainly one of a kind. Trouble was, she didn't have many friends she could confide in about his affairs, so she struggled with how to deal with them. At first she ranted and raved at him, and gave him ultimatums which he didn't take seriously. My dad was always only really interested in himself and doing what pleased him.' Not much had changed there, although after his dad's dizzy spell Jono was massively grateful that he had more time to forge some sort of relationship with his only living parent. 'After a while she seemed to grudgingly accept his behaviour. I guess she felt stuck—

we were living in Germany on the army base and dependent on him for money. But gradually things deteriorated and he started coming home late, or not coming home at all, and he didn't even try to hide that he'd been with other women. But, conversely, the more time he spent away from us, the happier they both were and I think Mum realised that too, because eventually she found the courage to leave him and we moved to be closer to her sister in Nottingham. It was just the two of us then for about eight years. Then, in my last year at high school, she was diagnosed with advanced ovarian cancer.'

'Oh, God, Jono.' Lexi's hand hovered over her mouth.

'She died a few days after my exam results came out. I always believed she was holding on until she knew I had the future she was hoping for. She was forty-two.'

'My God, that's younger than me. I'm so sorry.' Lexi's eyes glistened as she frowned, looking as if she really felt his pain. But you did well to get into medical school, especially Oxford, if she was sick during your last year. You must have worked damned hard.'

'I did it for her. She was all I had.' He shook his head and rubbed the wine glass with a little more force than was necessary.

Lexi obviously thought so too because she took it from his hands and placed it onto the wooden picnic table at her side. 'Oh, Jono. She'd be so proud of you. I'm sorry she's not here to see the man you've become.'

'Thanks.'

'And I'm sorry your dad wasn't a better man.'

'Ah, I probably didn't make it easy for him. Once we moved I saw him less and less. He'd make plans to come over then cancel or just not turn up. And when he did finally appear, sometimes late by days, months then years, I usually made some sort of scene.' He shrugged, remembering how angry he'd been at his dad when he didn't show up. 'I was a teenager, right? I wasn't capable of controlling my emotions back then. Once Mum died the visits fizzled out completely because she didn't insist on arranging them.'

'You had a rocky start, Jono.'

'It's in the past. I have a good life now.' Wanted one, anyway.

He hadn't noticed it happening, but somehow they'd edged closer. She was facing him, her feet tucked under his thigh. Her hand was on his arm.

He was acutely aware of her. Of the soft touch of her fingers, her heat. The way her drying hair was curling, framing her face.

'Yes, you've turned out okay. I guess.' She looked up at him, her eyes searching his, as if asking him an unspoken question. But he didn't know if he had the answer she was looking for. He had his own answer—which would be to hold her and to kiss her, but he didn't know what she wanted.

He ran a strand of her hair through his fingers, capturing her gaze. 'Only okay?'

'Better than okay.' She caught his hand, stroked the inside of his wrist, then up his arm, sending shivers of desire skittering across his skin. By the time her fingers reached his jaw he was hard and hot. She smiled as she grazed his cheek with her fingers, her gaze roving his face, settling on his eyes. 'Oh, I'd say you were pretty damned amazing, Dr Neale.'

The way she was looking at him rattled something loose in his chest, but he didn't want to get this wrong or put his own slant on the signs. 'Have you had too much wine?'

She shook her head, eyes wide. 'That was my first

glass. I didn't drink all evening in case someone needed a lift home.'

He wrapped his fingers around her wrist and stopped her caresses. 'In which case, I need you to think of the consequences of touching me like that. I'm trying hard to stick to our promise, but you're killing me here.'

'Our promise. Yes.' She studied him for a moment. 'I still believe in it.'

'That we're friends?'

'We are.' She stroked his cheek. 'We are friends first. Always. And I'm so glad I have you in my life. You're my best friend. I feel like I can tell you everything. Well…almost everything.' A corner of her mouth lifted ruefully.

'You see? You're right, this…attraction has changed us. Because once you would tell me absolutely everything. And now you're holding back.' Why he was trying to convince her to stop whatever this touching was, he didn't know, but he closed his eyes and counted backwards from ten, trying to regain control.

But all he was aware of was her ragged breathing, the heat of her hand. When he opened his eyes again she was still looking at him, lips slightly parted.

'I am holding back. Yes.' She swallowed. He watched the movement of her throat, mesmerised by her fine features. 'And it's killing me too.'

'Tell me what you're thinking.' He ran his fingers across her jawline and down her throat, wishing his mouth was there.

Her smile grew, wicked and hungry. 'You do not want to know what is in here.' She tapped her head.

'Hell, if you can't say it then write it to me, Lexi. I can wait. I will wait. Just tell me what you want, how you feel, in whatever way you can.' He sensed she preferred not to look at him when being absolutely honest and he got that. Refusing video calls because she said she looked awful after crying so much over the marriage break-up, she'd always written down her feelings, and he'd guessed it was also because she could be more open if she didn't have direct eye contact. Like the way she'd suggested he talk to his father around a shared interest instead of directly. 'But one thing I've learnt from this whole damned thing with my dad is that you have to say how you feel before it's too late. Don't be the one who looks back and says, *I wish I had*...be the one who says, *I'm glad I did*.'

'I don't want to spoil things.'

'I know. And neither do I. But, trust me, that kiss on the beach? It did not spoil a single thing for me. It only made things better.'

'Yes, but you...well, you have a history of kissing and forgetting, whereas I kiss and carry it...everywhere. It's driving me crazy.'

'I can see why it would. It was a good kiss. A kiss I'll never forget.'

'I wondered if you'd just jumped into it on impulse.'

'I didn't exactly plan it. No. Maybe that's how I acted years ago, but I hope you see that I've changed.'

'Yes.' She nodded. 'You really have.'

He wasn't the man he wanted to be. Not yet. But he was getting there. He stroked her hair. 'Honestly? I wanted to kiss you from the first moment I saw you on that train platform. It was all I could think about.'

She smiled up at him. 'It was the first time I'd taken that kind of risk in a very long time. Other than Ross, you are the only man I've kissed in over twenty years. It was a big deal to me.'

'It was a big deal to me too.' He tipped her chin up so

he could look her square in the eyes. He had no idea what
the future held for them, but he could give her this. Share
this. 'Lexi, I want you. I'm sick of pretending otherwise.
I'm sick of walking around the house averting my eyes
because I'm trying not to look at you all hot and sweaty
after your runs or fresh and damp after a shower. I'm
tired of not being able to tell you how amazing you look,
how amazing you *are*. I'm tired of not being able to pull
you onto my lap and hold you close after a long day.'

She stared at him, mouth slightly open, heat in her
eyes, her body trembling. The look in her eyes stole his
breath. She wanted him.

Then she moved.

'Like this?' She slid onto his lap, straddling him, her
face close to his.

'Yeah, just like this.' He fitted his palms to her waist
and held her there, dress fabric bunched in his hands, his
thumbs stroking her ribcage. If she moved closer she'd
be sitting on his erection, and man, that would feel so
good. But he knew he had to wait, even if it killed him.

It probably would.

She leaned even closer and put her cheek to his, whis-
pering, 'I want to kiss you again, Jono. I know that's a
crazy idea after everything we agreed, but I can't get it
out of my head. Every day I look at your mouth and I just
want to...' she leaned forward and pressed her mouth
to his '...do this...'

Then she ran her tongue along his bottom lip. 'And
this.'

He held steady. Would she regret this tomorrow?
Would he?

Never. Whatever happened, he was most definitely
in the *I'm glad it happened* camp.

He cupped her face and slid his mouth over hers, sinking into all the need and the want and the holding back he'd been doing for two long weeks.

'Jono…' Her voice was cracked and raw and filled with heat. '*God*, Jono.'

CHAPTER TWELVE

THIS KISS WAS wild and out of control.

Unable to hold back any longer, Lexi locked her hands at each side of his face and pressed her mouth against his. She relished the rough stroke of his fingers on her bare thighs, the heat of his mouth, the slide of his tongue against hers.

He groaned and took the kiss deeper, a hand now underneath her dress, exploring her body on a trail upwards to her breasts. She arched into his touch, wanting to feel his hands everywhere. When his fingers found her nipples she moaned. 'That feels so good.'

'You feel good,' he said against her mouth, then he slipped her jumper and dress over her head. Unclipped her bra and threw it to the ground. And she thanked her foresight for buying a cottage with a walled garden where no neighbours could see in.

His mouth found her nipples and she closed her eyes as he sucked in first one, then the other, sending shockwaves of need through her body.

She shifted on his lap and her soft core connected with his erection. Oh, God. He was so hard. So big. Could she even…?

Her heart hammered against her ribcage. Would she be any good at this? Would she be a let-down?

This was stupid. What was she doing? What were they doing? Would this put a stop to their friendship? Or would it deepen it? But Jono knew she couldn't have kids, so he clearly didn't want anything more from her than a fling. So they were both going into this—whatever this was—with no further expectations.

Or was she just finding excuses to have a wicked night with him?

All she knew was she didn't want the kisses to stop.

It dawned on her then that her ex had stolen more than her self-esteem; he'd taken her sense of who she was and he'd taken her sexual power. She'd had to create a whole new life from the ruins of the one she'd been building for years. She'd been rudderless and stuck but had reinvented herself. She knew her worth as a doctor and a friend, but as a sexual being? Enjoying it, rather than scheduling it purely to get pregnant?

Help.

Jono ran his thumb across her bottom lip and looked at her with eyes heavy with desire. 'Hey. What's wrong?'

'Nothing. I'm great.' She pressed her mouth to his but he pulled away.

'I know you, Lexi. I know when you're happy, when you're relaxed, when you're angry. And right now you've got that *I'm worried about something* look in your eyes.'

Great. Now she was ruining the moment. 'Do you have a condom?'

'In my room. Don't suppose you have anything in your dress pockets?'

Heat rippled through her. So they were going to do this. Or maybe they weren't because… 'Nope. Nothing. I haven't had sex in years; I didn't think I'd ever have it again.'

'That would be a damned shame.' He tipped her chin

and kissed her again and again until she couldn't think straight, never mind worry about how this would affect their relationship. Then he pulled away. 'I think you should have a lot of sex, Lexi Fisher. A lot, a lot of sex. With me.'

And he kissed her again, masterful and confident. He led and she followed. He was so good at this. And she was…overthinking. Her heart hurt for the young man who'd lost his mother and the pain caused by his father. She hadn't thought she could feel even more for him than she did, but wow…the emotions were so vivid and bright. And they seemed to have a hold on her— *he* had a hold on her. And it was dangerous to be this enthralled by someone but she didn't care. He was so much a man, so much a survivor and a fighter, and she only wanted more of him.

She pressed against him, bare skin to bare skin, running her hands over toned muscles, across his shoulders, down his chest. His hands stroked down her belly, fingers hooking into her panties and ripping them off. Then sliding his fingers down to her core. She breathed in so he wouldn't see her non-Becky tummy. But he groaned as his fingers sank deep into her.

She felt herself tighten around him instinctively and his next kiss was ragged and breathless and hot. So hot she almost came. But she held on, regaining control, and tugged at his belt.

He shook his head. 'No. No, Lexi. This is all about you.'

'But what about the condom?'

'We're nowhere near needing that.'

'We're not?' She buried her face in his neck, her body going slack. 'Oh, Jono, I'm sorry. I don't know what I'm doing. I am so not ready for this.'

He slid his hand between her legs again. 'Oh, I'd say you were exactly ready for this. Do you want to go upstairs?'

She looked up at the moon and stars and the inky black sky. 'I think it would be special it we stayed outside.'

He laughed. 'Really?'

'It's a beautiful night. Can we? Can we stay out here?'

'Are you sure? The grass is damp. The lounger is too narrow. It's cold and I'm fairly sure it's starting to rain.'

She giggled and put her forehead against his. 'This is not going the way I imagined things happening.'

'I can't help the weather.' He dragged a blanket over his shoulders, then pulled her down to hold her. 'What did you imagine?'

'I don't know. So many things. Fast and out of control. Or slow and dreamy. I didn't think we'd talk about the weather. But it's fine. It's so…us.' She'd imagined it so many times. Imagined him naked and inside her. A perfect melding of their bodies and minds. The reckless abandon she'd seen in films—definitely not the time-tabled sex she'd had with Ross. But she hadn't imagined rain or feeling so nervous she rambled on about the weather.

This was her fault. She was ruining everything. Again.

Thick raindrops splashed on her forehead. 'And now it's definitely raining.'

'Right. That's it.' He lifted her from him then stood up, slid his hands under her thighs and picked her up in one swift action. 'We are going upstairs.'

'But—'

'No buts.' He carried her upstairs and into his room. Laid her onto the bed and climbed over her, his eyes glittering with intense need. 'You want fast? Tell me what you want. I'm all yours.'

'I want to savour every moment.' She gripped her hands around his neck. 'You're right. It's warmer here.'

'Lexi…' There was humour but also a growl in his voice. Censure.

She was putting up barriers, and she couldn't seem to stop herself.

This was so bad. What if the sex was terrible? What if she was awful? She hadn't expected to feel so clunky and uncoordinated and self-conscious. 'I'm nervous, Jono.'

Positioning himself next to her, he propped himself up on his elbow and cupped her cheek with his free hand. His eyes roved her face, calm now and understanding. 'I know.'

'And you're so confident.'

'Lexi, I want to kiss every part of you, to rock deep inside you. I want to hold you. But you know what? I'm the first guy to make love to you since your husband. The man who drew you away from us. The man I watched you marry. The man you clearly adored for years. Who possessed you so much you were completely heartbroken at his betrayal. I know what you felt for him. So do you not think I might get a little performance anxiety too?' He tapped her nose. 'But I have absolute faith in the way I feel about you that everything will be pretty damned awesome.'

He leant forward and kissed her. A mind-warping, mesmerising kiss that made her limbs feel like jelly and her insides tighten with need. She wanted him inside her. *Oh, yes.*

Had he really just said that? That he wanted to be inside her?

But then he pulled away and looked at her.

Panic ran through her again. 'You've changed your mind.'

'I have not changed my mind.' He pressed his lips together as if trying not to laugh.

'So why are you looking at me like that?'

'Because I want to sear this into my memory. This is *us*, Lexi. You and me. Naked. In bed. Doing this.'

'It's a disaster. The grass was wet. We're doing too much talking. No, I'm doing too much talking. Maybe it's a sign—'

'Hey.' He put a finger to her lips. 'There isn't a protocol or prescription for this. It doesn't have to be like it is in the books or the movies. It just has to be about us. We can do it any way we want to. I love that we have fun and can talk and we have enough sexual experience not to expect stars and lights…although, hold on to your hat, baby. Because you just might.'

'Oh, Dr Modest?' She flicked her hand against his chest and giggled. 'Are you really that good?'

'Give me a chance and I'll show you.' He ran a fingertip down her nose, then traced a line all the way down her jaw, her chest and to the space between her breasts. He stroked and teased first one nipple then the other, his eyes on her the whole time. 'To me, it couldn't be more perfect like this. You couldn't be more perfect. Because you are being pure Lexi and I really like you just the way you are.'

Her whole body tingled with heat. This amazing man liked her…like this? All wobbly and uncertain? 'Wow, you really know how to say all the right things.'

She expected him to say that he'd had a lot of practice but he didn't. He just gazed at her. 'It's the truth. You are everything, Lexi. We talk. We laugh. We care for each other and about each other. And even now we can both be vulnerable and know it'll be okay.'

Was this what he'd meant about wanting someone to accept him? Because, yes, she did not want to be here doing this with anyone other than Jono Neale. He was her person. Absolutely.

Her chest filled with warmth and she cupped his cheek. 'To be honest, I'm surprised, Jono. In a good way. I didn't expect this side of you.'

'No. Me neither.' He laughed and dipped his head to suck in her nipple sending more electric shockwaves through her body before saying, 'I didn't expect any of this, Lex. It's amazing. I have so many things I want to do to you and with you.'

Whilst she believed Jono and knew he found her attractive, *felt* his attraction, Ross had crushed her self-esteem, leaving her vulnerable for any other relationship. Making her hate herself and the things she couldn't do with her body instead of celebrating the things she could. Making her second-guess everything about who she was and what she could do and what she could offer anyone else. Suddenly she needed to tell Jono, to warn him that she wasn't as perfect as he thought she was.

She placed her hand on his shoulder. 'I'm not...you know, Becky young. All pert and swishy.'

'For God's sake. Trust me, I've seen you in a bikini; your body is the best thing I have ever laid eyes on in my entire life. But I'd still be here doing this whatever you look like, because it's *you* that turns me on: all of you, not just your body.'

'Thank you. But still… I'm not sure how I feel about you seeing me naked.'

'Hey.' Mirroring her action, Jono pressed his palm to her chest too, right above her heart. 'You've lived, Lexi.

You've suffered more than others and I'm so sorry for that. But everything you've been through has made you into this amazing person that I care about, that I absolutely want to kiss and make love to and wake up with tomorrow.'

Overwhelmed by a flood of emotions, she buried her head in his chest. She'd never thought she'd be able to do this again. Certainly had never thought anyone would tell her that she was attractive and amazing. *Amazing?* She couldn't believe it. But she felt exactly the same about him.

'Okay, you can stop with the compliments now. I'm hot and extremely fabulous.'

'One hundred per cent. But, for the record, that was just about the most soppy thing I've ever said, even though I mean every single word.'

He jokingly winced, as if embarrassed by admitting something so deeply personal. And she got that, because even in his emails and messages when he'd opened up to her, he'd never admitted that any of his liaisons were serious or that he'd thought much of his dates. It made his words all the more precious as she stored them in her heart, making more space for him right there.

And then he got serious, dipping his head to her neck, pressing slow, sensuous kisses towards that sensitive spot just below her ear. She felt his erection hard against her thigh. The heat of his body pressed tight against hers. She arched her back, relishing the sensation of his skin against hers, not wanting any space between them. Wanting him deep inside her. There was no more denying it, no more ignoring it; she wanted this man. So much. Too much.

And so she got serious too. Taking back control, just

so she could lose it all again...this time in the kissing and the sex and not in the excuses.

Taking back the power Ross had stripped from her, she reached for Jono and crushed her mouth to his.

CHAPTER THIRTEEN

SHE WAS NERVOUS. Well, hell, it was a big deal to him too. This was his best friend. This mattered. Jono wasn't worried about getting it right, because their bodies knew exactly what to do, but he wanted to get it right *for her*.

She was putting her trust in him and that was like a damned medal of honour.

She was so exquisite and precious and he couldn't think of anything past sinking deep inside her. As they kissed, a desperate, raw moan came from her throat and he felt her press against him. Suddenly the awkwardness and stalling and nervousness stopped and her kisses became raw and hungry.

He dragged his mouth from hers and kissed down her beautiful body. Stopping at her nipples, laving hem one at a time.

'Oh, my God. Jono…' Her voice was ragged and hoarse and it spurred him to kiss lower. But she pulled him back to face her. 'I have to kiss you. I can't stop kissing you.'

Her mouth was so hot and her kisses so wet he wanted to drown in her. Not moving his lips from hers, he stroked down her body and slid his fingers into her wet centre.

And almost lost it.

She was so hot, so wet, and her urgent kisses spurred him on. He ached for her. He'd never been so hard or so desperate to be inside a woman before. But this had to be about her. He could wait until he'd given her the pleasure she deserved. But then he looked at her sex-drunk smile and he wasn't so sure he could wait at all.

He slid his fingers into her again and matched the rhythm of her hips as she ground against his hand. Faster and faster, her eyes tightly closed as if she just wanted to feel not think, her kisses a hot mess of desperation and delight. Hungry. Deep. No finesse. Just need.

'You want it like this? Tell me what you want, Lexi.'

'Faster.' She angled her hips just a fraction and his fingers slid in again and again. She was hot and tight. 'Like this?'

'Oh, God. Oh, God. That's. Just. Amazing.' Her muscles tightened around his fingers.

'Like this?' he growled against her neck, then took her mouth again, her scent filling the air so much he could taste it.

'Yes. Yes.' She gripped his shoulders. 'Oh, Jono.'

And he watched as she finally let go, her mouth slackening, her head lolling back, her body pulsing against his. She clung to him, her body slick with perspiration, her breathing fast and irregular. And he held her right back, his thoughts spiralling to her emails and her anguish from years ago and how that connection had brought them to this moment. Her ex was an idiot. But also a hero, because if he hadn't left her then Jono wouldn't be here.

It made no sense though. How could anyone ever want to betray her or discard her for something else? Because surely there wasn't another woman alive who could better Lexi Fisher. She was so damned hot. So intuitive. So sexy. *Man*, she was everything he'd ever wanted.

But what was this for her? Someone to help her get over her ex? Someone to help her regain her sexual confidence?

Head spinning with need, he grasped her tight against him as a swell of emotions rose inside him, landing hard and thick in his chest, a mess of emotions bundled up tight. They all began and ended with her.

After a few moments she nuzzled her head against his neck and sighed, all panting and breathy. 'That was out of this world.'

'Yeah, I'd say.' He leaned back so he could look at her, stroked her hair away from her damp face, then cupped her cheeks with both hands. 'Damn, you look so fierce and strong and sexy when you come.'

She giggled and her hand slid down his shorts to palm his erection. 'I want to watch you now.'

'Okay.' On a groan he captured her bottom lip between his teeth.

'Yes,' she whispered, then licked his top lip.

Not knowing which to concentrate on, hands or mouth, his brain went to mush. She tugged down his shorts and boxers then took him in her hand.

'Oh, man, that feels good.' His voice was raw, a growl and a groan. He didn't want her to stroke him because he didn't want this to end so soon, but hell, he couldn't stop her stroking him either. He closed his eyes and retook control, but her hand moving up and down brought him nearer and nearer to the edge.

But then she stopped and his eyes blinked open. She was watching him almost lose it and she smiled wickedly. 'Jonathan Neale, you are magnificent.'

'Lexi.' A breathless warning now. He was going to

come before he'd ever had the chance to be inside her. He stayed her hand and leaned over to his bedside table, grabbed a condom and sheathed.

'I can't believe this is happening. But I'm bloody glad it is,' she whispered as she pulled him in for another kiss.

She raked her fingernails down his back, making him arch and wince and grin, because he wanted to feel *everything*. Then he slowly entered her, pausing to allow her to get used to the feeling and the stretch.

But she moaned and tightened around him. 'You don't have to treat me like I'll break.'

'I don't want to hurt you.' To be fair, he just didn't want to ruin the moment by finishing too soon. And he was on the edge of that. His vision was filled with her, naked and beautiful. Her dark hair was splayed over the white pillow like something from a painting, her scent was everywhere. And yet it still wasn't enough because he wanted to be in her, on her, with her.

He lifted her arms and anchored them above her head, covering her body with his. He wanted to imprint his skin with her scent. With her sex.

She gasped as he thrust into her again and again. 'This…is the best… I've ever felt…in my whole life.'

'This is just a getting-to-know-you appetiser. Wait for the main act.' He laughed and thrust and his whole body tingled and tightened until he thought he was going to go crazy with the feeling of being inside her.

'I hope you're good at encores too.' She laughed, the sexiest, guttural, most sensuous laugh he'd ever heard. And his chest swelled some more. He made her feel this good? Well, hell, the pleasure was all his.

He picked up her rhythm. Found her mouth again and kissed the smile until it blurred with moans and cries for more and more and more. And he lost himself in her as he rocked harder and faster. Deeper and faster. When she cried his name he splintered into a thousand tiny pieces, her name a gasp on his lips. 'Lexi. Lexi. Lexi.'

And he clutched her to his chest, her hair in his face, her scent on his skin. Lexi Fisher, lodged pure and deep in his heart.

'We were so wrong. So very wrong.' Lexi lay back on the bed, trying to catch her breath through a giggle. Who knew sex could be such fun as well as intense and beautiful? 'I did have stars and lights. And it was just like every movie and book. Better, in fact.'

'I know, right? I didn't believe in all that…until now.' He chuckled and wrapped an arm over her waist, spooning her and cuddling close.

This was unbelievable. Incredible. That they could be friends and lovers. That they were so in sync. That this was only enhancing their friendship in ways she hadn't thought about.

Her knowledge and understanding of his background was deeper because the trust between them was developing all the time. Her admiration for him only grew. She imagined how damaging it had been losing his mother and her heart ached for that teenage boy, the same age as Tyler, trying to come to terms with death and the destruction of his family. It was a miracle he'd become the fun-loving guy she loved to spend her time with. *He* was a miracle.

This was a miracle. They'd managed to break through her reticence and hesitancy and proven just how amazing they could be together.

'You asleep?' His breath whispered across her shoulder blades and a host of goosebumps prickled her skin.

She didn't want to go to sleep. She wanted to stay awake and revel in the wonder of this.

'No. I was thinking about your childhood. You didn't deserve the way you were treated by your father. It makes me so angry.'

'Ugh. Don't ruin a brilliant night with that. I was thinking of something altogether different.' His hand slid over her breast.

'So soon?' She turned round to face him, nose to nose, mouth almost to mouth, then brushed her lips across his. Registered his sexy groan and the long slow strokes of his fingers over her belly. 'You really are phenomenal.'

'What can I say? I just like to make the most of any opportunity.' He teased her nipples with his fingers and the fire in her belly rekindled. 'Now we've finally got here I can't keep my hands off you.'

After sex, Ross had got into the habit of turning over and falling asleep as if there hadn't just been intense closeness between them. Of course he hadn't always been like that, but things had just sort of…deteriorated.

She needed to stop comparing.

Because, really…how could anyone compare to Jono? She turned to face him and he pulled her tight against his naked body and kissed her, long and slow, almost lazily and oh, so sexily, and she let herself fall back into the dreamy space that existed when she was cocooned in his arms. As if nothing could ever hurt her again.

When he pulled back he looked at her intently. 'Thank you for putting your trust in me. I know how badly hurt you were by Ross and what a big step this is for you.'

And even though she'd spent many, many words on her husband's betrayal, particularly in her emails to Jono, she felt encouraged to say a few more. And then this would be the last time she'd give her ex any space in her thoughts again. She put her hand on Jono's chest. 'I think I lost faith in my ability to trust people for a long time, but I hope it's coming back. I want it to. I want to trust you.'

'You can. I'd never hurt you, Lexi.'

'I know you don't want to. And I don't want to hurt you at all. Ever. But we don't know what's down the road. When I said my wedding vows I meant every word, and yet look how that turned out.'

Jono frowned. 'Not your fault.'

'Oh, I'm not so naive that I think I was blameless. Sure, he had the affair, but we'd been going through tough times long before that. I was devastated I couldn't conceive naturally and became one of those IVF sex-only-in-the-fertile-window planners. Our lives revolved around my hormones and clinic appointments and periods. We lost the fun of being us. And never got to be the us we'd imagined, with a family. So in the end it wasn't just finding out about the affair, although that was bad enough, but the news that she was pregnant broke me. I couldn't compare with that.'

He gave her an empathetic smile. 'Did you have any inkling he was having an affair?'

She tried to remember but everything was hazy and clouded with the emotions she had after he'd dropped his bombshell. 'There were probably signs, but I refused to look too hard. Even though we were having regular sex because we were so desperate to get pregnant, we'd grown apart. I spent most of my life at work, as did he... probably trying to avoid coming home to our sad reality. We passed like ships in the night, barely speaking. It was like we'd stopped knowing what to say to each other. And now I wonder if a baby would have actually healed us or whether it would have been a huge mistake to bring a child into the world with parents who'd grown so far apart there was no coming back.'

'Maybe it was as simple as you just outgrew each other. People change over time.'

'Maybe. Maybe he'd have left me for Lauren anyway. His secretary too. Such a cliché.'

Jono winced. 'But I guess, statistically, most people meet their partners at work.'

'True. At least they had the good grace to move to a different part of the country.'

She thought about that time of her life when everything had tipped sideways, leaving her grappling for stability and then finding it not from anyone else but within herself. It had taken a lot of work, was still taking work, but she no longer relied on anyone else to define or validate her. 'Actually, one of the hardest things was sharing out who got what when he moved out. We'd bought everything together. Built our life together. Then we had to unpick all those carefully woven threads completely apart. Watching him walk out of the door with his suitcase almost killed me. And now it's as if we were never married at all. Apart from the hurt.'

Jono rubbed her back gently. He knew all this, of course, but it was good to say it out loud. For the last time. It felt as if she could finally breathe properly again after years of tightness.

'In hindsight, perhaps I shouldn't have bought him out; we should have sold this place and I could have started fresh somewhere else.'

'No. You did the right thing by staying here. This place is great. Close to work and the shops, but feels like you're in the countryside. It's the kind of house I would have chosen. It feels like a home. I like what you've done in this room.' Jono pointed to the grey and saffron-coloured Roman blinds and the geometric print wallpaper on the feature wall with pops of the same red-orange as the soft furnishings. 'It's bright and happy.'

Should have been bright and happy and alive with the sound of baby giggles, then toddler laughter.

If they'd been successful on their first attempt their child would be ten now.

A lump formed in her throat. She had to stop bringing the past into her present. 'Glad you're pleased with it.'

'I love it here, but you're probably sick of having me under your feet.'

She wasn't sure what she should say to that. Was he saying he wanted to go? Or asking to stay?

And just like that the closeness they'd forged was being chipped away by the awkwardness of this new intimacy. 'Have you looked for anywhere else to live yet?'

She knew he hadn't. The man had only just completed a week in his new job, then his spare time had been spent either visiting his father or planning the party here. She also knew that if they hadn't just shared a very special evening, if they'd remained just friends, she'd be able to ask him outright and without experiencing the pain in her heart.

She scanned his face for any tell-tale signs of how he was feeling about moving out but he just shrugged and said, 'Not yet. But I'll have a look tomorrow.'

After what they'd just done and the way her body and, she had to be honest, her heart ached for him, she didn't think she could cope with watching another man walk out of her house.

It's temporary. She knew this. There was no point hoping or wishing for anything other than that. She had to accept he'd walk away at some point. And she'd started to trust again, sure, but she would always keep a little part of her untouchable, because she was not going to let herself be hurt again. Ever.

'There's no rush. You can stay as long as you want.'

'Thanks. I do like it here.' He put his forehead to hers and kissed the bridge of her nose. Then he slid his hand in between her legs and parted them. 'I especially like it right here.'

'I like you being there too.' She giggled. Because how could she resist?

He kissed her fully then and all thoughts of her past were erased. All she could think about was this amazing man, this tender moment. This opportunity they'd been given.

She pulled back, captured his gaze and held it, thoughts of their deepening relationship flitting through her mind like a film reel. The brush of fingertips. Their beach kiss. His story. His father. Jono's commitment to his work. His laugh. God, she loved his laugh and the casual cheekiness he won everyone over with. But he'd especially won her. Totally. Heart and soul.

He was so much more than she'd ever imagined. He believed in her. He'd supported her through the worst of times. He made her laugh. He made her feel protected, supported. He made her feel beautiful.

This was so different to what she'd had with Ross. She was falling deeply into…something. Something she refused to put a name to because she couldn't be the woman he wanted: the mother of his kids. She couldn't let him see just how *much* she felt for him.

But just for tonight she was going to let herself fall. Tears pricked the back of her eyes and her throat was raw. She stroked his cheek. 'Thank you.'

'Don't.' He took her hand and kissed her knuckles, his eyes heated and yet soft.

But she was confused. 'Don't what?'

'Thank me for anything. You have no idea what a big deal this is for me too.'

He pulled her closer and kissed her again. She could feel his erection and pressed against him, wanting him deep inside her again.

Then he quickly sheathed and was inside her. And this time it was slow and beautiful and when they tumbled over the edge together she knew that, despite what she'd been trying to convince herself earlier, she didn't want him to leave. Ever. She wanted to go to sleep in his arms and wake to every fresh start with him lying next to her.

Always.

Her best friend. Her lover.

After, he held her until their breathing normalised and the world took on a sharper edge.

If only we could spend for ever wrapped in each other's arms.

Such a silly, romantic notion, but she couldn't help her thoughts straying to what-ifs and hopes. Everything was muddled now, all mixed up with no defined edges, and her heart contracted at the thought. She'd been so turned on, so desperate for more of his kisses and for him to be inside her she'd glossed over all the reasons why they shouldn't.

'Hey, it's well after midnight. Tomorrow is the new today.' His words fanned over her cheek. 'Can this be our new start?'

'Ah, yes. Your mum always said to make the most of every new day.' She stretched out, her ankles crossing his. 'Today can start like this.'

But tomorrow? The next day? Next month? How long before he disappeared to a different house? Country? Another place where he tried to put down roots? Or to another woman? Like Ross had. To the one thing she couldn't compete with.

A family.

CHAPTER FOURTEEN

LEXI LOOKED AT the four-year-old boy sitting on Chantelle's knee at the nurses' station, tears streaming down his puffy cheeks, and her heart melted. 'Hey, Enofe, you're back. Were you missing us?'

Chantelle ran her hand over his cropped hair. 'I think Enofe loves being here with us, don't you, little fella?'

The boy looked up at them with his huge but sunken brown eyes and solemnly nodded.

They all knew he didn't want to be here all over again, with grown-ups taking his blood and making rules about what he could eat and drink and stopping him from playing football in his garden at home.

Chantelle looked at Lexi over Enofe's head. 'Admitted last night with a relapse of his nephrotic syndrome. Dr Calder put him on steroids and a no salt diet and we're monitoring his fluid balance. I'd say he's a little brighter than when he was admitted, but he's feeling pretty sorry for himself.'

'I don't blame him.' Lexi pouted in sympathy at the little boy. His body was swollen from fluid retention, which no doubt made his skin hurt. He would also probably have nausea and dizziness and generally feel lousy. 'Feeling yucky?'

Enofe nodded and fisted away the tears on his cheeks.

'Okay, I'll take a look at his notes.' Lexi turned back to Chantelle. 'Is mum around? How's she doing? Isn't she pregnant? How's that going?'

'Ah.' The charge nurse nodded. 'It doesn't rain but it pours for some of our families. Mum's just gone into premature labour and is down on the labour ward. Dad's in Nigeria on business but is trying to get a flight back as soon as he can. Nana's coming up from London, but she can't drive, so she's catching the train and at the mercy of their timetable and line works. So he's here on his own, poor little fella. I'm trying to do some paperwork, but he needs a friend to chat to.'

Lexi bent down so she could be at Enofe's level. 'Oh, poor you.' He hid his face in her scrubs and her heart cracked. 'Hey, come here.'

He slid his arms round her neck and hugged in close. She stroked his back until her left leg went to sleep. 'Hey, you, I've got to stand up now.'

And look at his charts, assess his medications and vital observations, plan his further treatment, as well as deal with the other children in her care. But she couldn't leave him on his own either. She glanced around, noting that all the other staff were busy too. She'd just have to stay later to finish the day's work. And that was okay with her.

Still saying nothing, Enofe put his arms out to be picked up. Her heart just about melted into a puddle in her chest. It amazed her how so many of her patients put all their trust in the hospital staff, even though most of them would rather be anywhere but here.

Sometimes being a paediatrician hurt her heart too much. Every time she saw a child in pain, or neglected or sick, she ached to help them. But it also healed, to some extent, the yawning space in her chest that she'd hoped to have filled, once upon a time, with a child of her own. If she couldn't have kids, she could spend her life helping them.

She lifted Enofe up, being careful not to dislodge the cannula in the back of his chubby wrist. 'Okay, come on. Let's have a look in the toy corner and see what we can find to play with.'

She started to make her way across the ward when she heard someone call her name. Not just someone. Jono. Her heart did a little jig at the sound of his voice. 'Lexi. Hey.'

She turned to see him smiling and happy and her whole body responded. They'd had six amazing nights together and she didn't think she'd ever felt this satisfied, or sleepy or happy, all rolled into a very pleasant sexual exhaustion. As she made eye contact with him the rest of the world faded just a little. Nothing was as bright and vibrant and perfect as Jono Neale. 'Hi there.'

He strode over and gently ran his fingertip over Enofe's little fist. 'Who's this?'

'This is Enofe. He's here while we make him feel better and fix his kidneys. He's got congenital nephrotic syndrome.' She turned to the boy. 'This is Dr Jono. He's my friend.'

She lifted her eyes to Jono's and saw so much care and affection and tease there it took her breath away and it took all her effort not to press her mouth to his.

The way she felt about him was almost indescribable. A satisfaction and yet a yearning. A restless desperation to be with him and yet a settled calm deep in her bones that he was in her life. As if her whole body whispered on a sigh, 'There he is,' every time she looked at him.

Almost indescribable, because she knew what it was.

She'd known it that first time they'd made love and refused to put a name to it, but she couldn't ignore it any more.

She loved him.

Sure, she'd always loved him, as a friend. They'd hung out at medical school, worked on the same rotations as house officers. He'd been part of her friendship group. Then latterly she'd looked forward to his messages, and she'd needed him to prop her up when she'd been so very sad.

But now—now—she was *in love* with him. Deeply. Totally. Utterly.

The kind of love that made her weak with desire, made her fiercely protective of him with his father's antics, made her hate the idea of him being with any another woman. Wingmanning be damned.

The kind of love that should be protected, revered and cherished.

Bone-deep, heart-wrenching, life-changing love.

The admission made her world tip sideways. No, not tip sideways. Lurch so hard she actually gripped the back of a chair to steady herself.

How could she have allowed this to happen?

But, truth was, she hadn't been able to stop it. She'd been swept along by the fun and the sex and the laughter and the emotion. But…to be in so deep? Especially when she knew the realities of their lives and the disconnect with what they both wanted long-term.

And…he was her best friend. Friends didn't have sex. Friends didn't kiss the way she and Jono kissed. It had gone way beyond anything they'd be able to salvage their friendship from. Any rejection now would be a deep personal wound.

She hated the thought that he wouldn't be in her life more than if he had another woman in his.

Panic spiralled through her.

Oblivious to the storm raging inside her, Jono winked at Enofe. 'Pleased to meet you, Master Enofe.'

'Hello.' The little boy looked up at Jono with something akin to adoration too. Was that how she looked when she gazed up at Jono?

Was it so obvious to him? To everyone?

'Enofe's mum's just gone downstairs to deliver him a baby brother or sister and he was feeling a bit sad being left on his own,' Lexi told him. 'He didn't fancy playing with any of the other kids, because he doesn't know them. But he knows me so we're going to find something to play with.'

'You've got Lexi to make you feel better. Good choice. She makes me feel better too.' Jono threw her a cheeky, sex-filled smile.

Heat sped through her and she glared at him to stop. But also to keep going. Because, despite herself, she wanted to bask in the heat of those dark eyes. Wanted to kiss him for the rest of her life. Wanted him, so badly, to be part of her future.

Jono grinned.

She dug very deeply to find him a grin back, trying to smile away the whirlwind in her head. Thinking about last night. And this morning. How they had become closer than ever in such a short space of time. And how exposed her heart was. How much she'd tried not to think about anything past the moment, when she should have always been thinking about the future and about protecting herself.

Jono's eyes were full of *later, later* promises. He swallowed and focused on Enofe. 'Bricks are good. I like building things. Bet you like building things too, don't you?'

'Yes.' Enofe managed a smile. 'And football.'

'Enofe is football mad.' Lexi pointed to the boy's Oxford United shirt.

'Good choice.' Jono gave him the thumbs-up sign. 'Then we can build a football stadium. Come on.'

'Oh, no, seriously. You don't have to.' Lexi slid the boy to the floor and sat down with him and Jono. 'I'm sure you've got loads of things to do.'

'I have thirty minutes spare. I was going to take you for a coffee before I take my dad home, but we can do this instead. Enofe is far more important, aren't you, mate?' He gave him another wink and started to rummage through a bucket of brightly coloured bricks.

She watched him play with Enofe, chatting so naturally, his eyes sparkling as he taught the boy how to stack the bricks, and laughed heartily when the stadium they'd so carefully built was demolished in a second because Enofe wanted to build a dinosaur park instead. Jono had a real and natural way with children and it made her heart ache to watch them together.

She'd come to terms with having a child-free life but what did he really want? At the wedding he'd talked about a family. He was still so young and had a zillion chances to build what he dreamt of. She, on the other hand, had no chances left.

Her heart shoved hard against her breastbone. She'd been fooling herself, pretending things would be perfect between them. Because how could they be?

How could she let herself fall more deeply under his spell, when all that existed for them was heartbreak?

She heard him whistling as he opened the front door and her heart squeezed. He sounded so happy. Clearly things must have gone well with his dad.

That was one less thing to worry about. Good.

She busied herself in the kitchen, trying to give the impression she'd been working hard on dinner and not trying to work out how to have the conversation they absolutely, definitely had to have.

She forced a smile as he grazed her lips with his. 'You're in a good mood. I take it your dad didn't bite your head off?'

'Kiss me first. I've been thinking about you all day. Wanting to strip your clothes off.' He wrapped his arms around her and pulled her hard against him. 'You feel so good. Fancy a quickie?'

Oh, yes. Always. But she tapped his chest and pulled back to look at his face. 'Honestly, you have a one-track mind.'

'It's your fault. You make me so horny.' As he kissed her his hand slid under her T-shirt and he pushed her against the kitchen counter where, only yesterday, they'd made love.

Love.

That was the problem.

Closing her eyes so he wouldn't see the sheen of tears threatening to spill, she pressed her mouth to his. Allowed herself to sink into his embrace. To commit to her memory his taste, his scent, the feel of him in her arms, so big and strong and steady.

I love you. So, so much. Don't hate me.

She pulled away again and forced words through a throat that was thick with unshed tears. 'Ahem. Right. Your dad?'

'Yeah. Good, actually. I think he must have been whisked into hospital without any notice because his house was a bit of a mess. Not up to usual army standards.' He stood to attention and saluted, laughing.

From somewhere she found a smile she hoped looked genuine. She was happy for him, absolutely, but it was breaking her heart seeing him so positive, knowing the conversation she had to have with him. 'I'm sure you soon remedied that.'

'If nothing else, my father taught me about the importance of keeping everything neat and tidy. Although that was ironic given his chaotic personal life. It's all a bit sad now though, because he didn't have anyone visit in hospital other than me. He had no family photos on the walls. Nothing. And no one.' He grimaced. 'I think I'm the only person he's got.'

'I hope he's grateful you're giving him a second chance.'

'I wouldn't say that exactly, but he did thank me for taking him home and eventually admitted he wasn't the father he should have been.'

'Oh, Jono. That's something, right?'

His eyes glittered with hope. 'Absolutely, although he didn't go into specifics and I'm not sure I want to go there anyway. What's the point in bringing up all that pain when we should be looking forward? Fresh starts, right? We like those.'

Her heart twisted some more. He looked at her with a teasing grin and she couldn't summon any words so she mutely nodded.

'Oh, and he asked where you were. He's still got an eye for the ladies.' Jono laughed ruefully. 'But seeing his house and how he lives and the lack of visitors made me finally realise that I'm not really like him at all. I wondered if I couldn't commit to a place or a person because I had his genes, but I do care about people other than myself. I care about you, Lexi, and my friends and my patients and I care about him enough to keep turning up, like you suggested. Thank you for that.'

He'd wanted an end to the father-son impasse so badly because underneath all the playful vibes Jono was actually a softie with a very big heart. A man who deserved the family life he craved. She smiled, even though her chest felt heavy. 'I'm so glad it went well.'

'Will you come with me to see him tomorrow? I think having you there would really cheer him up.'

Panic radiated through her. That would only underscore her and Jono's relationship when, in fact, they needed to stop it.

Trying to buy herself some time, she pulled a salad out of the fridge then handed him the steaks she'd put on the counter to bring to room temperature. 'Crank up the barbecue, caveman. And let's eat. I'm starving.'

He took the steaks from her and sauntered out of the kitchen into the back garden.

She took the chance to brace herself for what she was going to say. Gripping the countertop, she closed her eyes, took a deep breath and started to let it—

'There's no salt on these.'

'Oh.' She opened her eyes.

Had he seen her taking stock? He slid a kiss onto her cheek, his smile wide and broad. He looked so content, so calm. So clearly he hadn't noticed her anguish.

Her heart hammered hard, like rapid fire against her ribcage. When would be the best time to say the things she needed to say?

'First rule of a good steak is to season it well before cooking. Then the salt creates a tasty coating.' He ground salt over the slabs of beef. 'I said I'd get fish and chips on the way over to see him. We could all eat together and watch the football. You know how it is; eating gives us something to do instead of sitting in an awk-ward silence. Of which, I'm sure, there will be many. My dad is a man of few words.' He gave her a wobbly kind of smile. Apologetic but determined.

And her heart started to crumble because, in that pre-vious life where she and Jono were just friends instead of lovers, she'd have happily agreed to visit his dad with him. 'Actually, I've got a nightmare day tomorrow and I wouldn't want to hold you up. You should probably go on your own.' She ran trembling fingers over her fore-head, trying to smooth away the start of a tension head-ache. Here she was, making up excuses. Lying to him.

He put the plate down, stepped closer and wrapped his arms round her, hugging her against his chest. 'Lexi, what's wrong?'

'Nothing.' She pushed away from him. 'I'm fine.'

'Really, you're not. What's wrong? You're holding something back and I'd like to know, if it's so impor-tant, if I can help.'

No one could help her. That was the problem. She was all out of ways to resolve this.

'Jono. Please.'

Her heart rattled and her chest seemed to turn itself inside out. But she couldn't avoid it any more or go on pretending they could get by without the honesty and the truth that was the elephant in the room, in their lives. He wanted a family. She couldn't give it to him. He had a chance—he was young, he could find a woman, fall in love and have the family he craved. The family he deserved. She couldn't hold him back. She loved him too much for that.

She didn't just love his ideas and thoughts and words—she loved the way he kissed the tip of her nose before they left for work every morning. The way he always had her coffee waiting for her when she got back from her run. She loved the hollow of his throat, the way he kissed, the way he tasted. She loved the chats they had after making love. The way he snuggled against her before they went to sleep. She loved looking at him when she woke up, the way her chest felt light when she was with him, the way she looked forward to everything because he was fully in her life.

And because she loved him like that, she had to do this one thing for him.

She had to let him go.

CHAPTER FIFTEEN

HOT DAMN. SHE was retreating from him. Closing down right in front of him. Pretending to concentrate on fixing a salad, eyes firmly on the bowl and not meeting his gaze.

Truth was, he'd told himself that the main reason he'd come back to Oxford had been to see his father, but his friendship with Lexi had made him want a closeness he hadn't found in Australia. It wasn't the place or the people; it was him and his issues. He'd wanted to go back to where it had all started and sort it out.

And he'd wanted to see Lexi too. She'd been the one bright thing that had enticed him to buy the ticket, the embodiment of hope he'd had when he'd stepped off the last interminable flight, looking forward to seeing her face and catching up in person. Although he hadn't expected it to develop into more.

Certainly not a week of amazing sex, of heart-to-hearts, of working and living together. He loved going to sleep with her in his arms and waking up to her smiling face. He loved the way he could make her laugh. And the way his heart felt full every time he looked at her.

But she was still holding something back. She didn't trust him entirely. He could see the hesitancy in her eyes. And if he was being honest, he wasn't sure he was giving everything too. Because he'd seen her hesitancy and felt it and didn't know if he could put his heart on a platter only to have it smashed.

Or whether he deserved to hold her heart in his hands. Whether he even could. Because he'd never been in love. He'd never stayed the course. He liked the chase but didn't know how to see it through to the end. He'd never been a constant in anyone's life, not like Lexi. She'd been in a long-term committed relationship. She knew what it took to keep things together and how badly hurt you got when you failed.

He had a bad feeling he was way more involved than she was. Which left him exposed and at risk, which he'd never been before with a woman because he'd never allowed anything to get this deep, this fast. But he wanted to try to make it work, to be the guy he'd always wanted to be. The guy she deserved.

And yet here she was, looking at him as if her heart was about to break.

He shook his head, his heart pounding against his chest. 'Hey. Talk to me, Lexi. What's the matter?'

She'd stepped away but he craved her closeness. As he moved towards her she took a step back. And another. Eventually she raised her hand. 'Look, Jono, we've been avoiding talking about it, but we can't avoid it any more. The absolute truth is, I have eight years on you.'

'And so?' She was beautiful. So beautiful it made his heart contract just to look at her. Beautiful and wise and funny and sexy. 'How old you are doesn't matter to me. I've told you so many times. Seriously, age is nothing to me.'

She closed her eyes and looked as if she was fighting back tears.

His gut tightened at her reaction. What the hell was this about? Why was she almost crying?

When she opened her eyes again she looked directly at him, her expression filled with sadness. But there was resolve there too, as if she was forcing herself to say words she really, really didn't want to. Giving bad news.

He knew the signs. He'd done it himself.

He'd been given it too. His mother's death. The doctor's slow intake of breath, the deliberately soft voice. The desperate expression of not wanting to say the words, but also wishing they could take your pain away.

Losing the only person in the world that you loved.

'It doesn't matter in a cerebral sense, no. And it wouldn't have mattered years ago at medical school, or in ten years' time. But right now...*right now...*' she jabbed her finger towards the floor '...you're in your prime, Jono. You have so much to look forward to. You can find a woman younger than you, hell, even a couple of years older than you, and you can have the family you want. But I'm out of time. I've run out. I can't have kids; I'm probably even too old for IVF if I'm honest.' She shook her head. 'No—actually, I can't do that again. Not for me, not for you. It was too hard and too painful, putting everything else in my life on hold. Timetabled sex. Cancelled holidays because we'd just secured an unexpected appointment for yet another chance. The injections. The hormones... My God, the hormones. And all that hoping and wishing, only to be let down month after month. I've just got my life back. I can't go there again.'

'But the only thing that matters is us two.' Surely she understood that? 'I don't care about having children. I just want to be with you.'

She blinked quickly and a tear slipped down her cheek. 'You might think that now, but you may not think that further down the track. One of the first things you said to me when you came back was that you wanted the whole family thing.'

He trawled through his memory banks, pulling up conversations they'd had about things like this. The wedding. Walking back down the aisle. The pang in his chest as he watched the happy couples. 'I think I said something along the lines of, *I'm ready to settle*.'

She nodded, her eyes so dark. 'Right before you and Emma had a conversation about having kids.'

'What? I don't remember that.'

She nodded, her fingers gripping the salad servers. 'I heard you.'

'We talked about weddings and…' raking over what had been said '…wait…no. You can't have heard me say that, because I didn't. She did ask if I wanted kids. I said it wasn't a deal-breaker and that I was probably far too selfish to share my stuff and she laughed. Because I was probably right. At least I *was* too selfish to share, now I'm actually really happy to share things with you. Everything, Lexi.'

'No.' She blinked, holding her hand up again to shut him up. 'This is so hard to say, but you have to listen. Please. You might think having kids isn't important to you now, but what about in two years? Five? The truth is, I can't give you the kids you want. The future you've come home for.'

She was actually serious. A solid darkness bloomed in his gut. 'We could adopt.'

'I'm too old to adopt babies. Ross and I talked about it, looked into it. There are so many hoops to jump through.'

'There are ways. If not babies, then toddlers…like Enofe. We have options.'

'Yes, we do. And I'm choosing mine.' She dropped the servers onto the countertop and wrapped her arms around her chest, blocking him from any approach or attempt to touch her. 'You have to move out. I'm sorry. We can't keep doing this.'

'Whoa. You're not listening to me, Lexi.' The darkness clouded his thoughts.

After everything they'd been through she clearly didn't see him as anything but the old Jono who didn't take things seriously, who played around, who changed his mind and acted selfishly—like his father had. But he wasn't Gordon Neale. 'You don't think I'd stay with you?'

'Ross didn't.' She looked away.

'You want to know what I think? That you keep throwing up your age as a barrier, and when I tell you it's not important you tell me you're doing this for my own good. Then you put up other barriers like kids and ideas of family that I never even said I wanted. But, in reality, the truth is, deep down you don't trust me. You don't want to take a risk on me.' This was what happened when you tried to reach out to someone, when you finally and willingly gave your heart?

You got it stomped on.

'I...' She inhaled a shaky breath but no more words came out.

He exhaled, trying to keep in control. 'There's my answer. You don't want to take a chance, do you?'

She didn't trust him. Maybe he was wrong and she could see through to his core; maybe he was every bit like his father after all and wouldn't be able to settle down with one woman.

But he knew he was not that man. The only woman he'd ever want was Lexi.

She pressed her lips together. Then, 'I'm hoping we could stay friends...once the dust has settled. That we can start again and be what we were for each other, before we let our hearts rule our heads.'

'You want to be my friend? After everything we've done and shared? How do you imagine we could get back to that? Next minute you'll be asking to be my wingman again. We're in too deep, Lexi. Way too deep to go back to being just friends.' His chest felt as if a huge chasm was opening up inside it. 'And I don't even get a say in this.'

'Don't you see? I'm trying to preserve something of us. I don't think I could bear to lose you, Jono, if we committed to something and then you changed your mind. If you left me for someone younger and pregnant.'

'I'm not bloody Ross.'

'I know. But years of being a couple, a wedding band and marriage vows couldn't keep us together. Now he's just someone I used to know. We're just exes. Not friends. Not even a little bit. I cherish your friendship more than anything. You're the best person I have in my life and I don't want to risk losing that.'

He wasn't going to resort to begging but, surely in hell, she could see how good they could be together? 'You don't think we could make it even better? Friends and sex? Hasn't that got to be worth fighting for?'

'I'm fighting for the future you were planning before we got carried away and tumbled into bed. Fighting for that Jono who was so excited at the prospect of starting a fresh life here, the guy who wanted what Emma and Mark have. What Preeti and Bhavesh have.'

'Look.' He slammed his palm on the counter and immediately regretted it because sharp words wouldn't convince her. It was a struggle but he softened his tone from desperate to something he didn't recognise. Strangled? 'I don't know if I came back to settle down. But now, when I look back, it's obvious that I came back to you. To my dad, sure. But the pull back to Oxford wasn't the thought of a grumpy old man who doesn't even know me; it was you. It was always you, Lexi. At the wedding I watched Preeti and Bhavesh, Emma and Mark, and I was envious of what they have. I may have translated that into the whole family package, but I'd be happy... I'd be absolutely satisfied and content and not want anything more than this. You and me talking about things that matter. Laughing together. *Living* our lives together. Being kind to each other. Loving each other. That's the future I want.'

Wow.

Every word was true. Especially the loving bit. Because, hell, if that wasn't what this feeling in his chest was, he didn't know what else to call it.

Love. He'd been shying away from it ever since his mother had died, because he had never wanted to care so much for someone and then feel that kind of loss again. Or that bleakness. But he couldn't deny it was the way he felt right now. Along with a jumble of joy and fear, of certainty and shaky ground. Of pain and loss and yet... something so complete and pure that he couldn't deny it. Knowing someone, truly knowing them, admiring them, craving them, wanting to be with them for ever, whatever. An unshakeable truth.

He swallowed as *his* truth sank in. He'd fallen in love with her, even when he didn't believe love was possible for him. She was his anchor; she steadied him. She was the future he wanted to cling to. Lexi.

He reached to cup her cheek. 'And maybe *that* was

the soppiest thing I've ever said. But hold onto your hat because there's more... I—'

'No.' Fear clouded her eyes. She shook her head and covered her mouth with her hand but he still heard her say, 'Please don't. Please don't, Jono.'

But maybe, just maybe, this might convince her. Because if she knew how he felt, surely she wouldn't push him away? Words he'd never said to another single soul spilled from him. 'I love you, Lexi.'

She stared at him, her hand dropping to her side, her mouth a flat line. She shook her head. Her lips quivered. More tears slid down her cheeks. She swallowed, made a strange choking sound. Her nose dripped. She shuddered on her exhale.

He waited for her to say those words back to him. If she did there would be some hope. Something they could hang these threads of their lives onto.

But she edged out of his reach. 'I'm sorry, Jono. But no. I can't do it.'

Right.

He stepped away.

She didn't want him. Hell, if he didn't already know how *that* felt. His heart was just about blown into pieces.

His brave, beautiful Lexi was too scared to take a risk. And there was absolutely nothing that he could do about that. Nothing.

He stared into her dark eyes, and remembered all the amazing things they'd shared: the passion and the softness, the laughter and the serious times. And she was willing to throw it all away for a dream he didn't know if he wanted any more.

Okay. There were no words to describe how this felt. He'd gone into this for a bit of fun and now he was in so deep he couldn't navigate a safe passage out. He was just…lost.

So he turned and walked towards the door, leaving his heart right there in the kitchen. 'I'll go and start packing.'

Lexi sat at the bottom of the stairs and listened to the slide of drawers and the thump of his rucksack hitting the floor. The steps to the bathroom for toiletries, the scrape and jangle of metal coat hangers.

It was déjà vu on repeat. And it took everything in her not to run upstairs and tell him to stay. But she couldn't, because this was the only possible course of action.

But, for the record, she was never going to do this again.

Never.

Never going to let a man into her heart.

Never going to allow a man under skin or into her bed. And definitely never to move into her house.

Because watching them leave just about broke her.

But this time she was the one doing the breaking up. And it hurt so much more to watch Jono walk down the stairs, his rucksack banging against the wall, when she could say the words to make him stay.

She fisted her tears away with her cardigan sleeve and looked up at him. His face was stone, his eyes haunted. 'Where will you go? To your dad's?'

'Are you for real?' He shook his head, disappointed in her. 'A hotel is far more preferable.'

'It's summertime; they'll be full of tourists.'

'I've already booked a room.' He hoisted the rucksack onto his back and stepped around her off the bottom step. His movements were stiff, as if he'd built a wall around himself already. She'd never seen him like this before, her carefree, fun-loving Jono barricaded inside this shell.

When he reached for the door handle she stood. Put her hand on his shoulder. 'I'm sorry, Jono. I'm really, really sorry.'

He turned his head to look at her. Closed his eyes briefly as if trying to regain some control. 'I know. That's what makes this whole thing crazy.'

Then he opened the door and stepped out into the night. She managed to hold it together as she watched until he disappeared round the corner.

She remembered the way he'd played so joyfully with Enofe.

It's the right thing to do. It has to be. You'll thank me in the end.

Although it was cold comfort right now. She hadn't just lost her heart, she'd lost her best friend. This time she would have no Jono to help her heal. No Jono to brighten her day.

Except, of course, she'd see him every day at work. From a distance she'd watch him heal, watch him flirt, watch him…maybe marry. Watch his family grow.

I love you.

She closed the door behind him. Then slid down the wall onto her haunches and finally let her heart break.

CHAPTER SIXTEEN

JONO WAS TRYING very hard not to let his dad get on his nerves, but every day it felt as if Gordon Neale was trying to stomp on each one individually.

Okay. So it wasn't his dad that was the problem. It was Jono. He softened his tone before speaking. 'I appreciate that the diuretics make you go to the loo more often. That's their job, Dad.' Every day it was the same complaints. The diuretics, the bad food, Jono was too late or too early. Every day they went through this.

A harrumph from the grumpy corner. 'I just get comfortable and then I'm up and going again.'

'They keep the fluid from settling round your heart. So peeing is a good thing. Okay?'

'Still not heard anything from her then?' Across the dining table his father pierced him with a questioning look.

Lexi. The other half of his heart.

Jono was about to change the subject, but he got the feeling his dad would niggle away at it so he acquiesced. 'That obvious?'

'Your mood has worsened by degrees since you moved out of her house. I think we're at peak feeling sorry for ourselves right now. At least I hope so. I don't think I can put up with much more of this.'

Say what? Jono bristled. *He* was getting on his father's nerves? 'It's difficult, that's all.'

'Spit it out. Tell me.'

And now he wanted a heart-to-heart? This was surreal. His life had done a weird one-eighty twist, where his father was now his confidant and Lexi was the person he couldn't talk to.

Since losing his best friend and starting a new job where he didn't know people well enough to mope around them, he'd had no one else to confide in. And he just wanted to talk about her.

He blew out a slow breath. 'Where to start? I see her across the hospital café. I hear her voice in the emergency room. I can smell her perfume on my clothes. I dream about her. I can't seem to get her out of my head. Every little thing—her gestures, her laugh, her eyes. I don't know how to move on from this. And why I'm telling you this I don't know.' He put his head in his hands and laughed, because that was all there was left to do.

'Me neither,' his dad agreed. 'Because you won't listen to whatever I say anyway. But I'll give it a go. Tell her what you think, how you feel.'

Jono looked up. 'I already have and she threw me out. Trust me, I don't want to go through that again. She doesn't want me. She's decided we're not going to have a future and once she's made up her mind there's no convincing her otherwise.'

'Almost as stubborn as you then.'

'Pot. Kettle. Black.' Jono met his father's eyes and wondered if he'd realise Jono was joking. They'd come a long way but there was a longer road to travel yet. He waited for the angry outburst.

But his dad just shook his head sadly. 'I can't tell you how much I wish I'd done things differently. How I wish

I had the chance to rewind and tell people what I really felt. You know…be able to get the words out.'

Whoa. 'What words, Dad?'

'You know which ones.' His dad reached across the space between them and patted Jono's hand. 'You're a strong and capable lad. You'll get through this.'

'You think?'

'I know. A Neale heart is made of strong stuff.' He lifted his hand from Jono's and leaned back in his chair. 'Right. Come back tomorrow and bring something decent for supper. That pie had too much gristle in it.'

And so he was summarily dismissed.

Outside, Jono took a moment to work out what the heck had just happened. Had his dad tried to tell him he cared? He wasn't sure, but he was choosing to read between the lines.

He'd also told him how much he regretted not saying things to the people he loved.

Jono was not going to be like his father. So he was going to work out exactly how to fight for Lexi. And then he was going to do it.

He was going to fight for them.

'Want Jono to play.' Enofe put the red brick on the floor and looked up at Lexi with plaintive eyes that told her she wasn't exactly up to scratch on this building a football stadium game.

Great. Jono's fan club was still in full swing then.

Well, yes, it was. And she was still a card-carrying member.

So it was doubly frustrating that she came to work to forget him but bumped into reminders of him at unexpected turns. Like this little fella who wanted to play with him. Her heart hurt—she looked at the boy and shared a sad smile of solidarity—almost as much as Enofe's. 'He's not here, honey, I'm sorry. How about we find something else to play with?'

'Actually, we're just going to take him down to see mum and his baby brother in NICU.' One of the nursing assistants trotted over and held out her hand, which Enofe took like a lifeline.

'Give him a kiss from me,' Lexi called after them and waved. Sometimes even her job didn't give her all the positive feelings she wanted from it.

Then she scrambled up from where she'd been sitting on the floor and wandered over to the nurses' station, looking for a distraction from her current turbulent thoughts about Jono.

Trouble was, there was no distraction from a broken heart. Only time.

And not having constant reminders of him. Everywhere.

'Lexi. Hi, there honey. Just in time for cake.' Chantelle's voice brought her back to earth. The charge nurse was cutting a huge pink cake into pieces and sliding them onto plates. She handed one to Lexi. 'Becky's birthday. She left this for us.'

'That was nice of her.' Lexi took a bite. White chocolate and raspberry icing. It should have been delicious, but nothing seemed to taste good any more. And wow, she was miserable if cake didn't taste good.

She put the plate on the desk. What was he doing today? House-hunting? Visiting his dad?

She had to admit he'd been steadfast in trying to get his relationship with his father on track. Not taking no for an answer. Turning up every day. The way he had for her.

He knew what she'd been through, he'd shown how

much he cared for her over and over. He wouldn't say he loved her if he didn't mean it; he knew how hard that would be for her.

God, she missed him.

She loved him.

'Okay, missy.' Chantelle turned her swivel chair to face Lexi, knee to knee. 'It's Saturday and you're not on call, so please tell me why you're here.'

'I'm catching up.'

'Gazing into space is catching up. Right. Good.' A pause, during which Lexi was actually worried about what was coming next and she was pinned here with no escape. 'Is this something to do with your holiday souvenir?'

Lexi made an involuntary little laugh-sob sound. 'He's moved out.'

'I thought I hadn't seen him up here for a while. Used to pop in every day and now…nothing. You two had a fight?'

Lexi inhaled and blew out slowly, trying to control the inevitable swell of sadness inside her. 'I ended it.'

'Say what?' Chantelle looked at her as if she'd spoken in a foreign language. 'That is a good man. Or…did he do something wrong?'

'No. He did everything right. But he talked about having children and I immediately put the skids on our relationship. I can't have them, and I don't want to hold him back and have him resent me down the track.'

'Aw, honey. That's hard.'

'I don't know what to do. I miss him so much. We used to talk all the time. Say things to each other we'd never say to anyone else. I want him in my life, so much. Somehow. But how do I try and fix something when it's actually unfixable?' She'd known from the start that any romantic entanglement would destroy their friendship and she'd been right.

Chantelle's eyebrows rose. 'Is it unfixable?'

'I don't know. He said we could adopt or try surrogacy but I'm emotionally exhausted at the thought of that. He also said he'd be happy with just me. I don't know what to do.'

'Um...you could try believing him.' There was a reason why doctors had a lot of respect for charge nurses. Once they pinned you with their formidable stare you were completely in their thrall.

Lexi shrugged. 'I heard him. I can't pretend I didn't.'

'What exactly did he say?'

'He wants what our friends have.'

Chantelle leaned forward. 'Which is?'

'Preeti and Bhavesh have this really tight relationship. They've always been so good together. Soulmates, really. And they have a cute family. Twin girls and one boy and another baby on the way.'

'So they're soulmates. Okay.' Chantelle looked at her expectantly.

'And Mark and Emma have just got married, so they don't have kids or anything. They have each other. They have this way of looking at each other as if nothing else in the world matters.' Lexi sighed. It was what she wanted too. Didn't everyone?

The charge nurse nodded sagely. 'They love each other.'

'Wildly.'

'Any kids?'

'No. I don't know their plans.'

'I assume neither does Jono. But he wants what they've got?'

She could see where Chantelle was going with this. 'But what if he does want children, later down the line?'

'If he knows it's not on the cards, then I assume he'll accept it won't happen. Did he know you couldn't get pregnant before you two got involved?'

'Yes.'

'So, if he knew and he was already thinking about his future, do you think he'd have started something with you if having kids was a deal-breaker?'

'I don't know.'

'Come on, Lexi. I know you've been badly hurt before but don't let that colour your judgement here.'

Lexi said it out loud. 'I'm scared.'

'Good.' Chantelle smiled and took Lexi's hands in hers. 'Everyone should be scared at least once in their life. This is big. It's a risk. But is he a risk worth taking?'

Lexi fought back the tears. 'Without a doubt. Yes.'

'And what do you want to say to him now?'

'That I miss him, I love him. That I need him in my life. That he was right.' Lexi chuckled. 'He'd love to hear that. But I don't know how to say it. What if he hates me? I pushed him away. Like the only other significant person in his life.'

'It's been what? A week? Two?'

'More than two.'

'And you think he's going to hate you by now?' Chantelle tsked again. 'How did you two get so close in the first place? I thought he was in Australia for years.'

Lexi laughed. 'I feel like I'm in the psychiatrist's chair. We wrote to each other. Emails, texts. I was going through a breakup and I started to write to him.'

'Not phone?'

'No. The timing wasn't always right to actually chat. But there was this connection between us that felt so right. I told him everything and he did the same. We got each other through some messy relationship stuff.'

'Then try that. Write to him again. Get back in that zone.'

'You think?'

Chantelle picked up a plate of cake and dug her fork in. 'If you love him like you say you do, then anything is worth a try, right?'

And Lexi had to admit the woman had a damned good point.

Jono strode into his office on Monday morning after a weekend of house-viewing and his father's incessant complaining, neither of which had left him in a good mood.

'Morning Jono.' His secretary handed him an envelope. 'This came for you. It says private so I thought you'd better open it.'

No postmark, so hand-delivered. Jono turned it over and over. Who would physically write a letter instead of typing one these days?

But the handwriting was eerily similar to the shopping list on the fridge door in Lexi's house. Could it be from her?

His heart did a loop-the-loop as he opened it and read.

Saturday 21st August
Oxford

Hey, Jono,
 It's been a weird couple of weeks. The house seems so empty without you in it. No one to charcoal my meat. I have to make my own morning coffee. No annoying whistling.

No Jono.

I'm so sorry about the way things ended between us. Above all else, you're my best friend and I want us to be able to be there for each other the way we used to be. I know that it's my fault and I'm processing everything you said to me.

You know what I went through with Ross so I won't bore you again, but I'm scared to take a risk. Chantelle tells me I'm stupid for letting you go, but I'm trying to be fair to you because I care so much for you and want the right thing, for you.

I guess what I'm saying is I miss you more than I can say. You're the only person I've ever been able to be completely honest with, so I'm trying to make things right between us. I want us to try to get our friendship back on track. Somehow. I know it will take time.

Oh, your little friend Enofe needs a better stadium builder than my sad effort. If you could pop up to see him he'd love it. I won't be there on Tuesday or Wednesday afternoons as I have an outpatients clinic.

Where are you living now?

Anyway, I miss you. I miss us.

Lexi xxx

Jono read and reread the letter, trying to see a lifeline there that told him how she truly felt. She was processing. What did that mean? She missed him, but she gave him times she wouldn't be around for him to go see Enofe. How should he read that?

He didn't know.

His heart swung from happy to sad to unsure. No *I love you*. No *I want to be with you*.

But she'd reached out to him.

It was a start.

After dropping her letter off to his secretary Lexi didn't know what to expect from Jono and spent the whole day on tenterhooks, frantically checking her phone for any messages. But none came.

Would he think she was being silly? Had he moved on? She'd wanted to start the conversation. Had she said enough? Too much?

Finally, exhausted from a long day at work, she cycled home and found an envelope waiting for her on her doormat. Oxford Vista Hotel was printed on the front, above her name.

Her heart almost burst out of her chest as she tore the paper open.

Lexi, hi

Definitely a weird couple of weeks.

I'm looking for a place to rent but nothing has quite worked, so I'm still here at the hotel. It's walking distance from the hospital, which is great, but my room smells of boiled cabbage and the bed is lumpy.

It's been good weather, though...as I'm sure you know. This is crazy, right? I'm talking to you as if you're across the world when in fact you're almost in touching distance and you know exactly when it's been raining or sunny here. I'm also talking about the weather...what's happening to me?

I've taken to going for walks down by the river any chance I get and I smile to myself when I re-

member our day out on the punt. It was the best day. But I have to be honest and let you know. I lied to you; you are a terrible punter.

I'll make sure I visit Enofe. He's a good kid and makes me smile. Plus, who doesn't like building stuff with bricks?

Oh, and I've bought a car. A huge, luxurious Tesla which makes my dad almost spit every time I drive over to see him, because he can't see what's wrong with petrol. Although I think he'd be cranky about anything I did. I'm choosing to believe it's his unique way of saying I love you.

Talking of...

Her heart jumped as she turned the page over. Talking of...love?

...my dad. His health is improving day by day. Although clearly his mood isn't. I'm taking the approach that if he didn't have me to rail at he'd have nothing to live for. So at least I'm keeping him alive.

I hope you're okay. I think of you all the time. I miss you and our nightly chats. I miss everything.

Love always,

Jono xx

Sunday 22nd August
Old Marston

Jono. Hey.

I'll have you know that my punting is second to none. If I'd left it up to you we'd still be in the middle of the river going round in circles. It's a beautiful place.

It was the best day.

I hope you find a better place to live soon. A lumpy bed is no good. Cabbage is even worse.

I'm glad your dad is getting better and it sounds as if the two of you are perfectly matched. I can imagine you both sitting there pretending to be cross with each other because you can't say the words you want to say out loud.

Maybe he's just scared and he doesn't want to make himself vulnerable. Telling someone how you feel is so hard, but rejection is even harder. It undermines everything: your self-worth, your self-belief and your hope. And, yes, I speak from experience.

I'm okay. I think. I'm not sure. Work is the same. As you know, it's my constant. It's my happy place, or at least it has become so because my personal life sucks. My fault, I know. But I had to make some choices that I originally thought were for the best.

Now I'm having second thoughts. So many second thoughts.

Thank you for writing to me again. I've missed this part of us. I miss a lot of us. So much.

I miss you. Your smile. Your bad jokes. I'm going to stop there because otherwise you'll get all big-headed.

Tell me what's happening with you.

Your Lexi xxx

DrJonoNeale@gmail.com
Monday 23rd August 11.39 p.m.

Lexi,

We had a crash call this afternoon. It was tough. We lost the patient and I've been feeling off-balance ever since. I know it's something we face every day but he was a young guy with an undiagnosed arrhythmia. He had his whole life to look forward to, had made so many plans. He was due to get married in a couple of months.

It got me thinking.

I shouldn't think.

I miss you. I miss all the plans we never made but could have. I miss your scent on my pillow and your body curled around mine. I miss making you laugh.

I've told you how I feel and I'm pretty sure you feel the same way and yet here we are. I don't know how to convince you that it's all of you that I love, not just the bits that work the way they're supposed to. I know I can't prove to you that I will be by your side for ever unless you give me the chance to be there, next to you. But I want to be, with everything I am and everything I have. I'm your guy. Your person. You are mine.

We might decide to adopt or to try surrogacy, we might decide to live our best life, just the two of us. Those are conversations we need to have, but I want you to know I can only have my best life if I'm with you.

We don't know what's round the corner and we should grab every bit of happiness we can. I want to grab you…yes, in every way you can think of.

You said you made choices you thought were for the best. What are your second thoughts? In case you need more help making a decision, I wanted to let you know, my feelings aren't getting any less. I've loved you for as long as I can remember and I want to be in love with you for ever.

Yours always,

Jono xxx

DrJonoNeale@gmail.com
Tuesday 24th August 12.37 a.m.

God, sorry, Lexi.

I shouldn't drink and email. Had a crappy day today...oh, yesterday now.

I should stick to sending you emojis of aubergines, right? Or something.

Normal service will be resumed as from now.

J xxx

Jono pressed send and cringed. What an idiot.

She'd been processing. She'd been having second thoughts and she was too clever, too damned smart, to jump into something if she didn't give it careful consideration. She wasn't like him; she needed time.

So his plan had been to give her what she needed and hope like hell she'd realise what an amazing chance they had here, but now he was pushing her. And, knowing Lexi, she'd back further away.

Fuming with himself, he closed the laptop lid and walked the short distance across the hotel room from the desk to his bed.

The phone on the bedside table suddenly rang out its shrill soulless tone, making him jump. He grabbed the receiver, his heart hammering against his ribcage. Lexi? His dad? 'Hello? Room 213.'

'Night porter here. You called for a doctor?'

What? 'I...er...sorry?'

'There's a Dr Fisher here. Says it's an emergency.'

His heart just about stalled in his chest and a brightness bloomed there instead. 'Send her up.'

It probably only took five minutes, but time seemed to go in slow motion. He stood at the open door, telling himself it was because he didn't want her knocking to wake up his neighbours, but in truth he wanted to see her the moment she turned the corner from the lift.

And then she was there. Hair flowing loose round her shoulders, a light blue wrap over that yellow summer dress he'd stripped from her after the party.

Was that coincidence or by design? He hated that he couldn't read her these days.

As she got closer he whispered, 'Lexi?'

'Jono.' She nodded and walked into the room ahead of him, her scent wafting behind her, making him inhale over and over. He wanted to wrap her in his arms and kiss a trail from her throat to her mouth. To be inside her, making her moan, his name on her lips.

But he stood a few feet away. Looking at her. Waiting. Winding in all urges to press against her, to hold her. To tell her the things he felt.

She blinked up at him and nodded. So serious. Was she here to bawl him out about his email? 'Is everything okay, Lexi?'

'No, it isn't. I'm not okay, not at all.' She wrapped her arms round her chest. And he noticed then that her eyes were red and she was shaking.

'Oh.' This was not what he'd expected.

'I love writing to you, Jono. I love receiving your messages back. And I'm so, so sorry you had a crappy day. I know it sucks, and I know it doesn't help when I say you did your best. But you did.'

Ah. So she was here because she felt sorry for him. He ran his hand over his hair. 'It happens. Sorry for the email. I'd had one too many whiskies.' And they were still sloshing around his gut, burning the lining. Acid joined them now too. He pointed to the little padded chair tucked underneath the desk in this cramped space. 'Take a seat.'

'No, I need to say this out loud, and for some reason I can only do it standing up.'

'Sure. Go ahead.'

'I've watched you grow up, right? From a gangly eighteen-year-old to a committed, caring and compassionate doctor. But in the front of my mind I've always thought of you as someone who loves having fun and can't settle down.'

Was she going to talk herself out of this? 'Lexi—'

'No.' She held her hand up. 'Hear me out. The way you've committed to your love of medicine through everything, the way you've been a loyal constant in my life, and the way you've stuck with your dad even when it must have been hard, has made me look at you from a completely different place. Of course, I didn't see it until I thought harder about it.'

'You missed the bit about being great in bed.' He stepped closer, his chest alight with hope.

'I'm getting to that.' She gave him an uncertain smile. 'I'm older than you and I have no baby prospects and I've been bruised and hurt and I know I'm guarded. And I'm sorry I'm not an easier person to get to know. But you see me. You see me as a whole person. And you like me. Which is a miracle all of its own.'

'There are bits of you I like more than others, I have to admit.' He stroked up her ribs, tiptoeing fingers towards her breasts.

She gazed up at him. 'I have to take it on trust that you mean what you say.'

She'd trusted another man with her heart and he'd broken her. Jono pressed his mouth to her forehead. 'Hell, Lexi, I mean every damned word.'

Her voice was wobbly now. 'And you're right. Life is so short and I want to live my best life too, and I can only do it with you.'

It was everything he'd wanted to hear but... 'You need to be sure. I've had too many people push me away in my life. I'm not prepared to let it happen again.'

'Oh, I'm sure, Jono. And I'm going to show you just how sure I am every single day. I love you. I love your smile, your hope, your optimism. I love your commitment, your willingness to give me time. I love the way you show up despite wanting to run, and the fact you are hopeless at punting.'

'Hey—'

She silenced him with an earth-shattering, mind-melting kiss.

When she pulled away, all pink-cheeked and breathless, she said, 'And I love the way you are *great* in bed.' She ran the back of her knuckles down his cheek. 'I love you, Jonathan Neale.'

Words he hadn't heard from anyone for so long.

The pieces of his shattered heart began to fit back together again. Lexi was the glue. The constant. The beginning and the end.

His very best friend.

EPILOGUE

A year later

'Oh, YOU LOOK so beautiful.' Chantelle wiped away a rogue tear as she fastened the sapphire and silver bracelet around Lexi's wrist. 'Here's something blue.'

'Oh, that's so kind. It's beautiful.'

'From the team at work.'

Lexi ran her fingers over the silver. 'I wish I could have invited them all, but the reception room doesn't hold that many guests.'

'Hey, everyone's fine with it. They just asked me to take some pictures. Smile.' Her colleague clicked a few snaps on her phone. 'The backdrop is stunning. The little fishing village and the tiny private beach are picturesque. You picked the right place.' She looked at the screen and grimaced. 'It's getting late. I'd better go. Your mum and dad are downstairs, fussing about being on time.'

'Thanks. Tell them I'll be out in a minute.' One more minute before she became Mrs Fisher-Neale.

Lexi followed Chantelle's gaze down to the beach and she could just about make out the exact spot where she'd first kissed Jono. Or he'd kissed her…or they'd kissed anyway and started this journey to the happiest she'd ever felt in her entire life. Her heart danced. She turned back and looked in the full-length mirror at the long white dress. Who would have thought she'd be doing this again? It was some sort of miracle that she'd found him, that he'd fallen for her as much as she'd fallen for him.

And that he'd accepted her just the way she was, faults and all. But wasn't that what love was about? No judgement, but acceptance. He'd promised he'd be by her side every day and he had been. When they'd been to the surrogacy appointment and been told the chances of finding a surrogate were slim. When they'd enquired about adoption… Well, they were still filling out the forms, so it was very early days. But they'd agreed that, whatever happened, they'd be happy and fulfilled with each other, living their best lives together, a family of two.

They'd come full circle back to this place, because hadn't she once said it was the perfect venue for a wedding? She opened her crystal-covered handbag and found Jono's most recent note, scribbled on a napkin from this very hotel and pushed under her door this morning.

Fancy a quickie?
 Seriously, I can't quite believe I am so lucky as to have you in my life. I love you with everything I have. Heart and soul.
 Can't wait to be married to you.
 J xx

Even though they talked freely and with love every moment they were together, she still treasured the things he wrote to her. She kissed the napkin and slipped it into her bra for luck. Something new.

'Right.' She took a deep breath and smiled. 'Let's do this.'

She walked down the stairs towards the lobby and her waiting parents, and bumped into a taller, smarter Tyler. 'Hey, there, Dr Lexi. You look great.'

'Thanks, Tyler.' She kissed his cheek and didn't miss the rush of redness growing up his neck. 'No broken arms this year?'

'I was extra careful all week because I knew your wedding was coming up. Dad says hi.'

'Tell him hi back. We'll come visit him tomorrow.'

'He's planning on walking to the gate to meet you. Oh…' Tyler pulled a face '… I probably shouldn't have told you that, but he's been practising for the last month. He wants you to see him out of the wheelchair.'

'I'm so looking forward to seeing that. He's done so well. Tell him three o'clock and we'll bring wedding cake.' She loved this place; it was like a home from home. These people were like family too.

'Come on, love.' Her dad took her elbow. 'It's time.'

She gave Tyler a wave and set her sights on the makeshift aisle, thanking whoever was in charge of the weather for such a sunny day.

The flower girls, Preeti and Bhavesh's gorgeous three-year-old twins, were the real stars of the show, tossing petals in front of her as she walked down the aisle on her father's arm.

And there he was. The absolute love of her life. Her soulmate. Her everything.

She inhaled deeply, not nervous at all, not anything but delighted to be walking towards him. Maybe being more mature meant you savoured every bit of joy in every day because you didn't take anything for granted.

He was waiting under a canopy of white satin. His

smile said everything she knew already. *I love you. My best friend.*

She waved to Gordon at the front, dressed up in his uniform, standing as straight as he could, given his medical issues. He nodded back. Things still weren't easy between father and son, and maybe they never would be, but Gordon had insisted on being here today and that said a lot.

Then it was just the two of them making heartfelt promises to each other under a beautiful Cornwall sky, surrounded by friends and family.

And with a lifetime of happiness ahead of them.

* * * * *

COMING SOON!

We really hope you enjoyed reading this book.
If you're looking for more romance, be sure to
head to the shops when new books are
available on

Thursday 21st
July

To see which titles are coming soon, please visit
millsandboon.co.uk/nextmonth

MILLS & BOON®

Coming next month

FALLING FOR THE VILLAGE VET
Rachel Dove

'I've really enjoyed our date. I wanted to say that before we start talking about Portaloos.'

She burst into guffaws of laughter. He watched her with a very amused smile on his face. His hair was a little messed up, making him look more casual than usual. Ruffled.

'You're a goofball deep down, do you know that?'

'Yep. Just like you.' He looked her up and down slowly. 'Minus the colourful clothing.' He bit at his lip. 'I'm not all bad. I wish you'd known me before, when I was younger. I was different then.'

'Things change us in life,' she soothed.

'Nothing's changed you.'

She laughed again. 'Not now, no. It took me a while after my divorce to lick my wounds. I bought this place and just hid away at first.'

'Doesn't sound like you.'

He spoke as if he'd known her much longer than he had, but it sounded right to her too. They had seemingly been studying each other. Judged each other, yelled at each other, but yet here they were laughing, working on the charity drive together and enjoying the evening.

'It wasn't,' she breathed. 'I'm glad you came to live here. I'm not sure if anyone's actually said that to you yet.'

'It is nice to hear.' He was so close now. His eyes were taking her in, and she felt the stirrings of attraction sparking. 'Especially from you.'

'Your harshest critic,' she near whispered. They laughed again. 'What a battle-scarred pair we are.'

He laughed softly again, and something changed. It was so slight, so minuscule that she could easily have missed it, but he tore his gaze from hers, and poured them both a glass of wine.

'We'd better get on with the planning, then—I need to get back to Hendrix.' He wasn't rude, or surly. He was the man she'd come to know. The man who was so buttoned-up, she didn't think he'd ever get free. She hid her red face behind her wine glass, taking a good long pull. Trudy was coming to sort the dogs tomorrow, so she could sleep all day and then hide in work. Then she hid her disappointment at the date that wasn't a date. The non-date that had turned into a hot date and then back into a non-date. Just as she was starting to feel... Well, it wasn't anything, obviously. She sat up on her couch, pulled a pen from the pile on the table, and flipped open her notepad. Closing her heart at the same time.

Continue reading
FALLING FOR THE VILLAGE VET
Rachel Dove

Available next month
www.millsandboon.co.uk

MILLS & BOON

THE HEART OF ROMANCE

A ROMANCE FOR EVERY READER

MODERN

Prepare to be swept off your feet by sophisticated, sexy and seductive heroes, in some of the world's most glamourous and romantic locations, where power and passion collide.

HISTORICAL

Escape with historical heroes from time gone by. Whether your passion is for wicked Regency Rakes, muscled Vikings or rugged Highlanders, awaken the romance of the past.

MEDICAL

Set your pulse racing with dedicated, delectable doctors in the high-pressure world of medicine, where emotions run high and passion, comfort and love are the best medicine.

True Love

Celebrate true love with tender stories of heartfelt romance, from the rush of falling in love to the joy a new baby can bring, and a focus on the emotional heart of a relationship.

Desire

Indulge in secrets and scandal, intense drama and plenty of sizzling hot action with powerful and passionate heroes who have it all: wealth, status, good looks…everything but the right woman.

HEROES

Experience all the excitement of a gripping thriller, with an intense romance at its heart. Resourceful, true-to-life women and strong, fearless men face danger and desire - a killer combination!

To see which titles are coming soon, please visit

millsandboon.co.uk/nextmonth

JOIN US ON SOCIAL MEDIA!

Stay up to date with our latest releases, author news and gossip, special offers and discounts, and all the behind-the-scenes action from Mills & Boon...

 millsandboon

 millsandboonuk

 millsandboon

It might just be true love...